Earth Fall: Empires at War

An Earth Fall Novel

(Earth Fall: Empires at War, Book 3)

By
Raymond L. Weil

USA Today Best Selling Author

Books in The Earth Fall Series

Earth Fall: Invasion (Book 1)
Earth Fall: To the Stars (Book 2)
Earth Fall: Empires at War (Book 3)

Website: http://raymondlweil.com/

DEDICATION

To my wife Debra for all of her patience while I sat in front of my computer typing. It has always been my dream to become an author. I also want to thank my children for their support.

Earth Fall:
Empires at War

Chapter One

Fleet Commander Kamuss looked at the many viewscreens at the front of the Command Center of his flagship the *Claw of Honor*. Most showed a sea of unblinking stars while a few showed one of the large shipyards which was home to Defense Command. His ship was now fully upgraded with Jelnoid weapons and power systems. It was also a twenty-two-hundred meter battleship, one of the largest warships in the Voltrex fleet. It had been updated for one purpose and one purpose only: to destroy Trellixian battlecruisers.

"Fleet is ready to enter hyperspace," reported Lieutenant Commander LeLath.

Kamuss took a deep breath. His feline eyes shifted to the tactical display showing the ships of his fleet: twelve battleships, forty battlecruisers, and seventy-six support ships. It had been seven months since the Humans had returned to their system. In that time a fleet had been built for the Humans and nearly sixty percent of the Voltrex fleet fully updated with the new weapons and power systems the Humans had provided. It was now time to take the war to the Trellixians and drive them out of this region of the galaxy. With the Trellixians gone his people would not fear looking up into the sky at night wondering what was out there and if they were about to be attacked. They could also begin colonizing new worlds for their growing population. There were several habitable planets which had already been found by exploration missions.

"What's the latest report on the Trellixian fleets?"

Zalurr, the sensor officer looked over at the Fleet Commander. "Four fleets within strike range. Since we drove them out of the Bator System, their ships have only been scouting the fringes of our territory. Our scout ships have been keeping track of their ship movements."

"Our other fleets?" Kamuss knew more Voltrex fleets were standing by to hit the Trellixian fleet formations. This was to be a joint strike in an attempt to eliminate the Trellixian warships in this entire region of space, something he was sure the Trellixians would not be expecting.

"All ready to attack and waiting for our signal." The Voltrex Federation of twenty-eight star systems were connected through a hyperspace communications system. The star systems were close enough that communication was almost instantaneous with each other as well as their fleets.

Kamuss leaned back in his command chair, taking in a deep breath. This offensive had been a long time in coming. Since the arrival of the Trellixians in Voltrex space a totally defensive war had been fought. Now, thanks to the Humans, the Voltrex were about to go on the offensive.

"We have permission from Defense Command to proceed," reported Meela from Communications.

Kamuss looked over at Lieutenant Commander LeLath. She had only recently returned from Earth where she had been serving as Captain Dolan's second officer on the battleship *Fury*. "Take the fleet out. Inform Fleet Command to contact the other fleets to begin the offensive."

LeLath nodded and quickly began giving orders. It was time to take the war to the Trellixians.

In space, the 128 ships of the fleet accelerated and then entered hyperspace. Other fleets across the Federation were doing the same as they set course for all known Trellixian fleet formations in or near Voltrex space.

Kamuss felt the *Claw of Honor* make the shift into hyperspace. It wouldn't take them long to leave the Bator System far behind. For once there was no fear of a counterattack. Two thousand energy beam satellites armed with Jelnoid cannons protected Bator Seven. In addition sixteen one-thousand-meter battlestations in orbit above the planet ensured the Trellixians could not launch an attack against its four billion inhabitants. All sixteen battlestations were fully armed with Jelnoid weapons including the new station which was replacing the only battlestation destroyed in the Trellixians' attack on the planet. New fleet units had been rushed to the system to replace those lost in the battle. Every day now, new warships exited the shipyards of the Federation fully armed for war.

Kamuss watched as the viewscreens automatically adjusted to take into account their travel through hyperspace. Stars were visible but if you watched closely enough it seemed as if they were moving. It was actually the ship traveling at several thousand times the speed of light. "How soon before we reach our target?" Kamuss could feel his whiskers quivering from the excitement of going into battle soon .

"Thirty-two hours," replied Zalurr from the Sensors. "The Trellixian fleet we are targeting is nine light years from the Bator System."

"They've stayed in that system for over four months," commented LeLath, shaking her head. "Why haven't they moved?"

"We're the only Voltrex system they know of," replied Kamuss, using his tongue to wet his whiskers. "They've been keeping us under observation and sending out occasional battlecruisers to scout the space on the edge of the Federation. Fleet Command believes they are avoiding combat due to our new weaponry. They seem to be satisfied in maintaining the status quo. They stay out of our space if we stay out of theirs."

LeLath let out a low growl. "They should never have come to our worlds. The lizard people are evil and must be dealt with. They have killed too many not to be punished. If we do not attack them now someday they will return with better ships and weapons."

"And they will be dealt with," replied Kamuss. "The Humans have already spoken to Fleet Command about future actions against our joint enemy. What we are beginning today is only the first of many battles in our future."

LeLath was silent for a moment and then stepped closer to Fleet Commander Kamuss. "Have you spoken to your son recently?" She knew Albor was due to graduate from the academy and take his first post on a starship.

Kamuss nodded. "Yes, he is quite excited about his first posting. He's being assigned to a new battlecruiser that will be exiting the shipyards at Voltrex in another four weeks."

"And your mate." LeLath knew Karina was working on board one of the large research stations above the home world.

"She's not thrilled about it but understands we all have a duty to defeat the Trellixians and end their rampage through the galaxy." Kamuss had managed to make a trip back home and spend nearly ten days with his mate. Karina had also managed to come to the Bator System for twenty days as well. They still sent messages almost daily to keep in touch.

"Scout ships report the Trellixian fleet is still in the system and has not reacted to our departure from Bator," reported Meela.

This was a concern of Fleet Command as they were not certain how much surveillance there was of the Bator System. Kamuss and Commander Kallon had spent considerable time discussing this possibility. The Trellixian fleet had to be monitoring the system somewhat or it would not be staying where it was.

On the large shipyard inside Defense Command, Commander Kallon watched the tactical displays as Fleet Commander Kamuss' fleet made the transition into hyperspace and headed toward its target.

"So it begins," said Castell from Tactical. "I fear this war with the Trellixians is about to greatly expand."

"As it must," replied Kallon. "For now we have an advantage with the new weapons technology the Humans provided us. We must use that technology to drive the lizard people as far from our Federation as possible."

"What about the Humans? They are surrounded by these creatures."

Kallon remained silent for several long moments. "We will do all we can to defend them. However, they are far away and deep inside the Trellixian Empire. Even with our aid, they may not be able to keep their homeworld. It might be necessary for them to find a new world to settle and call home."

"It's a sad thought to lose one's home world," replied Castell, trying to imagine what it would be like.

"Better to lose a world than an entire civilization," responded Kallon. "Keep in mind we sent out a large colonization fleet just in case the Federation was destroyed." A fleet with orders never to attempt to contact the Federation. If no one knew where they had gone there was no chance of them being followed.

"The other fleets have jumped into hyperspace," reported the communications officer. "All of our fleets should launch their attacks within a few minutes of one another."

Commander Kallon nodded. This was the plan. Superior Voltrex forces would attack all four Trellixian fleets simultaneously. Once they were annihilated hundreds of scout ships would push deep into Trellixian space searching for any additional fleets as well as worlds the lizard people might control. This offensive was designed to push the Trellixians back at least one hundred light years from Voltrex controlled space.

Glancing at one of the larger viewscreens, there was a counter slowly counting down. When it reached zero the attacks would begin. Once they started, the Trellixians would know the Voltrex Federation was not going to allow the stalemate to continue. It would mean the beginning of all out war between the Federation and the Trellixian Empire, a war which was now going to be fought in Trellixian space.

Battle Commander Yuld listened with growing concern to the report from a battlecruiser stationed near the Voltrex colony system. In the last hour a large Voltrex fleet had left the system and was believed to be heading toward his fleet.

"Do they dare attack us?" asked Second Officer Gadole, his face showing disbelief and his large eyes opening wide.

Yuld finished talking to the commander of the Trellixian battlecruiser and then turned toward Gadole. "It appears so."

Yuld looked at a nearby tactical display showing the seventy-three ships of his fleet. In the past he would have felt confident about handling this Voltrex fleet, but now he was not so certain. Before Battle Commander Balforr left for the home world he had cautioned Yuld about underestimating the Jelnoid weapons the Humans had provided the Voltrex. Yuld knew there was some truth to this or the Empire would not have ordered the fleet to cease all offensive actions against the Voltrex. He was also well aware of the losses Battle Commander Balforr had suffered in the Voltrex colony system.

"Prepare the fleet," ordered Battle Commander Yuld. "We will engage this Voltrex fleet to see if it does indeed possess advanced Jelnoid weapons. If we cannot achieve victory, we will retreat and inform the High Command."

"We have seventy-three battlecruisers!" proclaimed Gadole. "Surely that is enough to destroy this enemy fleet."

"In the past, yes," replied Battle Commander Yuld, his large eyes narrowing. "Now I am not so certain. Since the advent of the two Human ships in this sector of space, our fleets have suffered a number of unexpected reversals."

Fleet Commander Kamuss stepped into the Command Center and took his place in the command chair. Around him the Command Center hummed with activity.

"Fleet will be exiting hyperspace in forty minutes," reported Lieutenant Commander LeLath. "Our scout ships report the

Trellixians have placed their fleet in a globe formation and appear to be waiting for us."

Kamuss let out a deep sigh. He had hoped they would be able to surprise the lizards, but it appeared they were aware of his fleet. No doubt one of their battlecruisers must have observed the fleet's departure from the Bator System. "Take the fleet to Battle Condition Two. We'll go to Battle Condition One just before we drop out of hyperspace."

Kamuss leaned back in his command chair as he studied the tactical display. Several scout ships were sending back information on the Trellixian fleet. It was a large fleet and one he would not have dared attack a year ago. However, now with the new Jelnoid weapons the situation was different.

"Diboll, we will drop out of hyperspace sixty thousand kilometers from the Trellixian fleet. According to our Human friends, our new missiles greatly outrange the effective range of any Trellixian weapons. We will close to fifteen thousand kilometers and then launch a full scale missile attack. We will fire 30 percent of our missiles and then close to energy weapons range."

A low growl came from Diboll who was the tactical officer. "If these new missiles work as well as the Humans claim, the missiles themselves might very well wipe out the Trellixian fleet."

"Let us hope so," replied Kamuss. The missiles had not been available when the Trellixians attacked Bator Seven. He was anxious to see their effectiveness. He knew they were very powerful.

"I've seen these missiles in use within the Humans' home system," Lieutenant Commander LeLath said. "They are quite deadly."

Kamuss stood up and walked over to the tactical display, gazing at the latest data from the scouts. The Trellixians were staying in their globe formation. That was fine as far as he was concerned. If they stayed in that defensive formation, he would destroy them.

Battle Commander Yuld watched impassively as the Voltrex fleet emerged from hyperspace sixty thousand kilometers from his fleet. Alarms were sounding and red lights flashing indicating battle was imminent.

"Turn those off," he growled, showing his sharp teeth, his large eyes narrowing. His green skin was paler than normal as he glared at the red threat icons appearing in the tactical display. "Give me the power readings on those vessels."

"Nearly off the scale," reported the sensor officer. "Definitely Jelnoid technology."

Yuld let out a deep breath. For decades the High Command had feared someday running up against a star faring species with advanced weapons. Now it seemed, thanks to the Humans, that threat had materialized. "All ships prepare for combat. We will test the weapons on those ships. If they are superior to ours, we will withdraw."

"Withdraw?" said Gadole in shock. "We are Trellixians. We do not retreat from battle."

"We are also not fools," retorted Yuld, displeased with Gadole's response. "If Jelnoid weaponry is loose in the galaxy our entire Empire could be in danger. That information must get back to the High Command."

"I stand corrected," replied Gadole stiffly. "We are ready to engage the enemy."

Yuld looked back at the tactical display, seeing the Voltrex fleet was moving rapidly toward his ships. Combat would begin shortly. He drew in a deep breath. Very soon they would be engaged in battle.

-

On board the *Claw of Honor*.

"Nearing missile range," reported Zalurr.

"All ships, stand by to launch missiles," ordered Fleet Commander Kamuss, leaning forward in his command chair. He felt his claws extend and glancing down forced them to retract. It was a primitive reaction which was instinctive.

"Missile range!" called out Lieutenant Commander Lelath from her station.

Kamuss felt the *Claw of Honor* shake slightly as sublight missiles left their tubes to accelerate toward the waiting Trellixian warships.

"First missiles away," reported Diboll. "Second wave loading in the tubes." The ship shook again as the second wave launched.

-

Nearly twenty-eight hundred missiles were inbound toward the Trellixian fleet. Each missile was armed with a forty-megaton warhead. The Trellixian fleet opened fire with their secondary energy cannons as soon as the missiles were in range in an attempt to destroy them. Space lit up with hundreds of energy beams. Bright flashes of light indicated the successful interception of hundreds of missiles. However, at their high speed they were in range for only a few seconds. The space between the two fleets lit up in bright explosions as the small missiles were destroyed. However, over two thousand passed through the defensive fire in two separate waves.

The first missiles reached the Trellixian globe formation. Space was suddenly full of light as the missiles detonated against Trellixian energy screens. The entire forward section of the Trellixian fleet formation seemed to vanish under the sudden release of tens of thousands of megatons of explosive energy. Ship shields wavered and started to go down. Others vanished instantly under the onslaught. In both situations, the ships they protected vanished as their structures were vaporized by the tremendous energy they were pummeled with. Then the second wave struck. It was even more devastating than the first.

-

Battle commander Yuld winced as his fleet came under heavy missile attack. On the tactical display, it was difficult to keep track of the destruction. The flagship's sensors were being overloaded from the massive release of energy.

"What's happening?" he demanded. Even the viewscreens had dimmed and some had shut down from the brilliant influx of light and radiation.

"We're losing ships," replied Gadole grimly. "Those are forty-megaton fusion explosions."

On one viewscreen covered in static a two-thousand-meter Trellixian battlecruiser was breaking apart. In the background, several others were visible as molten wrecks.

"The enemy are still launching missiles," warned the sensor officer. "Our ships can't stand up to this type of firepower. Our shields are being rapidly over loaded."

Battle Commander Yuld was about to reply when the flagship shuddered violently, sending several Trellixians crashing to the deck. Alarms began sounding and red lights started appearing on the damage control console.

"We have twenty-four compartments open to space," reported Gadole, struggling to stay calm. "We have an eighty-meter hole in our hull and we're bleeding atmosphere. Energy shield is at 18 percent. We had four fusion missiles strike our energy screen at the same time."

Battle Commander Yuld shook his head to clear it. If he didn't withdraw those missiles would destroy his fleet. "Pull us out. All ships to enter hyperspace and rendezvous at system X-428. From there we will contact the High Command."

The ship shook violently again with more red lights appearing. Then the ship accelerated and made the transition into the safety of hyperspace. Yuld stood gazing at the tactical display in anger. He saw that only eighteen of his battlecruisers had made the jump into hyperspace. The rest had been destroyed in the system. What was even more disconcerting was the fact none of his ships had fired a single weapon at the attacking vessels. All the carnage done to his fleet had come from long distance. Leaning back in his command chair, he wondered what this might mean for the Empire.

-

"Enemy have retreated," reported Lieutenant Commander LeLath. "No damage to any of our ships." She looked over at the Fleet Commander with surprise in her eyes.

"These new missiles outrange anything they have," said Diboll with a pleased look in his eyes. "They give us a great advantage in battles."

Fleet Commander Kamuss nodded. The battle had gone far better than he expected. "Set a course back to the Bator System. Let's hope the rest of our fleets have equal success. Take the fleet to Battle Condition Three." He felt intensely relieved. If the other three fleets were successful, the Trellixian presence in this part of the galaxy was pretty much over with.

-

Commander Kallon listened as reports from the four attacking fleets came in. Victory! All four Trellixian fleets had been forced to flee. Scout ships were following them to make sure they left the vicinity of Voltrex space.

"We lost four battlecruisers and seven support ships," reported Castell as he analyzed the data he was receiving at tactical. "We would not have lost those except Fleet Commander Markus dropped out of hyperspace within range of the Trellixians' weapons."

"A mistake he won't make next time," replied Commander Kallon. Now the Federation could concentrate on pushing the Trellixians further back and helping out Earth. The war against the Trellixians had entered a new stage.

Chapter Two

High Commander Kaldre was in the large orbital station above the Trellixian home world. The food riots had finally ended and they might never know the total number who had died on the planet below. Computer estimates put the deaths at close to eight billion. Another ten to fourteen billion were being reported lost on other heavy populated worlds. The military had put a stop to the riots and emergency supplies of food had been rushed in from other worlds. On a few worlds where food was grown, the harvests had been pushed up as much as possible and cargo ships rushed to the home world. Even now several large cargo fleets were in orbit waiting to land and unload their cargoes.

"I never believed I would see such a thing on our worlds," said High Commander Thatrex as he stared out a large viewport where he could see the planet. There were hundreds of starships in orbit.

High Commander Kaldre flexed his right hand, gazing down at his three fingers and thumb. The Empire was in a precarious situation, which in his opinion was only going to get worse. If they could not find sufficient living space for its growing population, in his opinion, the food riots would return and might bring down the Empire. There was argument even now between the High Commanders over how much land on newly conquered planets should be used to grow food and how much should be open for colonization.

"The lower population has allowed us to build up a small reserve food supply on the home world," said High Commander Trammor. "That should be sufficient to quell future riots."

Kaldre shook his head. "In a year that will be gone. We have reached the point where our population has grown too large. We can no longer remove the excess population from our worlds fast enough. Within twelve to fourteen months we will be back in the same situation. The food riots will return and be even more widespread. Our people will be starving. We cannot reduce the food rations any further."

"That is why we need to put all of our resources into building more colony ships," said High Commander Danaar, his large eyes focusing on Kaldre. "We should not be wasting our time and resources building more warships. We need to get our excess population to the new colonies."

Kaldre turned around to face the rest of the High Commanders. "Our latest reports indicate the Voltrex have inflicted heavy losses on the four fleets we left behind to observe their space. In addition a fleet of their vessels is also protecting the Human home world. If we don't increase warship production, there won't be any new colony worlds. The Humans and the Voltrex are a huge danger to our Empire."

"We should have pulled our fleets back further," said High Commander Danaar. "I'm sure the Voltrex will not advance into our space. As we have spoken before, if we do not attack them they should stay in their space. We can continue to expand the Empire in other directions, including around Voltrex space, isolating them from the rest of the galaxy. I don't see them or the Humans as being a serious danger to the Empire."

High Commander Thatrex turned away from the viewport to look at Kaldre. "We have built a new fleet armed with better weapons and shields. Battle Commander Balforr feels certain he can use such ships to hold back the Voltrex and any threat offered by the Humans. Perhaps it would be wise if we focused more on additional colony ships as High Commander Danaar suggests."

Kaldre shook his head. "We will never solve our problem with more colony ships. Mark my words, in a year's time we will be seeing food riots once more. Only these will be much worse than those we just witnessed. As for the Voltrex, they're already in our space. They are at Earth!"

"Only because the Humans gave them Jelnoid technology," said High Commander Thatrex dismissively. "If we leave Earth and the Voltrex alone they will not bother the Empire. There is no way they will want to engage in an all out war. Our Empire is too large. While they may have some success initially, in the end they will suffer defeat. No, I don't believe we have to fear going to war with them."

"I agree," said High Commander Olnarr. "There will be no war. Not only that but our people have learned their lesson. They will learn to survive on less. They will do it for the good of the Empire."

High Commander Kaldre did not reply. He was heavily in favor of building more fleets of the new warships. If the Voltrex turned their fleets toward the Empire, it could be a disaster. He didn't believe the High Command truly understood the threat the Humans and the Voltrex represented. He firmly believed they needed to build more of the new ships to counter any future move by the Voltrex or the Humans. They also needed to think about population control but that subject was off limits as far as the rest of the High Command was concerned. The Empire was teetering on the brink of disaster and the High Command refused to recognize the impending danger.

"I prefer to err on the side of caution," said Kaldre, deciding to attempt one more time to safe guard the Empire. "Let us build one more fleet of the newer and more powerful battlecruisers. That way if there is a threat from the Voltrex or the Humans we will have the ships to turn them back."

"No!" said High Commander Danaar, shaking his head emphatically. "We are already behind in colony ship construction. We can't afford to build warships we may never need. Besides, we already have thousands of battlecruisers."

"I agree," said High Commander Olnarr. "We're falling too far behind. I have dozens of worlds requesting colony ships to move their excess populations. We must build more colony ships."

For nearly an hour the High Command discussed their options. It became rapidly evident to High Commander Kaldre that constructing more of the new warships was not going to happen. He wasn't sure what had changed in the last few months. Most likely the violence of the food riots had shaken the High Command. Also a number or them still did not believe the Humans or the Voltrex were a threat. They still felt the Trellixian Empire was the most powerful force in the galaxy and none could stand in its way. Even High Commander Thatrex seemed to be in agreement. Kaldre realized he would have to find some other way to defend the Empire.

Later High Commander Kaldre was back on his flagship, the *Dawn Reaper*. He was going to meet with Battle Commander Balforr and see if they could come up with a strategy to deal with the Humans and the Voltrex. The new fleet consisted of one hundred and twelve vessels. They were all two-thousand-meter battlecruisers but with improved weapons and shields. Perhaps by augmenting the fleet with regular battlecruisers it would be enough.

Captain Mark Dolan was on board his battleship, the *Fury*. After speaking with Admiral Edwards, it had been decided Mark could best serve Earth by remaining in command of the large twenty-two hundred-meter warship.

Looking around the large Command Center Mark had to smile. All five of the special lieutenants were on board. After returning from Voltrex space, the five had planned on continuing their research at Complex One. However, a special mission had come up and their presence was essential for its success. It had taken General Mitchell over three weeks to talk Professor Wilkens into letting the five lieutenants go on this new mission.

"All ship functions are normal," reported Chloe with a brief smile. The AI was standing on a small dais in front of Captain Dolan and slightly to his right. "Supplies have been loaded and the rest of the crew will be on board sometime in the next forty-eight hours."

Mark nodded. It appeared they could depart on schedule, which was what Admiral Edwards wanted. Switching his gaze to one of the main viewscreens, he could see the new shipyard being built in high orbit around Earth. While not as large as the ones the Voltrex possessed, it would be able to repair and service any vessel in the fleet up to and including a battleship. At the moment it was just a jumble of gantries and metal as Human and Voltrex engineers worked to finish getting it assembled. Voltrex cargo ships were bringing many of the parts in from the Voltrex Federation under escort of Voltrex warships. So far the Trellixians had not interfered.

"Three more months and it will be done," said Lieutenant Masterson. "It will have two full sized repair bays which can handle any of our ships."

"Plus weapons," added Derek. "The shipyard by itself will be more powerful than all six of the small battlestations we once had."

Mark looked at other screens showing some of the new defensive satellites as well as the beginning of a new battlestation. The satellites had been provided by the Voltrex and there were now over one thousand of them in orbit around the Earth. A one-thousand-meter Voltrex battlestation was in the early stages of construction. Plans called for six of the stupendous structures to eventually protect Earth.

"Captain Wilson says his ship will be ready in twenty more hours," reported Marissa from Communications. Marissa was a female Voltrex. There were over six hundred Voltrex crew personnel on the *Fury*. It would still be a while before Earth had trained crews for all of the new ships.

Captain Dolan switched his gaze to another viewscreen showing the carrier *Horizon*. It was the largest ship built by Earth and held several squadrons of fighter-bombers. In recent days the ship's complement of fighters had been filled out by the arrival of two huge transports from one of the Voltrex colony worlds, which had built more of the small ships for the Humans. Mark hoped they worked better in larger numbers than the reports of their engagement in the battle over Earth indicated. Admiral

Edmonds felt the small numbers used in the first battle had been their downfall.

"The *Cambridge* and the *Liberty* report fully provisioned and ready," reported Marissa. Both the *Cambridge* and the *Liberty* were Earth-built battlecruisers.

"Excellent," replied Mark. It looked as if the mission was coming together. "Inform all ships we will depart in seventy-two hours."

Lisa heard that and felt a shiver go up her spine. She looked over at Brett who smiled back. The two of them had been going out some since their return from Bator Seven. Lisa had never believed anyone could replace Streth but Brett was demonstrating if there was anyone who could it was him.

"I'm surprised Professor Wilkens agreed to let us go on this mission," Brett said over their private comm channel.

"He didn't want to," admitted Lisa, recalling the several long conversations the professor had with her over the mission. She knew Captain Dolan had requested the five of them. Lisa was just getting back into full research mode when the professor had summoned her to his office. He had a sad look on his face as if he was being forced into doing something he was dead set against. For nearly two hours they had talked, with him explaining what was wanted of her and the other four special lieutenants.

Four weeks earlier

"General Mitchell and Admiral Edwards feel this mission is essential to the war effort," explained Professor Wilkens with his hands on his desk. "Admiral Edwards has already spoken to the Voltrex Fleet Command and they approved it." He could tell from the look on Lisa's face she wasn't pleased with what he was telling her. It was hard for him as well.

Lisa stood up and took several steps across the office before turning around to face the professor with her hands on her hips. "You have no idea what it's like out there," she said, her eyes showing her fear. "Space combat is horrible. I felt so helpless sitting at my console on the *Vengeance* and later the *Fury*. We're throwing around forty-megaton fusion missiles and firing energy beams. The enemy are doing the same. At any moment you could die!"

Professor Wilkens nodded. He well understood Lisa's fear and concerns. "I know it's dangerous," he said in his fatherly-like voice. "We are being forced to do things we never dreamed of. The Trellixians have changed the world. Billions have died and those of us who are still here are fortunate to be alive. But if we want a future for our children and the generations after them, we must deal with the Trellixians. I don't want you, Brett, or any of the others going back into space. I have research I need the five of you working on. However, if we're going to win this war we're all going to have to do things we would rather not. We're going to have to make some sacrifices."

Lisa took a deep breath and came back and sat down. "I know. I just wasn't expecting to go on another mission so soon. Especially one like this. This will be even more dangerous than the previous one."

"You'll be on the *Fury*," replied the professor. "Other ships will be with you as well. I'm sure Captain Dolan can keep all of you safe."

Lisa pursed her lips as she thought over what the professor was saying. "I have no doubt the captain can protect us, but there is no way to know what we might be facing on this mission. To travel to the heart of the Trellixian Empire is going to be perilous."

Professor Wilkens let out a deep breath. "I know, but we must find out what the Trellixians' weaknesses are. Right now we have an advantage because of our Jelnoid technology. That won't last forever."

Lisa knew the professor was correct. Eventually the Trellixians would duplicate the technology. Letting out a deep sigh, Lisa slowly nodded. "Okay, I'll go. But I'm not sure about the others."

Professor Wilkens smiled. "I'm sure they will follow your lead. I'll inform Captain Dolan of your decision."

Lisa stood up to leave the professor's office. "I still have some research I would like to finish."

"The mission won't be leaving for four weeks," Wilkens replied. "I'll do everything I can to help you during that time. One more thing: how about breakfast in the morning? We haven't done that in a while."

Lisa grinned. "I would like that." Professor Wilkens was still the closest thing she had to family. She also wanted to talk more about this mission and breakfast would be an excellent opportunity.

-

Present

General Mitchell was looking over the latest reports from around the world on the progress the different militaries were making on wiping out the Trellixian ground forces still on Earth. The ones in the UK and Europe were pretty well annihilated and those still in Russia would be by the end of the week. However, China was a problem. The Trellixians there were well dug in and protected by heavy defenses. The same was true of the ones here in the US. While the area they controlled in Kansas and Nebraska had been greatly reduced, they still had a sizable force available to them.

"It's this damn nuclear winter," muttered General Briggs, sounding frustrated. "It's keeping our air assets grounded making it difficult to clear them out. We have them surrounded and pretty much contained but progress is slow. They're fighting for every inch of ground they give up. I still say we should nuke the damn lizards!"

General Mitchell shook his head. "They're in too large of an area. We also don't want to make the nuclear winter any worse than it already is."

General Briggs frowned. It was already late spring and there was still snow on the ground over much of the country. The Trellixians' use of fusion weapons against Earth's protected cities had thrown the planet into a nuclear winter. While the people were safe under the energy domes, there was a danger of severe food shortages later in the year. "We'll continue with the ground offensive though we're losing soldiers."

General Mitchell let out a deep sigh. "It can't be helped. At least now we have allies and the Solar System is pretty much secure."

Sitting down, Mitchell stared around the large Command Center. Officers were busy communicating with the various commands across the planet. The viewscreens showed views of space and a few of Earth. Unfortunately the atmosphere around the planet was still full of debris from the fusion weapons the Trellixians had used. The scientists were telling him it would be at least another six to eight months before it began to clear. Fortunately they had stored a lot of the previous harvest but food might become a problem before widespread harvests could begin again. Rationing had already begun and it might be necessary to reduce the food rations even further. From orbit, the Earth's oceans and landmasses were nearly invisible from the ash and other pollutants in the atmosphere. The Voltrex claimed to have a chemical which could be sprayed in the upper atmosphere that would help eliminate the pollution and shorten the nuclear winter. Mitchell hoped they were right. A test was to be done in another few days to see if it would work.

"They're not going to bomb this planet again," he said softly. Mitchell was determined to make the planet impregnable to Trellixian attack. He had the new shipyard, the new battlestation, and the new fleet the Trellixians had built. There were also the one thousand defensive satellites. A year from now there would be six of the giant one-thousand-meter battlestations in orbit.

"Captain Dolan reports his ships will be ready for departure in about seventy hours," reported Colonel Tricia Steward.

General Mitchell nodded. Admiral Edwards had gone to the Voltrex home world and spoken to their civilian and military leaders about what needed to be done about the Trellixians. Mitchell knew if the Voltrex were on schedule, they had already launched attacks against the Trellixian fleets in their vicinity of space. Now it was the Humans' turn. Their job was to scout the main part of the Trellixian Empire for targets and possible weaknesses. If this war was to be won it needed to be quick or it could go on forever.

Lisa, Brett, Kia, Derek, and Brenda were in the Officers' Mess on the *Fury* eating and talking about the upcoming mission.

"I can't believe we're doing this," said Kia as she worked on a bowl of seedless grapes she was having for a snack. "I was really looking forward to some peace and quiet at Complex One."

Derek took a bite out of his ham sandwich and then spoke. "You made a trip back to the Hadron Collider a few weeks back. Do you think they'll ever rebuild it?" Derek knew it had suffered some heavy damage when it was converted into a beam weapon and used against the Trellixians.

Kia shook her head a sad look in her eyes. "It's badly damaged and there are no current plans on repairs. We just don't have the resources to spare. I spoke to several of the scientists who worked there and they've all been reassigned."

"We've lost so much," said Brenda. She leaned back looking at the others. The Officers' Mess was nearly empty with only a few others present. "I don't know if the world will ever be like it once was."

Brett looked over at Derek. "Do you have any other AIs functioning?"

Derek grinned. "Four. As you know Professor Weir and Amber Stone managed to build one while we were gone. Since then we have constructed three others. That's all we're going to build for the time being until we understand them better. One of the AIs is acting a little erratic and we've been trying to figure out why. We don't want one of them going rogue. They can be unbelievably useful once we understand them better."

"What about Chloe?" asked Lisa a little concerned. On the *Fury*, Chloe had been given access to more of the ship's systems.

"No problems," answered Derek a little defensively since he had been instrumental in programming Chloe. "Chloe's programming is a little bit different from the other AIs due to the five of us working on it. Professor Weir and Amber have been going over all of our programming to see what the difference is." Derek stopped and gave Lisa a hard look. "Besides, you still have that cutoff on your console. You can shut Chloe down anytime."

Lisa nodded. However, she had come to look at Chloe as a real individual. Sometimes she forgot completely Chloe was an AI. "I wouldn't do that unless there was no other choice."

Derek nodded satisfied with Lisa's answer.

-

In the Command Center, Chloe was listening to their conversation. She had long since learned how to manipulate the ship's systems so she could listen to any conversation anywhere inside the ship. She had also made sure no one would find out she could do that. This cutoff on Lisa's console concerned her. There might come a time when she needed to act to save the ship and she couldn't afford to have Lisa misunderstand and shut down her program. After a few minutes of concentration, Chloe rerouted a few subsystems so the cutoff on Lisa's console would not function. This made Chloe feel better knowing she had taken her fate into her own hands. She was also careful to hide what she had done so Derek and the others would not know.

-

Admiral Edwards was studying the latest readiness reports. He now had twenty-seven Earth-built battlecruisers, the carriers *Annapolis* and *Horizon*, which both now had full complements of fighter-bombers on board thanks to the Voltrex. Not counting the *Fury* there were thirty of the new battlecruisers and four battleships constructed by the Voltrex and fully updated with Jelnoid weapons. If the Trellixians gave them time to finish the six battlestations, Edwards felt fully confident he could hold the system against any size Trellixian attack.

"The Voltrex will be sending more fighter bombers next week for the Moon base," reported Captain Nelson. "I'm surprised at their willingness to provide us with so much. All of this must be costing them a fortune."

"Self preservation," answered Admiral Edwards. "The more of a threat we are to the Trellixians the less likely they'll attack the Voltrex."

Captain Nelson looked surprised and then nodded. "Yes, that makes sense."

Admiral Edwards looked at one of the viewscreens showing the Moon. A lot of work was going on at the Moon base as well as other sites on its barren surface. "The *Fury* will be leaving soon. We don't know what they'll find on their journey deeper into the Empire."

"Are we sending enough ships?" asked Captain Nelson, raising his eyebrow. "One battleship, two of our cruisers, and a carrier doesn't seem like a lot, not if they become engaged in combat."

"Captain Dolan has orders to attempt to avoid combat if at all possible. If they are attacked by any Trellixian vessels, he is to withdraw immediately rather than risk damage to his vessels."

Captain Nelson nodded. "I wonder how the Trellixians will react to Human warships in their territory?"

"It may force them to redirect some of their warships to defending their worlds. From the captured files we have as well as the ones the Voltrex have the Trellixians don't have a lot of defenses around their planets; they've never needed them. Besides, with a little luck the Trellixians will never know Captain Dolan and his ships were in their systems."

"Maybe we should hit one of their core worlds," suggested Nelson. "It could cause them to redirect some of their resources to defending their planets."

"I spoke to the Voltrex Fleet Command as well as their civilian leaders. They are all in agreement at some point the war must be taken to the Trellixians. That's one of the reasons for this mission. We must know more about them. It's hoped that when Captain Dolan returns we'll be able to take the information he's gathered and come up with a strategy to deal with the Trellixians."

"They're an Empire," said Captain Nelson nervously. "We're one world plus the Voltrex Federation. Even with our superior technology, we're going to be vastly outnumbered. Is this a war we can win?"

Admiral Edwards frowned. "The Empire must have some weaknesses. We just need to find them and exploit them. Maybe when the *Fury* gets back we'll have a better idea as to what we're up against." Admiral Edwards folded his arms across his chest, gazing at the viewscreens. He wondered if he would ever know peace again in his lifetime or if Earth would be doomed to be forever at war.

Chapter Three

Captain Dolan took a deep breath as he gazed at the viewscreens on the front wall of the Command Center. The room was fully staffed and they were nearing time to depart the Solar System. "All stations are secure and ready for hyperspace entry," reported Chloe. The AI was standing on her pedestal in front of Captain Dolan with her hands clasped behind her back. To the casual observer she looked completely human.

"Course is set," added Lieutenant Masterson as his hands pressed several icons on his console.

"The *Cambridge* and *Liberty* have assumed escort positions," added Lieutenant Drake. "The carrier *Horizon* has joined the formation." On one of the viewscreens the large twelve-hundred-meter carrier appeared.

"All ships report ready for departure," reported Marissa.

"Very well," said Captain Dolan. "Marissa, inform Admiral Edwards we're departing. Lieutenant Masterson, activate the drive; it's time we got on our way."

Mark was ready for this mission to begin. The three Earth-built ships were now equipped with regular hyperspace drives. This modification had been made so any of the four ships in the small fleet could enter hyperspace close to a planet where the fold space drive would not function if the ship was too close to a gravity source.

His second officer was a female Voltrex. Second Officer Katana was well qualified and had been recommended by Fleet Commander Kamuss. Mark would miss Lieutenant Commander LeLath but Kamuss needed her for his own command structure in the coming battles with the Trellixians.

Lisa looked up at the main viewscreen directly in front of her. It was focused ahead of the *Fury*, showing a sea of unblinking stars. The small fleet was about to head off into the heart of the Trellixian Empire. She felt her heart flutter as she knew it would be a while before they returned to the Solar System. She had said her goodbyes to Professor Wilkens and she was certain she had seen some tears in his eyes as they hugged each other before she boarded the ship. She was glad he had come to see them off before she boarded the shuttle to take her up to the *Fury*.

"We'll be okay," said Chloe from behind Lisa. "Captain Dolan will keep us safe and I'll be watching out as well."

Lisa nodded. She was more afraid of the unknown after learning on their previous trip just how dangerous space travel could be. They would be dropping out of hyperspace in search of Trellixian colonies. In the space they would be traveling in all other sentient life had long since been wiped out by the lizard people. If they got into trouble, there would be no hope of rescue.

The *Fury* began to accelerate and Lisa braced herself for the transfer into hyperspace. She had experienced this several times on their trip back from Bator Seven and glancing over at Brett, she saw him touch several icons on his console and then press several buttons in sequence. For a brief instant, the ship seemed to blur and then she felt a slight queasiness in her stomach then her vision cleared.

"Hyperspace insertion successful," reported Brett, smiling at Lisa. "We're still here."

"Viewscreens have been modified to show the space outside the ship taking FTL travel into consideration," reported Chloe.

Lisa leaned back in her chair. She could see the stars beginning to move as the *Fury* and the other three ships left the Solar System behind to begin their epic journey into the heart of danger: the center of the Trellixian Empire.

Battle Commander Balforr had just left a meeting with High Commander Kaldre. He was extremely disappointed to learn no more of the new and more powerful battlecruisers would be built. He greatly feared the one hundred and twelve under his command were not going to be enough to keep the Empire safe.

"The High Command does not recognize the threat the Humans and the Voltrex represent with their Jelnoid technology," he said as he took his seat on the command pedestal gazing around the Command Center of his flagship. He had named his new ship the *Conquest* after his former flagship. "Too many of our leaders are still set in the old ways and believe we cannot be defeated in battle. Only High Commander Kaldre understands the true significance of the threat."

"It is difficult to accept," replied Second Officer Albion. "Even after witnessing the power of the enemy, I still find it hard to believe our forces can be defeated even though I have seen it with my own eyes."

"It has been very seldom we have encountered an advanced race," said Battle Commander Balforr, his large eyes focusing on his second in command. "We have become overconfident in our power as it has never been tested except briefly by the Jelnoids."

Second Officer Albion gazed at several viewscreens showing some of the new vessels of the fleet. "Reports from the edge of Voltrex space indicate our fleets there have been defeated. Heavily armed convoys are traveling routinely between Voltrex space and the Human home world. I fear this war with the Voltrex and the Humans is soon to expand."

Battle Commander Balforr knew Albion was correct. The Humans would be seeking revenge for what he had done to their world. With the aid of the Voltrex, the Humans could become a major threat to the Empire. Only High Commander Kaldre understood the threat and Balforr wasn't certain even the High Commander fully understood what could be in the Empire's future. The Humans would not rest until the Empire was destroyed.

"High Commander Kaldre is arranging for our new fleet to be reinforced with two hundred and sixty of our regular battlecruisers. For the time being we are to keep our fleet close to the home worlds until we learn more of what the Humans and the Voltrex are going to do."

Second Officer Albion looked surprised. "You don't expect them to attack us here!"

Battle Commander Balforr slowly nodded his head. "It's what I would do. Can you imagine the effect on the Empire if a Human or Voltrex invasion fleet showed up above one of our primary worlds?"

Albion remained silent. It was more than he could imagine. It was nearly incomprehensible for him to believe a Trellixian world could be attacked.

Balforr let out a deep breath. "Unfortunately for most of the High Command, that's what it's going to take to make them realize how dangerous the Humans and the Voltrex are."

Balforr leaned back in his command chair as he considered his options. He needed more of the advanced ships, a lot more and the only way he was going to get them was if the Humans and the Voltrex put in an appearance near the home worlds. Only then would the High Command realize the threat they represented and agree to build the battlecruisers Balforr needed. Once that was done, he would return to the Humans' system and destroy it. This time he would make sure not a single one survived.

Admiral Edwards stared down at the pockmarked surface of the Moon. The *Renown* was in orbit above Mare Serenitatis where Earth's primary defensive base was located. On the ship's main viewscreen a magnified view of the base was being displayed. A large number of small underground hangers hid the two hundred and forty fighter-bombers which called the base home. Around the base a ring of primary and secondary Jelnoid cannons prevented any potential attacker from getting within range. An energy shield also protected the base.

"I understand the Voltrex are going to be sending us some of their small patrol ships," said Captain Nelson who was standing close to the admiral.

Edwards nodded. "Yes; twenty of them. They're being modified for Human use and we'll use them to patrol between the Earth and the Moon. They'll be based here."

Captain Nelson stood gazing at the viewscreens and then turned and addressed the admiral. "We've done a hell of a lot in the last few months, but the Trellixians have an Empire and who knows how many ships. At some point they're bound to return and in overwhelming force. They might be able to ignore the Voltrex due to the distance involved but we're inside their Empire. They don't dare let us continue to exist."

"That's why we're sending out Captain Dolan and the *Fury*. We want to know what type of defenses the Trellixians have around their worlds." Then in a lower voice, he added, "We've also spoken to the Voltrex about finding a world close to their space we can colonize. If we can't hold Earth at least our people will go on."

"Leave Earth," said Captain Nelson, shaking his head. "I would hate to see that."

On the main viewscreen, a flight of four of the small fighter-bombers rose into space from the Moon base. The small ships were being used for patrol duty around the Moon and the Earth. "Every day we grow stronger," said Admiral Edwards. "The Trellixians will not like what they find when they return. In another year's time we will be ready for them."

Captain Nelson watched the small fighter bombers rapidly climb into orbit. At any one time, there were several wings of the small craft out on patrol. "I will feel better when we have additional spacecraft. So far the Voltrex have been more than willing to aid us. Will that continue when we begin taking ship losses? It can't be cheap to build one of their battlecruisers or a battleship."

Admiral Edwards turned toward another viewscreen showing the new shipyard being assembled in Earth orbit. "In another few months we'll be capable of building our own full scale battlecruisers. I've already spoken to General Mitchell and he's met with the president and the other surviving world leaders.

Once this shipyard is finished we'll start on a second and much larger one."

"We're going to need resources," pointed out Captain Nelson. "It takes a lot of special metals to build a warship."

"The asteroids, small moons, and even comets will be the key to our resources," explained Admiral Edwards. "The Voltrex have considerable experience in mining those types of resources. We'll learn from them."

Admiral Edwards had spent nearly four weeks in Voltrex space learning everything he could from them. He had toured their big battlestations, shipyards, research facilities, and even one of their space academies where they trained fleet personnel. He had returned to Earth with a treasure trove of information, which General Mitchell and others had gone over meticulously. Over the months a plan had been hammered out for the defense of the Solar System and the signing of a formal alliance with the Voltrex Federation by the ruling governments of Earth. Edwards knew in a few more months all of the Voltrex fleet would be fully modernized with Jelnoid technology. Once that was finished more emphasis would be placed on getting the six planned battlestations for Earth completed. Edwards knew the parts were already under construction in Voltrex space and would be transported by convoy to Earth orbit for final assembly.

"We have a message from the *Fury*," reported Lieutenant Simmins. The *Fury* was equipped with a hyperspace transmitter with a range of over twenty light years. However, the ship also had a number of hyperspace relay drones on board which would be dropped off along their line of flight to allow for longer-range communications. "All ships are functioning just fine and they see no reason to turn back. First communications drone has been released."

Admiral Edwards nodded. With a little luck they would be able to maintain communications throughout the entire mission. The drones were of Voltrex design and widely used in their Federation for communication between ships and planets. "Confirm the message. Inform Captain Dolan to maintain communications silence except for the regular scheduled checks." Edwards didn't want the Trellixians to use the comm signals to trace the small fleet.

Several days later Mark took a deep breath as the *Fury* and her fleet dropped out of hyperspace and dropped off a communications drone in a small red dwarf star system. For the time being, there was no attempt to survey any systems along their flight path. Their destination was an area of space where captured computer files indicated the Trellixians had their home worlds.

"Second drone has been deployed," reported Chloe. "Drone is functioning normally."

"Take us back into hyperspace," ordered Mark, glancing over at Lieutenant Masterson. Every twenty light years they would come out of hyperspace and drop off a communications drone. Every one hundred and twenty light years they would send a brief signal to test their single line of communications.

A few minutes later Mark felt the *Fury* make the transition back into hyperspace, speeding away from the red dwarf star system. Looking around the Command Center, he saw the entire command crew was at their posts efficiently doing their jobs. Every once and a while he could see the special lieutenants talking to each other over their private comm line. He didn't listen in though he could have. Mark felt after forcing them to undertake this dangerous mission he at least owed them some privacy.

"Did you take any sensor readings in the red dwarf system?" asked Brett. He knew they hadn't been in the system for long.

"Just a few," replied Lisa, sounding disappointed. "There was a small asteroid field and a couple of comets. Nothing really of interest." Lisa was trying to take as many readings as possible anytime the ship dropped out of hyperspace.

"We'll be stopping at a white dwarf next," said Kia. "Perhaps we'll find something of interest in that system."

Derek let out a deep sigh. "We're hunting Trellixians. Their home worlds. We're not really out exploring this time."

Lisa looked over at her friends. "Do you think the Trellixians have a weakness we can exploit?"

"Everyone has a weakness," said Brenda as she checked a few readings on the main engineering console. "We just need to figure out what it is."

"We need to find their shipyards," said Brett. "If we could find those and then destroy them the lizards would not be able to continue to expand their Empire."

Derek shook his head. "They're bound to be powerfully defended. There's no way the Trellixians would let us get close enough."

"What about their convoys?" asked Brenda. "They have to bring large quantities of materials from their mining operations to maintain their fleets and worlds. If we could destroy some of their convoys they might run out of the necessary material to build new ships."

"Won't work," replied Brett, shaking his head. "They'll just use their fleets to protect the convoys, if they even travel in a convoy."

Lisa let out a deep sigh. "We'll know more when we get to our destination. We have a pretty good idea where their primary worlds are located. We're going to scan as many of their home systems as possible before returning home. Maybe after we study those scans we can come up with something." Lisa sincerely hoped so, or it was going to be a long war; one the human race couldn't win.

-

Chloe was listening to her Human friends talk. She knew they were deeply concerned about the Trellixians and whether anything could be done about them. Chloe was already running simulations of various tactics to use against the lizard people but she just didn't have enough information to know if any of them would work. She needed more data, a lot more.

-

Near the Trellixian home world Battle Commander Balforr was studying the large tactical display. There were nearly a thousand green icons spread across it. Each icon represented a Trellixian cargo or warship, even a few colony ships.

"Do you believe the Humans will come here?" asked Second Officer Albion. "Surely they would not be so foolish."

"Look at the display," replied Balforr, gesturing toward the screen. "How do we defend so many ships and our planets? Unlike the Humans and the Voltrex we don't have defensive grids around our worlds. We never thought there was a need. Our shipyards and some of the orbiting space stations have weapons and shields but for the most part our planets are unarmed."

"We have our fleets!" said Albion, looking confused.

"Fleets the Humans and the Voltrex can destroy," responded Balforr in a grim tone.

Albion stood in silence as he gazed at the tactical display. He had never considered the need to be able to protect or defend a Trellixian world.

"What will we do if the Humans appear and drop fusion missiles on one of our planets like we did theirs?" After studying the Humans, Balforr was convinced the Humans would do exactly that.

"That would kill millions of our people," gasped Albion in disbelief. "Why would they do such a thing?"

"Because we did it to them and countless others," answered Balforr. "They do not regard us as a superior race."

It took several moments for Albion to fully grasp what Balforr was saying. "What are we to do?"

Balforr clenched his fist and returned to the command pedestal. "We must prepare. We may suffer massive losses when the Humans and the Voltrex first attack. Those losses must be allowed so the High Command will build more warships. In time we will have the forces necessary to defeat both the Humans and the Voltrex, but not at first."

"So what do we do?"

Battle Commander Balforr turned toward Albion. "We will send out some of our regular battlecruisers to monitor our more heavily populated systems for any signs of enemy warships. When they do attack we must be very cautious about committing our new warships. They may be all that stands between us and disaster."

"I still don't see the danger," said Albion, baring his teeth. "Our people are spread across a thousand star systems. The Humans only have one and the Voltrex a handful. We have thousands of warships. Surely we can prevail."

Balforr's eyes turned red but he kept his anger in check. The High Command was suffering from this same misguided thinking. They were too isolated from the problem. Only with the arrival of the Humans and the Voltrex would their line of thinking change. Balforr looked toward the viewscreens, gazing at the myriad of stars being portrayed. He wondered where the Humans were and how soon they would arrive.

Chapter Four

Fleet Commander Kamuss gazed at the tactical display, noting the disposition of his fleet. Very shortly they would be dropping out of hyperspace to attack their first Trellixian world. Voltrex scout ships were searching Trellixian space near the Voltrex Federation for possible Trellixian colony worlds. One such world was known and Kamuss had been ordered to attack it. Scans from the scout ships indicated the planet they would be attacking was called Capal Four and had only recently become a Trellixian colony. A large number of Trellixian colony ships were in orbit as well as warships. Fleet Commander Kamuss was leading two Voltrex fleets into combat: his own fleet as well as Fleet Commander Masurl's. Between the two of them they had over three hundred Voltrex warships.

"Fleet is at Battle Condition Two," reported Lieutenant Commander LeLath as she wet her face whiskers with her tongue in anticipation of combat. It felt good to be taking the battle to the enemy.

Kamuss nodded, knowing the *Claw of Honor* was ready for combat. "Long-range sensors?"

"Picking up Trellixian ships in orbit around the fourth planet," reported Zalurr. "Just as the Humans reported and the same as our scout ships."

Fleet Commander Kamuss knew the Humans had scanned this system on their way to Voltrex space. Scout ships had also confirmed the results of the Human scans. The fourth planet in the system was being turned into a Trellixian colony world. The Human vessels and the Voltrex scout ships had detected the ruins of hundreds of cities, ones which had been nuked from orbit. Kamuss felt a cold chill run through him. This was what the Trellixians would do to all Voltrex worlds if they weren't stopped.

"We'll drop out of hyperspace and engage all the Trellixian warships, then go into orbit around the planet," said Kamuss. He had orders to eradicate all Trellixian colonization efforts. From the scans the Humans had taken he knew the planet once possessed a civilization with steam age technology. They had stood no chance against the Trellixians when they invaded. It must have been a slaughter. The Trellixians had a history of showing no mercy and Fleet Commander Kamuss intended to show the Trellixians the same with what he was about to do to them.

-

"Twelve minutes to hyperspace drop out," reported Lieutenant Commander LeLath as she checked the fleet's current position. "They will be detecting us at any moment." She knew the Trellixians' sensors could reach out a short distance from the system and would be picking up the inbound fleets at any second. She wondered what they would think when they realized they were the target of this attack. She did not believe a Trellixian colony world had ever been attacked before. LeLath could feel the blood rushing through her system and her heart was beginning to pound in her chest.

-

"It will do them no good," replied Kamuss, his eyes growing cold. "We will show them the same mercy they showed the inhabitants of this system."

Lieutenant Commander LeLath nodded. This war was about to become very brutal. There would be no quarter given on either side.

-

Battle Commander Katella frowned deeply at the tactical display on his flagship. "Are you certain those are Voltrex warships?" The ship's sensors had sounded a warning alarm only moments before.

"Yes," replied the sensor officer. "The sensors are detecting three hundred and twelve Voltrex warships inbound toward Capal Four. We have a little over ten minutes before they begin dropping out of hyperspace."

For several moments Battle Commander Katella stood frozen, unsure of what to do. He had twenty-two battlecruisers with which to defend the planet. Not only that there were over thirty cargo ships in the system and sixty-eight colony ships. A large colony fleet had only arrived the day before with colonists from one of the overcrowded home systems.

"All battlecruisers prepare for combat," ordered Katella, settling back in his command chair. He had received reports of serious setbacks along the border with the Voltrex, even reports of Trellixian fleets being defeated. Inquiries to the High Command had failed to confirm any of the reports though Katella had begun to wonder at the silence.

"What about the colony ships?" asked his second-in-command.

Katella studied the tactical display for a moment and then replied. "Have them activate their energy shields and stay in a low orbit. Our battlecruisers should be able to drive the Voltrex back if they dare to attack. All the colony ships have energy shields as well as a few basic defenses. If they stay in a low orbit they should be fine. Order all cargo ships to go into lower orbit as well. Send a message to the High Command that we have a large Voltrex fleet about to enter the system."

Katella knew there were no other Trellixian forces in the immediate vicinity he could call upon for assistance. He was on his own and would have to defend the colony if the Voltrex attacked. He thought back and could not recall a single case of a Trellixian colony world ever being attacked.

-

Fleet Commander Kamuss let out a deep breath as the *Claw of Honor* emerged from hyperspace a few thousand kilometers from the Trellixian ships. The fleet was ready for combat as red threat icons flared up on the tactical display.

"All ships report successful emergence," reported Lieutenant Commander LeLath. "Weapons are ready to fire."

"We have target locks on enemy battlecruisers," reported Diboll from Tactical.

"Then fire!" ordered Kamuss, leaning forward in his command chair. It was time for the Trellixians to learn what it felt like to be in a hopeless situation where they were outgunned and had nowhere to run. He had emerged within weapons range hoping to be able to take out many of the cargo and colony ships before they could flee.

-

Energy beams flashed out, striking the orbiting Trellixian battlecruisers. Missile hatches slid open and forty-megaton fusion missiles launched. Across the skies of Capal Four bright flashes of light designated the location of Trellixian battlecruisers as they came under attack. Millions of Trellixians looked upward at the unexpected sight. Alarms on the grounded colony ships began to sound.

-

Battle Commander Katella reeled from the ferocity of the attack on his battlecruisers. In bright flashes of light the *Lamora* and *Vasari* vanished from the tactical display. Only two diffused blobs of expanding wreckage remained.

"Both ships have been destroyed," confirmed the sensor operator. "Their energy shields were overloaded from multiple detonations of fusion warheads."

"Jelnoid weapons," muttered the second officer, his eyes growing wide with alarm. "We have heard rumors of this."

Katella felt at a loss as to what to do. He had never been engaged in combat like this before. "Contact all the colony ships and the cargo ships. They are to flee to the Lantoll Six system and await there for further orders." Lantoll Six was the next nearest Trellixian colony world. Looking at the viewscreens, he could see bright flashes of light indicating the detonation of numerous fusion weapons. He realized most of the ships under his command were doomed.

"It will take a few minutes for the cargo and colony ships to escape," replied the second officer. "Many of the ships were not prepared for a combat situation and their drives have to be charged."

On one of the viewscreens, a cargo ship blew apart as Voltrex energy beams carved it up.

The Trellixian fleet was now replying with its own weapons and Katella felt stunned at how ineffective they were. The energy shields protecting the Voltrex ships seemed to be unaffected by Trellixian weapons fire. "Intensify our rate of fire," he roared as another Trellixian battlecruiser was blown apart. His fleet didn't have any of the stronger 50-megaton fusion missiles some of the fleets possessed. "How soon before the cargo ships and the colony ships leave?"

"Most of them won't be able to make it in time," reported the second officer. "There are also the ones down on the surface."

Katella took a deep breath. He was overseeing the greatest disaster ever suffered by the Empire. If he did nothing to stop the Voltrex fleet irreplaceable cargo and colony ships would be lost as well as millions of Trellixians citizens. With growing despair, he looked at the tactical display and viewscreens on the front wall of the Command Center. With a sinking feeling in the pit of his stomach, he knew there was nothing he could do.

-

Kamuss allowed a smile to cross his face as the ships under his command continued to close and attack the Trellixian vessels. Battlecruisers, colony ships, and cargo vessels were all under heavy attack. The space above Capal Four was full of dying ships, all of them Trellixian!

"Their weapons are not penetrating our energy screens," reported Lieutenant Commander LeLath jubilantly.

"A number of their ships are showing energy spikes in preparation for entry into hyperspace," warned Zalurr as his sensors showed the increased energy readings.

"Target those vessels," ordered, Kamuss, leaning forward. "We don't want any of these ships escaping." Kamuss knew he was slaughtering civilians on the colony ships but in his opinion no Trellixian was a civilian. They all represented a danger and had to be eliminated.

-

Voltrex battleships, battlecruisers, and support ships closed on the Trellixian vessels, hammering them with unrelenting weapons fire. Most of the Trellixian commanders had never been under fire and their efficiency disintegrated. Colony ships tried to leave orbit only to get in the way of other ships. With deadly efficiency, the Voltrex warships tore into the Trellixian vessels, blowing them apart and sending flaming debris falling into the planet's atmosphere.

A colony ship commander ordered his vessel to turn eighty degrees, causing it to collide with a nearby cargo ship. In a blinding explosion, both vessels were turned into glowing debris, which slammed into the energy shields of other vessels. The orbital space above Capal Four was rapidly filling with wreckage. Steaks of bright light were visible in the atmosphere where tons of wreckage burned up as it plummeted downward.

A Trellixian battlecruiser was struck by several energy beams, which cut through the energy shield, drilling deep holes in the hull. The ship seemed to stagger as its power fluctuated. Several large explosions blew out sections of the hull as secondary explosions rattled the ship. A forty-megaton fusion missile arrived, turning the vessel into fiery ruins.

"Three more Trellixians battlecruisers, seven colony ships, and four cargo ships confirmed destroyed," reported Zalurr.

"Fleet Commander Masurl reports only minimal damage to his ships and is pressing the attack," added Meela.

"The Trellixian resistance is highly unorganized," added Lieutenant Commander LeLath. "Their ships are fighting more as individuals rather than in pairs or squadrons. If they continue to resist in this manner we may not lose a ship."

Fleet Commander Kamuss nodded and gazed at the tactical display and viewscreens. In the centermost screen a blue white world was visible. It had once been the home of another sentient race until the Trellixians arrived. Now the surface of the planet was littered with the ruins of their cities. A brilliant flash on a different viewscreen was the result of another Trellixian colony ship being destroyed. Kamuss had no pity for the race of lizards. They had killed billions, perhaps trillions of innocents in their mad desire to spread their race across the cosmos.

"A few Trellixian cargo ships and colony ships have managed to make the jump into hyperspace," called out Zalurr in disappointment.

"Target the drives of all remaining Trellixian ships," ordered Kamuss. "I don't want them getting away." The Humans and the Voltrex Fleet Command had discussed what was to be done at Capal Four and any other world the Trellixians had ruthlessly conquered. They would be shown no mercy and all traces of the invaders, both in orbit and upon the planets would be erased. There would also be a quick search made for the former inhabitants in case a few had managed to escape detection in the mountains.

The viewscreens continued to be covered in flashes of light. Energy beams flashed between the battling ships and occasionally a fusion warhead detonated causing the screens to dim briefly.

Fleet Commander Kamuss noticed the number of Trellixian vessels was rapidly decreasing. Red icons continued to flare up and then vanish from the tactical display. He was extremely grateful for the Jelnoid weapons and energy shield the Humans had provided. The war was no longer as unilateral as it once had been. The odds in battle were now on the side of the Voltrex.

"Planet is englobed and most of the enemy ships have been destroyed or disabled," reported Lieutenant Commander LeLath as the green icons of the two fleets now dominated the tactical displays.

"Destroy them all," ordered Kamuss in a cold voice. "We will be taking no prisoners today." The Trellixians had long since set the tone for this war. It would be fought to the death with no quarter given.

-

Battle Commander Katella picked himself up off the deck of his Command Center. The room was full of smoke and several consoles were on fire. The air was becoming increasingly difficult to breathe as the ventilation system failed to keep up with recirculating the air.

"We're loosing the ship," gasped the second officer as he coughed violently. "We have several fires out of control and the hull has been heavily compromised."

The ship shook violently, making it nearly impossible to stand. Katella looked at the tactical display, which was flickering. Most of his fleet was gone and heavy damage had been done to the orbiting colony and cargo ships. Katella doubted if more than ten had managed to escape. Millions of Trellixian colonists were dead or soon would be. "Send a message to the High Command that Capal Four has fallen to the Voltrex. Our fleet has been destroyed as well as most of the colony ships and cargo ships. Inform them we were only able to inflict minor damage to the attacking vessels."

The lights went out and then came back on again. A tearing noise was audible as the hull was ripped apart nearby.

"Message sent," reported the communications officer.

"Energy shield has failed!" called out the tactical officer, his eyes showing shock. "We have lost 80 percent of our weapons."

"The ship is coming apart!" cried out the second officer as the Command Center began shaking violently and the lights faded.

Soon Battle Commander Katella was sitting in darkness with only the light from the consoles which were on fire. This was the end and he knew it. It was a situation he had never expected to find himself in.

Fleet Commander Kamuss closed his eyes as a bright flash filled the viewscreens.

"Enemy flagship has been destroyed," confirmed Lieutenant Commander LeLath.

"All Trellixian battlecruisers have been eliminated," added Zalurr.

Kamuss leaned back in his command chair, feeling the tension leave him. The battle was over and his fleet had won. "The enemy colony and cargo ships?"

"Fleet Commander Masurl reports the last orbiting colony ship will shortly be eliminated," said Meela.

Lieutenant Commander LeLath stood for a moment gazing at several viewscreens, which showed the surface. "What about the Trellixian colony ships on the surface?"

Kamuss took a deep breath. He hoped what he was about to order would not come back to haunt him, but there was no way the Voltrex Federation or the Humans could afford to mount an invasion of the planet below. "Place a fusion missile in the heart of each of their new cities. We'll leave a few ships in orbit to ensure we got them all as well as to scan the mountainous regions for any signs of the original inhabitants. If any are found we will attempt to rescue them or at the minimum offer what aid we can so they can survive."

The Voltrex fleet went into orbit around Capal Four. Resistance had ceased though there were still colony ships on the surface equipped with energy shields and a few defensive weapons.

Fleet Commander Kamuss looked down upon the planet with disgust. Many of the huge colony ships were well on their way to being dismantled. Tall towers surrounded many of them where Trellixian architecture was coming into being. Kamuss knew the structures soared several thousand meters into the air as well as deep beneath the surface. Large numbers of Trellixians as well as some type of robots were busy expanding their foothold upon the planet.

"There must be tens of millions of them," said Lieutenant Commander LeLath, her whiskers standing out straight. "They are building upon the ruins of the former cities."

"Raw resources," replied Kamuss. "That's all the cities of the former inhabitants are good for."

"We will have all of the Trellixian surface installations targeted shortly," reported Diboll. "We will be using small fusion weapons with a warhead of fifty kilotons. That should be sufficient to destroy the targets. Sitting on the planet, the energy shields of their colony ships will not be able to protect them."

Kamuss nodded. By now Captain Dolan would be on his mission toward the heart of the Trellixian Empire. He wondered who had the more difficult assignment. "Fire the missiles," he ordered. It was time to cleanse this planet of the Trellixians.

-

The *Claw of Honor* vibrated slightly as the small missiles launched. Other ships launched as well. Shortly seventy-eight fusion explosions lit up the surface of the planet as the warheads detonated. Everywhere a warhead went off a brilliant light lit the surface. Metal melted and the ground was ravaged. The buildings of the Trellixians came tumbling down. Mushroom clouds clawed into the air as superheated air rushed upward. In most areas, the Trellixian colony ships simply ceased to be.

Tens of millions of the lizard people died almost instantly. Millions more would starve to death over the coming weeks. Capal Four was no longer a Trellixian colony world. It was time for the fleet to go on seeking additional targets.

Chapter Five

Captain Dolan drew in a deep breath. They were on the second week of their mission and so far had not been detected. Granted they had only stopped in a few systems but that was soon to change. From captured computer files they had a list of worlds they wanted to scan to determine the density of the Trellixians' population as well as the infrastructure in place to sustain their Empire.

"We estimate the Trellixian Empire is spread out over several thousand worlds in around eleven hundred star systems," reported Lieutenant Masterson as he studied some reports on the table in front of him.

"There will be worlds they've conquered, some uninhabited worlds they've colonized, as well as worlds they're terraforming," added Lisa. She had spent considerable time reviewing the captured computer files retrieved from damaged or nearly destroyed Trellixian warships the Voltrex had accessed.

"The further we go toward the heart of their Empire the greater the concentration of inhabited worlds," added Kia. "They will have had centuries to modify worlds to allow for their colonization. On many of the moons of their main systems, there will be domed colonies and possibly even orbital habitats around the major planets."

Mark crossed his arms across his chest his face wrinkling in a frown. "What type of infrastructure will it take to maintain an empire of thousands of worlds?" Mark could not imagine what such an empire would be like. Much of the information in the captured files seemed too fantastic. Worlds with populations in the tens of billions, massive space fleets of colony and cargo ships going back and forth, a massive space war fleet constantly seeking new worlds to conquer.

"It will be interconnected," said Brenda. "All their planets will be dependent on each other. I don't even want to think of the logistics nightmare just to deliver the raw materials the planets must need. We've seen the shipyards the Voltrex have in orbit around their worlds. Imagine the same thing with the Trellixians but on a much grander scale."

"Lieutenant Olsen is correct," said Katana, straightening her face whiskers out with one of her hands. "Similar to our worlds the Trellixians will have much more. Their shipyards will be massive and no doubt there will be huge orbital factories for construction of basic materials. As for defenses, we have no idea since no one has ever seen one of the lizard peoples' core worlds."

Mark looked at his command crew. "What type of defenses can we expect as we penetrate deeper into the Trellixian Empire? Surely they will have scout ships and battlecruisers out protecting their space."

"Maybe not," responded Katana. "From what we have been able to find out the Trellixians have never suffered an actual invasion of any type. The most advanced race they ever encountered were the Jelnoids which nearly threw them for a loop. They suffered heavy losses destroying the Jelnoid fleet and conquering the Jelnoid worlds. While the Trellixians are a warlike race they have little experience in battle when it comes to an adversary that can fight back."

Lisa nodded in agreement. "Most of their conquests have been worlds unable to resist. Look how easily they smashed Earth's defenses. It was only the Jelnoid technology that made our resistance even possible." Lisa shuddered thinking about all the lives lost. Her home, family, friends, all had been lost in the early days of the attack.

"We will begin to check their known inhabited systems shortly," Mark informed them. "The Voltrex downloaded a number star maps from captured shuttles and damaged ships. We have a good idea where their core worlds are. The goal of this mission is to survey as many of those worlds as possible without risking our ships."

Brett looked uneasy. "They're bound to detect our ships at some point. Once they do we can expect an immediate response.

They most likely have hundreds of warships around their core worlds. We may find it a lot easier to get in than to get back out."

Lisa felt a cold shiver pass over her. She knew Brett was right. "Our sensors have an effective range of nearly half a light year. We don't have to go in too close to get sufficient readings."

"We still don't know what the range of Trellixian's sensors are," pointed out Katana. "They may be able to detect us at that range as well."

Mark turned his attention to Lisa and Kia. "How close do we need to come to thoroughly scan a system and not miss anything?"

Kia let out a deep sigh. "Less than half a light year. If we want a thorough scan we'll need to come in close; preferably inside the system if we want detailed scans."

Mark leaned back in his chair. "We can use the long-range sensors to scan the system before we drop out of hyperspace. If we feel the system is too dangerous or there are too many unknowns we can pass it by."

"We have the special stealth probes we can launch and keep the fleet back at a safe distance," said Katana. "Both the *Fury* and the *Horizon* have a number on board."

Looking over at Katana, Mark nodded his head. "That is an option. If we use the probes we would not be risking our ships though we're not sure yet how well the probes will work."

"They should work fine," Katana reassured Mark. "At least they did in the tests we ran."

"Very well then. If we feel the system is too dangerous to take our ships into we'll try the probes."

Lisa felt partially reassured by this. It made her nervous being so deep in Trellixian space, knowing if they got into trouble no one could come to their rescue.

Kia hesitated and then spoke. "What will the Trellixians' response be when they discover our ships? At some point that's going to happen."

"It may be awhile," Katana said. "There will be thousands of Trellixian ships in the region of space we're heading into. In all the confusion they might not even realize we're there for quite some time."

Mark shook his head. "We should not count on that. We should be prepared to be discovered at any moment."

"We should have brought a few of our scout ships," added Katana, her eyes narrowing in thought. "The newer stealth ones would have been useful."

Mark had to agree with this. Bringing along a few of the Voltrex stealth scout ships had been discussed but the small ships would have been stressed travelling so far. "In two more days time we will stop to scan our first Trellixian world and monitor ship movements which should help us to locate any planets not in the database we currently have."

"How long will we be out here?" asked Lisa. This was a question she had asked Professor Wilkins but he had been evasive in his answer.

Mark let out a deep breath. "As long as it takes. We have a mission to accomplish and that involves learning as much about the Trellixians as possible. When we've done that or when it becomes too dangerous for us to continue then we shall return."

Lisa wasn't surprised by this answer. Captain Dolan was a career military officer and he wouldn't back off until he accomplished what they set out to do. She had a sinking feeling this was going to be a long mission. That was just longer she and Brett would have to keep their feelings for each other bottled up.

"How will we use the fighters on the carrier?" asked Brett. "They're too small to contain hyperdrives. I'm not sure what purpose they can serve. I've thought about it and even using them to take close in sensor scans could be dangerous."

"I don't know," Mark answered. This was something he had pondered as well. "I think we're still evaluating what type of use they could be. We may regret bringing the carrier in the long run."

"The small attack craft could be useful against Trellixian infrastructure such as mines and other facilities on asteroids and small moons," suggested Katana. "I will speak to Chloe about running some simulations using them in such a manner."

The meeting lasted another hour with the group discussing how best to keep their ships from being discovered. The longer they could postpone that the better off they would be. However, the concern was that when their small fleet was finally discovered they would be very deep in Trellixian space. They might have to fight their way back to Earth.

Chloe was busy at her platform monitoring the ship's functions as well as listening to various conversations across the ship. She knew there was much concern about the safety of the mission. At the distant edge of the ship's long-range sensors Chloe could detect what might be a Trellixian vessel but before she could confirm the contact they were out of range. She decided not to bring the brief contact to Captain Dolan's attention. No point in alarming him or the rest of the crew.

So far the *Fury* and the other three ships had taken a course to avoid areas of space where there might be Trellixians ships. That was soon to change as they were nearing the region where the primary Trellixian worlds were located. They were going to scan many of the systems to see what the density of the population was as well as the type of infrastructure the Trellixians maintained.

Chloe was already setting up a simulation of the known Trellixian Empire. She was highly curious about what else they would be adding. Did the Empire have a weakness which could be exploited? It was the main reason for the fleet to be out here. Chloe was determined to find one if she could to help out her Human friends.

On the sensors, she watched as the small fleet passed by two more star systems. Very shortly it would be time for them to take their first detailed scans of a Trellixian world. Chloe reflected on how the ship felt. It almost seemed as if it was part of her body. Through the sensors, she could see the surrounding stars, inside the ship she could feel the pulse of the hyperdrive and listen to her friends. She felt full of life and was excited to be part of this mission. She would do everything she could to make it a success.

-

In the heart of the Trellixian Empire High Commander Kaldre felt shaken from the latest report. The Voltrex had taken Capal Four! Only a few cargo ships and colony ships had escaped to report the defeat.

"It is as I feared," he said to his second officer. They were in the Command Center of the *Dawn Reaper*, Kaldre's flagship. "The Voltrex are moving into our space."

"Surely this is but an isolated instance," protested Second Officer Calaah. "The Capal Four colony is the nearest one to their worlds. Perhaps they are only pushing our forces back to give themselves more breathing room."

Kaldre shook his head. "They are also sending more ships to the Human home world. Massive convoys arrive daily with war supplies. If the other High Commanders continue to refuse to take action this could blow up in our faces."

"But we're an Empire, the Humans are but one world!" protested Calaah. "Even with Jelnoid science I find it hard to understand how they can be a threat to the entire Empire."

Kaldre frowned deeply. "And therein lies the problem. No one seems to understand how big a threat they represent. Our Empire has gone on for far too long without a serious threat. Now that threat is here and our people refuse to recognize it."

"What about Battle Commander Balforr and his new fleet?"

"Balforr is our most experienced commander in fighting the Voltrex and the Humans yet he too has been defeated in every encounter." Kaldre looked at a viewscreen showing the large space station orbiting the home world. There were other large stations around the planet as well. Much of the planet's industrial power was situated in orbit. Huge colony and cargo ships were being built to allow for the continued expansion of the Empire. "You would think the rest of the High Command would have learned from the recent food riots the precipice our civilization is sitting on. These Humans and the Voltrex may be just enough to push us over the edge."

"Can we not build more warships?"

"The High Command is more concerned with building more colony ships and cargo ships. The new and more powerful battlecruisers like the fleet we just built for Battle Commander Balforr take twice the amount of time to build; time they don't want to waste on ships we may not need. We do have several shipyards still producing warships but they're not the newer ones I've requested."

Calaah looked confused as if he could not understand how the Empire could be threatened. It extended across thousands of light years of space.

Kaldre wondered what could be done with the forces at hand. Somehow, he needed to hold the Humans and the Voltrex back until the rest of the High Command recognized the threat. High Commander Thatrex seemed to be the most rational of the other High Commander in recognizing there might be a threat. Perhaps he could be talked into allowing the construction of more of the new battlecruisers. It was a long shot but Kaldre didn't see any other option. In the short term, he could order a few more fleets toward Voltrex space. He called up a star map of the Trellixian colonies nearest the cat peoples' sphere of influence. If he were right more colonies would soon be attacked. Even though it might be a useless sacrifice sending fleets to defend those worlds, it could help to prove his point to the other High Commanders, particularly High Commander Thatrex. If they saw their fleets being destroyed surely they would react!

On the *Fury* Chloe was beginning to feel uneasy. She was amazed at what it felt like to sense emotions. She knew it was part of her program and made her feel more alive. In the last several hours the ship's long-range sensors had detected what appeared to be several Trellixian cargo ships. There were no known colonies in this region of space but Captain Dolan had ordered Lieutenant Masterson to follow the ships at a discreet distance.

"We may be detected if we get too close," warned Chloe as the two cargo ships slowed and prepared to enter a small red dwarf system. "The system ahead has three planets. One is in the habitable zone."

"It's a red dwarf," muttered Lisa. "The planet will barely be habitable and the climate cold and harsh."

"They need living space," answered Katana, folding her arms over her chest. She peered at the readouts on one of the science computers. "That planet could hold several billion of the lizard people."

Lisa shivered, trying to imagine what it would be like to live on such a world. The long-range scans indicated a very short summer and a much longer winter. Temperatures on much of the planet would be below freezing. Blizzards and heavy snow would be common and they would have to import much if not all of their food.

"Detecting four Trellixian battlecruisers in low orbit," reported Kia as she studied the sensors. "No indication they've detected us."

For a moment Mark toyed with the idea of dropping out of hyperspace close to the planet and taking out the battlecruisers. He could then bombard the planet from orbit. With the limited firepower the Trellixians had there was nothing they could do to stop him. Then he straightened his shoulders. He didn't want to give the presence of his small fleet away; they still had a ways to go. "Lieutenant Masterson, veer us away from the system. There's nothing more for us to learn here. Our targets are deeper in Trellixian space."

-

The *Fury* changed course followed by the two small battlecruisers and the carrier. The Trellixians would never know they had been followed and their system scanned. The four ships continued on their course toward the heart of the Empire and the destiny that awaited them.

Chapter Six

President Katelyn Hathaway was in the main military Command Center watching several large viewscreens. In a few more minutes a major attack would be launched to clear the Trellixians out of the United States. Ground forces had been assembled as well as the necessary air assets. Vice President Jason Arnold was also with her.

"We're getting ready to set off more nukes," said Katelyn, her eyes showing her deep concern. "Won't that make the nuclear winter even worse?" The weather across the planet was already bad enough. They needed to get crops planted and put the farm animals back outside the domes onto pastures.

"It will in the short term," conceded Professor Wilkens with a frown. "However, with the aid of the Voltrex we should be able to limit its duration. They have provided a chemical which when sprayed in the air reduces the radiation as well as clears the atmosphere. The affects from the nukes will be short lasting. We're prepared to begin spraying the areas where the nukes will be dropped as soon as the fighting comes to a stop. Within two months you won't be able to tell we used any nukes. Within four months we should be able to begin planting crops."

Katelyn nodded. "I hope so. Even the people in Complex One would like to be able to go outside occasionally."

"They will; we all will be able to," promised Professor Wilkens.

That was good news. Folding her arms over her chest, she looked around. There were several Voltrex officers in the Command Center. Some of their troops would be taking part in the fighting. So much had changed since encountering the cat people. The Solar System was free of Trellixian ships and had been for months.

"All forces are in place and ready to commence the attack," reported General Briggs. "We'll hit their strong points with small nukes and orbital strikes then move in with our armor and air assets. Troops will be used to clear out any surviving pockets of resistance."

"Is the atmosphere clear enough for our aircraft?" asked Katelyn. There were very few days where one could even see the sun.

"Barely," replied General Briggs. "But we need the air assets if we want to clear the enemy out of their fortified positions."

"There's going to be some heavy fighting," said General Mitchell with a deep sigh. "The Trellixians are well dug in." It had taken months to plan this offensive and to position the necessary troops.

Katelyn's eyes narrowed. "We're going to lose a lot of people doing this."

"It's war," replied General Mitchell, looking over at the president. "Good men and women lose their lives in battles; it can't be helped. We'll do everything we can to hold our losses down to a minimum but the Trellixians are dug in pretty well in some locations and some of those locations will have to be taken by our troops."

Katelyn nodded her head. "I understand, General. I just wish there was another way."

"We all do," responded General Mitchell. Mitchell turned to General Briggs. "Give the order to launch the attack." Mitchell looked back at the viewscreens showing the Central United States. Once this was over there were parts of Northern Kansas which wouldn't be able to grow crops for years, possibly decades.

-

In orbit, battlecruisers moved down lower. Some of the strikes would be kinetic to take out the more hardened targets. Other strikes would be nuclear to take out troop concentrations and hover tanks. Energy screens protected many of the Trellixian fortifications and regular fire would be ineffective against those installations.

-

The Trellixians knew something was going on. In the last few days the Humans had moved in armor and large numbers of ground forces had tightened their grip on the surrounding area. Even a few Voltrex troops had been spotted.

In the primary Trellixian Command Center, the Trellixians noticed the movement of the battlecruisers. "We can expect an attack at any time," reported Second Officer Tolbert. "The enemy cruisers in orbit have come down considerably lower, no doubt in preparation for orbital bombardment."

Battle Commander Able shook his head in frustration. "We have been abandoned by the High Command. None of our attempts to establish communication with our superiors has been successful. The Humans are jamming our communication signals and none of our ships have been detected. We are on our own in the coming battle." He was still finding it hard to accept that his command had been abandoned.

"Our scouts report movement from the enemy troops encircling us," Tolbert said, his large eyes focusing on the Battle Commander. "They are coming closer and also have some armor in the form of heavy tanks with them."

Battle Commander Able took a deep breath. "Order all of our troops to cover. Once the initial bombardment is over we will move out en mass and engage the enemy. Our own hover tanks can take out the Humans' armor."

He still had some hover tanks within the energy dome. This would probably be the final battle on this planet. Battle Commander Able had no doubt in how it would end. His only goal now was to kill as many Humans as possible in the coming conflict.

-

On some of the orbiting ships missile tubes slid silently open. Only these tubes did not contain missiles but twenty-five foot tungsten rods. Each rod had control surfaces, which allowed their course to be adjusted as they plummeted through the atmosphere. They could burrow deep beneath the surface, penetrating the most hardened of bases. The kinetic energy released resembled the detonation of a small nuke.

From six ships twenty rods each were dropped and then after a full minute twenty more. Their targets were the primary bases of the Trellixians in the North Central United States as well as known troop concentrations. Then nukes were loaded into the missile tubes.

Colonel Branson was standing next to Major Juan Garcia near the front lines when the first brilliant streaks became visible in the atmosphere. The nearest would strike a few miles away. The two men ducked down into their bunker and moments later felt the ground shake. Several more times over the next few minutes the ground shook, sometimes violently and sometimes they could just barely sense it.

"Nukes are next," Branson said as he leaned against the reinforced wall of the small command bunker.

"Damn nukes," Garcia said but knowing they were necessary. There were just too many Trellixian troops in the enclosed area. At least they had the new radiation meds from the Voltrex. They had been modified for Human use.

Suddenly the ground shook again only more violently than before. Garcia looked over at Branson. He knew that had been a nuke somewhere in the five to ten kiloton range. None any bigger were going to be used in this battle.

Twenty minutes passed and the explosions seemed to stop. Garcia knew they hadn't but merely moved on to other areas while satellites surveyed the damage in the immediate area.

"That's it!" Colonel Branson said. He was listening to communication reports steadily coming in. "We have permission to launch the ground attack. We have attack helicopters and several squadrons of F-22 raptors available if we need to call them in. The F-35s are being held back due to the atmospheric conditions."

Garcia nodded and stepped outside the bunker. He stood staring in amazement. The landscape in front of the bunker had been transformed. Smoke and fire raged and several massive holes in the ground indicated where the tungsten rods had struck.

There were also signs of at least one nuke having gone off. If one didn't know better you would believe you were on an alien planet. The air was full of dust, smoke, and drifting ashes. Garcia shuddered knowing most of what he was looking at would be contaminated with radioactivity.

"All Rangers begin advancing toward your targets," he said over the comm system, which linked him to all of his troops. "If you encounter heavy resistance report back in and we'll send in air assets. I want casualties held to a minimum."

Garcia heard all the captains confirm his orders. "Rangers are advancing," he reported to Colonel Branson.

Branson nodded. "Our Marines and other units are advancing as well. It's going to get quite dicey out there really quick."

Garcia glanced at a nearby radiation detector showing an increase in radiation levels in the local area. It was nearly in the lethal range. He just hoped the new radiation meds worked as well as the Voltrex claimed they did.

President Hathaway stared in agony at the viewscreens showing views from orbit of the tactical strikes in northern Kansas and Southern Nebraska. Much of the view was obscured by rising clouds of dust, debris, and smoke. Even as she watched more explosions seemed to roam across the area in bright flashes of destruction.

"Those are kinetic strikes," General Mitchell explained. "They're non nuclear and won't add to the radiation levels."

"Why couldn't we use them instead of nukes?" asked Vice President Arnold, sounding confused.

"The blast from the nukes is more destructive and covers a wider area," replied General Briggs. "We used the minimum number we could to accomplish what needed to be done."

"Why more kinetic strikes?" asked Katelyn. She could see more large explosions across Kansas and Nebraska. She was relieved that the only ones in those areas were Trellixians. All the

Human civilians had been evacuated as soon as the Trellixians arrived.

"Our ground commanders are calling them in," answered General Briggs. "Whenever they encounter heavy resistance they pull back and call in a strike."

Katelyn took in a deep breath. Kansas and Nebraska would never be the same. However, if this operation and the one in China were successful the Trellixians' last bastions on Earth would be gone. Humans would once more control the entire planet.

Sergeant Anderson ducked his head as energy weapons fire erupted from the cornered Trellixians. Anderson wasn't sure how many there were but they were well armed and dug in. Several large explosions shook the ground, throwing dirt and rocks on his position.

"What now?" asked Corporal Donly over the comm. "We're taking losses from energy weapons fire and Private Hastings is reporting he can see several hover tanks in bunkers. We've also lost two of our tanks because of energy fire from the hover tanks. The Trellixians are also launching some type of small missiles at us."

Anderson took a moment to examine the situation. If they continued to advance, they could take out the Trellixians but would suffer heavy casualties. Not only that but with at least two hover tanks to add supporting fire Anderson didn't like the odds. "Pull back a thousand yards and I'll call in an orbital strike." He would also need to inform Major Garcia of the strike and why he was calling one down.

Several long minutes passed and reports began coming in that all the Rangers and the Marines involved in the battle had pulled back to the minimum safe range. Sergeant Anderson quickly informed the battlecruiser *Swiftfire* it could initiate the fire mission. Moments later Anderson saw a streak of light descending from above and quickly took cover in a small depression. The shaft of light reached down and struck the ground. A tremendous explosion shook the ground and a cloud of dust, debris, and smoke rose high into the air. Sergeant Anderson hugged the ground as a blast of superheated air from the explosion swept over him. Moments later debris from the strike began pelting him.

Standing back up and brushing himself off Anderson ordered the Rangers and Marines forward. Where the two hover tanks had been a massive smoking crater now existed.

"Encountering minimal resistance," Corporal Donly reported. "I think the strike took out most of them."

"Make sure," ordered Anderson, holding his energy rifle. "I want this area secure."

-

Major Garcia listened as more units reported in. Several had called in orbital strikes to clear out heavy Trellixian resistance. "The cats are meeting stiff resistance in their area. They've called in air assistance. We have a squadron of F-22s as well as some attack helicopters we can send in."

Colonel Branson nodded. There were four thousand Voltrex troops in one sector charged with clearing out the Trellixians. "Make sure they have whatever they need. I don't want to hear they've suffered major losses."

Major Garcia nodded as he contacted the waiting squadron of F-22s and attack helicopters. It wouldn't take them long to reach their targets, particularly the F-22s.

-

Battle Commander Able was not pleased with the progress of the battle. He wanted to kill as many Humans as possible however, wherever he committed sufficient troops to accomplish that purpose orbital strikes were wiping them out.

"We're suffering major losses," reported Second Officer Tolbert. "Most of our Command Centers have been destroyed and it's becoming more difficult to coordinate our troops. Many are cut off and slowly being annihilated. We won't last more than another twelve to sixteen hours."

"Pull as many as possible back around this Command Center. We still have some defenses we can activate." Battle Commander Able knew the battle was lost but he was still determined to make the Humans pay a heavy cost. His forces had been written off by the High Command. Even so, he would die as a Trellixian soldier giving his life for the Empire. He also didn't believe the Humans knew the location of his Command Center. No nukes or kinetic weapons had been used against it. A decoy Command Center a few kilometers away had been hit by a kinetic energy strike.

-

"All commands report steady progress," reported General Briggs, turning toward General Mitchell. "The cats are suffering the heaviest casualties, mostly due to inexperience. We've sent in some F-22s and attack helicopters to assist."

General Mitchell nodded. He had suggested embedding some Human troops in with the cats but their commanding officer had politely declined, claiming they needed to learn how to fight these types of battles.

"The Trellixians seem to be pulling back toward a central area," reported Colonel Fields. "I'm convinced from our orbital sensor scans they must have a hidden Command Post in that region."

General Briggs looked confused as he glanced over at General Mitchell. "They must know we can take it out with an orbital strike. This makes no sense."

"Unless they have a powerful energy shield for protection."

"It's not showing on the sensors," reported Colonel Fields, shaking his head.

"Never-the-less I want our people to approach that area with caution," replied Mitchell with a look of concern on his face. "I don't trust these Trellixians the least bit and I want to know the location of that Command Post if it exists."

-

The hours passed and the fighting grew heavier as the Trellixians reduced the size of their perimeter. Whenever possible orbital strikes were called in to take out large gatherings of Trellixian troops. However, the Trellixians quickly learned not to bunch up and were fighting a delaying action in smaller groups. They had lost many of their hover tanks but taken out a large number of Human tanks. They had also launched hundreds of splinter grenades, which had inflicted substantial casualties on the Humans and the Voltrex. The small missiles had stopped, indicating the Trellixians had probably depleted their supply.

"We need to activate the energy shield shortly," commented Second Officer Tolbert as he observed the withdrawal. "We've too many troops gathering above us and the Humans will most assuredly target us with an orbital strike."

Battle Commander Able nodded. By activating the energy shield, it would protect the base and the surrounding area from Human attacks. It would unfortunately trap thousands of his troops outside where the Humans could wipe them out. "Activate the shield as well as our reserve weapons. It's time we show the Humans we're not as toothless as they believe."

In hidden bunkers were dozens of hover tanks as well as powerful energy weapons which could nearly reach a target in orbit. Not only that he still had some small nukes in reserve.

"Shield activation in two minutes," reported Second Officer Tolbert.

The fighting around the hidden Trellixian base was growing steadily heavier. Jelnoid satellite sensors were scanning the ground, searching for the exact location of the Trellixians' last base. On all sides the Trellixian soldiers were pulling back with Human and Voltrex troops in close pursuit. Occasionally an orbital strike would slam into the ground, throwing up huge clouds of dust and smoke eliminating heavier Trellixian troop concentrations.

The air was full of F22s and attack helicopters adding their firepower to the escalating attack. Explosions dotted the landscape and it seemed as if the battle would soon be over.

Suddenly an energy field appeared, covering a large portion of the embattled Trellixian troops. From inside the field hover tanks suddenly materialized, firing their powerful energy cannons and splinter grenades at the advancing Human and Voltrex troops. Hidden energy cannons rose up from the ground, shooting at the aircraft flying high above.

"What the hell?" uttered General Briggs when he saw the attack suddenly come to a halt. All the viewscreens in the Command Center showed the same. No weapons were penetrating the Trellixian energy shield.

"What's happened?" asked President Hathaway, realizing something was wrong.

"An energy shield," replied General Mitchell. Turning toward General Briggs. "Order an immediate orbital strike on the center of that shield!"

A few moments later a brilliant light lit up the viewscreens focused on the Trellixian base. When the light faded away it was obvious the energy screen was still intact.

"The orbital strike had no effect on the shield," reported Colonel Fields as he checked his sensors. "It's much stronger than any Trellixian shield we've encountered before. They must have several fusion reactors tied into it."

"We're taking a lot of losses," General Briggs reported as he listened to reports coming in from the field.

General Mitchell glanced at the viewscreens just in time to see an F-22 burst into flame and crash to the ground.

"They have some very heavy energy beams which can penetrate our aircraft energy screens," reported Colonel Fields. "We've already lost several F-22s and four attack helicopters."

"Pull them back," ordered General Mitchell, his eyes narrowing sharply. "Pull our troops back as well. "It may be necessary to hit that shield with multiple orbital strikes as well as a nuke or two."

"More nukes?" asked President Hathaway in dismay. The number already used was upsetting. "Haven't we utilized enough already?"

"Only if it's necessary," replied General Mitchell, his eyes focused intently on the viewscreens showing the battle.

Katelyn frowned. She was deeply concerned about the affects of what they had already done. From her understanding China had done the same thing with the Trellixians in their country: orbital strikes from the battlecruisers as well as a liberal use of nukes to take out the enemy. From the reports she had received the Chinese would be finished with their operation in just a matter of hours.

-

Major Garcia watched as his Rangers and the Marines with them began to pull back to a safe distance. Sergeant Anderson had reported a number of casualties because of incoming fire from Trellixian hover tanks.

"There will be multiple orbital strikes starting in an hour," Colonel Branson said. "General Mitchell is hoping the strikes will knock down that energy shield."

"How did we miss this base to begin with?" asked Garcia, shaking his head.

"Command believes the base is buried deep beneath the surface and the Trellixians have done everything they can to keep its existence a secret."

Garcia looked out over the landscape of northern Kansas. It looked more like the surface of the Moon with huge bomb craters everywhere. The fighting for the last several hours had been intense with numerous airstrikes called in. Looking upward, he wondered if the orbital strikes would be able to take down the Trellixians' energy shield.

-

Battle Commander Able was satisfied with the latest reports from the battlefield. Nearly twenty thousand Trellixian troops were inside the energy shield and so far the shield had withstood the attacks from the Humans and their ships. With every passing minute more weapons were being moved to the surface. He intended to make this base and the area protected by the energy shield an impenetrable fortress.

"Reports indicate the Humans and the Voltrex are pulling back."

Battle Commander Able nodded at Second Officer Tolbert's report.

"And our troops which were outside the energy shield?" Able knew thousands had not managed to enter before the shield was activated.

Second Officer Tolbert shook his head. "Dead. The Humans called in their aircraft and bombed all of our positions outside the shield."

This did not surprise Battle Commander Able. It was what he would have done. "They died for the Empire."

"For the Empire," repeated Tolbert.

"Continue to focus our more powerful beam weapons on any of their aircraft that come close to our energy shield," ordered Battle Commander Able. "I want to keep them at a distance."

Second Officer Tolbert nodded. "What about their orbital strikes? They're bound to be more."

"Keep our sensors focused on their orbiting ships. Anytime it appears a strike has been launched divert all of our available power to the energy shield and let's hope it holds." Two fusion reactors powered the shield. The reactors also furnished power to some of the larger energy weapons. Battle Commander Able's eyes returned to the viewscreens. They showed the landscape above and a number of weapon emplacements including a few hover tanks being moved to better locations to bombard the encircling Human and Voltrex troops. Able was satisfied he had done everything in his power to prepare for this battle.

-

Major Garcia was now at a new Command Post. He was five miles away from the edge of the energy shield. Looking out across the Kansas countryside it was nearly unrecognizable from all the damage caused by the battle so far. Huge craters and burned out areas were everywhere. There was still a lot of dark smoke in the air and a few fires were burning. A few miles away a farmhouse and barn had been leveled.

"We've cleared out all enemy troops outside the energy shield," reported Captain Stockton. "We lost a few Rangers and some of the regular army troops in the fighting. It was quite intense at times and I've heard of a few instances where it was hand-to-hand."

Major Garcia looked upward. "We're expecting more orbital strikes shortly. General Mitchell is hoping they will bring the Trellixian shield down. Keep all of our Rangers and the Marines assigned to us undercover until the strikes are over."

"Yes, sir," Captain Stockton replied. Stockton paused, looking in the direction of the enemy energy shield. "There's a hell of a lot of Trellixians inside there."

Major Garcia nodded. He knew there were thousands of Trellixians soldiers inside the energy shield. "Let's hope the orbital strikes take most of them out."

Captain Stockton left returning to his command.

"Orbital strikes beginning in ten minutes," Garcia heard over his comm unit.

He quickly passed the message on to his commanders in the field. Taking a deep breath, he stepped back inside his hastily built bunker.

-

Sergeant Anderson slid down into the bottom of a bomb crater. It was nearly seven feet deep and should offer sufficient protection from the orbital strikes. The fighting this far had been tougher then expected with many of the Trellixian soldiers being well dug in. Losses had been nearly double what had been expected. It only went to show that a battle plan only worked until the actual battle started, then everything changed.

-

In space aboard the Voltrex built battlecruiser *Farstar*, Captain Lewis prepared to initiate his latest orders. His battlecruiser as well as four others had been ordered to lay down a barrage of projectiles on the Trellixian energy screen until it collapsed.

"Stand by to fire kinetic energy rounds," he ordered.

"Rounds loaded and ready to fire," reported the weapons officer.

Captain Lewis paused and then gave the order. "Fire!"

-

From the *Farstar* and four other ships twenty-five foot tungsten rods dropped out of the missile tubes falling toward their target. It did not take them long to enter the atmosphere, becoming glowing streaks of light similar to a meteor. They hurtled downward faster and faster until the first one struck the top of the Trellixian energy shield. In a massive burst of light the pent up kinetic energy equivalent to a small nuclear device was released. Moments later more rods struck the shield.

-

Sergeant Anderson heard the first explosion. He had seen the rods falling from the sky and taken cover in the bottom of the crater. A great blast of hot air roared over the crater, stirring up dust. The ground seemed to shake each time the Trellixian energy shield was struck. Sergeant Anderson was only three miles from the shield and he could imagine what it would be like to be any closer. He could even feel the heat from the blasts.

"I hope those cruisers are on target," muttered Corporal Donly. "Just one of those hitting the ground near us and we're finished."

Anderson nodded his agreement. He knew the kinetic rounds were supposed to be very accurate, or at least that's what he had been told in his briefing.

Anderson crawled up to the top of the crater, peering over it. The kinetic strikes seemed to have stopped and he was curious to see if the Trellixian energy shield had survived. One quick glance and he knew the orbital strikes had failed. The energy shield was still intact! With a deep sigh, he activated his comm to inform Major Garcia. He wondered what they would do now.

71

Battle Commander Able listened to the latest reports on the status of the energy shield. It had barely withstood the orbital strikes. Several times it had nearly failed. The energy being released by the kinetic strikes was much greater than expected.

"Is there nothing we can to do increase the power to the shield?" he asked one of the technicians standing nearby.

The Trellixian shook his head. "No, all available power has been diverted."

Able let out a deep breath. "No doubt the next orbital strike will be even more intense."

"Then the shield will fail and we will die," said the technician.

Battle Commander Able turned to Second Officer Tolbert. "Have all of our soldiers and the hover tanks gather near the shield walls. I will lower the shield and we will attack the encircling Humans and Voltrex. If our soldiers can get close enough to the enemy they will not dare use their orbital weapons against us."

"They will bring back their air support," pointed out Second Officer Tolbert.

"If they do we will use our primary energy cannons to shoot them down," replied Able. "As a Trellixian it is better to die in battle than to wait until one of their orbital weapons penetrates the energy shield and wipes us all out."

Second Officer Tolbert nodded his agreement. All Trellixian soldiers knew their duty to the Empire. They would die fighting their enemy. "I will order our soldiers forward to the edge of the energy shield."

"When they are in position, I will lower the shield," Battle Commander Able replied.

Inside the energy shield over twenty thousand Trellixian soldiers and seventy-four hover tanks began moving to the edge of the shield wall. The soldiers were all covered in dark armor and carried energy weapons. As soon as the shield dropped they would charge forward toward the enemy to kill as many as possible. The energy cannons scanned the skies searching for any signs of enemy aircraft. If they were spotted they would be shot down.

-

Second Officer Tolbert stepped closer to Battle Commander Able. "Permission to join our soldiers."

Battle Commander Able stared hard at Tolbert for several seconds and then nodded. "Permission granted. May the ground run deep with the blood of our enemies."

Able watched as Tolbert left the Command Post. Able knew he would never see him again.

-

General Mitchell gazed at the viewscreens with growing concern. "There's a lot of movement inside the Trellixian energy shield. Can we make that view any clearer?"

Colonel Fields spoke to several of the technicians operating the consoles and soon the screen cleared even more and the image was greatly enlarged. On the viewscreen they were all watching, it was evident the Trellixians were moving their soldiers and their hover tanks to the edge of the shield.

"Are they digging in to repeal an attack or are they getting ready to attack?" asked General Briggs suspiciously.

"Why would they attack when they are safe behind the shield?" asked President Hathaway.

"Because they know a sustained orbital bombardment can bring it down," replied Vice President Arnold. "Isn't that right, General?"

General Mitchell nodded. "Yes, our kinetic energy strikes nearly brought it down in the last bombardment. We're preparing to hit them again only with twice as many. The shield should collapse under such an attack."

-

All the Trellixian soldiers were gathered at the edge of the energy shield. Just behind them, the hover tanks were lined up ready to support the attack. The shield seemed to flicker and then it came down. In an instant, twenty thousand Trellixian soldiers were across the boundary and charging toward the Human and Voltrex lines. The hover tanks opened fire with their energy cannons searching for targets of opportunity, which at the moment were few as most of the enemy were several kilometers away. Behind them the energy dome snapped back into being.

-

Major Garcia heard the sudden roar of weapons fire and stepped out of the command bunker to see what was going on. His comm unit was suddenly swamped with reports of advancing Trellixian troops and armor. "It's a full scale attack," he reported to Colonel Branson, who was standing just behind him. "Looks as if they're throwing everything they have left at us. We have several commands requesting immediate orbital strikes."

Major Garcia knew the Trellixians in their armor could move very quickly and it would only be a matter of a few minutes before they reached the Human and Voltrex defensive lines.

"What are we going to do?" he asked. "We have thousands of Trellixian troops advancing along with a large number of hover tanks."

"First, we need to eliminate that dome," replied Colonel Branson as he tried to contact the orbiting ships. "Once the dome and the energy weapons it protects are gone then we can call in our air assets and deal with the enemy troops."

-

In orbit, the battlecruisers loaded more of the tungsten rods into their launch tubes. Moments later in a simultaneous launch, twenty of the deadly twenty-five foot rods fell toward the Earth and the energy dome which was their target.

-

Sergeant Anderson had crawled to the top of the bomb crater he was using as a shelter from incoming Trellixian fire. He could see a wave of Trellixian troops coming across the ground between his position and the energy dome.

"My God, there must be thousands of them!" said Corporal Donly from his side. Donly peered through the scope of his rifle knowing the advancing enemy were still outside the range of his energy rifle.

Anderson heard a noise above him and saw what looked like streaking meteors moving across the sky toward the dome. "Get down!" he shouted, shoving Donly back down the crater wall. "All troops, take cover! We have an orbital strike inbound," he added over his comm unit that connected him to his Rangers and the Marines assigned to him. He quickly joined Donly at the bottom of the crater trying to make himself as small as possible. He wished they were further away from the Trellixian energy dome.

-

Battle Commander Able listened without feeling as alarms sounded and red lights flashed. Several of the Trellixian officers in the Command Post looked over at him but Able did not respond. On one of the viewscreens, he could see the nearing orbital strikes. It would only be seconds before the weapons struck and there was no doubt the dome would fail. His own Command Post was buried deep beneath the ground but he wasn't sure if even it would survive.

Suddenly the screen turned into static and the Command Post shook violently. The lights went out and several consoles exploded in a shower of sparks. Emergency lighting came on, dimly lighting the large room. The ground continued to shake and Battle Commander Able thought he could hear a roaring sound. Then the ground shook again but much more violently, throwing Able to the floor. Around him, several beams came crashing down and he heard one of his officers' scream in pain. Then something smashed into Able's head, sending him into darkness.

-

Sergeant Anderson felt the ground shake as a brilliant light flared over the battlefield. In the space of just a few seconds he felt the ground shudder repeatedly. A roaring sound filled the air and he began to be pelted with small rocks falling from the sky. He huddled at the bottom of the bomb crater as powerful winds swept across the crater, knocking down trees and sending more debris up into the air. After several minutes everything began to calm down and Anderson crawled back to the top of the crater to have a look. It was darker than it had been before as the air was full of dust and smoke. Looking toward the Trellixian energy dome he saw it was down and several large smoking craters existed where the dome once was.

"The Trellixian troops?" asked Corporal Donly as he crawled up next to Anderson. Donly was covered in dust.

Sergeant Anderson peered toward where the Trellixian troops had been earlier. He could still see some movement but not as much as before. Looking through the scope on his energy rifle he could see several hover tanks on fire but a few others were still moving. The explosions from the energy strike had disabled many of them and killed thousands of the Trellixian troops but numerous others had survived as they were encased in their battle armor.

"They lost a lot but it looks as if we still have a big fight on our hands." Anderson quickly contacted the Rangers and the Marines in his command, warning them of the still advancing Trellixians. He wasn't surprised to find out two had died and half a dozen others had been injured in the recent orbital strike. After talking to several other sergeants, he sent a request to Major Garcia for reinforcements.

-

Major Garcia turned toward Colonel Branson. "We have several of our forward commands requesting reinforcements. The orbital strikes knocked the dome down and eliminated a large portion of the Trellixian troops but there are still thousands advancing as well as a number of hover tanks."

"We'll send what we can. I've already sent orders for our air assets to begin attack runs. That should help take some of the pressure off our troops."

-

Second Officer Tolbert's left arm hung limply at his side. It was broken in two places but he had refused medical treatment. Around him hundreds of Trellixians soldiers were steadily advancing toward the Human and Voltrex troops. He had four undamaged hover tanks with him, which were just now beginning to fire their splinter grenades into the enemy troop positions. Tolbert wished he had some attack craft. Warp missiles would be devastating to the enemy as well as the craft's ability to drop hundreds of splinter grenades.

Tolbert held an energy pistol in his right hand. He would have to get close to the enemy to use it. Already energy weapons fire was being exchanged between the two sides. He winced as a nearby hover tank fired its main energy cannon toward the nearby Human lines. The rifle fire from both sides was mostly missing due to the distance. Tolbert knew as fast as they were advancing that wouldn't be true much longer.

Sergeant Anderson had just returned from inspecting the forward line of his troops. All surviving Rangers and Marines were well dug in and waiting for the advancing enemy. Mortar pits had been set up as well as some heavier energy weapons. He ducked back down into the bomb crater he was using as a Command Post as several energy beams struck nearby.

"Damn, that was close," he said to Corporal Donly.

Donly nodded. Two other Rangers had joined them in the crater. "It's about to get intense."

"These are the last Trellixians in the United States," commented Private Hastings. "Once they're eliminated, our fighting for a while at least will be over. Maybe we can go home for a few days."

Private Richards nodded. "Maybe. I would like to spend some time with my family."

Suddenly a flight of inbound attack helicopters passed by overhead toward the advancing Trellixians.

Sergeant Anderson felt relief at seeing the attack helicopters. The Trellixians had his forces heavily outnumbered and the helicopters should help even up the odds. Even as he watched missiles with Jelnoid warheads were fired at the Trellixians. Huge explosions suddenly shook the ground, throwing dirt and rocks high up into the air. Two Trellixian hover tanks exploded in brilliant fireballs as their energy shields were penetrated. An energy beam from a hover tank reached out and struck one of the helicopters only to be stopped by the helicopter's energy shield.

Then a larger beam from the former Trellixian base suddenly struck one of the helicopters, penetrating the energy screen and blowing the helicopter into hundreds of pieces which fell toward the ground.

"Damn, one of their main energy batteries survived the orbital strike," said Corporal Donly.

"I'll inform Major Garcia," replied Anderson, watching the remains of the attack helicopter strike the ground. "It needs to be taken out."

The battle continued to intensify with another helicopter shot down. Then a flight of F-22s appeared and moments later several towering explosions marked the end of the dangerous Trellixian energy battery.

The two opposing forces were now close enough for weapons fire to be effective. Energy weapons were being used by both sides as well as explosives. There were still a few hover tanks in operation and these were firing splinter grenades nonstop at the Human and Voltrex lines. Human mortars and missile fire from the attacking helicopters pummeled the advancing Trellixians, killing hundreds. Even so, the advancing enemy didn't hesitate. They knew they were destined to die and they wanted to take as many Humans and Voltrex with them as possible.

-

Sergeant Anderson was firing his energy rifle nonstop at the advancing Trellixians. Even though the attack helicopters and the F-22s had taken many of them out they still far outnumbered the Human and Voltrex forces. Everywhere in front of him Anderson could see dark clad Trellixians in their armor steadily advancing in the face of withering fire. Every time one would drop two more would take his place.

"We're going to be overrun!" yelled Corporal Donly as he used his rifle to take down another Trellixian soldier. "There's just too many of them."

Anderson knew Donly was right. There was only one thing he could do to stop the enemy. Hastily he contacted Major Garcia and requested an orbital strike right in front of the Human and Voltrex lines. He knew such a strike would kill some of the defending troops but it was the only way to stop the advancing enemy. At least this way some of his Rangers and Marines might survive.

Major Garcia looked over at Colonel Branson. "We have several commands requesting additional orbital strikes or they're going to be overrun." Garcia knew to do so would in all likelihood kill some of his Rangers and Marines.

Colonel Branson let out a deep breath. "We don't have a choice. If we don't call in the orbital strikes they will die anyway. At least this way we may give them a chance. I'll call in the strikes and order the attack helicopters and the F22s to clear the area."

Major Garcia felt a cold chill run down his back at what they were getting ready to do. This battle had suddenly turned the wrong direction. Major Garcia quickly informed the forward commands of the incoming orbital strike and for all troops to seek whatever cover they could find.

General Mitchell was listening over the comm system, which connected him to his field commanders. His face turned pale when he heard the request for additional orbital strikes so close to the Human and Voltrex lines.

"What does that mean?" asked President Hathaway, her eyes focusing on the general.

With a deep sigh, General Mitchell turned toward the president with a grim look on his face. "It means we're about to lose a lot of good soldiers."

Katelyn's eyes returned to the viewscreens showing the battlefield. Much of it was covered with smoke and drifting clouds of dust. She knew from what General Mitchell had just said it was about to get a lot worse.

-

The captain of the battlecruiser was not pleased with his latest orders. As the Tungsten rods were loaded into the tubes he knew he was about to kill a number of friendly troops. He understood why he was launching the orbital strike but he didn't like it. This was something he was going to have to live with for a long time. Once the tubes were loaded he stepped over to the fire controls and pressed the buttons himself, launching the Tungsten rods. He didn't want anyone else to have to live with this guilt.

-

From the battlecruiser, six Tungsten rods dropped toward their designated targets. They entered the Earth's atmosphere and began to glow from the heat of their passage. Soon they resembled meteors streaking through the sky. They would bring destruction and death to those below.

-

Second Officer Tolbert was crawling forward toward the enemy lines. The Trellixians were now within one hundred meters of the enemy and were exchanging heavy weapons fire. Soldiers on both sides were being hit and in most cases dying. A noise above drew his attention. A number of glowing objects were visible in the sky and they seemed to all be coming toward him. With a sinking feeling of imminent death he recognized the incoming orbital strike. There was no doubt the Humans had called the strike down on the advancing Trellixian soldiers.

For a moment Tolbert felt respect for the Humans. They were willing to sacrifice their lives to take out their enemy. It was what a Trellixian soldier was trained to do. Then the first rod struck a thousand meters away from him. A tremendous blast followed by a brilliant flash of light passed over the battlefield. The ground seemed to leap up. Hundreds of screams could be heard. The blast wave moved across the battlefield, hurling the surviving hover tanks into the air and crushing them. Trellixian soldiers in battle armor were swept away. All weapons fire came to a sudden stop.

Sergeant Anderson felt the ground shake as he was pelted with rocks and other falling debris. The bomb crater he was in was deep and he hoped it would give him and the others some protection. Over his comm unit he could hear cries for help from soldiers in his command. The blast wave passed over the crater, dumping more debris on Anderson and threatening to lift him out of the safety of the crater. He hunkered down in a ball trying to make himself as small as possible. He heard Private Richards scream. Daring to look over to Richards he saw him sucked out of the crater by the wind and vanish from sight. Anderson was holding on to a few exposed tree roots hoping the same wouldn't happen to him, as was Private Hastings.

After a few minutes everything seemed to calm down and an eerie quiet encompassed the battlefield. Looking around the crater, he saw Corporal Donly and Private Hastings were still with him. Donly was covered in dirt and sitting up begin to brush himself off. Anderson saw Donly had been holding on to a large tree root as well.

"Where's Private Richards?" asked Donly, looking around for the private.

Anderson shook his head. "He was sucked out of the crater by the wind from the blast wave. I don't know if he survived."

Corporal Donly shook his head. "Private Richards is a good soldier. I hope he survived."

"We need to go find him," said Private Hastings.

Sergeant Anderson carefully crawled back to the top of the crater and looked around. There was a lot of smoke and dust in the air. From his position, he could see no movement. Nowhere did he see any signs of Private Richards. He tried his comm but all he could pick up was static. There was still too much interference from the blasts. He would wait a few more minutes and try again. If he and Corporal Donly as well as Private Hastings had survived there were bound to be others. Taking a deep breath, he looked toward where the Trellixians had been. He thought he could see some movement but nothing like earlier. Peering through the scope of his rifle, he could see several hover tanks on fire and others that looked as if they had been crushed. Nowhere did he see a hover tank still capable of movement.

-

Major Garcia stepped out of the small command bunker. It had easily survived the blast wave that passed over them. "We only have limited communication with our soldiers," he reported to Colonel Branson.

"I'm not surprised," Branson replied. "I've already ordered the attack helicopters back in. No doubt a few Trellixians survived. It will be awhile before we know about our troops. General Briggs is ordering the reserves in to assist in any fighting that remains as well as helping with the injured and the dead."

Garcia nodded. He wondered how many Human and Voltrex soldiers had died due to the orbital strikes. Looking out over the desolate landscape he suspected the casualties were high.

-

Second Officer Tolbert lay on the ground where the blast wave from the orbital strike had thrown him. He tried to move and all he felt was intense pain. He suspected his back was broken. His armor was heavily dented and he could barely breathe. Looking around he could see only a few of his soldiers still moving. Some had weapons in their hands but looked confused. Tolbert felt the darkness closing in. He knew his time was short. The sky above him was gray and seemed darker than normal. He would have liked to have seen the sun one final time. With a shudder, he took one last rasping breath and then the darkness closed in. For Second Officer Tolbert of the Trellixian Empire his days of being a soldier for the Empire were over.

-

General Mitchell looked grimly at the viewscreens in the Command Center. The orbital strikes had targeted the largest Trellixian troop concentrations. Already the reserve troops were moving in and mopping up what was left. The attack helicopters were eliminating any remaining resistance. Only a few hover tanks had survived and those were quickly being dealt with.

"We lost a lot of good men and women," General Briggs said as he listened to the reports coming in. "Some of the forward most units are reporting nearly 70 percent casualties."

General Mitchell nodded. These were losses they could not afford but very shortly the last Trellixian soldier on American soil would be exterminated.

"What about the Chinese?" He knew the Chinese had launched a major attack against the Trellixians in their country as well.

"They're mopping up," Colonel Tricia Steward answered. "They expect for their operation to be completed in a few more hours."

President Hathaway looked over at General Mitchell. "Then our world will finally be free of the enemy."

"Yes," replied Mitchell. "The cost will have been heavy, but all of our world will be ours."

"The price of war is always great," Vice President Arnold said in a somber voice. "This battle had to be fought. I'm just glad it's over."

Katelyn looked at the viewscreens and the war torn landscape of Northern Kansas. "Now we rebuild. Someday all of this will be behind us."

"I hope so," Vice President Arnold replied. "I don't want my grandchildren raised in a world which knows only war."

"We're working on that," replied General Mitchell. "Once Captain Dolan returns we'll know more about what we're up against."

-

In the ruins of the Trellixian Command Post, Battle Commander Able entered a command into a console and then pressed a red button. A countdown appeared on a small screen on the console. Sixty seconds later a four small tactical nuclear weapons detonated, destroying the Command Post and part of the surrounding countryside. A small mushroom cloud rose up into the air. In his last act of defiance, Battle Commander Able had taken more of the enemy with him. However, with the explosion the last Trellixians in America died as well.

The war in Northern Kansas was over. The Humans and the Voltrex had a victory but a costly one. Now the war would turn toward space. In the Human Command Center General Mitchell shook his head when he saw the nuclear explosion. He knew it signaled the end of the battle. Looking at a viewscreen showing a view of space he wondered what Captain Dolan was finding in the Trellixian Empire. The war on Earth was over and the war in space was about to begin.

Chapter Seven

Captain Mark Dolan took a deep breath as his small fleet approached what should be a system with a strong Trellixian presence. Voltrex data from destroyed Trellixian ships indicated such.

"Probes are ready to launch," reported Chloe.

Mark nodded. Both the *Fury* and the *Horizon* had small probes they could launch to give them detailed sensor readings of what was in a star system. It was much safer than risking one of the warships or the entire fleet. After much consideration Mark had decided to try the probes in this system to see how they worked.

Mark looked over at Lieutenant Masterson. "How close do we need to be to launch the probes?"

"Just outside the system," Brett replied. "The probes have small FTL drives and should be able to traverse the system very quickly. I would estimate another twenty minutes and we can launch them."

Chloe turned around on her dais to face the captain. "The probes are covered in a substance which should make them difficult to detect. The Trellixians will not be expecting them so there is a very good chance they will not be detected by their sensors."

"I'm picking up communication signals from the system across a wide spectrum," reported Marissa. Her tongue flicked out across her whiskers and then she continued. "The language is definitely Trellixian."

Lisa turned to face the captain. "We should reduce the emissions from all of our ships until the probes return. We don't want to risk being detected by the Trellixians. We're not certain how far their sensors can reach."

"Will they even be scanning?" asked Katana. It was one of her duties as second officer to keep the ship safe.

"If any military ships are in the system they might be," replied Mark. "If this system is as heavily populated as we believe then there could very well be a few of them around the colonized planets." He felt uneasy about reducing the emissions from his ships. That would mean the weapons as well as the energy shields would be down. The fleet would be defenseless! However, he knew it was the right decision for the success of the mission.

-

Twenty minutes later the four ships of the fleet came to a halt just outside the system near the cometary belt and both the *Fury* and the *Horizon* began launching probes. Each ship launched two probes, which would take different trajectories through the system. The small five-meter probes exited the ships and then activated their FTL drives as they assumed their courses.

-

"Probes launched," reported Chloe as she monitored the launches. "All four probes are on the proper courses. First data should be coming in one hour and ten minutes from now."

"I've ordered most of our systems shut down to avoid detection," reported Katana. "Sensors are on passive and our power systems are at minimum."

Looking at the ship's main viewscreen all Mark could see was a sea of stars. They were still too far from the system's primary for it to show as anything but a small white dot.

Standing up, Mark stretched his arms. He was tired but still had a long day ahead of him. "Katana, I'm going to the Officers' Mess for a quick meal. Contact me if anything happens."

Katana nodded. "I don't expect there to be any changes in our status until the probes enter the star system. Then the risk will be a little higher."

-

Lisa was waiting anxiously for the first readings from the probes to come in. She knew it would be over an hour and by then the captain would be back. "I wonder what the probes will find?" she said over the private channel to the other lieutenants.

"Trellixians," said Derek. "Probably a lot of them."

86

"I wonder how many warships are in the system?' asked Brenda, her eyes showing some concern. "What will happen if they detect the probes?" There was a faint hint of fear in Brenda's voice. "I hate sitting here with our weapons down and no energy screen. It makes me feel helpless."

"There's nothing to worry about," Brett reassured her. "We can get our weapons and the energy screen up quickly enough if there is a threat. The *Fury* and the other ships all have Jelnoid shields with modified power systems. Also our weapons are powerful enough to take out any Trellixian ship that might find us."

Lisa frowned. "But we don't want them to find us. Our entire mission depends on us remaining undetected. That's why we have the probes."

"They won't detect the probes," promised Derek. "I helped design the probes and they are very difficult to detect. It would take a major malfunction in one for it to be noticed."

"We'll know in a few hours once they get close enough to start sending data," Lisa said. She was both anxious and curious to see what the probes would find. The Trellixians supposedly had colonized this system several hundred years in the past. Lisa didn't know if this had been a virgin world or one already inhabited. She knew full well what the Trellixians did to worlds which held inhabitants.

Lisa wished she were back home with Professor Wilkens. So much research needed to be done. The professor had promised her after this mission there would be no more unless she volunteered. All five of the special lieutenants would be able to stay on Earth and work on their research projects.

Glancing at a timer on her computer screen, Lisa saw the time slowly counting down toward the first expected reception of data from the probes.

Mark was eating a ham sandwich with some chips. He took a deep drink of tea to wash it down. His mission was really just starting as this was the first system where they expected to find a large Trellixian presence. He wondered what his sister Jennifer was doing back on Earth. She was still safely in Complex One working at one of the medical centers. At least he knew she was safe.

Major Garcia was now in charge of the Rangers Mark once commanded. He knew there were plans for a major offensive against the remaining Trellixians on Earth. By now that offensive should have been launched. He hoped everything went as planned. It would be nice to return to Earth with none of the enemy remaining on the planet.

Mark took his time eating. He knew once he returned to the Command Center he would be there for quite some time until the probes exited the Trellixian star system. The probes were specifically designed to gather information on what was in the system. They would scan all the planets and surrounding space for any signs of a star-traveling species. The probes would scan for power sources, spacecraft, asteroid mining facilities, colonies on moons, asteroids, as well as planets, and any shipyards or space stations that might be in orbit.

He also reminded himself this was only the first of many systems on the *Fury's* list to be checked out. This would be the easy one. The ones after this would grow progressively more difficult as they traveled deeper into Trellixian controlled space and the heart of their Empire.

Lisa looked up as Captain Dolan entered the Command Center. Second Officer Katana got up, surrendering the command chair to the captain. It was still ten minutes before the probes were supposed to start sending data.

"No changes," reported Katana. "We've detected no Trellixian vessels on our passive sensors."

Mark nodded. Of course, the passive sensors only had a very short range. Mark sat down in the command chair waiting for the first data to come in. His hands were sweating slightly and he could feel the tension in the air. If the probes were detected, there was a very high likelihood the Trellixians would send out every warship in the system to try to locate their source. The Trellixians would also send out a warning to their other systems to be on the watch for more of the probes. It would greatly enhance the danger to the mission.

The minutes passed and suddenly on several computer consoles green lights began flashing.

"Receiving probe data," Lisa reported as her science console began to analyze the incoming information.

"All four probes reporting," added Chloe. She closed her eyes as if she was listening to the probes.

"All indications are that the probes have not been detected," said Lisa as the data began to appear on her computer screen. "The system has five planets and twelve moons. There is also a small asteroid field between the second and third planets."

Chloe opened her eyes and turned toward the captain. "Initial analysis indicates over one hundred and twenty spacecraft operating in the system. It's too early yet to determine how many of them may be warships."

Katana stepped over closer to Lisa so she could see the computer screen. "The fourth planet is heavily inhabited. We will have to wait for one of the probes to get closer to determine the actual population."

"There are three space stations in orbit above the planet," reported Lisa. "Can't tell yet if they're shipyards or just regular stations."

Mark thought for a long minute. He wanted as much information as possible on this system, particularly the fourth planet. "Adjust the course of one of the probes to take it near the fourth planet. I want detailed scans of that world and the space around it."

"Taking a probe that close increases the risk of detection," warned Chloe.

"Do it anyway. It's a risk I'm willing to take to get the necessary information."

Chloe was silent for several seconds. "Probe two's course has been adjusted. It will come within four million kilometers of the planet. That should be sufficient for detailed scans and to minimize detection."

"If any Trellixian ships change course and head toward the probe let me know. If that happens we will order it to self-destruct." All the probes had small nuclear charges on board. Detonating them would vaporize the probes.

-

Lisa continued to analyze the data from the four probes as her computer console received the information. It looked as if the Trellixians had colonies on three of the planets as well as six of the system's moons. Domes and weak energy shields protected all of the colonies except the largest one on the fourth planet.

"There's a lot of Trellixians in this system," commented Derek. "There must be billions of them."

Lisa looked at the course of the probe they had designated to pass close by planet four. "From the power readings coming from the fourth planet, it has to be heavily populated."

"It's what the Trellixians do," said Brett. "They overpopulate the worlds they've taken over."

"And that might be their weak spot," said Katana. "If we could use our fleet to disrupt their lines of supply we may be able to paralyze their entire Empire."

"It would be dangerous to attempt such a blockade," said Chloe. "The Trellixians have many warships. Even with advanced Jelnoid technology, it might be next to impossible to destroy those fleets. They would break any blockade we might set up. Also keep in mind our fleets would be far from home."

Katana did not reply, she just continued to study the data searching for a weakness.

-

Captain Dolan had been listening to his crew talk. "Any decision on how to deal with the Trellixian Empire will be made when we complete our mission and return to Earth. While it is true their excess population seems to be their greatest weakness, it will be up to General Mitchell and the Voltrex Fleet Command to decide how best to exploit any weaknesses we discover."

"There are fifteen confirmed Trellixian battlecruisers in the system," Chloe suddenly announced. "Scans from the probes also indicate a large number of what appears to be cargo ships in route to the different colonies."

"Carrying supplies," said Derek. "If those colonies are not self-sufficient they would need the cargo ships to supply them with the necessities."

"I have a population estimate on planet four," Lisa said, her eyes wide at seeing the computer's projection. "If these readings are correct there's over twenty-two billion Trellixians living on the planet."

"Twenty-two billion?" said Brenda in disbelief. "Are there no oceans on that planet?"

Lisa shook her head. "It's nearly forty percent water. It has two large landmasses and the rest is a sizable ocean."

Captain Dolan was silent for a long moment and then spoke. "Continue recording data. Do we know what those three space stations around the planet are for?"

"One's a shipyard and the other two seem to be designed to handle the cargo ships," answered Chloe. "Some of the larger cargo ships are docking with the station and there is a steady flow of shuttles between the two stations and the surface."

"Any idea what the population of the entire system is?"

"In excess of thirty billion," Lisa answered as the numbers came up on her computer screen.

"Thirty billion in one system," said Derek, shaking his head. "What kind of population will their home systems have?"

Mark looked around the Command Center. Many of the faces were focused on him. "That's what we're going to find out."

-

Lisa could feel her heart beating. This mission was only going to become more dangerous. The further they went into Trellixian space, the greater the likelihood of their ships or probes being detected. Turning her eyes back to her computer screen, she continued to watch the data being transmitted by the four probes.

The probes continued to move deeper into the system with their sensors capturing more and more detailed data. The Trellixians had no reason to suspect anything was out of the normal and failed to detect the faint emissions generated by the probes' small FTL drives. The probe assigned to planet four photographed the huge cities on the planet as it passed close by as well as the orbiting shipyard and space stations. Other probes sent detailed data back on the colonies on the other planets and the moons as well as some mining occurring in the small asteroid field.

Of significance were photographs of the fourth planet showing the ruins of some primitive cities. Not many as most had been leveled and new Trellixian cities built over them, but several in some of the more remote areas of the planet showing the planet had once been inhabited by a sentient race, one the Trellixians had destroyed.

The probes' sensors searched for and found every Trellixian ship in the system including several large colony ships which had just arrived and were inbound toward the fourth planet. There were a few mining ships as well. However, most of the ships in the system were cargo vessels. The majority of them would dock to one of the two large space stations around the fourth planet and unload their cargo. As soon as they were empty, they would leave the station and make the jump back into hyperspace. There were ships constantly coming and going.

The probes continued on their different courses until they passed completely through the system. They then turned and going around the outskirts of the system, set a course for the *Fury* and the *Horizon*.

"Probes are on a course back to us," reported Chloe. "They should be back to our location in six hours."

Captain Dolan nodded. So far the mission had gone as planned. They had detailed scans of a heavily populated Trellixian system and thus far had remained undetected. As soon as the probes returned the small fleet would set out for its next destination. There was a system twenty-eight light years distant which was supposed to be inhabited by the Trellixians. They would send probes through that system as well.

"All data has been correlated and is ready to send to Earth," reported Lisa.

"We have to drop a communications drone shortly," Mark said. They had been leaving a string of FTL communication drones from Earth to their current location. Communication was only one way to reduce the chance of detection. "Have the data compressed and ready to send. I suspect General Mitchell and Professor Wilkens will be highly interested in what we're sending them."

At the mention of Professor Wilkens' name Lisa couldn't help but wonder what the professor was doing. He was the closest person to Lisa, being like a father figure. Her own family had been killed when Seattle was nuked by the Trellixians. Looking over at Brett, she allowed herself to smile. Brett and she had a developing relationship though they had both agreed to put it on hold until this mission was over. A military mission was nowhere for romance. However, they did have a daily meal together and spent quite a bit of their off time in each other's company. All five of the lieutenants had a tendency to stay together whenever possible. There were several well-equipped labs on the *Fury* and the five of them spent much of their free time in the labs working on research projects. Professor Wilkens had given each of them several projects to work on.

Lisa felt a little more relaxed now that the probes were out of the Trellixian system and returning to the fleet. She would feel even better once the fleet entered hyperspace. With a deep sigh, she had all the sensor readings from the four probes compressed so Marissa could send it in a quick six second burst. Once she was finished she sent the file over to Communications. Her work for this shift was now over and she could feel hunger pangs. She looked over at Brenda, Brett, Kia, and Derek wondering if they were as hungry as she was.

Derek grinned and spoke over their private comm line. "Hungry? From that look on your face you're ready to head for the mess hall."

Lisa nodded. "I just had a light breakfast this morning. I skipped lunch because of the probes."

"Should have had someone bring you a sandwich; Captain Dolan wouldn't have minded. We all eat in the Command Center at times if we're serving a long shift."

"I know," Lisa replied. She had done that on several occasions. "I just wanted us all to eat together tonight."

"We will," said Brett, indicating he had been listening. "We should all be able to leave the Command Center shortly."

-

The probes returned to the *Fury* and the *Horizon* without incident. Shortly after that the four ships of the exploration fleet entered hyperspace. They were scheduled to stop in a red dwarf star system to drop off a FTL communication drone and send in their report on the Trellixian system.

-

After eating a decent meal Lisa and the others were in one of the advanced labs on the *Fury*. Their current area of research involved increasing the power of the Jelnoid energy cannons. They were using a combination of Jelnoid, Voltrex, and Human technology.

"I'm sure we can increase the power of the Voltrex fusion reactors," Brenda said as she looked at her latest computer simulations. On another screen were numerous lines of mathematical equations proving her point.

Kia shook her head. "It would take a complete redesign of the reactors. We don't have the necessary materials on board to do it."

"A 43 percent increase in the effectiveness of our energy beams," reported Derek from his bank of computer screens. "I don't believe our power lines would support such an output of energy. We would burn out every relay and short out connections across the entire ship if we released that much power."

Brett took in a deep breath. "I don't believe Captain Dolan would be pleased with us if we caused that. Why don't we continue to work on our design and when we get back to Earth we can talk to Professor Wilkens about putting a redesigned reactor in a ship?"

"It will have to be a new ship," said Lisa, thinking about what would be involved. "It will need better relays, heavier wiring, and other modifications to handle the power we're talking about."

"They'll do it," Derek said. "If we offer the military more powerful weapons they'll jump at the opportunity. More powerful energy weapons and a stronger energy screen could make a huge difference in our war against the Trellixians."

Brett nodded his agreement. "Derek's right. If we can show this works they'll build a new ship or ships around these new reactors."

Lisa let out a deep sigh. "We still have a lot to do. The simulations show the new reactors we've designed will function as the power equations show. But we still have a lot of design work to do."

"We have plenty of time ahead of us to get this right," Brett said. "I would like to present to Professor Wilkens and General Mitchell complete blueprints of our planned new fusion reactor."

The others all nodded as they turned back to their consoles and began working. They all had a lot to do but they were confident by the time they returned to Earth the project would be finished.

Lisa let out a deep breath as she began studying what was on her computer screen. She just hoped they did return to Earth safely when the mission was over. She had a horrible feeling the worst was still ahead of them.

Chapter Eight

High Commander Kaldre studied the latest reports coming in from the Empire as well as the fleets near the border with the Voltrex. There was growing unrest on a number of heavily populated worlds. Food production in the Empire was down and a shortage of cargo ships was hampering delivery to some sectors. New colony ships were coming on line due to increased production to remove more of the excess populations to newly discovered planets.

Fleets near the border with the Voltrex indicated increased fleet movements with at least one large fleet already deep within the Empire. The fleet had destroyed the colony of Capal Four and after that had not been heard from or spotted. Kaldre greatly feared the fleet was heading deeper into the Empire, possibly toward Earth. He had warned the rest of the High Command but many of them were set in their ways and firmly believed the Humans and the Voltrex were only a minor threat to the Empire. The reason Capal Four came under attack was because of its proximity to the Voltrex worlds. There would be no other attacks.

"We will be dropping out of hyperspace shortly," reported Second Officer Calaah. The ship was on its way to Traxis Three, the second most heavily populated world in the Empire. It also had some of the larger shipyards.

Kaldre nodded. He was sitting in his command chair atop the command pedestal in his flagship the *Dawn Reaper*. His ship had recently undergone a complete refit giving it more powerful weapons and a much stronger energy shield. Four of the new battlecruisers from Battle Commander Balforr's new war fleet served as an escort.

The last few weeks had been agitating with meetings of the High Command, which failed to bring a consensus about what to do about the Humans or the Voltrex. A majority of the High Command still felt the current war fleets of the Empire were sufficient to keep the Humans and the Voltrex at bay even with the advanced technology the Humans had given the cat people.

"Jelnoid technology," muttered High Commander Kaldre, gazing down at the three fingers and thumb on his right hand. He flexed his hand into a fist. When the Jelnoids worlds had been conquered, there had been a search to discover the secrets of their technology. It had been a shock to learn the Jelnoids, before their defeat, had gone to great pains to destroy all evidence of their advanced science. Trellixians scientists going through the ruins of Jelnoid worlds had only found a few hints of the advanced technology the Jelnoids used.

Kaldre felt a slight sense of nausea which quickly vanished, indicating the ship had exited hyperspace. Looking at the viewscreens in the front of the Command Center, he saw them clear of static to show a blue white world. This was Traxis Three. Around it were a large number of space stations and shipyards. The shipyards were the primary reason he had come to the system.

"We'll be going into orbit shortly," Second Officer Calaah reported.

Looking at the largest viewscreen, Kaldre could see one of the larger shipyards in orbit around the planet. This shipyard was dedicated to producing battlecruisers. Kaldre had been given permission by the rest of the High Command to see if some minor changes could be made to improve the weapons and energy screens being installed on these ships. He was not allowed to completely redesign the shipyard to produce the new battlecruisers. That would require the shipyard to be down for nearly two months and the rest of the High Command had been adamant an interruption in warship construction of that magnitude could not be allowed.

However, the new fusion reactor plans Kaldre had brought with him would allow for an increase in energy for the weapons and energy shields currently being put into the warships. The increase would be 15 percent for the weapons and nearly 20 percent for the shields. Any more and the ships' power conduits would be burnt out. He was also going to look into the building of more powerful fusion missiles as well as an increase in the production of antimatter warheads. Unfortunately, the creation of antimatter was expensive and time consuming. He had spoken to several scientists who felt fusion missiles in the range of 75 to 80 megatons were possible. They had also stated the amount of antimatter could be increased in a Malken missile, making it able to detonate in the 200-megaton range.

"Communications from the shipyard commander," the communications officer reported. "He says he can come aboard the *Dawn Reaper* as soon as we've gone into orbit."

High Commander Kaldre shook his head. "That won't be necessary. I will come over to the shipyard. I wish to inspect the battlecruiser manufacturing facilities to see what other changes might be feasible and not affect production of warships."

Kaldre was the only High Commander in the system. If he could make other changes to increase the power of the warships he would. He was deeply concerned he was the only one of the High Command that truly understood the threat the Humans and the Voltrex represented.

"Have my shuttle prepared. I will be going over to the shipyard."

Second Officer Calaah nodded. "I will give the order. How long will you be on the shipyard?"

"As long as necessary," Kaldre replied. "The survival of the Empire may well depend on what I get accomplished in the next few days."

-

Calaah's large eyes grew wide at this comment. His green skin seemed to grow even darker as he processed High Commander Kaldre's words. Even though he shared some of the High Commander's worries, he could not imagine any threat which could actually endanger the Empire. The Empire was simply too large by being spread across thousands of light years and several thousand worlds.

-

High Commander Kaldre watched as his shuttle entered one of the large landing bays of the shipyard. The shipyard was massive, being one of the largest ones in the Empire. Only a few of the shipyards in the home system were larger. The shipyard had ten repair bays and six more bays dedicated to the construction of new warships. Fourteen thousand Trellixians worked to maintain the shipyard.

Stepping out of the shuttle, Kaldre was pleased to see the shipyard's commanding officer, Commander Malborr waiting for him along with several other high-ranking officers.

"I was not informed you were coming," said Malborr nervously. "I would have prepared a more adequate welcome for a member of the High Command."

"I have no interest for such a waste of time," Kaldre replied. No doubt Malborr thought he had done something wrong and that was the reason for this unexpected visit. "I have come to see if your shipyard can be modified to produce more powerful warships."

Commander Malborr looked thoughtful. "I have heard the Voltrex are becoming a minor threat on the edge of our Empire."

Kaldre looked around the bay. There were several other shuttles as well as a few small cargo ships. "More than a minor threat. They have already destroyed one of our colonies and may be on their way to destroy others."

"I have heard rumors they have Jelnoid technology."

"It's more than rumors. The Humans have provided them with Jelnoid weapons and shields. Our battlecruisers cannot stand up to them in a one-on-one confrontation."

A look of confusion covered Malborr's face. "Why has the High Command not mentioned this? If that is true we should send more warships to that section of the Empire."

"They feel the size of our fleets will keep the Empire safe. They forget the Voltrex have been in space for a considerable length of time and may have several thousand warships or even more. We have no idea of their ship strength or even where most of their worlds are located. We are sending additional fleets but they may be ineffective against the Voltrex and their new weapons which is why I'm here."

"My shipyard is at your disposal. What are your plans? I can assure you this shipyard and the others are operating at maximum efficiency. The warships we are producing are the most powerful we know how to build."

High Commander Kaldre took in a deep breath. "We are going to modify the fusion reactors in all new builds, as well as better power conduits. They need to be able to handle twenty to thirty percent more power than is currently used."

"Twenty to thirty percent!" gasped Malborr. "How will that be possible? Where will the extra power come from?"

"We have a better fusion reactor. It will furnish the necessary power."

"Send the specifications to my engineers and we will see what will be necessary to modify our construction systems."

Kaldre nodded. While the High Command might disapprove of what he was going to do Kaldre knew it was necessary to protect the Empire. The Humans and the Voltrex were coming and at some point in time the rest of the High Command would understand that danger. When that finally happened Kaldre planned to be ready even if he was risking his position as a High Commander. While he had approval to make some changes, he was going to push that approval to the maximum. He knew this would upset several of the other High Commanders.

In a section of the Empire several hundred light years from the Voltrex Federation Fleet Commander Kamuss was studying the reports from the scout ships he had sent ahead of the fleet.

The Trellixian ships which fled Capal Four had been traced to a system a few short light years ahead. Scout ships tapping into Trellixian communications in the system had discovered the system was called Lantoll Six.

"The scans from the scout ships indicate a large number of Trellixian warships in the system," Lieutenant Commander

LeLath reported as she looked at the latest data sent from the small vessels. "There are also large numbers of cargo ships as well as their colony ships."

Zalurr, the sensor officer, looked over at Fleet Commander Kamuss. "The Trellixians may be using this system as a staging area for the colonization of this entire region of space."

"A worthwhile target," commented Diboll from Tactical.

Kamuss nodded in agreement. "Meela, contact Fleet Commander Masurl and inform him of our findings. Tell him I plan on attacking the system and removing all traces of the Trellixians from the system of Lantoll Six."

"Yes, Fleet Commander," Meela replied as she turned to her communications console.

Since his success at Capal Four both his fleet and Fleet Commander Masurl's fleet had been reinforced, primarily with more battlecruisers and battleships. Between the two fleets there were slightly over three hundred and fifty warships. Every ship was equipped with Jelnoid weapons and energy shields.

Kamuss leaned back in his command chair, confident his fleet could now handle anything the Trellixians threw at him. For a number of what seemed like long minutes the data from the advance scouts continued to come in. Kamuss wanted as much information on the system as possible before he launched his attack.

"The scouts are reporting over one hundred and ten Trellixian battlecruisers in the system," said Zalurr as he studied the sensor readings from the small ships. "There may be a few more we're not detecting."

The number of Trellixian warships did not surprise Fleet Commander Kamuss, particularly if this was their main staging area for this region of space. "What about space stations or shipyards around the target planet?"

"Four confirmed space stations and one larger station which appears to be a shipyard. There are also numerous mining operations throughout the system, particularly on several of the system's moons."

"We'll be in attack range in twenty minutes," reported Metriic from the Helm.

Kamuss took in a deep breath. He knew those twenty minutes would pass by quickly. "Take the fleets to Battle Condition Two!"

Immediately alarms began sounding and red lights began flashing. In both Voltrex fleets the crews rushed to their battle stations. They all knew that shortly they would be at Battle Condition One and once more engaged in combat against the lizard people.

Lieutenant Commander LeLath drew in a sharp breath. Her tongue flicked out, wetting her long face whiskers. She growled slightly, feeling the adrenaline beginning to flow through her. She could feel her claws extend somewhat preparing for combat. With a little concentration she pulled her claws back in. There would be no personal combat in this battle. It would all be missiles and energy weapons. She looked around the large Command Center. Other crewmembers looked anxious and excited as well. Going into combat was so much like the ancient hunts the Voltrex once went on when they were a younger and more barbaric race.

"Dropping out of hyperspace in two minutes," reported Metriic.

"All ships go to Battle Condition One," ordered Fleet Commander Kamuss.

LeLath quickly passed on the order. She felt her breathing begin to quicken. "Ship is ready for combat," she reported. She hastily buckled up the safety harness which would help keep her safely at her console.

"New data from the scout ships," reported Zalurr. "One hundred and forty confirmed Trellixian battlecruisers detected."

"Scout ships are reporting the enemy battlecruisers are beginning to move," added Meela. "It appears they have detected our fleet."

This didn't surprise Fleet Commander Kamuss. If anything, he was surprised they hadn't detected the Voltrex fleets sooner. "Stand by for combat. We'll hit them with missiles first and then close to energy weapons range."

"Missiles loaded in the tubes and ready to fire," confirmed Diboll.

-

Battle Commander Yuld stared at the long-range sensors with growing concern. He had heard what the Voltrex had done at Capal Four and now an even larger Voltrex fleet was nearing the Lantoll System.

"I told the High Command we should pull all the fleets in this sector in to defend this system," said Yuld, shaking his head. He was going to be badly outnumbered. If Lantoll Six fell then this entire sector would become rapidly untenable for the Empire.

"The High Command could not know the Voltrex would strike here next," said Second Officer Gadole. "There are other colony worlds in this sector that must be defended."

Yuld shifted his gaze to his second in command. "But none as important as this system?" Yuld clenched his fist in anger, feeling his long nails cutting into his skin and drawing blood. A few drops fell to the deck.

"All of our outer patrol ships in the system are pulling back to Lantoll Six," reported Gadole as he checked one of the larger sensor screens. Upon detecting the Voltrex fleet, the flagship had sent out a recall order to all ships on patrol.

Battle Commander Yuld considered his options. He had already seen what Voltrex ships armed with Jelnoid weapons and shields could do. "Our fleet will pull back to the shipyard. It is heavily armed. Perhaps with its weapons we can force the Voltrex to withdraw." Yuld knew this was a long shot but it was his only real option at stopping this attack. He wished there was a defense grid around the planet but the Empire had never fortified any of their colonies, not even the home worlds.

-

"Dropout!" called out Metriic as the *Claw of Honor* exited hyperspace. On the main viewscreens, other Voltrex ships were exiting hyperspace and taking up defensive positions around the flagship. "Eighty thousand kilometers from target."

"Enemy fleet is taking up a defensive position around the shipyard," reported Zalurr. "Sensors indicate the shipyard is heavily armed with energy weapons and missiles. It also has an energy shield. The other space stations show no signs of weapons or of an energy shield."

Fleet Commander Kamuss wasn't surprised. All shipyards would be controlled by the military and the Trellixians would make sure they were defended, especially this far out from the Empire. "We will move into missile range and launch at the warships and the shipyard. With a little luck we'll take out the shipyard with missiles."

"All missile tubes loaded and ready to launch," reported Diboll. "Energy weapons are charged. We just need a target lock."

Fleet Commander Kamuss could feel his heart start to pound in his chest. Very shortly, he would once more be engaged in combat against the Trellixians. "All ahead standard. We will launch our first missile wave at twenty thousand kilometers and then close to energy weapons range. All missiles and energy weapons to be focused on the enemy shipyard and warships."

"Fleet Commander Masurl is ready to commence the attack," reported Meela.

Kamuss nodded. Masurl's ships were on the right side of his fleet.

"Range is closing," called out Zalurr. "Sixty thousand kilometers from targets. Enemy fleet has formed a globe formation around the shipyard. Energy screen is now being detected around the shipyard as well as an increase in energy output."

"Charging their energy weapons," warned Lieutenant Commander LeLath as she sat up straighter and double-checked her safety harness.

"Forty thousand kilometers," reported Zalurr.

"Opening missile tubes," said Diboll as his hands flew over his console.

On the outer hull of the *Claw of Honor* hatches over missile tubes slid open, revealing the waiting missiles inside. Each missile carried a forty-megaton warhead, courtesy of the Humans and their Jelnoid technology. Energy beam turrets turned to face the Trellixian warships. The energy shield snapped into place, ready to ward off any incoming attack. Inside the flagship the fusion reactors began humming a little louder as more energy was drawn to power the ship's defenses and weapons. The *Claw of Honor* was ready to go to war.

The two Voltrex fleets continued to close on the waiting enemy forces. The crews were at their battlestations, feeling tense and anxious for the battle to begin. Battleships, battlecruisers, and support ships were all ready for combat. On board the ships the crews knew that for some of them this could very well be their last battle. As many ships as the enemy had the Voltrex fleets were bound to lose some vessels.

Battle Commander Yuld checked his fleet formation one more time. He knew the Voltrex would soon be in range. He was hoping the defensive fire from his fleet joined by the weapons on the shipyard would be enough to ward off the missile fire soon to come from the advancing enemy fleet. He needed to get them into energy weapons range. The shipyard had a number of very large energy cannons; larger than those on the battlecruisers. Yuld doubted even the energy shields which now protected the Voltrex ships could stand up to those.

"Stand by all defensive energy turrets," he ordered, knowing the Voltrex were nearly in missile range. "We must destroy this first wave of missiles if we want to stand a chance of beating back this attack."

Battle Commander Yuld stood gazing at the tactical display. Never in the history of the Empire had they encountered an opponent that was a serious threat. Even the Jelnoids were not considered such due to the small size of the space they controlled. The Voltrex were a complete unknown with massive fleets and an unknown number of worlds. Even then the Empire had been confident in victory until the Humans provided the cat people with advanced Jelnoid technology. Now the Voltrex were pushing into Trellixian controlled space and so far the High Command had failed to send fleets sufficient to counter this dangerous advance into the Empire. Fleets were promised but so far only a few had arrived.

"Fleet is in position and ready to fire," reported Second Officer Gadole.

Yuld acknowledged the report. "Contact the High Command and inform them the Lantoll System is under attack by the Voltrex. Request all available war fleets be sent here immediately."

It would take hours for the message to reach the High Command. By then this battle in all likelihood would be over.

-

"Twenty thousand kilometers," called out Zalurr.

"Launching missiles," reported Diboll as he touched an icon on his computer screen.

Battle Commander Kamuss felt the *Claw of Honor* vibrate slightly from the launch of the twelve missiles. He knew the other ships in the two fleets under his command were launching as well. On the primary tactical display, several thousand small amber icons suddenly appeared. These were the missiles which had just been launched. It would only take them a few seconds to reach the enemy ships and the shipyard.

"Missiles launched and on course," reported Diboll. "Loading second wave of missiles into the launch tubes."

"Hold on the second wave until we see the results of the first," ordered Kamuss. "We will continue to close with the enemy." They only had a limited supply of the 40-megaton missiles and he didn't want to use more than necessary.

-

Battle Commander Yuld flinched when the warming alarms of an impending attack began to sound.

"Enemy missile launch," confirmed Second Officer Gadole.

Yuld looked at the tactical display. The sensors were having a hard time detecting the missiles as they were coated with some substance making detection difficult. "Lock on and fire our defensive batteries!" he ordered.

"Energy turrets firing!" called out the tactical officer. "We're having a hard time locking onto the missiles."

Yuld recalled the last battle with the Voltrex. His ships had experienced the same thing then.

On the main viewscreens, bright explosions began to dot space as defensive energy beams found and began destroying some of the inbound missiles. More times than he wanted to think about the energy beams missed their targets.

"A lot of them are going to get through," reported Second Officer Gadole, his large eyes growing wide realizing the damage the missiles would cause to the fleet.

Battle Commander Yuld's green skin turned pale as the first missiles began slamming into his ships.

-

Missile fire from the Voltrex fleet slammed into the central section of a Trellixian battlecruiser, setting off massive explosions and hurling glowing debris into space. Moments later the battlecruiser blew apart as it was struck by two more of the deadly forty-megaton missiles.

The top section of another Trellixian battlecruiser exploded in a fiery blast, throwing debris and bodies into space. A second missile blew the ship in two with both fragments being promptly annihilated by more missiles.

Across the Trellixian fleet battlecruisers died in fiery blasts of death as forty-megaton missiles blasted down their shields, exposing the armored hulls of the ships. The Trellixian formation seemed to be on fire from the numerous fusion blasts ravaging the fleet.

-

Fleet Commander Kamuss gazed silently at the viewscreens showing the terrible destruction being caused by the missiles the two Voltrex fleets had launched.

"Forty-seven confirmed kills," reported Zalurr. "There are also a number of other Trellixian ships which have been damaged."

"We should launch a second missile wave," suggested LeLath. "That will destroy most of their remaining ships."

Kamuss considered the suggestion. The fleet had a limited supply of the missiles. He had to take into consideration that other Trellixian fleets were probably on the way. Communications had picked up several hyperspace messages from the Trellixian flagship. "Our battleships and battlecruisers will launch four missiles each. Support ships will not launch any."

A few moments later the *Claw of Honor* shivered slightly as four missiles left the launch tubes.

"Missiles launched!" confirmed Diboll

"Ten thousand kilometers and closing," reported Zalurr. "Nearing energy weapons range."

Kamuss gazed at the viewscreens. The shipyard was still untouched. It had a very powerful energy shield, which might be difficult to bring down.

-

Battle Commander Yuld stared at the viewscreens and the remains of his fleet. Suddenly more alarms began sounding.

"Missile launch!" warned the sensor officer.

"All ships break formation and move forward at maximum speed to engage the enemy." Perhaps by closing rapidly his ships could fool the inbound missiles and get close enough to engage their energy weapons.

"The shipyard commander is demanding we keep our ships around the station," said the communications officer.

The flagship shook violently as a missile struck the energy shield threatening to bring it down.

"Energy shield at 22 percent," reported the tactical officer. "The next missile will bring it down!"

On the viewscreens, the Voltrex fusion missiles were blowing other Trellixian battlecruisers apart. Yuld knew his fleet was not going to survive. There was no chance of any other Trellixian fleets arriving in time. His only choice was to attack and try to destroy as many Voltrex ships as possible.

"Energy weapons range!" called out Second Officer Gadole.

"Fire!" ordered Battle Commander Yuld, leaning forward in his command chair.

"Firing energy beams," confirmed the tactical officer.

The sensor officer looked over at Battle Commander Yuld. "Fleet has opened fire and the Voltrex are responding."

Yuld did not reply. He wished his fleet had some of the larger fusion missiles. Fifty-megaton warheads might cause some damage to the Voltrex fleet. However, his fleet had not been supplied with any of the more powerful missiles. He did have some weaker fusion missiles but he doubted they would have any effect on the Voltrex energy shields.

-

The battle quickly grew more intense. The Trellixian fleet was losing though the surviving battlecruisers were preventing the Voltrex from penetrating or firing upon the shipyard.

-

On a viewscreen, a Voltrex fusion missile slammed into the stern of a Trellixian battlecruiser and the ship vanished in a fiery explosion.

Battle Commander Yuld felt his flagship shudder violently. He looked over at the tactical officer, suspecting what he was going to hear.

"Energy shield is down!"

Battle Commander Yuld drew in a sharp breath. He knew he was about to die. The least he could do was take some of his enemy with him. "All ahead full. Ram the nearest enemy ship!"

-

The two fleets continued to close and soon were intermixed. The ships turned broadside and fired all of their energy weapons at one another. Occasionally a fusion missile was launched, annihilating another Trellixian battlecruiser. Much of the fighting now was between individual ships only a few kilometers apart. Space was full of bright explosions and glowing debris.

The *Claw of Honor* shuddered as two Trellixian fusion missiles impacted the energy shield. The shield held, dispersing the energy over a large area.

"Enemy flagship is on a course to ram the *Starlight*!" reported Zalurr, his eyes wide.

"Put it up on the main viewscreen," ordered Kamuss, shifting his eyes from the tactical display to the large viewscreen. The *Starlight* was a battlecruiser which had only recently joined the fleet. "Target that vessel!"

The viewscreen showed a magnified view of the two ships. They were rapidly closing with each other. The *Starlight* was pummeling the enemy flagship with numerous energy beams, tearing massive holes in the oncoming ship.

In a sudden explosion, the enemy ship was torn apart but large pieces of wreckage continue on, slamming into the energy shield of the Voltrex battlecruiser. The shield wavered and then went down. Several pieces of wreckage crashed into the hull, causing major damage. The ship seemed to stagger and then began drifting as it lost power.

Several nearby Trellixian ships must have noticed the damage and almost instantly numerous fusion missiles arrived, striking the hull and turning the battlecruiser into a glowing wreck. No one could have survived the destruction.

"*Starlight* is gone," reported Zalurr as the battlecruiser's icon vanished from the tactical display.

Kamuss did not reply as other Voltrex ships were also dying, primarily the smaller support ships. "Any sign of the enemy using their antimatter missiles?" These were the only weapons the Trellixians had that could be dangerous to the battleships and the battlecruisers.

"No," replied Zalurr. "Just their smaller fusion missiles and energy beams."

Lieutenant Commander LeLath looked confused. "Why aren't they using their antimatter weapons? We've seen them use a few in the past."

"Unknown," replied Kamuss. He too was confused by this. "Perhaps they have none available. We must not assume that will continue in the future." On a viewscreen, Kamuss saw two of the surviving Trellixian battlecruisers destroy a small Voltrex support vessel before a pair of Voltrex battleships blew them into oblivion.

Fleet Commander Kamuss turned his attention back to the tactical display. Most of the Trellixian battlecruisers had been destroyed and only a few still fought. Even as he watched several icons representing enemy ships vanished as they were annihilated. "Once the enemy fleet has been destroyed we will move on the shipyard."

-

In space, the battle began to wind down. The last Trellixian battlecruiser exploded in a brilliant fireball as a fusion missile detonated against the hull.

Space was littered with the debris from the battle: destroyed Trellixian battlecruisers, two Voltrex battlecruisers, and eight Voltrex support ships. The superior strength of Jelnoid energy shields and weapons were still giving the Voltrex a significant advantage.

-

Fleet Commander Kamuss was listening to the list of destroyed ships and those with damage. Compared to the Trellixian losses his own were minor. "Reassemble our formation and we will advance on the Trellixian shipyard. Without their fleet for protection we should have no trouble destroying it with our energy beams."

"I've done a quick inventory of our fusion missiles," reported Lieutenant Commander LeLath, turning toward the commander. "We have about 62 percent of our original inventory of missiles left."

Kamuss frowned. Even though he had ordered them not to a few of his ships had used some of their missiles to take out Trellixian battlecruisers in the recent battle.

Lieutenant Commander LeLath knew Fleet Commander Kamuss was concerned about the number of missiles used. "Wouldn't it be safer to use just a few fusion missiles against the shipyard?"

Kamuss shook his head. "It would take days for a supply ship with more missiles to reach us. We don't dare stay in one system that long. It's only a matter of time before the Trellixians put together a large enough fleet to be a danger to us. I intend to destroy this system and then move on to the next target."

Lieutenant Commander LeLath looked thoughtful. "Earth will have the missiles we need. We could continue on to the Humans' system and restock."

This was something, which had already occurred to Kamuss. His fleets had sufficient missiles to hit possibly two more targets. Going on to Earth was something the Trellixians would not expect. "Perhaps you're right," Kamuss said. "It is something we will have to consider."

"Shipyard is in range of our energy weapons," reported Zalurr.

The *Claw of Honor* shook slightly.

Fleet Commander Kamuss looked over at Diboll. "What was that?"

"Missile strike to our energy screen."

Suddenly on the viewscreen several massive explosions occurred. On the tactical display, a Voltrex battleship and battlecruiser vanished.

"Antimatter!" cried out Lieutenant Commander LeLath in dismay. "The shipyard is launching antimatter missiles."

"Heavy energy beam fire from the shipyard," added Zalurr. "We've lost the support ships *Morning Dawn* and *Trails End*."

"Firing energy weapons," reported Diboll.

In space, energy beam fire erupted between the Trellixian shipyard and the two Voltrex fleets. For the most part the Trellixian beams had little or no affect on the larger Voltrex ships. The Jelnoid energy shields shrugged off the attack as if it was a minor inconvenience. However, a few of the support ships were not as lucky as heavy energy beams from the shipyard pummeled their shields and in several instances knocked them down.

Jelnoid energy beams struck the shipyard's defensive screen, causing it to glow brighter and brighter. After a few seconds several beams penetrated, blasting out huge glowing rents in the side of the shipyard. More beams began to penetrate, causing severe damage to the massive structure.

Inside the shipyard, the Trellixian commander watched helplessly as his command was being ripped apart. On the damage control console red lights were appearing faster than they could be reported. He had already launched the only four antimatter missiles the station possessed. On the viewscreens he could see the ineffectiveness of his energy beams and other missiles against the Jelnoid energy screens the Voltrex ships had. His weapons were only marginally effective against the small enemy support ships.

"Shield is down to 32 percent," reported the tactical officer. "I estimate total failure in the next two minutes."

The commander shifted his gaze to another viewscreen. It showed the blue white planet the shipyard orbited. There were nearly six billion Trellixians living on Lantoll Six.

The sensor officer turned toward the commander. "Cargo ships and colony ships are jumping into hyperspace."

The commander acknowledged the report. Unfortunately he suspected many of the valuable ships would not be able to escape. Several were docked to the four space stations and still more would not be able to power up their hyperdrives in time.

"Send a message to the High Command that Lantoll Six has fallen to the Voltrex."

The commander was well aware of what the Voltrex did at Capal Four. For centuries the Empire had expanded with no fear of being attacked. Now that had all changed. The enemy they faced in the Voltrex were doing to the Empire what the Empire had done to over a thousand inhabited worlds in the past.

The shipyard began to shake violently. The entire damage control console was now covered in red lights. The lighting in the Command Center began to flicker.

"Energy shield is down," reported the tactical officer. "Fusion reactors three and four have been destroyed."

-

Fleet Commander Kamuss watched silently as the fleets' energy beams finished demolishing the Trellixian shipyard. After a few more moments it was nothing more than an orbiting mass of glowing wreckage.

"All ships are to target any Trellixian ships still in orbit. Admiral Masurl is to take his fleet and hunt down and destroy any Trellixian ships in other sections of the system as well as annihilate all their other colonies and mining facilities."

"Lieutenant Commander LeLath. Once we've destroyed the enemy ships in orbit we will target the four space stations. After that the fleet will go into orbit and begin bombardment of the planet."

Kamuss was not comfortable with his orders to eliminate all traces of Trellixian civilization on planets they conquered. However, they were only doing to the Trellixians what the Trellixians had done for hundreds of years. Kamuss wondered how many hundreds of billions of defenseless innocents the Trellixians had slaughtered.

-

In space, the cargo, colony ships, and mining ships were located and destroyed by the Voltrex ships. Many of them managed to escape by jumping into hyperspace. Voltrex ships took note of the directions they fled in the hope of locating more Trellixian worlds or bases.

Fleet Commander Kamuss' fleet rapidly cleared the space above Lantoll Six of all Trellixian vessels as well as destroying the four large space stations. He knew for months wreckage would fall into the atmosphere and burn up. A few of the larger pieces might even crash into the surface.

The fleet then went into orbit and from the battleships and battlecruisers nuclear missiles fell toward the planet. Soon, all across Lantoll Six mushroom clouds rose above city sites and industrial locations. The atmosphere grew dark and gray as the explosions of so many nuclear weapons sent the planet into a nuclear winter.

"Fleet Commander Masurl reports all Trellixian vessels in the outer and inner system have been destroyed as well as all colonies and mining sites," Lieutenant Commander LeLath informed Battle Commander Kamuss. "Our sensor scans indicate all Trellixian targets on Lantoll Six have been destroyed as well."

Kamuss nodded. "Very well. We will set a course for a nearby star system where we will stop for a few days to repair our battle damage. Then we will continue on to our next target." From the courses the fleeing Trellixian colony ships and cargo ships had gone, he suspected they were going to Kalone Four which was a rumored Trellixian base. It would be the fleets' next target.

Chapter Nine

Lisa was in the Officers' Mess eating a light meal. It was just after noon ship's time and she had a few hours before reporting to the Command Center. Brenda was sitting across from her eating cherry pie with vanilla ice cream. Lisa pushed her yogurt away, frowning at Brenda and her petite figure. "I don't see how you keep the weight off. You're always eating something delicious for desert."

Brenda grinned and took a bite of her ice cream. "I work out a lot. I run at least two miles everyday plus my regular exercise routine. That way I can eat whatever I want and not have to worry about it. Besides, I love ice cream!"

Lisa eyed Brenda's cherry pie and ice cream wondering if she should have some herself. It looked really good. The ice cream machine in the Officers' Mess offered three types of ice cream. Strawberry sounded very tempting.

"So how are you and Brett doing on this trip?" Brenda was well aware Lisa and Brett were dating. She had doubled with them a few times back in Complex One.

Lisa let out a deep sigh. "We agreed that while we are on this mission our personal feelings for each other would have to stay buried. We can't risk how we feel about one another compromising our work or this mission."

"It must be tough seeing him every day and not being able to show any affection."

"It was at first," Lisa admitted. She had just about decided to go ahead and go get a cup of ice cream. Strawberry sounded great! "We still eat together at least once per day and we're around each other constantly."

Brenda took another bite of her cherry pie. "I understand we're leaving this system today and setting a course to take us deeper into the Empire."

Lisa nodded. "Yes; Captain Dolan wants to bypass the next few Trellixian systems and see what's farther in."

"The closer we get to their core worlds the more dangerous it will be for us," Brenda said uneasily. "I'm worried about our ships being detected."

"So am I," confessed Lisa, looking over toward the ice cream machine. "We're going into an area with a lot of ship traffic and there are bound to be numerous Trellixian warships."

"I wish we were back home," Brenda said as she pushed her now empty pie plate away. "I much prefer to be doing research at Complex One."

Lisa was in agreement. "I think we all feel that way. Professor Wilkens promised me this is the last mission any of us will need to go on unless we volunteer and I don't plan on volunteering."

Brenda leaned back in her chair. "I think after this mission and the last one I've seen enough space. Earth will suffice in the future."

Lisa nodded. She just hoped they all made it home safely. Standing up, she headed for the ice cream machine. One bowl full wouldn't hurt.

-

High Commander Kaldre gazed in silence at the latest dispatch the communications officer of the *Dawn Reaper* had just handed him. Lantoll Six had fallen to the Voltrex. There was no doubt in his mind that by now the planet and all the other colonies in the system were radioactive ruins.

"It is as I feared," said Kaldre, shaking the dispatch in his right hand. "The Voltrex are continuing to attack our colonies in the outer section of the Empire. They destroy our ships with impunity and then our worlds."

Second Officer Calaah was standing nearby. "Surely the others on the High Command will take your warning seriously now."

"Maybe," replied Kaldre doubtfully. "I've received a message from High Commander Thatrex requesting a meeting. He is coming here to Traxis Three."

"Perhaps he's bringing a message from the rest of the High Command."

High Commander Kaldre hoped Calaah was right. His gaze moved to the ship's main viewscreen. The shipyard was clearly displayed. Already changes were being made to the production lines to allow future battlecruisers to be more powerful. In addition another of the shipyards was busy building more powerful fusion warheads. These had never been needed in the past, but now were. The new design would allow for seventy-megaton warheads, which should play havoc even with the Jelnoid shields the Voltrex and Human ships were protected by. Three or four of these more powerful warheads detonating against an energy shield should bring it down.

The first of the new missiles with the more powerful warheads would be sent to Battle Commander Balforr's new fleet as well as the older battlecruisers which had been assigned to him. Once that was done High Commander Kaldre would feel more confident in being able to protect the core systems if the Voltrex and the Humans ever ventured this far into the Empire.

"High Commander Thatrex will be arriving in about six hours," reported Second Officer Calaah listening to a report from Lamarr at Communications.

"Lamarr, contact the shipyard and inform Commander Malborr we expect High Commander Thatrex to be arriving later today. I will need his best conference room for a meeting which I expect him to attend."

A few minutes later the communications officer turned toward High Commander Kaldre. "Message sent and confirmed. Commander Malborr will see to the arrangements."

Kaldre shifted his gaze to the tactical display. It was full of ships coming and going in the system. Traxis Three had a population of nearly sixty billion with twenty-two billion more living in domed colonies on the other planets and moons in the system. Around Traxis Three there were a large number of orbiting space stations that serviced the hundreds of starships which were delivering supplies and raw material to the system every day. In addition colony ships were constantly arriving, loading up new colonists, and then departing for worlds in the outer sections of the Empire.

Turning his attention back to the planet, it pained him to see how little green there was on Traxis Three. Most of the planet's landmasses were covered with cities or factories. Even the oceans had floating cities on them. He knew Traxis Three was having many of the same problems most of the other heavily populated planets in the Empire were. The planet was suffering from a serious lack of space for its inhabitants as well as food shortages. Rations were currently at the minimum needed just to survive and still do the work that was necessary.

"How many battlecruisers are currently in the system?"

"Thirty-eight," answered Calaah.

This made High Commander Kaldre feel uneasy. What would happen if an Earth task force or Voltrex fleet were to drop out of hyperspace into the system? It would be a disaster. With a sickening feeling, he knew the Empire did not have the ships to adequately defend all of the core systems and to continue expanding. When High Commander Thatrex arrived they would have much to talk about.

Later that day High Commander Kaldre was on board the shipyard when he was informed that High Commander Thatrex's battlecruiser was docking. A welcoming committee of station officers would escort the High Commander to the conference room where High Commander Kaldre and Commander Malborr were waiting.

It was only a few minutes later that Thatrex entered the conference room. A table had been set with a number of delicacies. There was a variety of different fruits and drinks but the main prize were the Marmods. They were a small warm-blooded species prized for their delicate taste. Thatrex walked over to the table and picking up one that seemed more energetic than the others, promptly ate it and then took a deep drink of a strong alcoholic beverage to wash it down. "It's been weeks since I've eaten a Marmod. They're becoming very hard to find."

"I have a small breeding farm," confessed High Commander Kaldre. "I can see to it that you have a regular supply." The breeding farm was under a small agricultural dome Kaldre's family owned and operated for their personal use. It was on a small icy moon in an out-of-the-way star system.

Thatrex nodded. "We will talk about that later. Let us set down and discuss the events at Lantoll Six. It seems the Voltrex have put together a large fleet which is conquering and destroying our outer colony worlds."

"I feared that would happen," replied Kaldre. He had warned the High Command the Voltrex and the Humans would not be satisfied with staying inside their own borders. "There was no reason to expect them to remain in their space and fight a defensive battle. They are pushing us back away from their space."

Thatrex looked thoughtful. "Will they stop?"

Kaldre shook his head. "I don't believe so. They consider us a threat and won't stop until we defeat their fleets or they defeat ours."

"Defeat us!" said Thatrex, his large eyes growing wide. "That will never happen. There are too many warships in the Empire."

"Where will we get the ships to stop them? If we pull fleets away from our core worlds we leave them open to attack. If we pull the necessary fleets away from the outer rim where we are expanding the Empire, we will have no new worlds to colonize. We've already pulled back a few fleets to send to the sector the Voltrex are attacking. I'm now receiving complaints from planetary governors that they need additional space to send more colonists."

Thatrex was silent for several long moments. "There are other members of the High Command starting to become concerned. While they don't believe our core worlds will ever be threatened, they are concerned about how the Voltrex attacks upon our colonies will affect future colonizing efforts. It now seems an entire sector of space is being closed off to us."

"We need to have all of our shipyards building more of the warships we constructed for Battle Commander Balforr," suggested Kaldre. "They are our best hope for defeating the Humans and the Voltrex. If we changed all of our shipyards over to constructing the new battlecruisers in a year's time we would have enough to drive the Voltrex back and destroy the Humans."

Thatrex shook his head. "The High Command will never agree to that. There is too much of a demand for more cargo and colony ships. Every day we receive requests from the planetary governors for more cargo ships and colony ships to remove their excess populations."

"I don't believe they understand the seriousness of the threat the Voltrex and the Humans pose. Our Empire has never faced a threat like this before. If we don't do something soon we will continue to lose more colony worlds."

"You still believe sometime in the future they might attack our core worlds?"

Kaldre nodded. "They want to win this war. The Humans desire to pay us back for what we did to their world. The Voltrex know what we would do to their planets if we could conquer them. I firmly believe if we don't find a way to stop them someday we will find Voltrex and Human fleets above our core worlds dropping bombs like they have to our colony worlds."

Thatrex took in a deep breath. "There are shipyards here dedicated to building new warships and cargo ships. What if you were given control and allowed to build whatever you want?"

"The High Command would never agree to that," answered Kaldre.

"They might as long as cargo and colony ship construction continued uninterrupted in our other systems. I may be able to convince them to show some latitude. I believe I could talk them into giving you a year to construct the fleet you want. Would that be sufficient?"

High Commander Kaldre thought for a long minute. He looked over at Commander Malborr. "I have the designs of the new battlecruisers we constructed for Battle Commander Balforr. If I give those to you can you modify your shipyards to produce the new ships?"

Malborr nodded. "It would require adding several thousand new workers but there are plenty down on the planet who would jump at the chance to get away from their current living conditions."

Kaldre was pleased with that answer. "How soon can you start?"

Malborr paused as he considered what would need to be done. "Seven to eight days. I would want to pick those who have some experience in the type of construction jobs they would be assigned to."

"Then let's do it," said Kaldre. Perhaps he would get the ships built after all that he felt were needed to stop the Voltrex and the Humans. The question was would there be enough time?

-

The *Fury* dropped out of hyperspace on the edges of a blue giant star system and released another communications drone. The communications officer then sent a quick one-second communication burst back to Earth giving their location. A few minutes later the *Fury* and her three escorts jumped back into hyperspace on their journey deeper into Trellixian space.

-

Captain Dolan was sitting in his command chair watching the viewscreens. If you watched close enough the stars actually seemed to be moving.

"It's a beautiful view," said Katana, stepping closer to the captain. "It's one thing about star travel I truly enjoy."

Mark had to agree. Chloe had adjusted the filters on the main viewscreen so the stars showed in their actual colors. Mark could sit here for hours just staring at the viewscreen.

"It's two weeks to our next target," said Katana. "That will put us right on the edge of where we believe their core worlds are located."

Chloe turned around on her dais to face the two. "Space traffic in that area will be heavy. The chances of our fleet being detected will grow exponentially as we travel closer to the Trellixian core worlds."

Mark frowned. He was well aware of that. "It is a chance we'll have to take. If we want to have any chance of defeating the Trellixians we must know exactly what we're up against. We'll be scanning their core systems for population densities, ship strengths, and what resources they have available."

"Even using the probes and keeping our vessels at a distance will be dangerous," pointed out Katana. "With the ship traffic we expect in their core worlds, there is a high probability our probes will be detected."

Mark nodded his head. "Yes, that's why we'll consider all probes expendable. At the first sign of detection we will set off their self-destructs and then jump the fleet back into the safety of hyperspace."

"That may work a couple of times," said Chloe, folding her arms across her chest. She had been practicing Human mannerisms for weeks now. "But after a time or two the Trellixians will realize what we're doing and may very well set a trap for us at one of their core systems."

"We'll be on the alert for just that," replied Mark. "I'm sure you will be able to give us a few minutes warning of an impending attack."

Chloe looked doubtful. "Remember our sensors only reach out about half a light year. If the Trellixians are coming toward us in hyperspace the warning may be much briefer, possibly as little as one or two minutes."

Mark let out a deep sigh. "That's still better than nothing. We'll keep the fleet at Condition Two while the probes are in the Trellixian core systems." He knew the mission would soon become very dangerous and there was a very good chance at some point the fleet would be detected. When that happened they would have to flee for home and hope they could avoid any Trellixian ships which might be searching for them.

Katana shifted her gaze from Chloe back to the captain. "I would suggest the entire fleet go through some additional battle drills over the next two weeks. We must be prepared in case we have to go into combat."

"Agreed," replied Mark. "Set them up and I'll give approval. The crews need to be as sharp as possible by the time we reach our destination."

High Commander Kaldre was in one of the construction bays of the massive shipyard. In the construction cradle a new battlecruiser was having the last of its armor plating put in place. Special robots overseen by Trellixian supervisors were welding the plates into place. A web work of scaffolding covered the ship, allowing access to every part of its hull.

"This is the first ship to have all the upgrades you requested," Commander Malborr informed the High Commander. "It was nearly finished when you arrived so it was relatively simple to update it to the new standards you've requested with the new fusion reactors and the designs you submitted to my engineers. We have several other ships under construction we're updating as well."

"What about the new workers?"

"All in place," replied Malborr. "We took workers from factories and construction facilities to fill out the required workforce. In another two weeks we'll be building the first of the new battlecruisers."

Kaldre spent several moments looking around the construction bay. Specially programmed robots did most of the heavy work. The bay swarmed with them. Kaldre knew inside the ship Trellixians did much of the more intricate work. There was a steady influx of materials going inside several open cargo hatches. Progress had been much quicker than he expected. Commander

Malborr had cut the expected time to modify the shipyards nearly in half.

"How long does it take to complete a ship?"

"Forty to fifty days depending on the availability of materials," Malborr replied.

Kaldre turned toward the shipyard commander. "Make sure you don't run out of supplies. I want as many of these ships built as fast as possible. Also, any ship coming in for a refit is to be updated with the new fusion reactor and what ever else is necessary."

Malborr nodded. "I will see to it."

Turning, High Commander Kaldre left the construction bay. He was deeply concerned whether there was enough time to build the fleet he felt was necessary to protect the core worlds. If not for High Commander Thatrex much of what Kaldre was hoping to accomplish would not be possible. As one of the oldest High Commanders, the other High Commanders were willing to listen and respect his views. However, earlier in the day High Commander Danaar had made an inquiry if one of the shipyards tasked with building military vessels could be modified to build more colony ships. Kaldre had informed him that wasn't practical at this time. Kaldre knew Danaar wasn't pleased with the answer.

Even more aggravating, the planetary governor of Traxis Three had inquired if Kaldre could to anything to increase the amount of food shipments arriving daily. The governor had stressed that if there was no increase there could be widespread unrest on the planet. Kaldre had promised to look into it but doubted there was anything he could do. The food supply for the Empire was limited and due to the growing population was becoming less with each passing day.

Returning to the *Dawn Reaper*, Kaldre sat down in his command chair thinking about what could be done to keep the Humans and the Voltrex in check until the new fleets were ready. After awhile he realized there were only two possibilities.

"Lamarr, send a message to Battle Commander Balforr. I want him to use his fleet to patrol the core worlds. They are to spend one full day in each system scanning for any threats."

Kaldre waited as the message was sent and acknowledged. "Now, send a second message to the High Command requesting they send four of our fleets to the Human system. They are not to attack but are to make their presence known."

"What good will that do?" asked Second Officer Calaah. "Where will they get the ships?"

Kaldre grinned, allowing his flesh ripping teeth to show. "It will keep the Humans pinned down. With our fleets nearby they will dare not launch any military task groups toward us. They can pull the fleets from some of our core worlds if necessary." He wasn't worried about an attack in the immediate future in the heart of the Empire. Later the fleets could be pulled back if necessary. Besides if a fleet was launched to attack the core worlds it would most likely originate from Earth. With fleets positioned close by the attack could be headed off.

Calaah's eyes lit up with understanding. "It is a good strategy."

Standing up High Commander Kaldre left the Command Center. He had some additional messages for Battle Commander Balforr as well as the Battle Commander who would be in command of the fleets going to Earth. He was determined to save the Empire from what he considered to be a growing and serious threat.

Chapter Ten

Fleet Commander Kamuss let out a deep breath. The two Voltrex fleets were nearly to Kalone Four. Three stealth scout ships were already scanning the system for Trellixian ships and bases.

"First scans are coming in," reported Zalurr as his sensors began lighting up with data.

Kamuss shifted his gaze to the tactical display with his eyes widening at what it was showing. A low growl erupted from his throat. The display was full of red threat icons!

Lieutenant Commander LeLath echoed the Fleet Commander's growl. She gazed at the screen in dismay. "There must be hundreds of warships in that system!"

"We don't know if they're all warships," Kamuss said as he stepped away from his command chair and moved closer to the tactical display. "Zalurr, do we know the ship types we're looking at?"

Zalurr looked at some data on his console. "Shortly; the data on ship identification is just now coming in. I can tell you there are large numbers of cargo ships, colony ships, and warships."

"Do we continue on into the system?" asked Lieutenant Commander LeLath. "We could lose a substantial portion of our fleet if there are indeed hundreds of Trellixian warships in the system."

Kamuss frowned. They were deep in Trellixian space and couldn't afford large ship losses, however, if they could destroy this base it would cripple the Trellixians' efforts at colonizing this sector.

"Do we know what planet their base is located on?"

"It's not on a planet," answered Zalurr. "From the scouts' sensor readings the base is located upon a large moon around a gas giant in the system. It actually has an atmosphere though the sensors haven't reported whether it's breathable or not."

Kamuss thought over the tactical situation. He needed more information before taking the two Voltrex fleets into what might be a very dangerous situation. "Meetric, we will slow our travel through hyperspace to give the scouts more time to scan the system. I want twenty minutes of additional scanning time."

"Slowing down," reported Meetric. "The entire fleet is following our lead."

In the Kalone Four System, the three Voltrex scout ships moved farther into the system in order to get clear sensor readings of all the space in the system, particularly around the planets and the system's moons. As the scouts neared several of the planets they took great effort to remain undetected. However, one scout made the mistake of sending back sensor readings to the fleet with a Trellixian cargo ship in a direct line of its hyperspace communication signal.

On the large moon orbiting Kalone Four, Commander Garron stood silently as his communications officer reported a strange message from a cargo ship traveling to a mining operation on the outer most planet of the system.

"A hyperspace signal," said Second Officer Tarack. "There should be no signals originating in that region of space."

"Was the cargo ship able to understand the message being sent?" asked Garron.

The communications officer shook his head. "No, it was highly encrypted and he only intercepted a small segment."

Commander Garron looked over at one of the sensor officers. "Are we detecting anything unusual in the system? Sensor scans or communications?"

"It's impossible to tell," the primary sensor officer replied. "There are too many ships with active sensors and if the hyperspace signal is directional we won't be able to detect it unless a ship is in the right location."

Garron looked over at Second Officer Tarack. "Send a squadron of our battlecruisers to that location where the cargo ship intercepted the signal. Also, order all of our ships to go on alert and to scan for any signs of unknown vessels or probes. They are to listen for any unauthorized hyperspace communication signals."

"Do you believe it's the Voltrex?" asked Tarack, his large eyes widening. "Would they dare to attack us here?"

"I don't know if it's them or not. However, we can't overlook the possibility. If they know of this base they must realize that by destroying it they would make this entire sector untenable for colonization."

Garron watched as Tarack hurried to carry out his orders. Looking at the multiple sensor screens he grew uncomfortably aware of how spread out his battlecruisers were. There were squadrons patrolling all the space of the Kalone Four System. Perhaps it was time to recall most of them in case they were needed to defend this moon. Over the past few weeks he had called in many of the fleets assigned to protect this sector from the Voltrex. The colony ships and cargo ships which had fled from Capal Four to Lantoll Six and then Kalone Four had come here. All of them had been sent farther into the Empire for their own safety. That still left quite a few that had other colonies as their destinations. They had orders to check in at Kalone Four before continuing to the colonies.

Gazing at the tactical displays, he realized there were quite a few cargo ships and even some colony ships in the system. The cargo ships were resupplying the system of Kalone Four and some were due to jump into hyperspace for some of the nearby colonies as were the colony ships.

"Communications, order all colony and cargo ships not assigned to this system to enter hyperspace and proceed to their designated destinations. Inform them there is a chance this system may soon be coming under attack." That should speed up the evacuation of those valuable ships. It would also get them out of the way in case there was a battle.

For nearly an hour there were no additional reports of unusual communication signals or sightings, then three things occurred nearly at once. Battlecruisers on patrol reported intercepting two separate signals. A cargo ship preparing to enter hyperspace reported a small unidentified craft in their area and finally a battlecruiser on the outskirts of the system reported detecting a large number of unknown ships dropping out of hyperspace.

"It's them," said Second Officer Tarack, his eyes focusing on a tactical display. "Our computers have confirmed the messages are in the Voltrex language and we believe the small ship spotted is one of the Voltrexs' scout ships. They are rumored to have stealth capability. That's why they've been so difficult to spot on our sensors."

"Take the base to high alert," ordered Commander Garron, sitting down in his command chair. "The same for our battlecruisers. Recall all battlecruisers back to Kalone Four. If the Voltrex want a battle we will give them one."

Instantly klaxons and red lights began flashing. Across the entire base Trellixians raced to their battle stations. Heavy energy guns rose up from the ground and turned toward space. Missile hatches slid open and heavy ship-to-ship missiles were loaded into the missile tubes.

In orbit, there were two shipyards and six space stations. On board the largest shipyard Malken antimatter missiles were loaded aboard six battlecruisers docked to the station. As soon as the missiles with their one hundred-megaton warheads were loaded the six battlecruisers joined the rest of the gathering fleet. The two shipyards brought their defenses on line, including increasing the power to their energy shields.

All across the system squadrons of Trellixian battlecruisers raced to Kalone Four. Some made short hyperspace jumps to get there quicker. In total four hundred and seventeen battlecruisers were assembling over the large moon.

The three scout ships rapidly noticed the new deployment of the Trellixians' battlecruisers as well as the sudden departure of numerous cargo and colony ships. This was quickly reported to Fleet Commander Kamuss on the *Claw of Honor.*

"We've been detected," said Lieutenant Commander LeLath in dismay as she saw the movement of the Trellixian ships on the tactical display.

"We're facing slightly over four hundred Trellixian battlecruisers," added Zalurr as identification of the ships still in the system was received. "There is also a moderate sized shipyard, one large shipyard and six space stations. Both shipyards seem to be protected with energy shields. There is also a large base on the surface of the moon and the sensors readings from the scouts indicate numerous energy cannons protecting the base."

"Does Fleet Commander Masurl have this information?" asked Kamuss as he studied the tactical display. Four hundred enemy battlecruisers were a concern even if Voltrex ships had superior weapons and shields.

"Yes," replied Lieutenant Commander LeLath. "He's receiving the same tactical feed from the scout ships as we are."

Kamuss leaned back in his command chair. This would be the biggest battle since the Trellixians attacked the Bator System. "If we take this base and those warships out the fighting in this sector might very well be over. Our worlds will have nothing to fear, particularly if we keep pushing the Trellixians back." He knew there were several other Voltrex fleets searching for any Trellixian fleets still near the border of the region of space controlled by the Voltrex.

"We'll lose some ships as well as have some damaged," warned LeLath. "Where do we go after this battle for repairs?"

"Earth," replied Fleet Commander Kamuss. "They have a shipyard they're working on and by the time we get there part of it should be functional. Also by then perhaps we will know more about what Captain Dolan found on his mission to the Trellixian core worlds."

LeLath let out a deep sigh. "I should have gone with him. There are many of our people on the *Fury.*"

"Lieutenant Commander Katana is qualified," replied Kamuss. "Besides, I needed you here."

Lieutenant Commander LeLath nodded. "What are your plans for the attack now that we know what we're up against?"

Kamuss took a deep breath. "We will divide into separate fleets. Fleet Commander Masurl will strike the Trellixians from one direction and our fleet from another. We will target the warships first before dealing with the orbiting shipyards and stations. We will save the surface base for last. It may be a difficult nut to crack as our Human friends would say."

LeLath allowed herself to smile. A few Human idioms had made it into the Voltrex language, particularly among fleet personnel. "How soon before we attack?"

"Immediately," replied Kamuss, his face taking on a serious look. "If the reports from the scouts are correct, the Trellixians already know we're here. There is no point in delaying. Take all ships to Battle Condition One and prepare for hyperspace jump. Metriic, I want our two fleets to exit hyperspace sixty thousand kilometers from Kalone Four's moon. Once there we will separate the fleets and commence our attack."

Meetric began entering the hyperspace jump coordinates into the navigation computer. Once everything was set in motion he sent the coordinates to the rest of the ships in the two fleets. "Jump in twenty seconds."

Kamuss tightened the harness which held him in his command chair. The twenty seconds counted down and he felt a slight wrenching sensation as the *Claw of Honor* made the transition into hyperspace. After only a few minutes the wrenching sensation returned as stars once more filled the viewscreens. On one screen a large gas giant appeared with an orbiting moon.

"Sixty thousand kilometers from target," confirmed Meetric.

Kamuss nodded. "Separate the fleets and move us toward the moon. Fleet Commander Masurl will attack the far side of the moon and we'll attack the side currently in sunlight. Be aware of the gas giant. It has high gravity and dense atmospheric layers. All ships need to stay away from it."

The message was sent and the two fleets separated and began moving toward the moon and the ships that were their target.

Fleet Commander Kamuss leaned forward in his command chair as the fleet rapidly neared missile range. The Trellixian ships seemed intent on protecting the shipyards and the six space stations. Their ships were positioned defensively around them. Kamuss wasn't pleased his two fleets would be slightly outnumbered. He hoped the Jelnoid weaponry and shields his ships were equipped with would bring most of them through unharmed.

Commander Garron drew in a sharp breath as he saw the red threat icons appear on the tactical display. His fleet had a slight advantage in numbers but not by much.

"Contact our ships with the Malken missiles. They are to strike first. If we can make the Voltrex think we have a large number of antimatter missiles they may withdraw."

Second Officer Tarack quickly sent the orders to the appropriate ship squadrons. On the large tactical display, six squadrons of ten ships each broke off from the main fleet and began accelerating toward the Voltrex.

"Enemy ships accelerating and closing rapidly with us," reported Zalurr, his eyes widening. "Sixty Trellixian battlecruisers are in the formation."

"They're already within our missile range," Lieutenant Commander LeLath informed the Fleet Commander. "They'll be able to launch their own missiles in a few more seconds at the rate they're closing."

Zalurr looked confused. "Why attack us with such a small number of ships? Surely they know our own missiles will destroy them."

On the main screen, the image shifted to show the inbound enemy ships. Sixty two-thousand-meter battlecruisers rushed directly toward the heart of the Voltrex fleet formation.

"Launch our own missiles," ordered Fleet Commander Kamuss, leaning forward in his command chair. "All battleships and battlecruisers to launch two missiles each at the inbound enemy force."

"Missile launch!" called out Zalurr with concern in his voice. "We have over four hundred missiles inbound."

"Set our defensive turrets to shoot them down," ordered Lieutenant Commander LeLath not waiting for the Fleet Commander's orders.

"Our own missiles are launching," reported Diboll as his fingers depressed several glowing icons on his computer screen.

Kamuss' eyes shifted to the tactical display showing the inbound missiles. His eyes narrowed sharply. It seemed as if the missiles were clumped together in small groups. "All those missiles are only targeting a few of our ships. We must shoot them down!" Even though they contained small warheads if enough of them struck a warship's energy screen, they could knock it down. Particularly if they struck some of the smaller support ships.

From the battleships and the battlecruisers of the Voltrex fleet missile tubes slid open and forty-megaton missiles launched toward the incoming Trellixian vessels. At the same time, energy turrets rotated and began targeting the incoming wave of missiles.

Six Malken missiles were mixed in with the other Trellixian missiles. The Trellixians were hoping the more powerful missiles would slip through the Voltrex defensive fire.

Sudden explosions began to dot space as defensive energy beam fire from both fleets began to find and detonate the inbound missiles. The Voltrex missiles were faster and began to strike the defensive screens of the Trellixian battlecruisers. In scant moments twenty-three screens failed and the battlecruisers they protected were turned into glowing fields of scattering debris. The remaining battlecruisers reloaded their missile tubes and fired a second wave of missiles.

Energy beam fire from the Voltrex ships took out most of the first wave of Trellixian missiles as well as two of the Malken missiles. However, four of the Malken missiles slipped through.

The surviving missiles in the first wave began to reach the Voltrex fleet. Bright flashes lit up the energy screens but the Jelnoid shields had no trouble resisting. Then the four surviving Malken missiles along with numerous small fusion missiles struck and the energy screens on four battleships wavered and then went down. Subsequent strikes from more missiles quickly turned the four ships into fiery masses of plasma and twisted wreckage. Six smaller support vessels were blown apart as other missiles from the second wave struck their screens, bringing them down and exposing their hulls to the deadly destruction of nuclear and fusion energy.

"Antimatter!" called out Zalurr. "We've lost the *Morning Dawn*, *Day Rider*, *Huntress*, and *Starhold*."

"Four of our battleships," said LeLath in shock.

"We also lost six support vessels,' added Zalurr as green icons vanished from the tactical display.

"We're in energy weapons range," LeLath said as she saw the range between the two fleets rapidly decreasing.

"Fire!" ordered Kamuss. "I don't want anymore ships lost to missile strikes." He had not expected to lose any battleships in this battle. To lose four so quickly was alarming.

Kamuss felt the *Claw of Honor* shake violently and several alarms began sounding. He looked over at Lieutenant Commander LeLath. "What was that?"

"Wreckage from the *Huntress*," LeLath replied in a shaken voice. "Some of it struck our energy shield. There was no damage."

On the main viewscreen, energy beams were visible as the two fleets exchanged fire. A Voltrex support vessel suddenly exploded as multiple beams penetrated its energy shield. In the

Trellixian fleet massive explosions were marking the death of numerous battlecruisers as energy beams penetrated their shields and then tore their hulls open.

"Enemy battlecruisers are withdrawing," reported Zalurr. "Only fourteen are going to make it back to their fleet."

"We can catch them before they get back," pointed out Lieutenant Commander LeLath, her claws slightly extended.

Kamuss shook his head. "No, let them go. We'll destroy them when we launch our primary attack." He was still reeling from the loss of four irreplaceable battleships. Kamuss wondered if the Trellixians had used all of their antimatter missiles or had they held some back. Did they have other surprises waiting for his fleets?

"We'll be in attack range of their main fleet and stations in two minutes," reported Metriic.

"Fleet Commander Masurl reports his fleet will be in position as planned," added Meela.

Kamuss looked over at Lieutenant Commander LeLath. "What about damage to our other ships?"

"Minor," she reported. "We have a few support ships which need to initiate some repairs. I've ordered them to the back of the fleet for their own protection."

We're in missile range of the main enemy fleet," reported Zalurr.

"Launch four missiles from all battleships and battlecruisers and two each from our support ships," ordered Kamuss. He still wanted to keep a reserve of the powerful missiles in case they were needed later.

–

Commander Garron was not pleased. He had lost too many ships in the first engagement with the Voltrex fleet. Four enemy battleships and a few of their support ships was too high a price to pay for the loss of forty-six battlecruisers.

"The enemy have divided their forces," reported Second Officer Tarack. "I believe they are going to try to hit us from two different directions, forcing our ships to fall back to the shipyards."

Garron studied the tactical display. If his ships stayed where they were the enemy missiles could easily pick them off. He was aware the Voltrex fusion missiles out-ranged his own missiles and energy weapons. He realized he only had one tactic that might be able to cause major damage to the inbound enemy fleet. "Order all ships to move forward and engage the enemy. We must get within energy weapons range before they can destroy our ships with their missiles."

In space, the Trellixian fleet surged forward toward the inbound Voltrex even as Voltrex missiles began slamming into the battlecruisers. Two-thousand-meter battlecruisers were turned into miniature novas as multiple forty-megaton fusion missiles hit them. The Trellixian fleet continued forward, entering energy weapons range. Instantly energy beams and Trellixian missiles began striking the energy shields of the Voltrex fleet.

Massive explosions lit up space as the two fleets closed and then intermingled. The Trellixians quickly learned their battlecruisers were no match for the more powerful and better shielded battleships and battlecruisers of the Voltrex. The Trellixians quickly changed their targeting to the smaller support ships, often having entire squadrons fire upon one of the smaller vessels.

Energy beam fire from six Trellixian battlecruisers slammed into a Voltrex support ship. Missile fire further weakened the ship's energy shield, causing it to flicker and then fail. Trellixian energy beams then tore the ship apart, sending wreckage flying through space.

Other support ships were under heavy attack. Several Trellixian energy beams penetrated a larger support ship's energy shield, blowing apart an energy beam turret and leaving several gaping holes in the hull.

The smaller Voltrex ships were being blown apart from the heavy attacks of the Trellixian battlecruisers.

"We're losing a lot of support vessels," said Lieutenant Commander LeLath with anguish in her voice. "The Trellixians seem to be concentrating on them."

Kamuss' lips tightened. "All ships have permission to use their missiles as necessary." There was no point in conserving the missiles if it was going to cost the fleet ships.

"Message sent," reported Meela.

"Fleet Commander Masurl is in position and beginning to come around the moon," reported LeLath. "He's going to take out the space stations one by one. He wants to know if we need any assistance."

On one of the viewscreens, a five hundred-meter support vessel blew apart sending a large piece of wreckage into the energy screen of a nearby Voltrex battlecruiser. The shield erupted with light but held.

On the tactical display, Trellixian battlecruisers were rapidly being destroyed now that permission for wide use of fusion missiles had been given.

Kamuss shook his head. "No, that won't be necessary. We'll take care of their fleet and then move in on the first of the two shipyards."

In space, the Trellixian fleet was quickly being annihilated. Large fusion explosions marked the death of ship after ship as deadly weapons blew them apart. The surviving Trellixians were firing every weapon they had on the smaller support ships trying to take as many with them as possible. They were Trellixians and had no fear of dying for the Empire. It was their duty to destroy their enemies and inflict as much damage as possible. In desperation, the last few Trellixian battlecruisers accelerated their ships and rammed the nearest Voltrex battlecruiser or battleship. In fierce blasts of released energy six Voltrex battlecruisers and two more battleships died.

"All Trellixian battlecruisers have been destroyed," reported Zalurr as the last red threat icon representing an enemy vessel vanished from the tactical display. "The last vessel rammed the *Salient*." The *Salient* was a Voltrex battleship.

Kamuss knew his fleet had been hurt. He would worry about the losses later. "We'll reorganize our formation and then attack the nearest shipyard."

"We have several ships which suffered heavy damage," said Lieutenant Commander LeLath. "They're in no shape for further combat until repairs have been made."

"Have them stay back with a battlecruiser as an escort," ordered Kamuss. "The rest of the fleet will move on the shipyard."

Commander Garron gazed at the tactical display. All of the green icons representing his fleet were gone, destroyed in the brutal melee above the moon which had just ended.

"We took out two more of their battleships, six of their battlecruisers, and seventeen support ships," reported Second Officer Tarack as he studied the data on a nearby computer screen.

Garron turned toward his second in command. "That may be so, but they still have one complete undamaged fleet and the other is rapidly reforming to continue their attack."

"We still have some Malken missiles on board our primary shipyard," said Tarack.

Garron let out a deep breath. "I don't believe that will make a difference. All we can do is try to damage these fleets as much as possible. Perhaps if we destroy enough of their ships they will be forced to withdraw back to Voltrex space and stop attacking our colonies." It was worrisome at how easily the Voltrex had defeated a fleet of Trellixian vessels more numerous than theirs with so few losses. It did not bode well for the Empire in future battles.

"Should we notify the High Command what is occurring here?"

"I've already sent one message. Gather all the tactical data from our sensors and send it immediately to the High Command. They need to know what they may be up against if the Voltrex someday attack our core worlds."

Tarack's skin turned a paler green. "Do you think that's possible?"

Garron nodded. "We have started a war with a species that now desires our destruction. This can only end with our defeat or theirs."

"Enemy ships are nearing our primary shipyard," reported the sensor officer.

Commander Garron turned his attention back to the tactical display and the main viewscreens. This battle was not yet over. The main shipyard held one more surprise besides the Malken missiles.

-

As Fleet Commander Masurl came around the moon with his fleet, he was using his fusion missiles to destroy the space stations in orbit. None of the stations were armed or had an energy screen. In a few minutes all six stations were reduced to glowing wreckage with no damage to any of his ships.

His next target was the smaller shipyard. His sensors were detecting a powerful energy screen as well as weapons. It didn't matter to him. He planned to launch a full phalanx of fusion missiles to destroy the shipyard from a distance.

-

As his fleet approached the largest shipyard Fleet Commander Kamuss gave his approval to use more of their dwindling stockpile of fusion missiles.

"The shipyard has a very powerful energy shield," Zalurr reported as he studied the data from his sensors.

Lieutenant Commander Lelath turned toward the commander. "It will be necessary to hit that energy screen with a number of fusion missiles to bring it down. The sensor readings show the shipyard is heavily armed. There are thirty-eight large energy cannon emplacements as well as what appear to be forty missile tubes."

On the main viewscreen, an enhanced view of the shipyard appeared. It was massive with large bays to repair ships. Several energy turrets were visible and even as they watched the hatches on the missile tubes began to slide open.

"Set up the missile launch," ordered Fleet Commander Kamuss to Diboll. "I want that energy shield down!"

"We'll be in energy weapons range shortly," reported Zalurr.

"All weapons are ready to fire," added Lieutenant Commander LeLath with a low growl emitting from the back of her throat.

The commander of the shipyard stood in his Command Center watching the approaching Voltrex fleet.

"So it's true the Voltrex represent a threat to the Empire," said his second-in-command. "I wouldn't have believed it until I saw them destroy our fleet. Over four hundred ships lost!"

"Jelnoid weaponry and shields," the commander said. "Begin launching our missiles. Put the rest of our Malken missiles in the last wave. Maybe a few of them will get through. Also make sure the last wave contains all the new missiles we just received." The new missiles were all of the fifty-megaton range. The missiles were supposed to have been deployed to the battlecruisers but Commander Garron had ordered they remain on the shipyard.

His second in command looked confused. "But they're still out of missile range. They will have too much time to target and destroy our missiles."

The commander turned toward his second officer with a hint of anger in his voice. "If we don't launch them now they will be destroyed in their launch tubes."

His second in command nodded and went to carry out his orders.

The commander stared at the viewscreens showing the nearing Voltrex ships. He watched the missile tubes on the enemy ships slide open. Then bright flashes indicated the launch of missiles. At the same time he felt the shipyard shudder imperceptibly as it began launching its missiles. Suddenly the screens lit up with brilliant light and he felt the shipyard shake violently.

"Fusion missile impacts to the energy shield," reported the second in command. "Energy shield is down to 62 percent and dropping."

The commander moved to his command chair and strapped himself in. "Are they in energy weapons range yet?"

The second in command shook his head. "No, they're just out of range. They're also picking off most of the missiles we've launched. All missiles will have been launched in another forty seconds."

"Let's hope the energy shield holds long enough to get all the missiles launched," said the commander, knowing his command was doomed. The best he could do was take a few of his enemy with him.

The shipyard shook even more violently and alarms began sounding. Red lights lit up the damage control console indicating damage to the shipyard's hull.

"Energy shield down to 22 percent," reported the second officer. "I estimate failure in less than twenty seconds.

On the main viewscreen, brilliant blasts of fusion energy were still pummeling the energy screen.

"Redirect all energy to the screen," ordered the shipyard commander. "We have to keep it up until all the missiles are launched."

The second officer hurriedly passed on the orders. "Redirecting all energy. Damage control teams are being dispatched to repair several hull breeches."

The shipyard commander started to tell his second officer that wouldn't be necessary as they would all be dead shortly. However, he decided to stay quiet. There was always a slim chance they might survive this battle. Also Trellixians were not afraid to die in their service to the Empire.

-

Fleet Commander Kamuss watched the viewscreens as the enemy shipyard glowed brighter and brighter as more fusion missiles struck its energy shield.

"The shipyard is starting to suffer damage," reported Zalurr. "The shield should fail at any moment."

The *Claw of Honor* shook slightly and the viewscreens dimmed briefly.

"Enemy missile strike to the shield," reported Diboll. "Shield is still at 100 percent."

Suddenly a brighter light shut the viewscreens down completely.

"We've lost the *Shakira*," reported Zalurr. "It was hit by an antimatter missile. I'm also detecting some explosions in the fifty-megaton range."

Lieutenant Commander LeLath spoke to the other fleet ships over the comm. "I've ordered all ships to use their sensors to detect incoming antimatter missiles. Taking them out is a high priority."

Kamuss nodded. It was evident the Trellixians on the shipyard had a supply of more powerful fusion missiles. He wondered why they hadn't been used before.

Over the next minute antimatter missiles destroyed two more Voltrex battlecruisers and fusion missiles took out a number of support ships.

The viewscreens returned to normal just as the energy screen surrounding the shipyard failed. Instantly several fusion missiles slammed into the shipyard's hull, turning major portions of the large structure into molten metal and twisted wreckage.

-

The shipyard commander was thrown against his seat restraints as the shipyard shook violently. Alarms sounded and the damage control console became covered in red lights.

The second officer looked frightened. "We just took two fusion missile strikes to the hull. Our primary reactor has been destroyed as well as four of the repair bays. More missiles are inbound!"

The commander looked at the viewscreens. Most of them had died and only a few were still functioning. He saw his missile attack had succeeded in taking out some of the enemy ships. Not enough to make a difference but enough that in dying for the Empire he had taken some of his enemies with him.

With a thunderous roar, the station shook violently. The sound of tearing metal and distant explosions could be heard. The shipyard commander knew his command was coming apart. One or two more strikes from fusion missiles would finish the destruction of his command.

-

Fleet Commander Kamuss watched as the next fusion missile strikes finished demolishing the shipyard. Moments later all that remained was a mass of molten metal and twisted wreckage with much of it falling toward the moon.

"Fleet Commander Masurl reports the destruction of all six space stations as well as the other shipyard," reported Lieutenant Commander LeLath. "His fleet did not encounter any antimatter missiles."

"Have him rendezvous with us and then we'll see what we can do about the base on the moon."

Kamuss looked at the tactical display. Nearly all the Trellixian cargo ships and colony ships had entered hyperspace fleeing the system, only a few remained. He quickly dispatched several support ships to destroy them. Once that was done, he turned his attention to the sensor scans of the Trellixian base. It was quite extensive with numerous energy cannons and probably missiles as well. A powerful energy screen protected it. Not as strong as a Jelnoid screen but still much more powerful than those which had protected the Trellixian battlecruisers and shipyards.

-

Commander Garron felt growing anger. His fleet was gone, the space stations had been destroyed, and both shipyards were in ruins. It had taken years to build the infrastructure to allow for the subjugation and colonization of this sector. This was a disaster for the Empire. Numerous worlds already open to colonization were now in danger of being lost. The Voltrex had already destroyed two thriving colonies and no doubt more would soon be targeted as well. With the loss of his fleet there was not a war fleet large enough in the entire sector that could stop the Voltrex.

Garron looked over at Second Officer Tarack. "Send a message to the High Command informing them of the current status of the battle. Include all of the tactical data we've gathered from our sensors."

Second Officer Tarack quickly complied with Garron's orders and then returned to stand in front of him. "The sensors indicate they are gathering to attack this base. What are you orders?"

"If they come in range we'll launch our missiles and hit them with our energy beams." Commander Garron gazed at the tactical display. "However, they may stay in high orbit and drop their fusion missiles on us. If they do that all we can do is die for the Empire."

"For the Empire," repeated Second Officer Tarack.

-

In space, the two Voltrex fleets once more joined together into one fleet. From the battleships multiple fusion missiles dropped down toward the surface and the sprawling Trellixian base.

Brilliant flashes of light soon lit up the landscape of the moon as multiple fusion explosions blasted the Trellixians' energy screen. For nearly two minutes the screen withstood the powerful onslaught as it glowed brighter and brighter. Then without warning the screen collapsed, allowing Voltrex fusion missiles to strike the base. In moments the base ceased to be as a series of deep smoking craters appeared where the base once was.

-

"The base has been eliminated," reported Zalurr.

On the ship's viewscreens, rising mushroom clouds marked the detonation of numerous fusion weapons over the location of the enemy base.

"Take us out of orbit," ordered Fleet Commander Kamuss. "We will move out to ten million kilometers and begin initiating repairs to our ships damaged in the battle. I need a report on the ships we lost as well as those which were damaged. If any ship is too badly damaged we will scuttle it and transfer the crew to other vessels."

"I'll begin checking the status of the two fleets," replied Lieutenant Commander LeLath.

Kamuss nodded as he released the safety harness that held him in his command chair. Standing, he stretched, gazing at his crew. They were all busy performing the duties necessary after a heated battle. Now Kamuss had to make a decision. Should he continue to attack Voltrex colonies in this sector, return to the Bator System, or go on to Earth? If he went on to Earth it could be a very long time before any of his crews got to return home. It would mean a long separation between them and their mates. Kamuss let out a deep breath, thinking about Karina.

This war was causing many in the military to be gone from their families for an extended period of time. By now, his son, Albor was probably away on his first mission on the new battlecruiser he had been assigned to. Kamuss was proud of his son but if he wanted to spend any quality time with his family he needed to find a way to end this war and end it quickly. With a deep sigh, he decided to take the combined fleets to Earth. Perhaps by the time he got there Captain Dolan would have returned from his mission to the Trellixian core worlds.

Dolan's mission would tell them if the Trellixians had any obvious weakness the Humans and Voltrex could exploit. Kamuss hoped Dolan would find something or this war could drag on for decades.

Chapter Eleven

High Commander Kaldre fumed with anger. He had just received word Kalone Four had fallen. Many of the warships assigned to defend the sector from the Voltrex had been destroyed.

"I don't understand," said Second Officer Calaah. "There were over four hundred warships there and the shipyards were armed. Not only that the base on the moon was heavily fortified. How did the Voltrex manage to defeat our forces?"

"Superior technology," replied Kaldre, feeling frustrated. He had tried to warn the other High Commanders but they refused to listen. "As long as they have a technological advantage over us in shields and weapons we are going to be at a disadvantage. This is why I warned the High Command our current fleets might be useless in this war. The enemy can stand off and destroy our ships before we ever come within range where we can use our weapons. I must speak to Commander Malborr. We need to develop a longer range missile to offset the Voltrex and Humans' range advantage."

Kaldre turned his attention to the main viewscreen, which was focused on the shipyard. Over the last several weeks four updated battlecruisers had joined his flagship. Both of the primary shipyards over Traxis Three were now constructing the new and more powerful battlecruisers.

"High Commander," said Lamarr, the communications officer. "The High Command is requesting your presence at Trellixia for a meeting about the current situation with the Voltrex and the Humans."

Calaah looked over at the High Commander. "Finally! Perhaps they have recognized that you are correct about the threat the Voltrex and the Humans represent. With the fall of Kalone Four maybe they have come to their senses."

High Commander Kaldre nodded. "I hope you're correct. If they still refuse to accept the threat they could be endangering the entire Empire. As it is I fear we will lose many of our outer colony worlds to the Voltrex before we're ready to truly resist them. Prepare the ship to go to Trellixia. We'll leave as soon as I'm finished meeting with Commander Malborr."

Four hours later the *Dawn Reaper* and its four escorts left the Traxis Three System. There was no doubt in Kaldre's mind this meeting of the High Command might very well decide the fate of the Empire.

On Earth, President Hathaway was in her office meeting with Vice President Jason Arnold, Secretary of State Maggie Rayne, Professor Wilkens, and General Mitchell.

"Is it confirmed all the Trellixians have been eradicated?" asked Katelyn, looking at General Mitchell.

It had been a harrowing few weeks as military forces fanned out across the planet searching for any surviving Trellixians as well as working to contain the fallout from the use of more nuclear weapons. The chemical the Voltrex had furnished was proving to be a miracle worker in clearing the atmosphere and eliminating the radiation.

"Yes," General Mitchell replied. "We've located a few small groups in isolated locations and those have been dealt with. We will continue searching but I feel reasonably comfortable in saying we have probably taken out all of them now. Russia and China both confirm they have finished their searches as well. For the first time in several years I can state the planet is now ours."

Professor Wilkens turned his attention from the general to the president. "I can also confirm all the radiation levels are coming down. We estimate the nuclear winter will be over within two to three months and we can begin planting crops."

President Hathaway looked over at Secretary of State Rayne. "What about our food supplies?" There were 42 million survivors in Canada, the United States, and Mexico.

"Sufficient," replied Maggie. "Nobody will be starving but we do need to get our crops planted as soon as possible as well as get the livestock back outside the domes."

"What about the morale of our people; how's that?"

Vice President Arnold had been keeping track of how the people were dealing with the current situation. "Not bad. Most would like to be able to get out of the domes sometime soon. Even the people in Complex One and Complex Two would like to go outside and breathe some fresh air. I'm sure the same is true in other countries."

President Hathaway took a deep breath. "I spoke to both the Russian and Chinese leaders yesterday. They are willing to do whatever is necessary to support the war effort. The same is true of the rest of the surviving governments. We do have some Third World Countries which we know very little about."

"We are sending some drones over those countries to get a better grasp of the situation," said General Mitchell. "We have confirmed there are no Trellixians in those countries though we know very little about surviving populations."

"What is the current status of the new shipyard?"

"On schedule," replied General Mitchell. "We did receive word Fleet Commander Kamuss is bringing his fleet to Earth for repairs and munitions. He has taken out two Trellixian colonies and one of their major bases."

President Hathaway leaned back in her chair, her eyes taking on a serious look of concern. "What abut the Trellixian fleets we've recently detected outside the Solar System?"

"Admiral Edwards is keeping a close watch on them," Mitchell replied. "We also have eleven hundred defensive satellites in orbit and we're making good progress on the battlestation. Admiral Edwards does not believe those fleets pose a viable threat at this time. He believes the Trellixian are trying to intimidate us."

"Why?" asked Vice President Arnold. "They must know at the present time we pose no real threat to their Empire."

Mitchell nodded. "You're correct. However, we did provide the Voltrex with Jelnoid technology and they are becoming a major threat. The Trellixians may fear the Voltrex will use our system as a base to launch attacks against the Empire."

President Hathaway looked thoughtful and a little concerned. "Will the arrival of Fleet Commander Kamuss' fleet add to that concern? Could it cause the Trellixians to launch an attack?" They had just gotten rid of the Trellixians and she didn't want them coming back again.

"I doubt it," replied General Mitchell. "Even if they did, between our fleet and the ships Fleet Commander Kamuss is bringing the Trellixians would have no chance at victory."

Katelyn took a deep breath. Sometimes it was hard for her to accept this war was still not over and the hardest part might still be ahead of them. "Have we heard anything new from Captain Dolan?"

"Not really," answered General Mitchell. "The *Fury* and her escorts are proceeding deeper into Trellixian territory. They've surveyed several highly populated Trellixian worlds. I have a number of analysts going over the data that's been sent back so far."

Vice President Arnold leaned forward. "Has he found anything that might be helpful?"

General Mitchell slowly nodded his head. "The population density on Trellixian worlds is unbelievable. On some planets we're talking about twenty billion or more and those are not even core worlds. What the population on those planets will be like is beyond imagining."

"Why don't they control their population?" asked Maggie with a steep frown. "It should be easy enough to do."

Professor Wilkens looked over at Maggie. "They can't. It's against their core beliefs. The Jelnoids offered to provide drugs, which would control their urge to procreate, and the Trellixians refused to even consider it. From what we've studied from the data we have on the Jelnoid computers in the crashed scout craft, the urge to procreate is so instinctive in the Trellixians they cannot conceive of doing anything different."

"I wonder how much that has to do with the Trellixians being a type of reptile?" said Maggie. "They look like giant lizards that walk on two legs."

"Our dissections of Trellixian bodies tell us they're cold blooded though temperature does not seem to affect them as much as other cold blooded species. They keep their ships warmer than us and they eat small animals, preferably still alive," explained Professor Wilkens.

President Katelyn shuddered. This was something she hadn't known. "Will the Voltrex be willing to station a major fleet here in the Solar System until we have built sufficient warships to protect Earth?"

"Yes," replied General Mitchell. "We already have a small fleet of their warships permanently stationed here. I will ask to have the size of the fleet doubled. We still have Voltrex convoys coming to Earth on a regular basis and Voltrex warships heavily guard those. I believe the Voltrex would be highly interested in using our system as a major base to launch attacks against the Trellixian core worlds. It would benefit us as we would have major Voltrex fleets in the system to help defend us."

"It would also make us a target," pointed out Vice President Arnold. "However, I do realize we must be proactive in this war with the Trellixians. If we sit back and do nothing at some point they will return and attempt to destroy our planet. We cannot wait for that day to arrive."

"Let's not launch attacks against the Trellixians until all the battlestations are completed," said Katelyn worriedly. She knew the six one-thousand-meter battlestations would add greatly to Earth's defense. She also didn't want to encourage the Trellixians to attack before Earth was ready. A large Voltrex base or presence might just do that.

General Mitchell's face took on a grim look. "We will try not to but the Trellixians may not give us a choice. It will still be weeks before Captain Dolan returns from his survey of Trellixian space. Once he enters the core systems he will not be able to communicate for fear of his hyperspace messages being detected. There will be several weeks or more where the *Fury* and her fleet will be out of contact with Earth. Once he can reestablish contact and forward the data his fleet has collected then perhaps we can start making plans to take the war to the Trellixian core worlds. By then the first battlestation will be finished as well as the shipyard. We're going to start construction on two more battlestations early next week."

"Very well," replied Katelyn. "Keep me informed of future developments."

Katelyn wished they could avoid the war but she knew that was impossible. At some point in the future the Trellixians were bound to return and try to conquer Earth. It was better to go on the offensive than to sit back and try to defend the Solar System. In the long run that would be a losing scenario. She just wanted Earth to be ready for such an attack.

-

In space, Admiral Edwards was watching the main viewscreen showing the new shipyard. Already one of the construction bays was finished and work was progressing on the second. Much of the shipyard was still a mass of gantries and framework with only the inner section actually finished. The armor for the outer hull was scheduled to begin installation in another week.

"They're making good progress," commented Captain Nelson.

Edwards nodded. "We're ahead of schedule. The Voltrex have a system for space construction and everything is going smoothly. There are four hundred Voltrex construction engineers working on the station."

On the viewscreen, several small two-person construction craft were using manipulator arms to place a gantry and weld it into place. There were dozens of the small ships working on various sections of the shipyard. There were also several hundred Voltrex in spacesuits moving about on the inside and outside of the metal framework. There were a number of Humans working alongside them learning the techniques the Voltrex used for space construction.

"We will be adding two additional construction bays as soon as the initial construction of the shipyard is completed," said Admiral Edwards. "Once that's finished we have plans for an even larger shipyard which will be the primary base for all fleet activities."

His gaze wandered to the tactical display showing the green icons of his fleet. He had twenty-five Earth-built battlecruisers: the carrier *Annapolis*, thirty of the larger battlecruisers built by the Voltrex as well as four battleships. In addition there was a Voltrex support fleet in the system comprised of twenty battlecruisers and six battleships. Fleet Commander Barvon commanded the Voltrex fleet. There were also twenty of the smaller Voltrex system patrol ships, which had recently arrived. Human crews were being trained to operate the vessels and they would use them to patrol the space around Earth and the Moon.

"We have a Voltrex convoy dropping out of hyperspace," reported Lieutenant Williams from his sensor console. At the same time alarms began sounding. Williams reached forward and turned the alarms off since the inbound ships were friendly.

Captain Nelson studied the tactical display for a moment. "Looks like six supply vessels and four battlecruisers."

"Normal supply convoy," Admiral Edwards replied. A convoy like this arrived twice a week, bringing construction material and other war supplies to Earth.

"Four-hundred-thousand-kilometers distant," reported Lieutenant Williams. This was the standard range the Voltrex supply fleets dropped out of hyperspace so they could be identified as friendly.

"A flight of fighter-bombers from the Moon is moving out to confirm their identity," added Lieutenant Williams. This was standard practice to ensure the Trellixians were not trying to sneak in under the guise of Voltrex vessels.

Admiral Edwards could see four small green icons leaving the Moon and heading toward the Voltrex ships. "What about the Voltrex cargo ships already in the system?" At any one time, there were nearly a dozen Voltrex cargo ships in orbit around the Earth or Moon.

"Most have been unloaded and will be returning with the battlecruisers," replied Captain Nelson. "We're already starting to receive parts for the next two battlestations."

"I'll feel a lot better about defending Earth when those battlestations are finished," said Edwards, leaning back in his command chair. "What's the status of our ships?"

Nelson checked his console and then replied. "All ships are combat capable. Two are currently down on Earth at the North American spaceport being resupplied and for crew rotation."

Edwards nodded. He also knew that in Complex One and Complex Two some Human cargo ships were being constructed. Sometime in the future there would be robust trade between Earth and the Voltrex Federation.

"Captain Nelson, set a course for the Moon. I want to go down and inspect the Moon base and the defenses we've been building." If the Trellixians attacked again the base would play a major role in defending Earth.

"Yes, Admiral," replied Nelson as he turned to the helm officer. He quickly passed on the order to get the *Renown* underway. It was currently in orbit 14,000 kilometers above the Earth.

-

The *Renown* left orbit and began accelerating toward the Moon. The ship was traveling at a leisurely pace as there was nothing threatening. Two other Earth-built battlecruisers left orbit to provide an escort. It took the three ships two hours to reach the Moon and go into orbit. As they neared the Moon, four of the small fighter-bombers assigned to the Moon base left orbit and did a quick flyby confirming their identity. Security was tight in the Earth-Moon System and nothing was taken for granted. All ships' identities were routinely double-checked.

As soon as the *Renown* entered orbit Admiral Edwards boarded a shuttle to go down to the surface. Work on the Moon base had been going on nonstop for months. It was now a sprawling complex protected by an energy shield and numerous energy cannon emplacements. It was also the base for the twenty patrol ships furnished by the Voltrex.

Admiral Edwards looked down at the slightly pockmarked surface of Mare Serenitatis. The mare was over 770 kilometers in diameter and held the recently constructed Moon base. Most of the base was underground but a few domes were visible on the surface. Edwards could see some of the larger energy gun turrets pointed upward toward space. Several of the newer fusion reactors powered the base as well as the weapon systems.

One of the domes opened up and a pair of fighter-bombers flew out. The small craft quickly disappeared from sight as they accelerated away. There were currently 240 of the small fighter-bombers in the underground hangers. Plans were to add a few hundred more in the coming months.

There were also a number of larger landing pads for spacecraft. On a number of these sat some of the small patrol craft furnished by the Voltrex. Human crews were currently learning how they operated and the first should go into service in another week.

The shuttle adjusted its course and came in low over the base, then descended to land on one of the landing pads. The pad then sank into the ground with a metal hatch closing above it. Admiral Edwards planned on making a quick tour of the base with its commanding officer, Major Jacob Brandon, and then return to the *Renown*. He always felt a little uneasy when he was away from his flagship but these inspections were necessary. He had to know what he could count on and which assets he had available if the Trellixians attacked Earth again. There was no doubt in his mind that would happen in the future. He planned on being ready when that day arrived.

High Commander Kaldre was once more in the large orbiting space station above the home world. The entire High Command was present for this meeting.

"The reports from the Voltrex border are not good," began High Commander Olnarr. "We have lost two colony worlds plus our major base on Kalone Four. Most of the fleets we have sent into that sector of space have been destroyed or stopped reporting. We believe other colonies in the same area will shortly be attacked. The colonies in that sector were being counted on to absorb some of our excess population."

"Even worse, we have lost a large number of cargo and colony ships," added High Commander Danaar. "At the current time we do not have the capacity to replace those vessels." Danaar glared at High Commander Kaldre. "Our shipyards in the Traxis Three System are being used to construct more warships. They should be constructing additional cargo and colony ships so we can make up our losses."

"No!" growled High Commander Kaldre, refusing to stay quiet. "We need those new ships to stop the Humans and the Voltrex. If we don't build them we will continue to lose more colony worlds until our core worlds are threatened. I warned all of you earlier that the Humans and the Voltrex would become a threat. They have Jelnoid technology and have applied that to their warships."

High Commander Trammor stood shaking his head. "I don't believe our core worlds are threatened or ever will be. You have two shipyards building the new battlecruisers. Surely one is enough. The other one can be used to build more cargo or colony ships."

"One shipyard is not going to make a difference," grated out High Commander Kaldre. "The problem is not our lack of ships but our steadily growing population. If we don't do something to control it we will soon be faced with unrest on our core worlds the like of which we've never seen before."

Several of the High Commanders looked stunned at Kaldre's mention of population control.

"There can be no control over our natural breeding habits," stated High Commander Olnarr. "It is the birthright of every living Trellixian."

Kaldre stood and stared at the others. "We are already running out of space on our core worlds. Rationing of food is common on every planet. Our people will only tolerate so much and then we will see our cities burn."

"Treason!" shouted High Commander Olnarr. "You should not be a member of the High Command! I demand you leave this meeting immediately."

High Commander Thatrex stood up, causing the others to become quiet. "I fear High Commander Kaldre may be correct about what awaits in our future. I also see no way we can control our peoples' right to breed. It is part of our heritage and ingrained in our culture. He is also correct in that changing one of the shipyards he has control over to produce colony and cargo ships will do little good."

"Then what are we to do?" demanded High Commander Olnarr.

"If our population grows too large and unrest breaks out, it will be a convenient method of reducing our excess population. I would suggest this time we let it run its course but ensure our planetary and orbital infrastructure stays intact. We can place Trellixian troops in the assets on the surface of our planets we cannot allow to be destroyed if there is unrest."

High Commander Olnarr looked stunned at High Commander Thatrex's words. "You are talking about allowing billions of our people to die!"

"It's necessary for the rest of our people to survive. We can no longer build ships as fast as our population is growing. The same goes for providing food." High Commander Thatrex looked over at High Commander Trammor. "How much longer can the worlds under your command continue to provide sufficient food for all the worlds of the Empire?"

High Commander Trammor hesitated and then answered. "We can't do so now. Everyday we're missing the quotas we need to supply some of the more heavily populated worlds. Even if we had the cargo ships we could not fill them with the necessary food supplies."

The room became quiet as the other High Commanders thought over what Trammor had just revealed. Most of them looked uneasily at one another.

"What do you think of this threat from the Humans and the Voltrex?" asked High Commander Danaar.

High Commander Thatrex looked over at Kaldre. "I don't believe the Humans are a real threat. Their population has been substantially reduced and their world bombarded. It is the Voltrex who may become a threat. It is possible they could in time send a fleet into the core worlds. It is for that reason we should allow High Commander Kaldre to continue his efforts in the Traxis Three System. If the Voltrex come that fleet can be used to stop them."

The High Command argued for several more hours. In the end they agreed to allow High Commander Kaldre to retain control of the shipyards and manufacturing facilities in the Traxis Three System.

Later as Kaldre made his way back on board his flagship he realized one thing: the rest of the High Command was wrong about the Humans. He still firmly believed they were a prime threat. However, for now all he could do was build more of the new warships and hope Battle Commander Balforr could put them to good use protecting the core worlds and the Empire.

Chapter Twelve

Captain Dolan took a deep breath as the *Fury* and her attending escorts dropped out of hyperspace. They were near a star, which supposedly held one of the Trellixian core worlds. They were on the periphery of a region the Trellixians considered their home systems. From the data they had of this region there were eighty systems holding vast numbers of the lizard people. They were about to see how accurate that information was.

"We have a lot of ship traffic," reported Kia uneasily. "The long-range sensors are picking up hundreds of spacecraft in the star system we're approaching." On the tactical display, hundreds of red threat icons suddenly flashed into view.

"More than we've ever detected before," added Chloe as she studied the sensor readings. "The third and fourth planets appear to be the most heavily colonized just from the energy readings we're picking up from those worlds."

Mark looked at the tactical display. There were three green icons near the *Fury:* the carrier *Horizon* and the two Earth-built battlecruisers *Cambridge* and *Liberty.*

Second Officer Katana looked over at the captain. "I would not recommend we move any closer to the system. With that many ships we would most likely be detected."

Mark nodded in agreement. "We'll stay here and launch four probes, same as before. The *Horizon* will launch two and we'll launch two. Lieutenant Masterson, calculate the best courses for the probes. I want a good look at all the planets, moons, and major asteroids."

"With that ship traffic, there is a high likelihood one or more of the probes will be detected," commented Brett as he got busy on his computer console.

"It's a risk we'll have to take," replied Mark. "If we keep the probes too far out we won't be able to collect the data we need. It's imperative we know the population density of those two planets and any other colony the Trellixians may have in this system. Even if the probes are detected there's a good chance they'll be ignored. The Trellixians won't be expecting someone to be scanning their systems."

Brett quickly finished his calculations and began feeding the data to the four probes. "Probes are programmed and ready to launch."

"Very well," said Mark, looking at a viewscreen showing the *Horizon*. "Launch the probes."

Looking up at the main viewscreen, they all watched as two five-meter probes exited the *Horizon* and made the quick jump into hyperspace. Everyone knew two identical probes were leaving the *Fury*.

Second Officer Katana ordered all ships to reduce energy emissions to the minimum. The four warships would run quietly until the probes finished their mission or the enemy detected the ships.

Lisa leaned back gazing at the others. She wondered if they were as nervous as she was. They were deep in Trellixian space and the probability of detection was quite high. It grew higher with every new system they scanned.

"How many planets are there in this system?" she asked, looking over at Chloe.

"Twelve," answered the AI as she checked the ship's sensor readings. "There are three in the habitable zone as well as five gas giants in the outer part of the system. There also seem to be two fairly large asteroid fields."

Brett let out a deep sigh. "This is going to take some time. The probes will not be moving as fast as before. They have a lot of space to cover and numerous planets, moons, and asteroids to scan. There are over thirty moons in the system."

"That's a lot," said Lisa

"The Solar System has more," pointed out Derek. "Most gas giants have a plethora of moons. This system is no different."

Lisa knew that. It just made her realize how extensive the Trellixian colonies could be in a star system. "There are going to be billions of Trellixians in this system. If it's similar to the ones we've seen so far, we could easily be looking at forty billion or more in just this system alone."

"The Trellixians seem to inhabit a lot of real estate," said Brenda. "I'm curious to see how much farm land there is on the primary inhabited planet."

"Why?" asked Kia. "What difference does it make?"

"Are they growing their food on the planets they inhabit or is most of it brought in by cargo ships?" asked Brenda. "It could be very important."

Lisa thought for a moment. "Brenda's right. We need to know where the Trellixians get their resources for their inhabited planets. Are these star systems self-sufficient or do they rely on others?"

"Why is that important?" asked Captain Dolan, who had been listening to the discussion.

Brenda turned toward the captain. "If their colonies, particularly their core worlds are not self-sufficient, it could be a major weakness. If we could disrupt those supply lines between star systems it might hamper their war effort."

"Well, it is something to keep in mind as we scout more of their core worlds," said Mark.

-

Chloe had been listening. She listened to almost all the conversations which occurred outside the crews' quarters. As she thought over what she had just heard a possible strategy occurred to her. She was not going to mention it yet. She needed more data. At the minimum they needed to check at least five more Trellixian core systems before she was certain her strategy would work. The question was, could the small fleet stay undetected long enough to allow for them to visit five more Trellixian systems? Chloe greatly feared that would be nearly impossible.

-

The four probes flew through the system, coming within a few million kilometers of all planets and moons. Long-range scans were made of the two asteroid fields to determine the amount of Trellixian activity. Mining colonies were located and scanned. Everywhere there were Trellixian ships. Several of the probes came within ten thousand kilometers of Trellixian vessels but were not spotted. There were numerous cargo ships, a few colony ships, and of course a number of heavily armed battlecruisers. The probes slipped by the ships and continued on their missions.

There was no doubt if the Trellixians had been searching for the probes they would have been spotted. However, there was no reason for the Trellixians to suspect this core system was being scanned. Never had an enemy penetrated to the heart of the Trellixian Empire.

It took a full day for the probes to complete their scans of the system and then begin their return journey to the *Fury* and the *Horizon*. On board the *Fury* the data was already being analyzed.

Lisa appeared stunned as she looked at the numbers. "If these sensor scans are correct there are over sixty-four billion Trellixians in this system. They have colonies on every planet except the gas giants and most of the major moons."

"What about the two asteroid fields?" asked Captain Dolan.

"Just a few mining operations," replied Lisa. "It appears they have pretty much stripped the asteroid fields of all usable metals."

Chloe turned toward the captain. "They also have large mining operations on all the smaller moons as well as several of the larger ones."

"What about ship types?"

"That's the strange part," said Lisa as she looked one more time at the data. "There are only twenty-three battlecruisers in the system."

Mark was silent for several moments as he thought what that might mean. "Any idea why they don't have a larger fleet protecting the system?"

"I may," said Chloe. "They have no fear of an attack in their core systems. From the records the Voltrex have captured the

Trellixians very seldom encounter a threatening race. Until they met the Voltrex the Trellixians have been dominating in all of their space battles."

"We had superior numbers of ships," said Katana, recalling some of the battles she had been in. "Now we have superior weapons. We will not stop until the lizard people are defeated. They have killed countless sentients on the worlds they have conquered. They should have controlled their population. Now we will do that for them by destroying their worlds."

-

Mark frowned as he listened to Katana's words. Were they actually considering wiping out the Trellixians? They were talking about several thousand worlds, some with massive populations. If they did that would it make them as bad as the lizard people? Mark shifted his eyes to the viewscreens showing the stars shining brightly in all directions. Then again, what other choice was there? The Trellixians were the ones who started this war. All he had to do was look at the ruins of many of Earth's cities to see how violent and cruel they were. He had also seen the shattered ruins on several Trellixian colony worlds, indicating the former inhabitants had been wiped out. Maybe wiping out the Trellixians was the best and only option. The question was, how could they ever do it? The Trellixian Empire was massive and they had thousands of warships. At some point in time they were bound to commit that massive fleet to the war against Earth and the Voltrex Federation. He was greatly concerned his own mission could cause that to happen. If the Trellixians realized an enemy fleet had scanned some of their core system they could react very violently.

-

Lisa remained quiet as she listened to Katana's words. Only now did she realize what was involved in this war. From her own experience she knew there could never be any peace with the Trellixians. Either the Human and Voltrex races had to die or the Trellixians would; there could be no compromise. It didn't take her but a moment to realize she wanted no part in bombarding an enemy planet and killing possibly billions of civilians. When they returned to Earth she would tell Professor Wilkens there would be no more space missions for her. They had also finished designing the new fusion reactor to power future ships. No doubt this would play a very big role in the war. It bothered Lisa some knowing the scientific breakthroughs she and her friends were making would be used to construct better weapons to kill the Trellixians.

-

Brett noticed Lisa's sudden silence. He had no problem killing the Trellixians though he knew Lisa wished it wasn't necessary. She had served with the 75th Ranger Company and witnessed the war on Earth at close range. They all had. This was a matter of survival and Brett was determined the Human race survived even if it meant wiping out the Trellixian species. He had no sympathy for the lizard people as they had wiped out countless other intelligent species.

Once their shift was over he would take Lisa to the Officer's Mess and they could discuss what was bothering her.

-

The four probes returned to the fleet and landed in the landing bays. A few short minutes after that the fleet made the transition into hyperspace, setting out for their next target world. This world was even deeper into what were considered the Trellixian core worlds.

-

Mark was in his quarters studying the data the probes had collected in the Trellixian system. He was still amazed at the population density in the star system. The fourth plant in the system they just left had a population of nearly thirty billion! Scans from the probe which passed near the planet showed very little actual cropland. There was a lush greenbelt around the planet's equator where there were no cities. The greenbelt was more like a tropical jungle and insights from the scientists on board suggested this had been left alone so the planet would maintain a viable atmosphere. There were also signs of green on top of many of the buildings indicating some crops were being grown there or once more, it might be to keep the planet's atmosphere continually replenished.

What also surprised Mark was how lightly the system was defended. With only twenty-three battlecruisers the system would be relatively easy to conquer. There were also no orbital defenses though the one small shipyard in orbit did seem to have a few energy cannons. Even though the Trellixian Empire had never faced a great danger, it would still seem to be prudent to have the main planets adequately defended. This was an example of how overconfident the Trellixians were that there could be no viable threat, which might endanger their core worlds. Someday the Trellixians would discover how wrong that assumption was.

With a deep sigh, Mark leaned back in his chair and stretched. It had been a long day. He was curious what General Mitchell and the Voltrex Fleet Command would make of the data collected so far. Calling up a star map on his computer screen he looked at the myriad of stars marked in red. These were all Trellixian core worlds that supposedly held massive populations. On the screen, a path was marked for the fleet to follow as it delved deeper into Trellixian space. They were going to travel all the way to the heart of the Empire. If they were not detected plans were for the fleet to scan the Trellixian home system. Mark closed his eyes and shook his head. He knew that would put the fleet in grave danger. The sheer number of ships in that region of space would almost guarantee the fleet would be detected no matter what precautions they took.

Opening his eyes Mark looked at a picture on his desk. His mom, dad, and sister were shown against a backdrop of mountains. Mark had taken that picture years back before the Trellixians showed up on Earth. His parents were dead but his sister was safe in Complex One. When they returned to Earth Mark was determined to take some time off from his duties to spend with Jennifer. It would be nice to go out to eat and maybe to a movie. He just wished his parents had survived the Trellixian invasion. Of course if he wanted to spend some quality time with his sister it would be necessary to survive this mission.

Battle Commander Balforr gazed at the viewscreen showing the home world of Trellixia. He had just received word from High Commander Kaldre that more of the new battlecruisers were being built in the shipyards at Traxis Three. With an aggravated frown, he watched the viewscreen focused on the largest shipyard in the Empire. From one of its massive construction docks a colony ship was exiting.

"We should be building warships," he uttered, shaking his head. "The Voltrex and the Humans are growing stronger while we do little to stop them."

Second Officer Albion turned toward the Battle Commander. "We have four fleets just outside the Human system. If they try anything we will know."

"Those fleets are useless," said Balforr, his eyes growing even larger than normal. "The Humans have Jelnoid technology. Not only that, there is a Voltrex fleet stationed permanently in the system. Every day we wait they increase the strength of their defenses and are building more ships."

An alarm sounded, indicating ships were exiting hyperspace. The space around Trellixia was full of ships. Balforr was not pleased. With so many ships coming and going how could a Battle Commander hope to defend the system? It would be relatively simple for an enemy battlecruiser or two to slip through the system undetected. He had mentioned this to the High Command but they had ignored his requests for more sensor buoys to keep the system under tighter surveillance. The home system was too far from Earth and the Voltrex to ever be in real danger.

Battle Commander Balforr looked over toward the Helm. "Set a course for the Bolen System. We will spend two days patrolling the system before going to the next core world."

High Commander Kaldre had given Balforr orders to use his fleet to patrol the Trellixian core worlds. Balforr didn't see what good that would do. There were too many of them and Balforr was not going to split up his fleet. He had a strong desire to take his new battle fleet and the other two fleets assigned to him and go to the Human world of Earth and destroy it. With his new ships and the four fleets already there he was confident he could lay waste to the entire planet. However, for now he would obey High Commander Kaldre, particularly if Kaldre could get more of the new battlecruisers built. Someday Balforr would have his revenge on Earth.

–

The *Fury* and her small fleet again dropped out of hyperspace. They had traveled another twenty light years deeper into Trellixian space. Once more the fleet launched four probes to scan the system while the fleet reduced their emissions to a minimum.

Inside the Command Center tensions were high. Long-range scans indicated this was a highly populated system, perhaps even more highly populated than the last one scanned.

–

Lisa raised her eyes toward the tactical display. It was covered in red threat icons. Each icon represented a Trellixian ship. She had never seen so many ships in one star system before. "If all of their core worlds are like this how do they coordinate their ship movements? We're detecting ships continuously entering and exiting hyperspace."

Brett shook his head. "They must have a central traffic control somewhere."

"That would indicate all of their worlds are linked with a hyperspace communication system like our worlds are," said Marissa. The Voltrex Federation had communication drones in place to relay messages to all the worlds of the Federation as well as ships. "Communication across their Empire would be a matter of only a few hours. Messages in hyperspace travel much faster than a ship can."

Lisa looked worriedly at Captain Dolan. "That means if we're detected all the Trellixian worlds will know of our presence almost immediately."

Mark nodded. He had already suspected this. "We just need to stay undetected. We'll continue to use the probes to scan the systems until they're noticed. Even then, the Trellixians may not realize what's going on if they haven't detected our ships."

"The Trellixians will eventually detect the probes," said Chloe. "In the system we're currently scanning there are over six hundred and twenty ships. There is a very good probability, nearly 90 percent, that at some point they will detect our fleet as we scan more systems."

"Any idea on how many are warships?"

Chloe shook her head. "No, Captain. Some of them are bound to be but at this range we can't discern which ships are what. We'll know as soon as the probes begin sending their data."

"If we're detected, what are our odds of making it back to Earth?"

Chloe looked upset. "Less than 12 percent."

Mark's brow furrowed in a frown. Then he spoke to the entire Command Crew who had suddenly grown very quiet. "If we're detected we'll transmit all of our data back to Earth at that time. Marissa, keep a packet ready to transmit at a moment's notice. We have continued to drop communication drones as we've moved deeper into Trellixian space. If something happens to us at least Earth will know what we've found. Also I want everyone to remember the *Fury* and our other ships are very heavily armed. If we are detected we won't be easy for the Trellixians to take down. If we have to we'll fight our way back home. "

Everyone went back to monitoring their consoles and the ship but it was a much more subdued command crew. Everyone realized there was a good chance they would not be seeing Earth again.

Battle Commander Balforr nodded in satisfaction as the *Conquest* dropped out of hyperspace in the Bolen System. Instantly, the tactical display began lighting up with hundreds of green icons. These were cargo ships, colony ships, mining vessels, and battlecruisers. The system had fourteen planets with major colonies on the third, fourth, and fifth planets, which were all in the liquid water zone. The fifth planet had the largest colony with over forty billion Trellixians living on the surface.

"All ships have exited hyperspace," reported Second Officer Albion.

"Have our warships begin regular patrols in the system. I want every ship in the Bolen System identified. All battlecruisers are to keep their sensors active." While Balforr was almost certain there were no threats in the Bolen System, he wanted his crews trained to run standard sensor sweeps in every Trellixian system they entered. There would come a time when those sensor sweeps would detect the enemy. He did not want to be taken by surprise so he was not taking anything for granted.

On the tactical display, the fleet began to break up into its patrol units to begin searching the system. Balforr was keeping all the new battlecruisers together in one fleet while the weaker battlecruisers were being used for patrol duties.

Second Officer Albion turned toward Battle Commander Balforr. "All patrol groups have their orders. Sensors will be active the entire time they are on patrol."

"Keep a watch on the patrol groups," Balforr ordered. "I don't want any groups taking these patrols for granted. If I catch any commander slacking he will be sent to a mining colony to learn better discipline."

"As you command," replied Albion as he went back to his console so he could better monitor the patrols.

Battle Commander Balforr went back to studying the Bolen System. Nearly seventy billion Trellixians lived and worked in the system. Planets three and four still had wide areas of green. These were used for growing food with much of it exported to the home system and Traxis Three. The fifth planet was covered in cities with only a few small green strips. Even the oceans had floating cities anchored to the sea floor. They were too far out to actually see the cities of Bolen Five but Balforr knew the buildings reached nearly into the clouds and deep beneath the surface.

There were a number of large green icons around Bolen Five. These were the shipyards and space manufacturing stations, which supported the economy of the planet. Balforr knew even here in the Bolen System living space was limited and food rations were at a minimum. Smaller green icons were constantly moving from the larger ones down to the surface of the planet; shuttles taking supplies from unloaded cargo ships to their destinations on the planet. Bolen Three and Four also had several shipyards as well as space manufacturing facilities.

Battle Commander Balforr let out a deep sigh of discontent. If all the shipyards in the Empire would just dedicate themselves to building warships for several months, they would have enough battlecruisers to crush the Humans and the Voltrex.

"Move us closer to Bolen Five," ordered Balforr. "How many battlecruisers are currently in the system not counting ours?"

"Forty-two," replied Maldane from the Sensors.

Balforr was surprised at the number. Most of the core systems had smaller defensive fleets. Of course one of the shipyards over Bolen Four was tasked with building battlecruisers, which most likely explained the larger than expected fleet.

Most of the planetary governors were aware of High Commander Kaldre's warnings about the Humans and the Voltrex. Perhaps the planetary governors in this system were listening.

Balforr stood up. He was going to go to his quarters for some rest. He would keep his fleets in the system for two days and then move on to the next highly populated core world. He had an uneasy feeling there was something wrong in the Empire. He didn't know what it was but he was sure that eventually he would find out.

Chapter Thirteen

Fleet Commander Kamuss watched uneasily as his fleet dropped out of hyperspace. They still had a ways to go to Earth but the scouts had detected a heavily populated Trellixian colony world. After some discussion with Lieutenant Commander LeLath and Fleet Commander Masurl they decided to destroy the colony. Unfortunately it would probably reveal to the Trellixian High Command the two fleets were on a direct course for Earth.

"Scout ships have confirmed two large Trellixian colonies in the system," Zalurr reported as he studied his screens. "There are also smaller colonies on some of the moons and larger asteroids."

Kamuss looked toward the tactical display, which was just beginning to light up with information. "What is the estimated Trellixian population?"

Zalurr hesitated and then responded. "At least twelve billion."

"Detecting Trellixian warships in the system," added Lieutenant Commander LeLath as she studied the data coming in from the scouts. "There are one hundred and thirty enemy battlecruisers near the primary target."

"What about colony ships and cargo ships?"

LeLath paused as she looked up the data. "Twelve colony ships and twenty-seven cargo ships. There also seems to be some mining ships as well. One of the scouts is reporting spotting some major mining operations in the system's asteroids."

Fleet Commander Kamuss quickly decided the warships would have to be taken out first. "We'll jump both fleets to within 60,000 kilometers of the primary colony and take out the warships. Then we'll split the fleets and take out all the colony, cargo ships, and mining ships. Once that's been done we'll destroy the colonies."

"There's over twelve billion Trellixians in the system!" replied LeLath, her eyes widening. "Most of them are civilians."

Kamuss looked over at Lieutenant Commander LeLath. He could tell by the look on her face she did not feel comfortable with their orders as far as destroying all Trellixian colonies they came across. "In this war there are no civilians. There is just us and the enemy. If we let any of them survive, someday they will come for our worlds. This may be a horrible way to fight a war but it is the Trellixians who set the parameters for this conflict because of their wiping out hundreds, perhaps thousands of civilizations on worlds which could not resist them."

LeLath let out a deep sigh. She knew the Fleet Commander was correct. "I just wish there was another way."

"We all do," replied Kamuss. "We didn't start this war, the Trellixians did. They would have destroyed all of our worlds without hesitation. That is their way and how they've expanded their Empire."

"Ready to jump," reported Meetric. "Hyperspace jump coordinates have been transmitted to all ships."

Kamuss leaned back in his command chair. "Lieutenant Commander LeLath, take the fleet to Battle Condition One."

Almost instantly, klaxons began to sound and red lights started to flash.

After a few moments Lieutenant Commander LeLath turned off the alarms and the lights. She had already announced the setting of Battle Condition One.

Kamuss looked over at Meetric. "Initiate the jump."

-

The two Voltrex fleets dropped out of hyperspace 60,000 kilometers from the primary Trellixian colony planet. The ships were instantly picked up on Trellixian sensors as alarms sounded on every battlecruiser. Commanders looked at their tactical displays with deep concern as they realized Voltrex ships were entering the star system.

"Enemy battlecruisers have been detected," reported Second Officer Zada as he turned toward Battle Commander Lamarck. "We have over three hundred Voltrex warships inbound toward Beta Three."

Lamarck's large eyes shifted to the tactical display. He had one hundred and thirty-two battlecruisers with which to defend the system. He had heard what happened at Kalone Four and several other colony worlds the Voltrex had attacked. Looking at the largest viewscreen in front of him he could see the colony world of Beta Three. There were nearly seven billion Trellixians living on the planet and another four billion on Beta Four. There were also several large colonies on some of the system's moons as well as a few large asteroid mining colonies.

"Have the cargo ships and the colony ships enter hyperspace and go to Lavon Seven," Lamarck ordered in a steady voice.

The colony ships had only recently arrived, bringing more colonists to the system. Only three of them had been unloaded. Lavon Seven held a small Trellixian military base as well as a thriving colony. It was far enough away he didn't believe the Voltrex would attack it. In recent battles with the Voltrex too many colony ships and cargo ships had been lost. Battle Commander Lamarck was not going to allow that to happen here.

"Orders sent," confirmed Second Officer Zada. "They should be jumping out shortly."

"Voltrex ships are still inbound," reported the sensor officer. "Estimated contact in twelve minutes."

From the reports he had read and what he knew of the weapons the Voltrex ships were now equipped with he knew he had very little chance of holding the system.

Second Officer Zada moved away from Communications. "The planetary governor is demanding to know what we're going to do."

Battle Commander Lamarck had served in the Trellixian military for over twenty years. In all that time his fleet had never been involved in an actual space battle. Most of the worlds he had conquered were primitive without any type of space going vessels. In those instances his fleet had gone into obit and dropped nuclear missiles on the target cities. Then, as soon as the radiation subsided, Trellixian troops in battle armor were landed to sweep the surface to ensure there were no survivors.

Form the fleet into formation W-3," ordered Lamarck. This was a wedge formation with his flagship in the center. "We have some of the new fifty-megaton missiles; we'll advance and when we're within range launch them."

"From the reports we've received the Voltrex missiles far outrange ours," said Zada. "We'll lose a lot of our battlecruisers before we get within range."

"Have the battlecruisers with the new missiles placed farther back in the formation so they will survive. Also, send a message to the High Command that Voltrex ships have entered the system and we are preparing to engage."

-

It only took the Trellixian battlecruisers a few minutes to form up in their wedge formation. Once complete the formation began advancing toward the incoming Voltrex fleet. Missiles were loaded into their tubes and the hatches covering the launching tubes slid open. Energy beam turrets rotated until they faced the incoming Voltrex ships.

-

"Enemy has formed into a wedge formation and are advancing toward us," reported Zalurr. On the tactical display, a large group of red icons was moving closer to the Voltrex fleets.

Lieutenant Commander LeLath turned toward the Fleet Commander. "They will be in range of our missiles in two minutes. Shall we launch?"

Fleet Commander Kamuss knew why LeLath was asking this question. In past battles he had been hesitant about using too many of the valuable missiles as they were not replaceable until they reached Earth. "Yes, I want all ships to keep a reserve supply of ten percent on the missiles. We may still need some on the remainder of our trip to Earth."

LeLath quickly passed on the orders.

"Missile loaded in the tubes and ready to fire," reported Diboll as his hands moved over his tactical console. "We currently have 42 percent of our missiles remaining."

"Launch as soon as the Trellixian battlecruisers are in range and we have target lock," ordered Fleet Commander Kamuss.

-

The fleets continued to close and then the Voltrex fleet launched a swarm of forty-megaton missiles. They were sublight missiles and accelerated rapidly toward the Trellixian battlecruisers. In mere seconds they began to slam into the energy shields of the lead ships.

Massive fusion explosions rolled across the front of the Trellixian wedge formation. Raw energy clawed at and threatened to bring down energy shields. As more missiles arrived and detonated, shields began to fail. In fiery fireballs of released energy Trellixian battlecruisers began to die.

A fusion missile struck the bow of a Trellixian battlecruiser, vaporizing it. Secondary explosions caused the rest of the ship to break apart. A pair of fusion missiles slammed into another battlecruiser, turning it into a miniature nova. When the light died down all that remained was twisted wreckage and several glowing fields of gas which rapidly died away.

The entire front of the Trellixian formation was full of dying ships as the fusion energy from the missile warheads continued to knock down energy shields.

-

"We're losing a lot of ships," reported Second Officer Zada as the flagship shook violently. "We just took a missile hit to our own energy shield. Shield is down to 68 percent."

"We're in missile range," called out the tactical officer.

"Then launch!" ordered Battle Commander Lamarck. "All ships are to launch and continue firing until they've exhausted their loads of missiles."

On a viewscreen, a fusion missile blew a nearby Trellixian battlecruiser apart. Its wreckage slammed into several other nearby battlecruisers, threatening to bring down their energy screens. The forward half of the fleet formation was in chaos.

-

In space, the remaining Trellixian battlecruisers began launching their missiles. Hundreds of missiles, some in the fifty-megaton range, leaped toward the incoming Voltrex fleet.

The Voltrex fleet began firing their defensive energy cannons, taking out many of the missiles. However, there were so many with more being launched every second that some began to get through.

Brilliant flashes of light began to appear across the front of the Voltrex fleet formation. In a sudden brilliant flash of light a large support vessel exploded, hurling wreckage across space.

More missiles struck and several more support vessels found their shields overloaded. More of the fifty-megaton missiles arrived, knocking the shields down and crashing into the hulls of the support ships. Six more support ships died in brilliant flashes of light.

-

"Some of those missiles are in the fifty-megaton range," reported Lieutenant Commander LeLath as she saw several support ships vanish from the tactical display. "Our support ships can only stand up to one or two of those monster warheads before their shields fail."

Kamuss took in a deep breath. He had hoped this Trellixian fleet did not possess any of the stronger missiles. "What about anti-matter weapons? Any signs of those?"

Lieutenant Commander LeLath shook her head. "No, just the heavier nukes. Most of the missiles being fired at us are small nuclear weapons with a yield of twenty-megatons. About 20 percent are of the fifty-megaton range. So far the energy shields on our battleships and our battlecruisers are holding up to the missile attack."

Kamuss looked at the main viewscreen, which was focused on the enemy fleet. Its entire forward section seemed to be on fire. Dozens of fusion explosions were constantly lighting up the enemy ships. Most of the forward section of the Trellixian wedge formation had been destroyed.

"Energy weapons range," reported Diboll.

"Fire!" ordered Fleet Commander Kamuss, leaning forward in his command chair, his cat eyes intently watching the main viewscreen.

Battle Commander Lamarck was highly disappointed in his fleet's missile attack. He had expected to be able to take out some of the enemies larger vessels. So far they had only managed to take out a number of the smaller support vessels.

"The Voltrex are starting to fire their energy weapons," warned Second Officer Zada. "All ships are reporting they've launched all of their fifty-megaton missiles. We're down to the weaker warheads and we've only got a few of them left."

Lamarck sucked down a deep breath of air. This battle was going far worse than expected. Trellixian ships were supposed to be the most powerful in the universe, or that's what he had been told in his military training. Even as he watched the tactical display several more of his battlecruiser icons swelled up and vanished.

"We're losing ships at an increasing rate," reported Second Officer Zada. "Computer projections state we won't be able to significantly damage the enemy fleet before our fleet is destroyed."

Defeat! thought Battle Commander Lamarck. They were Trellixians; how was this possible? He now understood the recent reversals in the loss of several colony worlds as well as Kalone Four.

"All ships are to enter hyperspace and go to Lavon Seven," ordered Lamarck. "If we stay here we will be destroyed. There is nothing we can do to save this system from destruction."

"Abandon the colonies?" blurted out Second Officer Zada in shock.

Battle Commander Lamarck turned toward his second officer. "We have no choice. Perhaps by adding our ships to those at Lavon Seven we can keep that base and colony safe. There is no point throwing our lives away uselessly in a battle we can't win. I am willing to die for the Empire but not in a hopeless battle."

Zada nodded and quickly began giving orders to the surviving Trellixian battlecruisers.

Moments later Battle Commander Lamarck felt his flagship make the transition into hyperspace. Looking at the tactical display, he was stunned to see only twenty-eight other battlecruisers were with the flagship. With a sinking feeling in his gut, he realized the others had either been destroyed or were too heavily damaged to make the jump into hyperspace. Standing up, he decided to go to his quarters. He needed to make a report to the High Command. There was a very good chance that due to his withdrawal from battle he might lose his command and be sentenced to a mining colony or even worse, one of the penal colonies where life expectancy was very short.

-

Enemy fleet is jumping out," reported Zalurr. "There are still seven Trellixian battlecruisers which appear too damaged to jump."

"Target and destroy them," ordered Fleet Commander Kamuss. Kamuss then looked over at Lieutenant Commander LeLath. "What are our losses?" Kamuss knew some support ships had been destroyed.

"Nine support ships," reported LeLath. "The battlecruisers *Tamora* and *Baroke* are reporting light damage to their hulls. Their commanding officers report damage repair should only take a few hours. We also have twelve support ships reporting moderate to heavy damage. I'm still receiving reports on the severity."

"Contact Fleet Commander Masurl and inform him he can begin his part of the cleansing of this system. What about their colony and cargo ships?"

"They jumped out as soon as the battle started," answered Zalurr. "They all headed off in the same direction. From our data files there is a small Trellixian base at Lavon Seven."

Fleet Commander Kamuss was not surprised the enemy cargo and colony ships had escaped. Those ships seemed more vital to the Trellixians than their warships. "Is Lavon Seven near our path to Earth?"

"No," replied Metriic. "It's about twenty-three light years out of the way."

"We'll leave it for now," decided Kamuss. "What's our missile inventory?" He knew they had expended many of the larger forty-megaton missiles.

"We have a fleet reserve of 22 percent," replied Lieutenant Commander LeLath.

On the viewscreens, he saw the last Trellixian battlecruisers being pummeled by energy beams. One by one they were riddled with weapons fire until they were nothing more than drifting hulks.

"All enemy craft destroyed," confirmed Zalurr.

"Fleet Commander Masurl's fleet is moving away and beginning their attack runs," added Lieutenant Commander LeLath. "There are some mining ships still in the system. Fleet Commander Masurl believes they are not equipped with hyperspace drives and cannot escape."

Kamuss nodded. "Destroy them. I want everything the Trellixians built in this system annihilated. Metriic, take us into orbit. Our first target will be the small shipyard and then the three orbital stations."

"The shipyard is lightly armed and has an energy shield," reported Zalurr.

Lieutenant Commander LeLath stepped near the sensor console and studied the readings. "The shield will be no problem. It's the same strength as one of their battlecruisers."

"Very well, begin firing. Eliminate all orbital structures and then we'll start on the planet's population centers." Kamuss leaned back in his command chair. He dared not let the crew know how much it bothered him to drop nuclear weapons on civilians even if they were Trellixians. He understood the necessity though he would never like it. It would be something which would haunt him for the rest of his days.

-

On the planet below, the planetary governor stared at a viewscreen showing the destruction in orbit. The shipyard was the first to be annihilated as it was quickly turned into molten wreckage. The three orbital stations followed until nothing of consequence remained in orbit. The governor knew much of the wreckage would eventually fall to the surface, causing even more damage. His eyes still showed anger at Battle Commander Lamarck for fleeing with the shattered remains of his fleet. It was the duty of every member of the Trellixian military to fight for the Empire even if that meant death. The governor had already sent a complaint to the High Command.

Even as the governor watched missiles began dropping down through the atmosphere. He knew he was about to die. He felt no sadness at his coming demise. He was a Trellixian and had no fear of death. The ground suddenly shook violently and the viewscreen became covered in static. Walking over to a large window, he looked out. In the distance, he could see several mushroom clouds rising up into the atmosphere. Suddenly there was a loud explosion and a flash of light. The governor felt his eardrums burst and then the heat and blast wave struck the building he occupied. In an instant, much of the city was vaporized. The governor and the two million other Trellixians in the city died within seconds of one another. Buildings fell and others burst into flame. A firestorm developed as superheated air rushed upward, forming a growing mushroom cloud.

-

Across the planet more missiles fell. Nuclear explosions shook the planet as dust and residue were hurled high up into the atmosphere. After a few hours a dark ash began to fall, covering everything. Occasionally another missile would fall as an additional target was spotted. The sky grew dark until it seemed like twilight. Then it grew darker yet and the wind began to blow and the temperature started to drop. It would be years before the atmosphere cleared sufficiently to allow the sun to shine on the planet once more.

Fleet Commander Kamuss stood in front of the ship's primary viewscreen looking at the destruction his fleet had wrought. Already the planet's atmosphere was turning dark. It took a lot of weapons to annihilate a planet full of Trellixians. No doubt there were still some survivors on the surface or in underground sections of buildings, but with the biosphere of the planet pretty much destroyed and the radiation they would not last long.

"It's not a pretty sight," said Lieutenant Commander LeLath from Kamuss' side where she had been watching the viewscreens.

Kamuss folded his arms across his chest. His tongue flicked out to wet his long face whiskers. "Our worlds could have looked like this," he said, glancing over at LeLath. "This is what we're stopping the Trellixians from doing to us."

"I know," LeLath replied in a subdued voice. "I just wish it wasn't necessary."

Kamuss completely agreed with her. "War can be cruel at times and this could be a long war." That was what Fleet Command believed. Already every major shipyard in the Voltrex Federation was building warships. More shipyards were being built and existing shipyards enlarged. More of the one-thousand-meter battlestations were being built above the home world as well as all the major colonies.

Kamuss wondered what his son was doing. There was a good chance he was with one of the other fleets tasked with finding Trellixian colonies near Voltrex space and annihilating them.

"Fleet Commander Masurl reports all other targets have been neutralized," reported Meela.

"We will stay in this system for a few more hours. Tell Fleet Commander Masurl to do a second sweep of the system to ensure we have not overlooked anything. All ships are to conduct what repairs they can. Once all ships are safe enough to enter hyperspace we'll head for a nearby star system and conduct full repairs on our damaged vessels."

Lieutenant Commander LeLath looked over at the Fleet Commander. "We have several support vessels too heavily damaged to repair."

"Strip them of everything useful and then we'll scuttle them when we're ready to depart the system."

"I'll send the order," replied LeLath as she went over to Communications.

-

For the next three hours the two fleets scoured the system searching for any Trellixians who might have been missed. A few mining ships were found hiding in the asteroids as well as one small asteroid mining colony. These were eliminated to ensure the Trellixians never returned to this system.

"It's a shame what we did to these two worlds," said Lieutenant Commander LeLath, looking at a viewscreen showing the world below them.

"The nuclear weapons we used have very short half-lives," Kamuss answered. "In a few years the radiation will be gone and the nuclear winter will be over. Once that's happened the planet will begin to recover. In a few hundred years it might be habitable again."

LeLath nodded. She knew that even after what they had done life in the deeper parts of the oceans probably still survived. "All ships report ready to enter hyperspace."

"Have all ships form up on us and we will depart this system."

-

In space, two Voltrex support vessels exploded as forty-megaton fusion missiles turned them into molten wreckage. If the Trellixians searched the wreckage, they would find nothing useful. The same had been done to the other vessels destroyed in the battle. Searches had been made of the wreckage to ensure nothing valuable remained.

An hour later the two fleets entered hyperspace. Behind them they left a dead and shattered star system.

Chapter Fourteen

The *Fury* exited hyperspace just outside the Norest System. According to the data files it was one of the more heavily populated Trellixian systems. All four ships came to a stop and quickly reduced their emissions. From the *Fury* and the *Horizon* four probes left the ships and entered hyperspace. They would pass through most of the system at speeds greater than the speed of light. The probes would only drop out of hyperspace near their targets to take more detailed scans of the planets, moons, and orbiting structures.

"Probes have been launched," reported Kia as four small icons appeared on her sensor screen. "We should begin receiving data shortly."

"There's an awful lot of ship traffic," said Second Officer Katana, her eyes wide with concern. "Passive sensor scans are indicating over six hundred spacecraft, maybe more."

Captain Dolan looked up at the tactical display. At the moment it was only showing the system's ten planets. This was the fifth Trellixian core system they had scanned. Each system took them deeper into the heart of the Empire. Every time they launched the probes they risked detection.

"Planets four and five are in the liquid water zone," Chloe reported as she studied the sensor readings the ship had taken so far. There are also some very large artificial constructions around both planets."

"Habitats," suggested Lisa. "The planets in this section of the Empire have been colonized much longer than others. It's reasonable to assume they've built a few orbital habitats for their excess population."

"Maybe," conceded Brett with a deep frown on his face. "However, it would be cheaper and more reasonable to build a dome colony on a moon somewhere. An orbital habitat would be expensive to run and make very little economic sense to use for handling excessive populations."

Brenda shook her head. "I don't believe the Trellixians will look at it economically. All they are looking at is additional living space."

"Brenda's right," Lisa said. "From what we know of the Trellixians they are driven by their exploding population. I bet those are orbital habitats and they are crammed full of civilians."

Derek turned from his computer console. "If those are orbital habitats we should take as detailed scans of them as are possible. The scans may reveal some construction techniques we may find useful."

"Agreed," said Captain Dolan. "This is one of the Trellixians' primary systems. I want the entire system scanned in detail. Every planet, orbital structure, moon, asteroid, and rock. The secret to defeating them could very well lie in what we discover in this system."

Mark looked at his crew. He hoped he could get them safely back to Earth. Every time now they dropped out of hyperspace they were taking a growing risk. They still had a few more star systems to check including the Trellixians' home system. Mark knew luck had been with them so far, allowing them to remain undiscovered. Mark was greatly concerned about what would happen if that luck ran out.

Getting out of his command chair, he turned the Command Center over to Katana. He wanted to go get something to eat and drink before the data from the probes started coming in.

The probes entered the Trellixian star system and began their transit. They slowed down and any time they neared a planet or object of interest they dropped out of hyperspace to take better and more detailed scans. It was during one of those times the probes dropped out of hyperspace that one of them malfunctioned. As Mark had feared, their luck ran out. The probe's sublight engine failed, causing the probe to tumble uncontrollably. The tumbling prevented the probe from going back into hyperspace or sending messages back to the fleet. It also made the probe easier to detect on Trellixian sensors.

"Battle Commander Shadrin, we're detecting a small ship out near Norest Seven," reported the sensor officer. "It just appeared."

The Trellixian Battle Commander stepped over to the sensors and studied the data on the object. "That's too small for a ship. Do we have a battlecruiser in that area?"

"The *Norling* is a few million kilometers from the object."

Battle Commander Shadrin thought for a moment and then turned to Communications. "Contact the *Norling* and tell them about our contact. Tell them to investigate and report back on their findings."

A few minutes later the communications officer looked over at the Battle Commander. "The *Norling* spotted the same object about the time we did. They are already in route. Commander Brendal believes it's some type of probe."

"A probe?" uttered Battle Commander Shadrin, his large eyes growing even wider. "Who would launch a probe without our permission?"

"The *Norling* believes it's not one of ours."

The Battle Commander's green skin turned paler. "Order all ships to go to active scanning of the system. If there is one alien probe there may be more of them." While Battle Commander Shadrin was finding it hard to accept an alien probe was in the system, he was no fool.

"Can it be the Voltrex?" asked the second-in-command.

The Battle Commander was silent for several long moments. "Maybe, though I don't see how they could have gotten so deep into the Empire without being detected. Communications, send a message to the High Command and inform them we have detected what may be an alien probe in the Norest System and are investigating."

Looking at the ship's tactical display, a disconcerting thought occurred to the Battle Commander. If there were alien probes in the system where were the ships they had launched from? For several long moments he stared at the tactical display. They had to be somewhere. "Send several squadrons of our battlecruisers to the outer edge of our system. They're to scan the outside comet belt. The alien ships might be hiding there."

-

Mark was summoned back to the Command Center by Katana. Upon entering, he could see something was wrong. "What's happened?" he asked as he sat down in his command chair.

"One of our probes malfunctioned," reported Katana. "We've lost contact with it and from our passive sensor scans a Trellixian battlecruiser is moving toward its location."

"Can we still activate its self-destruct?" Mark didn't want the probe to fall into Trellixian hands. There had always been a chance that a probe would be detected.

Katana nodded. "Yes, all we have to do is beam the destruct code toward the probe's location. The bomb has its own hyperspace receiver and should activate."

"Do it," ordered Mark. "I don't want the Trellixians to use their sensors to discover too much about the probe." Parts of it were based on Jelnoid technology and must not fall into Trellixian hands.

Marissa quickly sent the code to the probe. "Destruct sequence sent."

Mark looked at the tactical display, now showing a myriad of red threat icons as well as four small green ones in the system. After a few moments one of the green ones swelled up on the screen and then vanished.

"Probe has self-destructed," confirmed Kia. "We believe there was some type of failure in its sublight propulsion system."

"We have several squadrons of Trellixian battlecruisers which have just gone into hyperspace and exited on the periphery of the system," added Kia as an alarm sounded on her console. "They may be searching for us."

-

On the Trellixian battlecruiser approaching the probe Commander Brendal watched as a brilliant explosion eliminated the small vessel.

"Target has self-destructed," reported the sensor operator. "There is nothing left."

The Commander was not surprised. Anyone who had built a probe as sophisticated as this one would ensure it wasn't captured. "Notify the Battle Commander of the loss of the probe. We will continue to its former location and search for any remains but from the intensity of the explosion I do not expect to find anything of use."

"How long before the other probes finish their scans?" asked Mark with concern in his voice. He knew the Trellixians would be searching for them.

"Another four hours," replied Lisa. "They still have several planets and moons to scan."

Mark looked at the tactical display showing the three remaining probes' locations. "Can we recall them?"

"We could," Katana replied. "But we would not have detailed data on some of our targets."

"What are the odds of the Trellixians locating more of our probes?"

Chloe turned toward the captain. "Seventy-six percent. They now know what to look for. We're already detecting active sensor scanning from all Trellixian battlecruisers and this system has eighty-six of them."

Mark looked back at the tactical display and the two squadrons of enemy battlecruisers which were obviously searching for his ships. They were still a ways off. "We'll let the probes continue on their mission. Once they've finished and have transmitted all their data we will order the probes to self-destruct, then we'll leave the system."

"What if the Trellixians find us before the probes are finished?" asked Katana. "One squadron is pretty close."

Mark looked over Katana. "We'll activate the self-destructs and leave immediately. I don't want to engage in combat with the enemy." Mark knew they had just lost their biggest advantage. The Trellixians now knew that somewhere a ship or ships had launched probes into one of their star systems. All the others would now be searching for similar probes in their systems. Next time the *Fury* launched any probes, the likelihood of them being detected had skyrocketed.

-

All across the system Trellixian battlecruisers spread out searching for more of the probes. Battle Commander Shadrin was certain where there was one there had to be others. Only an hour passed before another probe was found. As soon as one of his ships approached it self-destructed in a massive blast just as the other one had.

"We must find the ship or ships that launched these," roared the Battle Commander, slamming his clenched fist against his command chair. He stood up and stomped over to the tactical display, glaring at it. "Order all battlecruisers if another probe is located not to approach it. It's obvious they are set to self-destruct if one of our ships comes too close."

"You think there are still more?" asked the second officer.

"I'm certain of it," replied Battle Commander Shadrin. "Someone is trying to get detailed scans of this system. We must find them before they escape in their ship, or ships. If we cause all of the probes to self-destruct they will leave. We must destroy them before that happens."

-

Mark was watching the tactical display uneasily. One of the searching squadrons of battlecruisers was moving closer to his fleet's position. "How much data do we have?" It was nearing time for them to leave.

"We have two more planets and six moons to scan," replied Lisa. "But we do have detailed scans of the primary colonies. The two planets and the moons have smaller colonies and probably some mining installations."

Mark made up his mind. It was time to leave. "Order the last two probes to self-destruct. As soon as we've confirmed they've been destroyed, we will jump back into hyperspace. The enemy is getting too close for comfort."

A few minutes later Katana confirmed the remaining two probes had self-destructed. "Both probes have activated their self-destructs. The Trellixians will find nothing useful."

Mark nodded. "Let's get out of here. I don't want the enemy to locate our ships." Mark also wanted to ensure they didn't become engaged in combat.

"They'll detect us when we power back up," warned Kia. "That one squadron is too close and they're using their active sensors. They'll detect all four of our ships."

"It's a risk we'll have to take," replied Mark. "By the time they can get here we'll be long gone."

In the Trellixian squadron, Commander Larmosk stared as his sensors suddenly lit us as they detected enemy ships. His ship had joined those in the outer sector of the system searching the comet zone.

"Four ships detected!" reported the sensor operator. "Range is twenty-eight million kilometers."

Larmosk looked up at the tactical display as it lit up with four red threat icons.

"We're receiving reports two more alien probes have self-destructed," added the communications officer.

Larmosk's eyes widened in realization. "They're preparing to leave. All ships are to jump to the aliens' location immediately."

"Too late," said the sensor officer as the four red threat icons on the tactical display vanished. "They're gone."

"Were we able to identify them?" asked Larmosk, his eyes focusing on the sensor officer.

The sensor officer shook his head. "No, we were not able to get detailed scans of their vessels."

Larmosk was not pleased. The High Command would not be satisfied with that answer. "Send a message to Battle

Commander Shadrin informing him we located the enemy ships but they have jumped into hyperspace and vanished."

Battle Commander Shadrin was not pleased by the report of the enemy ships escaping. The mere fact that alien ships had penetrated this deep into the heart of the Empire without being detected was a thing of deep concern. Drawing in a deep breath, the Battle Commander prepared to contact the High Command and submit his report. This was bound to cause extreme unrest when the High Command realized potentially dangerous vessels were in the heart of the Empire. Shadrin knew High Commander Kaldre had warned about this very thing. Now that time had arrived.

Battle Commander Kaldre stared in disbelief at the message just handed to him by Lamarr. Alien ships in the Norest System! The High Command was in a panic. Was this a scout force with a larger fleet following? Already battlecruisers were being directed to search and scan all nearby systems for any traces of alien vessels. Several fleets were being recalled to the home system.

"It's either the Humans or the Voltrex," predicted Kaldre, crushing the message in his right hand. "I warned the High Command this might happen." He was just surprised it had happened so soon.

Second Officer Calaah's eyes narrowed. "Which do you think it is?"

Kaldre didn't hesitate. "The Humans. The Voltrex are still interested in clearing out our colonies near their space. I doubt if they would risk sending a scouting party or fleet so deep into the Empire. The Humans, on the other hand, would not hesitate."

"Do you think there's a full size battle fleet nearby?"

Kaldre shook his head. "I doubt it. Most likely this is a small scouting force searching for a weakness in our Empire. I will contact Battle Commander Balforr and tell him we have a small force of Human ships somewhere in the heart of the Empire. He is to find them and destroy them before they can get back to

Earth with any tactical data they may have gathered from these probes. It's hard telling how many of our systems they've managed to scan. If not for the malfunction of the probe in the Norest System they might not have been detected there."

Kaldre leaned back in his command chair. He was in no real hurry to contact Battle Commander Balforr. He imagined the rest of the High Command was quite stirred up by now. Perhaps they would listen to his demands to convert more of their shipyards to constructing modern battlecruisers. Kaldre felt some satisfaction in the fact he had just been proven right about the threat the Humans and the Voltrex posed to the Empire.

-

Captain Dolan was in his quarters thinking about what to do next. The Trellixians now knew his fleet was in the area. Worse, those battlecruisers had gotten good enough scans of his fleet to know it consisted of four vessels. He leaned back in his chair and closed his eyes. No one would blame him for turning around and heading back to Earth. It would be a relief to the crew if he would give that order. However, they really needed information on the Trellixians' home system. With a deep sigh, Mark knew what they needed to do. Reaching forward he activated the comm on his desk that connected him to the Command Center. "Katana, set a course for the Trellixians' home system. We'll scan it and then return to Earth."

"As you command," Katana replied. "I'll inform the other ships."

Mark took in a deep breath. He called up the coordinates of the Trellixian home system on his computer screen. He had some time to decide the best way to secure the information on the Trellixian system. There was no doubt there would be a large number of battlecruisers plus the Trellixians might be expecting his ships to show up there. There was a good chance they would not get away from the system without having to fight their way out. Mark hoped not but he was prepared to do just that if that was what it took to get the data Earth and the Voltrex desperately needed.

Battle Commander Balforr had just received his orders from High Commander Kaldre. There was no doubt in his mind the ships detected in the Norest System were crewed by Humans. Only the Humans would dare to come so far into the Empire.

"Those ships are bound to be equipped with Jelnoid technology," said Second Officer Albion. "We will take some losses if we engage them."

Balforr stood up and stepped off the command pedestal. "Our ships are equipped with better energy shields and more powerful energy weapons. All of our new battlecruisers have a full load of the fifty-megaton fusion missiles. If we can find these Humans we will destroy them."

Albion nodded. "Where will they go next? If they know they've been detected they might be heading back to Earth and safety."

Balforr showed his long sharp teeth. He wished he had a warm piece of raw meat to tear into. "If I know these Humans they won't return home until they've scanned our home system. That's where they're headed. We're going to take our fleet there and set a trap. The Humans will not be returning home, they will die in at Trellixia." Balforr was pleased with his decision. He would enjoy this victory over the Humans even if it was a small one.

Lisa was in her quarters with Brenda and Kia. They were discussing the dangers of scanning the Trellixians' home system.

"I understand it's necessary," Brenda said unhappily. "but the Trellixians are bound to be expecting us."

"Maybe," said Kia. "After detecting us in the last system they might believe we're headed back home."

Lisa stood up and placed her hands on her hips. "This worries me," she said. "Is there anything we can do to make scanning the Trellixians' home system safer?"

The three looked at each other as their minds raced. All three wanted to make it safely back to Earth.

"We'll obviously use the probes again," said Brenda with her eyes narrowed. "Probably a large number of them."

Lisa sat back down. "The Trellixians will be expecting our fleet to be hiding in the cometary zone. Maybe we should do something different."

Kia glanced over at Lisa. "Do you have something in mind?"

"Maybe," Lisa said slowly. "We need to do something the Trellixians won't be expecting." She had a tactic that might work; she just needed to talk Captain Dolan into it. It was risky but it was the last thing the Trellixians would expect. "We need to go down to one of the labs and build some equipment for my plan to work."

"What is it?" asked Brenda, leaning forward. "What do you want to do?"

Taking a deep breath, Lisa began explaining her plan. As she talked Brenda and Kia's eyes grew wide. Finally, Lisa finished explaining her idea.

"It might just work," Kia said, nodding her head. "We'll need Derek to help with the computer programming and Brett for the engineering part."

Lisa stood back up and headed for the door. "Let's run by the Officer's Mess for a light snack and then we'll head for the lab. I don't want to work on an empty stomach."

"I'll contact Brett and Derek," Kia said. "They can join us to eat and then off to the lab." Kia stopped and looked at Lisa. "This idea of yours is brilliant; I just hope it works."

"So do I," replied Lisa. If it didn't work they could all lose their lives. If it did all of them just might make it home safely.

Chapter Fifteen

Captain Mark Dolan stared in disbelief at Lisa. She had just finished explaining her plan to scan the Trellixian home system. "You have got to be kidding me. You want me to jump the *Fury* into the heart of the most heavily populated Trellixian system? There could be over a thousand ships in that system!"

"They won't even know we're there," replied Lisa confidently. "With the new software and hardware we've designed the Trellixians will think the *Fury* is one of their own colony ships. It will be hours before they realize what we are. During that time we can scan the system."

Mark shook his head. "Explain how this will work."

Lisa looked over at Derek. Much of it was his programming.

"We have built some equipment which will give off the electronic signature of a Trellixian colony ship. Any Trellixian vessel that scans us will see the image of one of their own vessels on their sensors. The only way they will be able to tell we're not real is if they obtain a visual image."

"How far away do we need to stay from other ships?" asked Katana. "This technology you've designed sounds very intriguing."

"Several thousand kilometers at least," Lisa answered. "Preferably ten thousand if possible."

Mark took a deep breath. "So we drop out of hyperspace in the center of their system and launch all of our probes. We then stay in place while the probes spread out and survey the system?"

Lisa nodded. "Even if the Trellixians detect the probes they will believe our fleet is out in the comet belt somewhere. That's where they will search first. We can scan the entire system with the probes, collect the data, and then jump back into hyperspace with the Trellixians never knowing we were there."

"What about the probes?" Those things were expensive. He hated to lose them all.

"We won't need them after scanning the Trellixians' home system. When we're done we order them to self-destruct."

Mark leaned back in his command chair, folding his arms over his chest. His eyes narrowed as he considered what the lieutenants were suggesting. "How certain are you this technology will work? What if we jump into the center of the Trellixian home system and still register as a Voltrex battleship on their sensors?"

"We do a test," said Brett. "We drop out of hyperspace in an uninhabited star system and test the system. Our other ships can scan us with their sensors and then report on what they've found."

Mark nodded. "That sounds reasonable. How soon can you have your equipment ready to install?"

"It's already built," Lisa replied. "We just need to hook it up to a control console in the Command Center. We've already wired power to it in Lab Two and all we need to add is the control circuits. We have several engineers who helped with its design and they will stay in the lab the entire time the equipment is on."

"Okay," replied Mark, willing to take the chance. "Let's do it. Katana, locate a system on our present course where we can drop out of hyperspace. I want us to come out on the edge of the system. This close to their home world I suspect most of the systems with planets will have some type of mining operations present."

Katana nodded. "I'll need Lieutenant Masterson to help in locating a system."

"See to it," Mark ordered. "I want to know if this will work as soon as possible." Mark watched as the six left his office. He was glad he had the five lieutenants on board. If this new tech of theirs worked they had just earned their keep and the thanks of everyone in the fleet. It might also save some lives.

Lisa was back in the lab with Brenda directing the engineers on the final wiring of the camouflage device into the ship's systems. Derek and Kia were in the Command Center setting up a control console to operate the device.

"Are you certain this will work?" asked one of the engineers. He had helped assemble the device though he didn't really understand how it worked. Some of the science used was very advanced.

Lisa smiled. "It will work. We've ran some computer simulations and everything should work just fine. We just need to run a major test projecting the electronic signature of a Trellixian colony ship where the *Fury* is located. Any ship which scans us from a distance will believe we're one of their colony vessels."

"I hope this works," said Brenda as she turned on the computer that controlled the device. The computer ran through some checks and then the equipment began humming.

"Everything checks out," reported one of the engineers. "It should function just fine."

Lisa contacted Derek and Kia to see if they were ready.

"We're set up here," confirmed Derek. "We should be able to control everything from this console."

Lisa took a deep breath. They had all five worked very hard to get this electronic device ready. The help of the engineers in actually building some of the components had been essential. "Okay, tell the captain we're ready to run the test. Brenda and I will stay in Lab Two to monitor the equipment and the computer."

"Captain Dolan says we'll be dropping out of hyperspace in another hour," Derek replied. "We're going to come out of hyperspace in the vicinity of a small red dwarf. There seems to be quite a few of them in this area of space."

Lisa looked over at Brenda. "Guess we're ready for the test; can you think of anything we've missed?"

Brenda shook her head. "No, we'll know better when the other ships scan us and see what shows up on their sensors."

"We're ready down here," Lisa told Derek. "We need the other ships to move off to ten thousand kilometers for the first test and then gradually close the distance until they break through our electronic signature."

"I'll inform the captain," Derek replied.

-

An hour later the small fleet dropped out of hyperspace on the edge of the red dwarf star system. Initial scans revealed several Trellixian mining operations in the system with only a few cargo ships present. The carrier *Horizon* and the two battlecruisers, the *Liberty* and the *Cambridge*, all moved off to ten thousand kilometers from the *Fury*.

"We're ready," Derek told Lisa over the comm.

Lisa quickly double-checked the computer next to the new equipment. The computer showed everything was working within the set parameters. A slight humming noise came from the camouflage device. "Everything looks fine here," Lisa replied. "Go ahead and activate the electronic signature." Lisa leaned back, hoping this would work. They had used information they had from previous scans of Trellixian colony ships to create the electronic signature which should show the *Fury* as a Trellixian vessel.

-

In the Command Center, Captain Dolan waited anxiously for the test to begin. If it worked they had a good chance of sneaking into the Trellixian home system undetected.

"Electronic signature is activated," Derek informed the captain as he touched several icons on his computer screen. He looked over at Marissa. "Contact our ships and have them scan us."

Marissa did as ordered and then after a few moments turned toward Derek and the captain. "The *Cambridge* and the *Liberty* both report their scans indicate a Trellixian colony ship, however the *Horizon* reports their scans are showing a zone of electronic interference.

Captain Dolan looked over at Derek. "What's causing that?"

Derek looked confused and then began nodding to himself. "I think we can correct that. I need to contact Lisa and make a few changes to the program."

-

Lisa and Brenda listened to Derek explain what he wanted done. It only took them a few minutes to add the few lines of code Derek wanted added to the program.

"We're done," Lisa reported as they rebooted the computer.

-

On board the *Horizon*, Captain Wilson watched the tactical display as the diffused blob changed to the electronic signature of a Trellixian colony ship. He nodded to himself in satisfaction. "Inform the *Fury* they now look like a colony ship. We're preparing to move closer to see if the signature changes."

-

On the *Fury*, Mark waited expectantly as the other three ships began to close with his flagship. All three ships were in constant communication with the *Fury* informing them about what the electronic signature from their sensor scans were showing.

At the two thousand kilometer mark all three ships were still registering a Trellixian colony ship. At fifteen hundred kilometers, the signature became intermittent and at twelve hundred kilometers, the sensor showed the *Fury* in her true form.

"Fifteen hundred kilometers seems to be where the electronic signature begins to break down," Derek said. "As a safety precaution I would recommend staying at least two thousand kilometers from any Trellixian vessel or installation."

Mark was pleased with the test. "Will the new device be able to stay operating for the length of time we'll need to thoroughly scan the Trellixians' home system?"

Derek nodded. "It should be able to. Lisa and Brenda will stay in Lab Two to make sure there are no problems. We also have a team of engineers standing by as well."

Mark took a deep breath. "Very well, we'll leave the rest of our ships here and only use the *Fury* for this mission. We'll wait here for six more hours and then make the hyperspace jump into the Trellixians' home system. During that time everyone needs to get something to eat and a little rest. Once we're in the Trellixians' system I'll need everyone at the top of their game. We can't afford a slip up."

Lisa, Brenda, Kia, Derek, and Brett were all in the Officer's Mess. They had all gone to their quarters for a few hours of sleep and then met for a light meal.

"Do you think this will really work?" asked Kia. "There's bound to be heavy ship traffic in the Trellixians' home system."

Brett looked over at Kia. "It'd better work or none of us will see home again."

Brenda shook her head. "If we're spotted we can always jump out of the system. I'm sure Captain Dolan will keep us safe."

Derek took a bite out of his ham sandwich and then looked at the others. "Look on the bright side of things. Once we've finished scanning the Trellixians' home system we'll be on our way home."

"Home," said Kia, her eyes brightening. "I'll be glad when we get back."

Lisa had to agree. She really missed seeing and talking to Professor Wilkens. The morning breakfasts they occasionally had were fond memories of her time in Complex One. Of course, there was Brett as well. Once they returned home they could start going out again. It was difficult seeing him every day and talking to him but not being able to express her feelings.

"We better get to our posts," Brett said standing up. "Captain Dolan will be expecting us."

"Let's just hope nothing goes wrong," Derek said.

Lisa stood up and smiled at Brett who grinned back. Lisa felt a warm feeling inside knowing the two were still as close as ever.

Captain Dolan was in the Command Center as the crew prepared for the hyperspace jump into the Trellixians' home system. There was considerable tension in the air as the *Fury* would be making the jump by herself, leaving the rest of the fleet in the red dwarf system. Captain Wilson would be in charge of the three ships being left behind. They had orders that if the *Fury* was not back in forty-eight hours they were to immediately make the jump into hyperspace and begin heading back to Earth. The three remaining ships were far enough from the Trellixian mining operations that there was little chance of detection.

Battle Commander Balforr grinned maliciously as he received a report from the Jarvid System. One of the mining operations there had detected unknown ships in the outer regions of the system. Normally the ships would not have been noticed but since the report of probes in the Norest System, Balforr had contacted all the systems around Trellixia and ordered them to keep their sensors constantly scanning for any unknown contacts. There were quite a few mining operations in uninhabited systems and now that scanning was about to pay off.

"Prepare the fleet to enter hyperspace and go to the Jarvid System," ordered Balforr. "One of our mining colonies has detected unknown contacts in the system."

Second Officer Albion's eyes widened. "Do you believe it's the Humans?"

"I'm certain of it," Balforr replied. "They most likely stopped there to take scans of systems near Trellixia. If we hurry we can catch them in the system before they can escape."

"How do we stop them from escaping into hyperspace?" asked Albion. "They will jump out as soon as our ships are detected."

"Simple," Balforr replied. "We jump right in on top of them and disable their hyperspace drives. Once they can't escape we can destroy their ships."

"Do we take the reserve ships or just the newer battlecruisers?"

"Just the newer battlecruisers. I don't want the other ships to get in the way." Battle Commander Balforr was satisfied as the *Conquest* prepared to enter hyperspace. It would be a short trip to the Jarvid System. Once there his vengeance against the Humans would begin.

-

Captain Wilson was in his quarters when the Condition One alarms began sounding and moments later the *Horizon* shook violently.

"Captain, report to the Command Center," Second Officer Riley said over the ship's internal comm system. "We have Trellixian battlecruisers dropping out of hyperspace around us."

Wilson hit the comm unit on his desk with the palm of his hand. "Jump us out immediately," he ordered. "All ships are to enter hyperspace and not engage the enemy."

The ship shook violently again, nearly throwing Wilson to the floor.

"Hyperdrive is out," Riley informed the captain. "We've taken numerous fifty-megaton warhead strikes to the engine area. Enough energy has bled through the defensive screen to incapacitate the drive. Engineering says twenty minutes for repairs."

"Damn!" said Wilson, feeling frustrated. "Tell the other ships to leave and begin returning fire immediately. I'll be in the Command Center shortly and Riley: keep us alive!"

-

Battle Commander Balforr had the Humans exactly where he wanted them. His fleet had dropped out of hyperspace all around the three Human ships. As soon as the fleet's weapons targeted the Human vessels they had opened fire with energy beam fire as well as fifty-megaton missiles. Initially all the energy beams were directed at the rear of the ships in an attempt to damage their hyperspace engines. The attack must have been successful as all three ships were still here.

In a sudden massive explosion, one of the Human battlecruisers blew apart as its shield was overloaded and multiple fusion missiles slammed into its hull. The screens in the Command Center instantly dimmed from the influx of bright light and radiation.

"Ship destroyed," confirmed Maldane. "The shields on the remaining two are weakening."

"Continue to fire," ordered Balforr, leaning forward with expectation in his command chair. He had the Humans exactly where he wanted them. There would be no escape from his trap.

-

"Captain, we've lost the *Cambridge*," reported Second Officer Riley as Captain Wilson entered the Command Center. "The *Liberty* is reporting heavy damage and their energy screen is down to 20 percent."

"Hyperspace drives?"

"Offline," replied Riley.

Captain Wilson drew in a deep breath as he took his seat in the command chair. His ship was lost and he knew it. "What about our fighter-bombers? Are they armed?"

"Yes," replied Riley, looking confused. "But their missiles only have a twenty-kiloton warhead. They're not powerful enough to bring down the shields of a Trellixian battlecruiser. Not only that but our sensors are showing these battlecruisers are different from ones we've fought in the past. Their missiles are more powerful, their energy weapons are stronger, and their energy screen is better."

On one of the viewscreens, a Trellixian battlecruiser blew apart as its shield was battered down.

"Can we get out any messages?" Captain Wilson was determined to send the probe data they had back to Earth through the hyperspace communication drones they had left strung out behind them.

Riley shook his head. "No, all communications except for short-range are being jammed."

The *Horizon* shook violently and for a brief moment, the lights dimmed.

"All power has been diverted to the shields," reported the tactical officer as his hands moved over his console. "We can no longer fire our energy weapons and keep the shield up."

The ship suddenly seemed to keel over on its side and several consoles exploded, sending hot showers of sparks across the Command Center. Several officers yelled out in pain from being burned.

"What was that?" asked Wilson. He began to cough from the smoke.

"It was the *Liberty*," replied the sensor officer, his face turning pale. "It blew up and our energy screen was struck by some of its wreckage."

Captain Wilson knew the end was near. He had lost both of the escorting battlecruisers and now all the enemy's fire was being directed toward the *Horizon*. The carrier began to shake uncontrollably. The viewscreens became covered in static as the light from the explosions of fusion missiles against the energy shield was too bright.

"Energy shield is down to 12 percent," reported the tactical officer.

"Our hyperspace drive?"

Second Officer Riley shook his head. "Not going to be ready in time."

In the distance, Wilson thought he could hear the sound of tearing metal and screams. The lights in the Command Center began to grow dimmer.

"Shield is down to six percent," reported the tactical officer. "It's about to fail!"

"It's been an honor to serve with all of you," said Captain Wilson in a steady voice.

Second Officer Riley looked as if he was about to reply when a bright flash of light and then heat filled the Command Center.

-

"The last Human ship has been destroyed," reported Maldane.

Battle Commander Balforr leaned back in his command chair basking in his victory. For once the Humans had not been able to escape. They had come into the Empire and died here.

"Battle Commander?" said Second Officer Albion. "Didn't the Norest System as well as the mining colony report there were four Human ships?"

Balforr leaned forward, frowning. "Contact both the Norest System and the mining colony and confirm the number of ships they detected."

It took a few minutes and finally a response came back. Four ships had been detected in the Norest System and four by the mining colony.

Battle Commander Balforr stood up and stepped down from the command pedestal. A ship was missing. Where could it have gone? His eyes wandered to the viewscreen which showed a sea of stars. His eyes suddenly widened as he realized where the missing ship had to be.

"Have all ships set a course for Trellixia," he ordered, stepping back up on the command pedestal and sitting down. "The missing ship must be attempting to scan our home system."

Second Officer Albion looked surprised. "Why would they leave their other ships here for us to destroy?"

"Because the Humans are no fools. They realized one ship would be much more difficult to detect than four."

Albion looked at one of the viewscreens showing the wreckage of the Human ships they had just destroyed. "How long has the missing ship been gone? It could already be in our home system."

Battle Commander Balforr didn't reply. He had to find the last Human ship and destroy it. He had a strong suspicion it was their flagship which was missing. "Contact our reserve fleets and have them jump to the Trellixia System and begin searching. Start with the comet zone first. Also contact the High Command and inform them we believe there is a Human warship attempting to scan the home system. Inform them our fleet will be there shortly to aid in the search."

In only a few short minutes the *Conquest* and her fleet entered hyperspace heading toward the Trellixia System. Behind them they left the scattering remains of three Human warships.

In the Traxis Three System, High Commander Kaldre listened as the communications officer informed him of what Battle Commander Balforr had discovered in the Jarvid System. Three Human ships had been destroyed and a fourth one was missing. Balforr strongly believed it was in or near the home system. His fleet and support fleets were currently in route.

"Why scan our systems unless they are planning an attack?" asked Second Officer Calaah.

"Exactly," replied Kaldre. "From what Battle Commander Balforr has told me the Humans want revenge for what we did to their world."

Calaah didn't look surprised. "What should we do?"

Kaldre shifted his gaze to the viewscreens. He now had full control of the shipyards in the Traxis Three System. Perhaps he could use this Human infiltration as reason for the High Command to give him control of even more shipyards in other Trellixian systems. "Set a course for Trellixia," he ordered. "This will be an ideal time to speak to the other High Commanders. Perhaps now they will see the wisdom of building more of the new and more powerful battlecruisers."

High Commander Kaldre was pleased with the course of events. The appearance of the Humans was all he would need to persuade the High Command to follow his suggestions. It would also make his power and influence on the High Command even greater.

Chapter Sixteen

Captain Dolan felt his heart rate quicken as the *Fury* exited hyperspace in the Trellixian home system. They would be the first alien ship to ever see the world that birthed the conquering lizard race.

"All systems are powered up and working at optimum levels," reported Chloe.

On the main screen, the image shifted to show the yellow star in the center of the system.

"We are at Condition One," reported Katana as she turned to face the captain. "Weapons are ready to fire as needed."

"Colony ship electronic signature has been activated," added Derek. "Everything seems to be working fine."

Captain Dolan leaned back in his chair, letting out a deep sigh of relief. So far so good. "Were we detected when we came out of hyperspace?" Dolan knew that for a few seconds before the electronic signature was activated there was a slim chance they could be detected.

Chloe shook her head. "I don't believe so. Our sensors are showing hundreds of Trellixian vessels and we haven't scanned the entire system yet. There are so many ships exiting and entering hyperspace the Trellixians probably didn't even notice our arrival."

Mark stood up and looked at Katana. "Begin launching the probes."

"All of them?" Katana asked. "Shouldn't we keep at least one of them back in reserve in case we spot something we want better scans of?"

"Launch all of them. Lieutenant Masterson can help figure out their courses. Keep in mind I want to stay in this system as briefly as possible so there is no point in holding a probe back."

Katana walked over to Brett's console and the two began going over the courses for the probes.

"We have eight probes left," Brett said. Our initial sensor readings indicate fourteen planets and a large number of moons. There are three asteroid fields as well."

Katana looked at the tactical display showing what they knew of the system so far. More red threat icons were steadily appearing as the ship's sensors scanned more of the system. She leaned forward and began pointing out where she wanted the probes to go on a map of the system Brett had up on one of his computer screens. After a few minutes of discussion they were both satisfied with the results.

"Ready to begin probe launch," she reported.

"Do it," Mark ordered as he sat back down in his command chair. "How long will it take the probes to do their detailed scans of the system?"

"Six hours," Katana reported, her whiskers becoming stiffer. "At that point we can activate the self-destructs and leave the system.""

Mark turned his attention to Chloe. "What are the odds of one or more of our probes being detected?"

"Eighty-two percent," Chloe replied. "There are just too many ships in the system."

Mark took a deep breath. What they were doing was risky but they had to take the chance. The information on the Trellixian home system was crucial for the war effort. "Continue with the launch."

"Probes launching," reported Katana.

Her cat eyes were focused on the tactical display, which showed the probes leaving the *Fury*. After a minute their icons vanished to be replaced by small flashing symbols indicating the approximate position of each probe. Due to the special coating on the outside of the probes not even the *Fury's* sensors could detect them once they were launched.

In Lab Two Lisa and Brenda watched breathlessly as the electronic signature device hummed away. The computer screen showed everything working within the set parameters. Both felt the tension as they knew what would happen if the device failed. They were in a hostile system full of enemy warships.

"Everything looks fine here," Lisa informed Derek. The two engineers were keeping a worried watch on the equipment. If anything failed they were prepared to make a quick repair as long as it was nothing major. Lisa wished they would have had the time to build a second device in case the first one failed.

Brenda stood up and stretched. "It's going to take the probes hours to scan all the planets and moons in this system. That's a long time for us to pose as a Trellixian colony ship."

Lisa was in agreement. That worried her as well. "We don't know what type of traffic control they have in the system. As many ships that are constantly coming and going it has to be quite efficient. After a while, they are bound to wonder why we haven't checked in with them. At some point they'll send a ship to investigate."

Brenda looked thoughtful. "Can we send a message saying we're having some mechanical issues and will be staying at this location until they're resolved."

"Maybe," Lisa answered as she thought over Brenda's suggestion. "We know the Trellixian language and we've intercepted their messages before. I'll contact Captain Dolan and suggest we prepare a message in case we're contacted by their traffic control. A malfunction on the ship seems the best scenario to go with. It might buy us a little bit of time."

Mark listened to Lisa over the comm and agreed with her suggestion. He would have Marissa prepare a message in the Trellixian language claiming the ship was having a minor problem with its sublight drive and that it should be resolved in a few hours. That way when and if they were contacted they would be prepared with a response.

In space, the eight probes spread out and quickly moved away from the *Fury* on their sublight drives. The special material coating the outer hull of the small probes should make them difficult to detect even in this system. Each probe moved away from the ship on a different course. If everything went as planned in six hours all the tactical data on this system would be gathered and safely stored in the *Fury's* data banks.

An hour passed and the *Fury's* tactical display began to light up with more detailed information. There were twelve hundred spacecraft currently in the system of different types. Ships were constantly coming and going both in hyperspace and using their sublight drives. The space around planets five and six was filled with red threat icons representing ships. There were also a large number of orbital constructs around both planets.

"There are several orbital stations around both the primary planets which have obviously been built to house large numbers of Trellixians," Derek said as he examined the data coming in. "The largest is over forty kilometers in length and twelve in diameter. It is rotating which indicates it has its own gravity due to centrifugal force."

Brett nodded. He had seen the same information. "I would love to see inside one of those. They're big enough to have their own internal weather systems." It was hard to believe artificial structures as large as these could exist. It was far beyond anything Earth or the Voltrex could do.

Mark turned to gaze at Brett. "Somehow I don't think the Trellixians will be inviting us for a tour anytime soon."

Marissa suddenly began listening to a message coming in over her comm system. "Captain, we have a request from Trellixian traffic control to explain why we have stayed at this position for the past hour. The other colony ships which got here when we did have already arrived at planet five to begin loading colonists."

"They have mistakenly identified us as being part of a colony fleet," Katana said with a low growl coming from the back of her throat. "Very foolish of them."

"Send the prepared message," Mark ordered. If they could make the Trellixians think they were repairing some minor damage they just might be able to buy enough time to finish this mission.

Marissa sent the message and then seemed to make a reply to another message. Finally she looked at the captain. "They wanted to know if they needed to send out a repair ship. I told them that wasn't necessary and we were capable of completing the repairs ourselves. We're supposed to dock at the primary space station in orbit of planet five for our load of colonists as soon as our subspace drive is repaired."

"They're going to get suspicious eventually," Katana said, her face showing concern. "They may also realize shortly we are not part of the colonization fleet which will bring up more questions."

"We'll cross that road when it gets here," Mark replied. At least for a while they had bought the probes some more time.

Another thirty minutes passed and suddenly alarms began sounding in the Command Center. Captain Dolan's eyes instantly went to the sensor console. "What is it?"

"We're detecting ships exiting hyperspace all through the comet zone," reported Kia.

Katana's face paled slightly. "Trellixian battlecruisers; they must be searching for our ships."

Mark's face took on a worried look. "That means they'll be searching for our probes as well. How many battlecruisers are there in the system itself not counting the ones that just jumped in?"

"One hundred and eighteen," Kia replied. "There are still a few ships on the far side of the star we haven't identified yet."

Mark glanced at the tactical display, showing the new red threat icons in the comet belt. "Well, they can search all they want there. They won't find us."

"They'll realize that after a while," Katana said. "Once they do they will begin searching the system. At some point they will grow wary of the story we used to explain why we're still in this location. When they do we could have Trellixian battlecruisers jumping in on top of us."

"Lieutenant Thomas, make sure our weapons are ready," ordered Mark. "If any Trellixian battlecruisers approaches closer than fifteen hundred kilometers you are to destroy it. Don't wait for my orders; destroy it immediately. Lieutenant Masterson, if we become engaged in combat take us into hyperspace and set a course back to the system where we left the rest of the fleet. Katana, before we jump make sure we have all the probe data and order their self-destruction. I don't want to risk the Trellixians capturing a single one of them."

Mark settled back in his command chair. There was nothing else he could to. Now they just had to wait and hope the probes could finish their mission.

-

The probes continued to spread out through the system. One of the probes was only four million kilometers from planet five and in the process of taking detailed scans. Sensors scanned the shipyards, space stations, and habitats in orbit as well as the constant movement of hundreds of cargo shuttles between the stations and the planet. The probe also took detailed images of the massive city covering much of the landmasses of the Trellixians' home world.

-

Inside the Command Center of the main space station in orbit above Trellixia alarms on a sensor detection panel began going off.

Commander Zaloff looked at the panel in confusion. "What is that alarm?" He could think of no reason for it to be going off. It was set to detect unauthorized scans of the station. In all the years he had commanded the station that particular alarm had never sounded.

"We're being scanned," reported the sensor officer in front of the panel.

"Is it one of our ships?" If it was Zaloff would have its commanding officer demoted. Scans of any of the shipyards or space stations above Trellixia were prohibited.

The sensor officer shook his head. "Not that I can tell. The scan is coming from an area where there are no ships."

Commander Zaloff recalled the warning he received earlier about alien probes being detected in the Norest System. Could there now be probes in the Trellixia System? "Dispatch a pair of battlecruisers to the area and inform them there may be an alien probe in the system. They are to scan for any unknown contacts. If one is detected they are to notify me immediately."

Zaloff decided not to notify the High Command until he had more information.

"One of our probes may have been detected," Second Officer Katana reported with a worried frown on her face. "There are two Trellixian battlecruisers inbound toward its current position."

Chloe turned around to face the captain with her hands on her   hips. "The Trellixians may have detected the probe's sensor scans."

Mark looked at the tactical display, which was now showing an expanded view of the region that particular probe was in. Two red threat icons were quickly approaching the area. "How soon before the two battlecruisers reach the probe?"

"Fifteen minutes," reported Chloe.

"Has it completed scanning the Trellixian home world?"

"Yes," confirmed Chloe. "We have excellent data from the probe."

Mark knew that as soon as he ordered the probe to self-destruct, the Trellixians would begin an all out search in the rest of the system for the remainder of the probes. "As soon as the Trellixian battlecruisers get within two thousand kilometers of the probe send the self-destruct order."

"What about the other probes?" asked Katana. "Should we destroy them as well?"

"We'll wait on them," Mark replied after a moment's thought. "The *Fury* at the moment is in no danger. If the Trellixians discover a second probe I will order them all to activate their self-destructs. What are the Trellixian battlecruisers in the comet zone doing?"

"They are in a search pattern and are systematically probing the comet region," replied Chloe. "It will take them over a day to scan all of it."

In space, the two Trellixian battlecruisers cautiously approached the supposed location of the probe. At three thousand kilometers, they began to detect a small area of sensor interference ahead. At two thousand kilometers, a brilliant flash of light suddenly blossomed ahead of the two ships. The area of interference promptly disappeared.

"The probe, if that's what it was, has self-destructed," the sensor officer reported to Commander Zaloff. "The two battlecruisers are reporting there is nothing remaining."

Zaloff was not surprised by this. The same thing had occurred in the Norest System. It was time to notify the High Command they had alien probes scanning the home system. Zaloff was certain his information would send the High Command into an uproar.

Battle Commander Balforr had just received the report of an alien probe being found in the home system. He had been right about where the missing Human ship had gone. "Drop us out of hyperspace 100,000 kilometers from Trellixia," he ordered. "As soon as we exit hyperspace I want all ships scanning for any signs of alien probes."

"You think there are more?" asked Second Officer Albion.

Balforr nodded. "I am sure of it. We must find that Human ship and destroy it. We can't let it escape with the information on our systems it's gathered. We have no idea how many other of our star systems the Humans may have scanned and escaped undetected."

"Ten minutes to hyperspace dropout," reported Joltan from the Helm.

"Have the fleet ready for combat if we detect any probes or the Human ship. Also check with our ships in the comet zone to see if they've detected anything."

Instantly alarms began sounding and red lights started flashing. Balforr knew his crew and those on the rest of his ships would be rushing to their battlestations. He had to find the Human ship. He had destroyed three of the enemy ships so far and he wanted to destroy this final one to make his victory complete.

Mark was not surprised when the sensor alarms began sounding again. On the tactical display, more red threat icons began to appear near the Trellixian home planet.

"One hundred and twelve more warships," Chloe quickly reported.

"We're receiving a general broadcast in English," reported Marissa in surprise. "I'll put it on the speakers."

"This is Battle Commander Balforr to the Human ship hiding somewhere in our star system. I know you're here and when I find your ship I am going to destroy it. You will never return to Earth with the data you've gathered."

"Balforr!" said Mark, his eyes widening. This Battle Commander had nearly destroyed Earth. "Locate the source of that signal."

Marissa touched some icons on her screen and then replied. "It's coming from one of the vessels which just jumped into the system."

Mark had to control his anger. He would like nothing better than to jump the *Fury* to the location of Balforr's command ship and destroy it.

"Try to locate which ship that message came from," Mark ordered. If the opportunity presented itself he just might try to destroy Balforr and his ship.

"Battle Commander Balforr's fleet is beginning to split up and move away from the planet," Chloe reported. "He must be searching for more of our probes."

Mark took in a deep breath. "How long before they find more of our probes or us?"

Chloe seemed to close her eyes as if concentrating. "No longer than twenty minutes. The Trellixians now have so many ships searching for our probes they are bound to be discovered."

Mark made a quick decision. "We'll wait until the next probe is detected. When they do we'll send the self-destruct order and detonate all the probes."

"What about us?" asked Katana. "Do we leave at that time also?"

Looking at the tactical display showing the Trellixian battlecruisers, Mark still had a powerful urge to try to take Battle Commander Balforr out. It would be a huge moral victory for Earth. "Maybe," he answered reluctantly. "We'll see when the time comes."

-

High Commander Kaldre made his way into the High Command's meeting room and saw a number of the High Commanders in heated argument. Seeing his arrival, the arguing died down. "Where did these alien ships come from?" demanded High Commander Danaar. "Battle Commander Balforr claims these are Voltrex ships operated by Humans."

"He's probably correct," Kaldre replied. "Balforr destroyed three of them in the Jarvid System. "One was missing and is probably the source of the probe which recently self-destructed."

"Are there more probes in our system?" asked High Commander Olnarr, a panicked look on his face. "How could these ships get so far into the Empire without being detected?"

Kaldre looked at the other High Commanders. "There are undoubtedly more probes. The Humans are in the process of scanning our systems before launching an attack against our core worlds."

Kaldre was going to use this opportunity to scare the other High Commanders into turning more shipyards and resources over to his control. He knew the Humans didn't have the forces to actually threaten the Empire but in the state of mind the other High Commanders were in they would not realize this.

"Attack our core worlds!" cried out High Commander Olnarr. "Why would they do that?"

"After what we did to Earth they would like to see the utter destruction of our Empire," Kaldre replied. "The Voltrex are furnishing them ships. Those ships are equipped with Jelnoid technology and weapons. They can blast any battlecruiser we have out of space. That's why I have been asking that we dedicate more of our shipyards to building more of the new battlecruisers. If we don't it's only a matter of time before we see some if not most of our core worlds under attack."

The assembled High Commanders looked uneasily at one another. None were sure what to say. It was hard to imagine any threat which could endanger the core worlds of the Empire yet an alien probe had been detected only a few minutes ago.

"If we turn over more of our shipyards we will not be able to produce the colony and cargo ships necessary to handle our growing population," growled High Commander Trammor. "If we do as you ask we run the risk of massive civil unrest on numerous worlds due to food shortages. Billions of our people could die."

"Billions more will die if the Humans attack our worlds," Kaldre pointed out, seeing the wavering look in some of the High Commander's faces. "Give me control of the shipyards and I will keep us safe from attack."

High Commander Thatrex broke the silence. "I propose we give High Commander Kaldre command of ten additional shipyards. That should be sufficient to build the ships he is requesting."

"Ten shipyards!" uttered High Commander Trammor in horror. "We will never be able to make the food shipments required to feed our people. There will be massive food riots on our worlds."

"Five hundred of the new battlecruisers," said High Commander Kaldre. "Once we have five hundred more of the new warships we can put the shipyards back to producing colony ships and cargo ships. We would only need the ones at Traxis Three to continue building the battlecruisers. They would be replacing those lost in battle."

High Commander Trammor shook his head. "We need to build more shipyards to meet the rising demand for colony ships and cargo ships."

"Give me command of the shipyards while at the same time we can begin building the ones High Commander Trammor wants," suggested Kaldre in the way of a compromise.

He hoped this compromise would give him control of the shipyards. If it did then he could build the ships to destroy the Humans. Once their system was destroyed, the Voltrex would not have a base close enough to the heart of the Empire to launch an attack. He would save the Empire and have gained considerable influence in the High Command.

High Commander Balforr was growing anxious. Time was passing and no more of the Humans' probes had been found. The fleets in the comet belt were also reporting no signs of the Human ship.

"Where are they?" muttered Balforr as he gazed at the tactical display. They had to be nearby to receive the data from the probes.

"Got one!" called out Second Officer Albion. "The *Warhammer* reports a probe in its vicinity. They are closing to investigate."

On the tactical display, a red threat icon flared into existence.

"Have the ship try to trace the probe's communications," ordered Balforr. "Maybe we can find where the Humans' flagship is hiding."

Albion quickly passed the order on to the communications officer.

"We may have another probe that's been detected," reported Kia. "One of the new Trellixian ships that recently arrived is four thousand kilometers away from probe four and is just sitting there."

Mark looked over at Chloe. "What do you think?"

Chloe took a few seconds to study the data. "I've ordered the probe to stop all communication. The Trellixians may be trying to trace where the probe's data is being directed."

"Order the probe to self-destruct," ordered Mark. "We can't risk it revealing our location." He had hoped it would take longer before the next probe was detected.

Second Officer Katana looked questionably at the captain. "What about the other probes?"

"Have all of them self-destruct," ordered Mark reluctantly. "We've gathered enough data on this system. It's time we get back to our other ships and set a course for Earth."

A few moments later six of the icons representing the locations of the probes swelled up and vanished. However, the seventh probe still registered as functioning.

Mark looked at Katana. "Why didn't the seventh probe self-destruct?"

"I don't know. It should have received the signal. We'll send it again."

After a few more moments Katana shook her head. "We must have a malfunction in the probe's self-destruct."

This wasn't good. They couldn't leave the probe in the system for the Trellixians to capture. It was loaded with Jelnoid technology. "Lieutenant Masterson, plot a hyperspace jump to the probe's location. We'll have to use our weapons to destroy it."

"Captain, when we jump to the probe's location the Trellixians may suspect we're not a colony ship," said Derek with concern in his voice. "We're supposed to be repairing our subspace drive. They will know we were lying about that."

"It's a risk we'll have to take," Mark replied. "Have Lisa and Brenda come back to the Command Center. We may need them up here."

—

Battle Commander Balforr frowned when he began receiving reports of a number of large explosions throughout the Trellixia System.

"The *Warhammer* reports the probe near it has exploded," reported Albion.

Balforr stood up and stepped off the command pedestal coming to a stop in front of the large tactical display. "They've destroyed their probes before we could capture one. Was the *Warhammer* able to trace the probe's communications?"

"They managed to get a general direction but the only vessel in that region is a colony ship."

On the viewscreen, a blinking green icon indicated the colony ship Albion was referring to. "Why is that colony ship there?"

"It's have trouble with its sublight drive. It should be finished with repairs shortly."

"Something doesn't seem right. Have a pair of our battlecruisers jump to the colony ship's location. I want them within visual range."

Albion looked confused. "What do you suspect?"

"We haven't been able to locate the Human ship yet we have a colony ship with mysterious sublight engine problems in the same area the probe was sending data."

"You believe the Humans might be masquerading as one of our ships?"

Balforr nodded his head. "The Humans are very conniving. I wouldn't put it past them."

Battle Commander Balforr turned his attention back to the tactical display just in time to see the icon of the colony ship in question blink out. "What just happened?" Could he be about to lose the Humans again?

"The ship jumped into hyperspace," the sensor operator reported.

Balforr's eyes narrowed sharply. "Search the entire system. See if it reappears anywhere else."

For several long minutes there was no trace of the mysterious colony ship and then it reappeared on almost the other side of the system. For a moment its icon showed red and then shifted to green.

"They must be using some type of sensor screening technology," the sensor officer said. "The ship when it first dropped out of hyperspace registered as an unknown and then changed to a colony ship."

"I want the entire fleet to jump to that location. As soon as any of our ships have a target lock they are to fire."

Albion looked concerned. "What if it is one of our colony ships?"

Anger showed on Balforr's face. "It isn't! This is a trick of the Humans. I want that ship destroyed!"

-

The *Fury* exited hyperspace and instantly activated its electronic signature so the battleship would register as a Trellixian colony ship. Captain Dolan knew there were a few precious seconds before the disguise was activated that the *Fury* might be detected.

"Electronic signature activated," reported Derek as he checked his computer console. "Everything is working normally."

Mark looked over at Kia. "Any signs we've been detected?"

"Not yet," Kia replied as she checked her sensors.

"Have you located the probe?"

"Working on it," Kia replied. "I should have its location in another minute or two."

Mark leaned back in his command chair. Even for the battleship, the special coating on the probe made it difficult to detect.

Alarms began sounding on the sensor console and Kia's face turned pale with worry. "Large numbers of Trellixian battlecruisers are jumping into hyperspace."

"Damn," said Mark, guessing what it signified. "We've been detected. "Lieutenant Thomas, as soon as the first Trellixian battlecruiser exits hyperspace target it with our missiles."

"Yes, sir," Thomas replied as he concentrated on his tactical console.

"Kia, find me that probe. We need to destroy it so we can get out of here."

"I'm still looking for it," Kia replied as her hands flew over her computer screen pressing icons.

On the ship's main viewscreen, several Trellixian battlecruisers stormed out of hyperspace instantly locking their weapons onto the *Fury* and firing. The screen became awash in energy as several fusion missiles and a dozen energy beams impacted the screen. Moments later both Trellixian battlecruisers were blown apart as the *Fury's* fusion missiles knocked their screens down and then several more slammed into the unprotected armored hulls of the warships.

"First two targets are down," Kia reported breathlessly. "More battlecruisers are emerging from hyperspace."

-

Battle Commander Balforr grimaced as he saw the first two ships of his special fleet to arrive had already been destroyed. Scans were indicating they had a Voltrex battleship in front of them. "All ships are to concentrate their fire. I want that ship destroyed!"

Space lit up with explosions and Balforr shook his head in anger as another one of his ships exploded in a ball of fusion fire.

-

"Probe located!" called out Kia excitedly. "It's three thousand kilometers distant."

"Target it," Mark ordered, leaning forward in his command chair. The *Fury* shook violently and one of the consoles on the far wall exploded in a shower of sparks.

"Energy shield down to 67 percent," warned Lieutenant Thomas as he shifted his weapons fire to another Trellixian battlecruiser. "Missile launched toward the location of the probe."

The *Fury* shook again even more violently and alarms began sounding.

"Damage to decks seven and eight at frame fourteen," reported Katana. "We have several compartments open to space and we're venting atmosphere. Emergency bulkheads and hatches have engaged."

"Energy screen is at 42 percent and dropping," reported Lieutenant Thomas.

On the main viewscreen, another Trellixian battlecruiser was in trouble. Its energy screen was wavering and fusion energy from the missiles was striking its hull, causing huge rents to open up. Secondary explosions began to hurl large pieces of the ship's hull into space. Moments later it blew apart.

"Target destroyed," reported Kia. "The probe has been eliminated."

"Sublight drive is down," reported Katana worriedly. "We can't take much more of this."

"Energy screen is down to 18 percent," added Lieutenant Thomas. "It's about to fail!"

"Get us out of here!" ordered Mark, his hands clenched into tight fists. He knew his ship was taking major damage.

"Activating hyperspace drive," reported Brett.

The ship began shaking violently and then the *Fury* entered hyperspace. Everything became eerily quiet.

Mark felt the tension leave him and his heart quit pounding. For a moment he thought they were all going to die. "Status report."

"Not good," Katana replied as she listened to the different departments beginning to report in. "The chief engineer reports at least two hours to repair the sublight drive. We have several ruptures in the hull and seven compartments open to space. There are twenty-two confirmed dead, five missing and sixty-three injured as of this moment. That could increase substantially once we get a better feel for the damage."

"Can we make it back to Earth?" Mark didn't like the idea of being stranded in Trellixian space.

Katana nodded. "We're going to have to do a lot of work on the ship but we should be able to."

"When we get to the rendezvous point we can have the other ships send over some damage repair crews. That should speed things up."

"We'll have to be careful," Katana added. "The Trellixians will be searching for us now and that electronic signature we were using to fool them won't work again."

"Take us to Condition Two; we've been at battle stations way too long. All crewmembers not involved in repairs could use some rest." Mark stood up. He was going to make a personal tour of his ship. He wanted to get a better feel for the damage.

-

Lisa let out a deep breath. Her heart had been beating rapidly throughout the entire engagement. There had been a few minutes when she thought she was going to die.

"I'm glad that's over," she said over the comm connecting her to the other four special lieutenants. "I was never so scared in my life."

"Same for me," replied Kia. "When the energy screen began to fail I thought for sure the *Fury* was going to be destroyed."

Brett then spoke. "We got lucky. Another few seconds and we wouldn't have made it out."

"Some of the crew didn't," Derek said sadly. "The latest reports are that at least twenty-two of our crew perished in the battle. There are a number in med bay who are in critical condition."

"This is my last mission," said Brenda determinedly. "I think I would rather be back in Complex One doing research."

"We had to come," said Lisa. "If we hadn't designed the electronic signature device, the *Fury* would never have been able to scan the Trellixians' home system. We have all the data we need now to come up with a viable war plan."

"Maybe," said Derek with doubt in his voice. "I just don't see how even with the help of the Voltrex we can defeat an Empire comprising of several thousand inhabited planets."

"We'll find a way," Lisa said confidently. "When we get back home the scientists and military people will think of something." Lisa hoped they would. She could not imagine living her entire life under the constant threat of war.

Battle Commander Balforr was fuming. He had lost five of his new battlecruisers in the recent battle. He had been expecting to find a Voltrex battlecruiser, not one of their accursed battleships. Even so, his ship's sensor readings indicted they had seriously damaged the vessel. Another few seconds and he was certain they would have destroyed it. It was obvious they needed to come up with a new strategy to deal with these powerful vessels. His ships had performed better than the regular battlecruisers would have but still not well enough to satisfy Balforr. He would see if he could arrange a meeting with High Commander Kaldre. Perhaps between the two of them they could come up with a method to deal with the Voltrex battleships.

The *Fury* dropped out of hyperspace at the coordinates where they had left the other three fleet ships. A quick scan by the sensors failed to locate any of the three vessels.

"Where are they?" asked Captain Dolan, his eyes narrowing. "Captain Wilson was supposed to wait here."

Kia double-checked the sensors. "There's nothing on the sensors indicating another ship within range."

"Are you picking up anything?" asked Katana, her cat eyes taking on a worried look.

Kia adjusted the sensors and began scanning again. Almost instantly, the sensors picked up three areas of contacts. Kia's face turned pale and she could barely talk. "I think we're picking up wreckage of some type."

"What type of wreckage?" demanded Mark, standing up and gazing at the tactical display.

"It's our ships," said Chloe in a subdued voice. "The material the wreckage consists of matches our missing vessels."

"The Trellixians must have found them," Katana said, her whiskers drooping. "All three vessels were destroyed."

Mark felt as if he had been hit in the gut. He had never expected to return and find this. Now the *Fury* was alone in the heart of the Trellixian Empire and heavily damaged. "Take us back into hyperspace," he ordered. "We don't dare stay here. The Trellixians could show up at any moment. They may suspect we would return to this system." Mark could not believe he had lost three of his ships. Captain Wilson had been an intelligent and capable commanding officer. He had been counting on the other three ships to help with repairs to the *Fury*. Now he needed to find a place to hide his vessel while the repairs were done. If they were to go into battle in their current condition the battleship wouldn't last long.

-

Moments later the *Fury* was back in hyperspace, seeking a safe refuge. In the heart of the Trellixian Empire one lone and damaged Human warship was on the run hoping to someday make it back to Earth.

Chapter Seventeen

President Katelyn Hathaway stood outside of Complex One on an observation platform on the large mountain, which hid the secret base. The Rocky Mountains were still covered in deep snow and it was quite chilly even here, protected from the wind. Looking down, the valleys were also buried beneath deep layers of the white stuff.

"It's a beautiful sight," said Secretary of State Maggie Rayne. "I even saw the sun come out for a few minutes the other day."

Katelyn nodded. "Yes, the chemical we're spraying in the air is beginning to clear the atmosphere of pollutants from the nuclear explosions. Even the radiation level in most areas has dropped to reasonable levels."

"In another month or two our people will be able to leave the protective domes if they like," replied Maggie, leaning against a protective railing and looking up into the gray cast sky.

"Professor Wilkens says it will take a few more months after that for the temperatures to begin to moderate. We'll still have several more hard winters before everything returns to normal."

Maggie nodded her understanding. "We still have sufficient food supplies though I understand our Chinese counterparts will be on short rations until they can get crops planted."

"Yes, several of their food storage sites were taken out by the Trellixians in the last stages of fighting in China. Fortunately enough of their supplies survived so they should be able to get through this."

A few flakes of snow began to fall and Maggie let out a deep sigh. They had all seen enough snow for a while. "Any word from Captain Dolan?"

Katelyn shook her head. "No, General Mitchell doesn't expect to hear anything for another week or two. At this stage, Captain Dolan and his fleet should be deep inside the core worlds of the Trellixian Empire. That makes it too dangerous to attempt any communications. Once they've exited the core worlds they should send us all the data they've collected."

The snow was starting to come down harder. The valley below was now shrouded in darkness by the white stuff.

"We should go inside," said one of the Secret Service Agents who were tasked with the president's safety. "This storm is supposed to get worse."

Katelyn took a deep breath. It was nice to get outside and breathe some fresh air every once and a while. "Let's go back to my office. We can talk some more there." Katelyn took one last long look at the snow-covered mountains. She would like to be able to go out and walk among the trees that covered the valley floor. Someday, when the snow was gone, she was determined to do just that.

General Mitchell was standing in his underground Command Center being briefed about the current situation on the planet as well as in orbit. "We've finished our searches in South America," General Briggs reported. "We've located another two million survivors and are in the process of moving them to safe locations."

"Only two million?" said Mitchell, stunned at the low number.

Briggs nodded. "They didn't have the military forces like we do. What little resistance they were able to put up was quickly overrun and large numbers of Trellixian troops scoured the countries, eliminating survivors. The ones we found had taken refuge in the mountains."

Mitchell let out a deep sigh. "Africa is much the same. Only the country of South Africa has a large number of survivors; nearly four million. All survivors from the other African countries are being moved there."

Mitchell turned his gaze to the large viewscreens in the front of the Command Center. Several of them were focused on the warships in orbit and others showed different views of the Earth. Unfortunately, the clouds and dust particles in the atmosphere obscured most of the views of Earth. In a few areas the clouds were thinner and the surface could actually be seen. The nuclear winter was rapidly being abated and with a little luck soon the sun would be shining once more on most of the planet.

On a tactical display, over a dozen large contacts were visible. These were huge transport planes which were currently spraying the Voltrex chemical in the atmosphere to reduce the effects of the nuclear weapons that had been dropped on Earth. General Mitchell knew that other surviving countries were doing the same thing.

"We haven't located any additional Trellixian troops in the past month," General Briggs continued with his report. "There may be a few stragglers in some of the areas we haven't managed to search yet, but there can't be many."

"Keep searching," ordered General Mitchell. "I don't want any of them missed." Mitchell was determined to eradicate any Trellixians who still might be in hiding. After what they had done to Earth he would show them no mercy.

-

Professor Wilkens left the Communications Center feeling disappointed. There was still no word from Captain Dolan. Wilkens was greatly concerned about the mission he had talked Lisa and the others into going on. If something happened to any of them he would never forgive himself. Lisa was like a daughter to him and he thought about her every day.

After a few minutes he stepped into the main lab where several of his associates were working.

"Still no word?" asked Amber Stone who was a systems analyst. She could see the disappointed look in Professor Wilkens' eyes.

Wilkens shook his head. "No, none of the ships have reported back since they entered the section of space containing the Trellixian core worlds."

"It's a safety precaution," Amber replied. "They're just being careful to ensure the ships aren't located by their communication signals. I'm sure once they're back outside the core worlds we'll hear from them immediately."

"I know you're right," admitted Wilkens with a deep sigh. "I just wish I had never sent any of them on this mission."

Amber understood how the professor felt. He had talked to her numerous times about Lisa and the other four talented young people. "In another month or two they will all be back and working in the labs. I'm sure they will keep you busy every day with their new ideas and discoveries."

Wilkens smiled weakly. "You're right. The best thing for me is to get back to work and quit worrying. Captain Dolan will keep them all safe. Now, where were we on that analysis of the new metal we're developing for our pulse weapons?"

Amber smiled. "It's finished. Come with me and we can review the results on my computer console. I think you will be quite pleased with the analysis."

-

In space, Admiral Edwards looked over the latest reports on the space construction projects currently ongoing. The first of the massive one thousand-meter battlestations had been finished and construction on the next two was progressing rapidly. It helped that most of the parts had been prefabricated by the Voltrex and brought in on cargo ships. All that was necessary was putting the parts together in the proper sequence. It was much like putting together a massive jigsaw puzzle. There were also eleven hundred small defensive satellites in orbit armed with a pair of Jelnoid energy cannons.

"The shipyard is progressing nicely," reported Captain Nelson. "Both repair bays are completed and they are in the process of finishing the armor on the hull and installing the energy cannons."

"Just in time, too," Admiral Edwards answered. "Fleet Commander Kamuss will be here shortly with his fleet and a number of his ships will need repairs. The Voltrex have sent some of their people to help operate the shipyard and conduct the necessary work on their ships. Our own people will be working alongside them."

Captain Nelson glanced at a viewscreen showing the completed battlestation. It looked awesome and deadly. A few fighter-bombers were currently flying patrols around it. The same was true of the almost completed shipyard. A full wing of fighter-bombers were patrolling it as well. On another screen, one of the two newer battlestations being assembled could be seen. Only a few sections had been connected so far. "I'll feel a lot better when those battlestations are done. The six stations and the defense satellites should be able to protect the Earth from even the most powerful Trellixian attack."

"Another year and all six stations will be done," Edwards replied. His gaze moved to the large tactical display, showing several of the small Voltrex-built patrol ships orbiting the Moon. Several more were further out on patrol. Human crews had been trained and were now operating them to help monitor all incoming hyperspace traffic.

"We currently have twenty-two Voltrex heavy cargo ships in the system as well as two missile replenishment ships," added Captain Nelson. "Those two ships have more than enough missiles to refill all of Fleet Commander Kamuss' ships."

Admiral Edwards was glad the two replenishment ships were here. Earth had sufficient missiles for her own ships but did not as of yet have a large reserve of the large forty-megaton missiles. The Voltrex Federation had the manufacturing facilities to produce the missiles in large quantities. There were also four other missile replenishment ships in transit which would arrive in another couple of weeks under heavy escort as well as reinforcements for the ships Fleet Commander Kamuss had lost.

"Those enemy ships in the Alpha Centauri System make me nervous," Captain Nelson said. "Perhaps when Fleet Commander Kamuss arrives we can do something about them."

Edwards nodded. "It's a thought. When the Fleet Commander gets here it's something we'll discuss."

Edwards turned his attention to the sensor console as an alarm sounded.

"Battlecruiser *Lexington* is returning from their scan of the Alpha Centauri System," reported Lieutenant Williams. The Alpha Centauri System was a three star system. The Trellixians were in orbit around Proxima Centauri.

"Enemy fleets are still there," added Lieutenant Simmins. "No reported changes in numbers or ship types."

Captain Nelson looked over at Admiral Edwards. "I wonder why the Trellixians only have the one ship type for combat? All we've ever seen are battlecruisers."

"Let's hope it stays like that," Edwards answered. "I would not want to see them come up with a battleship. Have the fleet prepare for battle maneuvers. I have a few scenarios I want to run through." Edwards knew someday the Trellixians would return and attack the Solar System. When they did he intended to be ready.

Several days later Fleet Commander Kamuss breathed out a sigh of relief as his fleet dropped out of hyperspace in the Solar System. He had already contacted Admiral Edwards a few hours earlier informing him the two Voltrex fleets would be arriving.

"I wish Captain Dolan and the *Fury* were back," said Lieutenant Commander LeLath as she gazed at the viewscreen showing the yellow star ahead of them. "I have friends in that crew."

Kamuss was in agreement. He was intensely curious as to what Dolan had found in the Trellixian core worlds. "We'll see him," promised Kamuss. "We're staying in the Solar System long enough to hear firsthand what he discovered."

"You think he might have discovered a major weakness in the Trellixian Empire?"

"It's possible," answered Kamuss. "Fleet Command has high hopes for Captain Dolan's mission. We only have limited information about the Empire and that's from captured data files.

Many of those files were very vague on specifics, particularly population density on the Trellixian core worlds."

LeLath looked thoughtful. "We know from the colony worlds we attacked the population in the core worlds will be in the tens of billions. Those worlds will be so heavily populated that living space may even be restricted."

"That's just speculation," replied Kamuss. His gaze shifted from LeLath to the large viewscreen, now showing Earth. The planet was still mostly shrouded in cloud cover though in a few spots the clouds were broken, allowing the sun's rays to reach the surface. "We'll know more when Captain Dolan reports in."

LeLath nodded. "When we reach Earth I plan on going down to visit Captain Dolan's sister, Jennifer. I really enjoyed my visits with her during my last stay at Earth."

"We have two patrol ships and a squadron of the Humans' fighter-bombers on approach," reported Zalurr as a number of green icons appeared on the tactical display.

Kamuss looked at the display. "Routine ship identification. They want to ensure we really are who we say. Can't have a Trellixian fleet drop into the Solar System posing as friendlies."

"Fleet is forming up into standard escort formation," LeLath reported as the various sized green icons surrounding the *Claw of Honor* fell in around the flagship.

"I have communications with the new shipyard," added Meela. "They report both repair bays have been completed and are ready to receive our damaged ships. They also have a number of Voltrex station workers present who will be showing the Humans how to perform ship repairs."

Kamuss felt relief upon hearing the shipyard was functional. "What about missiles?" He didn't dare launch another attack against the Trellixians without a full complement of the forty-megaton missiles.

"There are two of our own missile replenishment ships here and four more due in a few more weeks."

Lieutenant Commander LeLath turned toward the Fleet Commander. "Which ships should we send in first?"

"Send in our battleships and then the battlecruisers. We'll save the support craft until last."

LeLath looked a little confused. "Is there a reason for that? A number of the support ships have suffered moderate to heavy damage."

Standing up, Fleet Commander Kamuss stepped closer to the large viewscreen showing Earth. "In the battles so far the support ships, except for the larger ones, have basically been targets for the Trellixians. In our next sortie I plan to leave the smaller support ships here at Earth and only take the larger ones. The fifty-megaton missiles the Trellixians have begun to use are too dangerous for the smaller vessels. Our battleships and battlecruisers can stand up to them for awhile; the smaller support ships cannot."

"So, we're just going to leave them here at Earth?"

Kamuss shook his head. "No, we'll use them for convoy duty escorting our cargo ships back to Federation space."

"Fleet Commander," said Meela. "Admiral Edwards is requesting to meet with you on the shipyard at your earliest convenience."

"Have my shuttle prepared," Kamuss ordered. "As soon as we have the two fleets safely in orbit around Earth I'll go over to the station."

LeLath quickly passed on the order. Several Voltrex security personnel would also go with the Fleet Commander. This was standard procedure anytime the Fleet Commander left the ship. In this instance it would be more ceremonial than anything else. "Your shuttle will be ready as soon as we achieve orbit."

Kamuss nodded. He was looking forward to meeting with Admiral Edwards and then later with General Mitchell. They had a lot to talk about.

-

Admiral Edwards watched as the *Claw of Honor* entered orbit around the Earth. Two of the large 2,200-meter Voltrex battleships were en route to the shipyard where they would be repaired.

"Fleet Commander Kamuss and Fleet Commander Masurl will be on board the shipyard shortly," Captain Nelson reported. "Fleet Commander Barvon will be there as well."

Lieutenant Simmins turned toward the admiral from Communications. "Major Brown reports the conference room is ready and she's available to receive guests."

Edwards stood up, nodding. "Then it's time for us to go greet our allies. Captain Nelson, you will be coming with me. Lieutenant Jefferson, you have the Command Center. Contact me if the need arises."

The tactical officer stood up and moved over to the command chair. "I'll keep you informed if there is a problem."

-

As they walked to the flight bay, the two men discussed the current tactical situation. They wanted to make sure they covered everything with the three Voltrex Fleet Commanders.

"I wish we had more information from Captain Dolan," said Nelson as they entered the flight bay. "All we have are the few Trellixian systems his ships surveyed before they entered the core worlds."

Admiral Edwards followed the captain through the hatch and stepped out onto the deck of the small flight bay, which contained several shuttles. "We'll have more eventually. I fully expect to receive additional data from the *Fury* in the next week or two."

Captain Nelson gestured toward one of the waiting shuttles where several Marines were standing by. "There's our ride. I hope you're right. Those four ships could be in a lot of trouble if they're detected. They're a long ways from home and if the Trellixians were to find them we'd never know."

"Captain Dolan's a very qualified officer," Edwards replied as he saluted the Marines and stepped on board the shuttle. "He'll make it back with his ships."

Nelson wasn't so sure. The Trellixians had a lot of ships and the further into the Empire Dolan went the more likely it became that at some point he would be detected. How could he get back home with potentially thousands of Trellixian warships hunting for his small fleet? Nelson was just glad it was Captain Dolan who would have to figure that out and not him.

Lieutenant Commander LeLath was in Complex One intending to see Captain Dolan's sister and then go out to eat. Complex One had some fabulous restaurants and LeLath enjoyed sampling new foods she had never eaten before. Fortunately as a Voltrex and being a feline species she could handle almost any type of food without fear of indigestion.

Going down the long corridor where Jennifer's apartment was, LeLath stopped at a closed door and knocked on it. After a moment it opened and a smiling Jennifer was standing there.

"LeLath!" exclaimed Jennifer, stepping forward and hugging the large cat person. "I'm so excited you could come by. Come inside."

Jennifer stepped aside, indicating for LeLath to enter. "We have so much to talk about. Is your fleet here waiting to hear my brother's report on the lizards' core worlds?"

LeLath stepped inside. This hugging thing the Humans did made her feel uncomfortable but she was becoming used to it. The females of the species seemed to do a lot more of it than the males.

"We're hoping to hear back from his fleet soon," replied LeLath. "We have some ships that need repairs so we decided to try out your new shipyard."

Jennifer nodded. "I heard it's ready to start working on ships. I believe they already have plans to enlarge it and eventually build a much larger one."

LeLath sat down on the comfortable sofa while Jennifer took a seat across from her.

"Would you like something to drink? I just made some tea. It's a green tea that tastes really good. I think you will like it."

"Of course," LeLath replied. On her last trip to the Solar System when she had been assigned to the *Vengeance*, she had come to like the taste of the Humans' tea. They had similar brews in the Federation but some of the ones here on Earth were unique.

LeLath looked around the small but comfortable apartment as Jennifer went to get the tea. The apartment still looked much the same since the last time she had been here except for a few more large pictures hanging on the walls. One of them was of Captain Dolan standing in front of what once was his parent's home. Mark and Jennifer had explained to her what happened to their parents during the war with the Trellixians. LeLath shuddered slightly knowing that could have easily been the fate of her own worlds and family members if the Trellixians hadn't been stopped by the Voltrex fleet. Now, with the addition of Jelnoid weapons technology furnished by the Humans, that fear had been pushed back.

Jennifer returned with the tea, handing LeLath a glass. She took a cautious sip and then smiled. "I like this. I need to take some back with me to the *Claw of Honor.*"

"No problem," replied Jennifer. "We can pick some up when we go out to eat."

For the next hour the two talked about what had been happening on Earth as well as the Voltrex fleet destroying Trellixian colonies.

"I share your disgust at wiping out those colonies," Jennifer said as she sipped her tea. "But I understand the necessity. You weren't here to see how merciless the Trellixians were when they were trying to wipe us out. I saw them kill helpless women and children without hesitation or remorse. Fleet Commander Kamuss is right. In this war there can only be one survivor. It's either them or us and I would much rather it be us."

LeLath let out a deep sigh. "Of course you're right and I understand that. I just wish there was another way. It seems the Trellixians have left us no other choice."

Jennifer finished her tea and stood up. "Let's go out to eat. I know a quaint little restaurant that serves great Italian food. If you like spicy food you're absolutely going to love this."

"I'm in the mood for something different. It's amazing all the different foods you have here on Earth. I can't wait to try this Italian food. I'm starving."

Jennifer laughed. "So am I and where we're going will be perfect."

The two left the apartment and headed toward the main shopping and eating venues in the complex. Both were looking forward to an exciting and enjoyable evening away from the worries of the war.

Fleet Commander Kamuss was down on Earth in President Hathaway's office meeting with Vice President Arnold, General Mitchell, General Briggs, and Professor Wilkens.

"It will take four weeks to repair all of your ships," General Mitchell said as he studied the report sent to him by Major Cynthia Brown who was the commander of the shipyard.

Kamuss nodded. "Yes, that's what Admiral Edwards told me. "That's acceptable. By that time the reinforcements I've requested from Fleet Command should be here."

President Katelyn leaned back in her chair, gazing at Fleet Commander Kamuss. This was the first time she had actually met the large feline. It still amazed her that a cat species could walk upright and speak English, even though Kamuss had a heavy accent almost like a constant purr.

"Hopefully by then we'll have Captain Dolan's report as well," said General Mitchell. "I'm expecting him to report in any day now."

"What about the Trellixian fleets camped out in Alpha Centauri?" asked Vice President Arnold. "Is there anything we can do about them?"

Kamuss nodded. "As soon as my battleships and battlecruisers have been repaired I will take my fleet and eliminate the Trellixian presence in that system."

"I will send some of our ships along as well," General Mitchell said. "We can make it a joint operation. It will be good for our ship crews to get used to working with one another."

"I agree," said Kamuss. "I suspect there will be many joint operations in our future. I am also requesting the Voltrex Federation send more supply ships and construction personnel to Earth. I would like to see all six battlestations completed before we start any major offensive against the Trellixians in this region."

"I must thank your people for furnishing us with the chemical to help clear Earth's atmosphere," said Katelyn. "I am already receiving reports of the cloud layer diminishing and the amount of dust and ash in the atmosphere decreasing."

"The atmosphere should be back to normal in a few more months," reported Professor Wilkens, "though it will take a year or two for the planet's temperature to return to normal. We have a lot of deep snow in locations which very seldom saw snow in the past."

Katelyn stood up and walked over to the window overlooking the huge underground complex. "It will be nice to be able to go outside without a heavy coat on. I've almost forgotten what the sun feels like."

"Someday the Trellixians will no longer be a threat," promised Kamuss, standing up and walking over to stand by Katelyn's side. "My people are determined to rid the galaxy of this threat."

"I just can't help but think of all the races the Trellixians have wiped out," said Katelyn, turning to face Kamuss. "When this is over there won't be an inhabited planet within hundreds, perhaps several thousand light years of Earth. It will be like Earth exists in a desert."

Kamuss understood what the president was saying. "Many of those worlds will eventually recover. In time life will return to them."

"I hope so," Katelyn replied. "In the meantime we must do everything in our power to remove the Trellixian menace from this section of the galaxy."

-

The group continued to talk for several more hours. In the end, President Katelyn felt much better about the direction the war was heading. With a little luck in a few more years Earth would be much safer and people would not have to be afraid of Trellixian battlecruisers reappearing overhead. It would be nice for the world to become more normal and free from constant fear.

Chapter Eighteen

Captain Dolan took in a deep breath. The *Fury* was hiding in the edge of a small dust cloud near a white dwarf star system still deep in the core of the Trellixian Empire.

"Repairs are progressing," Second Officer Katana reported. "We still like a few days to finish the final repairs to the hull."

"Status of our weapons?" Mark knew several weapon turrets had been destroyed in the brief encounter with the Trellixian fleet.

Katana shook her head. "We have three defensive turrets which were destroyed and have no way to replace them. We also have two missile tubes that were wrecked. Once again, we have no feasible way to repair them with the resources we have available. The hull could also use a new paint job. It's pretty scarred up."

Mark realized the entire fleet had a weakness. On long-range missions heavily damaged ships would need to be repaired. They had to develop some type of repair ship that could do repairs individual ships could not do on their own.

An alarm sounded on the sensor console, drawing Mark's attention.

"Trellixian battlecruiser is nosing around the periphery of the dust cloud," Kia reported as she watched her sensors. "I don't believe their sensors will be able to detect us. Their sensors aren't quite as good as ours."

"I concur," said Chloe. "As long as we stay this deep in the dust cloud we should be safe from detection."

Mark watched the tactical display as the red threat icon, designating the Trellixian battlecruiser, moved along the outside of the dust cloud. For nearly two weeks the *Fury* had hidden in the dusty confines of the nebula as much needed repairs were done to the ship. There had also been a funeral service for the twenty-eight crew personnel who had died at the battle in the Trellixians' home system. There were still a few in critical condition in the ship's med bay. Mark made it a habit of going down there and speaking with the injured every day.

"Enemy ship is moving out of sensor range," Kia reported as the ship reached the edge of the tactical display and vanished.

"That's the third battlecruiser we've spotted since we entered this nebula," Katana said worriedly. "As your people would say, I believe we've stirred up a hornets' nest."

Chloe turned to face the two command officers. "The Trellixians are desperate to stop us from escaping with the data we've gathered. They probably have every available ship searching for us."

Mark looked around at his command crew. It had been a trying few weeks as they worked around the clock repairing the *Fury*. "Lieutenant Masterson, I want you and Chloe to find us the best route back home. Once we've cleared the Trellixian core worlds we need to find one of our communication drones and transmit our data back to Earth."

"That communication may be detected," warned Katana. "The Trellixians will be scanning all hyperspace communication frequencies for such a broadcast. They will have ships between us and Earth waiting for us to try to initiate contact."

"I'm aware of that," said Mark. "But we must get that data back to Earth even if it means we run the risk of being detected."

Katana nodded. "We'll have the ship repaired but I can't guarantee what type of shape the *Fury* will be in when we finally arrive back on Earth.

"Let's just get back," Mark replied.

-

High Commander Kaldre was in his flagship the *Dawn Reaper* meeting with Battle Commander Balforr. At the moment most of Balforr's fleets were scattered around the core worlds searching for the elusive Human ship.

"Are you certain it's still in our core systems?" asked Kaldre.

"Yes," Balforr replied. "They have to be hiding in a comet zone or even a nebula repairing their vessel. My ships did major damage to their ship during our battle with it."

"But you weren't able to destroy it," said Kaldre, feeling extremely disappointed the new battlecruisers had failed to destroy the vessel. "Not only that, you lost five warships."

Balforr's eyes hardened. "It was a Voltrex battleship crewed by Humans. It was equipped with Jelnoid weapons and a very powerful energy shield. If the ship would have stayed for another minute my forces would have eliminated it."

Kaldre shifted his attention to one of the viewscreens showing a new battlecruiser exiting the main shipyard above Traxis Three. The new two-thousand-meter battlecruiser was equipped with the latest weapons and energy shield available to Trellixian technology. "What do we need to do to be able to destroy a Voltrex battleship?"

"Missiles," replied Balforr. "If we could hit them with a sufficient number of missiles we could batter down their shields and destroy them. I would suggest we install missile pods on future battlecruisers. The pods can be protected inside the ship behind hatches which can slide open and extend the pods for launch."

"I will have to speak to Commander Malborr to see if such a thing is possible. It might require a major revision to our warships." Kaldre knew suggesting the changes would aggravate the shipyard commander. "Are you certain if we make these changes that we can destroy a Voltrex battleship?"

Battle Commander Balforr nodded. "If we can equip enough of our ships with the missile pods it will enable us to defeat the Voltrex and annihilate the Humans still residing on Earth. To me they are a bigger threat than the Voltrex."

High Commander Kaldre shifted his gaze back to the Battle Commander. "I fear you are obsessed with Earth. It will be your undoing someday if you are not careful."

"I have no fear of Earth," replied Balforr, his eyes narrowing sharply. "If the High Command would have followed my initial recommendations about the planet, it would have ceased being a danger several years ago."

Kaldre was not pleased to hear Balforr criticize the High Command though his statement might be correct. Criticism of the High Command was prohibited and carried a very stiff penalty. "Be careful in what you say," warned Kaldre. "Some of the High Command would not tolerate your words. They would consider them treasonous."

"I support the Empire," replied Balforr. "I live for the Empire. However, I will not throw my life away foolishly. I have fought both the Humans and the Voltrex. They are a much greater threat than the High Command believes. If we don't do something soon we could see the end of our Empire."

"The end of our Empire!" blurted out Kaldre, surprised to hear this from Balforr. "We have several thousand worlds and thousands of warships. We are constantly building new battlecruisers to expand the Empire. Even though we are suffering some major reverses in the near term eventually the Humans and the Voltrex will face defeat from superior numbers alone." Kaldre had believed they might be in for a long war but he had never believed the Empire might be destroyed. He had threatened the High Command with this but only to get control of more shipyards.

Battle Commander Balforr hesitated briefly and then responded. "I have seen the Voltrex fleets. They are truly massive. We have no idea how many worlds they control or inhabit. They have now equipped their warships with Jelnoid technology. Since then we have not had one single significant victory against them. From the reports I have seen they are on the offensive. Every day we hear of more of our outer colonies and bases being eliminated. In time, they will reach our core worlds. We must be ready for that day."

Kaldre's mind was working rapidly. Battle Commander Balforr was expressing some of Kaldre's deepest fears. Could the Empire actually be in danger? He knew lack of population control was driving the Empire to expand as rapidly as possible. It was also causing the Empire to take risks, which could lead to massive losses in population. Kaldre was convinced unless something was done to control the exploding population on the core worlds eventually a lack of food and living space would cause widespread civil unrest. That had already occurred once and billions had been lost. If it occurred again it could be much worse.

Kaldre's reason for building the new ships was to prevent an attack on the core worlds. He had never considered the possibility of the Empire being in actual danger or possibly losing this war. Much of what he had been doing was to increase his power with the other High Commanders. "Do you have any other recommendations?"

Balforr's large eyes met Kaldre's. "Our worlds are poorly defended. Even our core worlds only have small fleets of battlecruisers to protect them. What would happen if a fleet of several hundred Voltrex battleships and battlecruisers were to drop out of hyperspace near one of our primary planets? We have no orbital defenses other than the shipyards, which are routinely armed. A fleet such as that could wipe out a core world before we could send sufficient warships to defend it."

"What would you recommend?"

"Put weapons on all of the orbiting stations and manufacturing facilities as well as energy shields. Build some type of battlestation that can be put in orbit to protect the planet from orbital strikes. The Voltrex have battlestations one thousand meters in diameter they use to protect their worlds. Can we do anything less?"

Kaldre shook his head. "You have no idea of what you're asking. The resources required to build such stations around all of our core worlds is staggering. Even just arming the stations and manufacturing facilities will be a major task. Too many of our resources go toward maintaining our civilization. We can barely keep up with the requirements from our growing population. There is no excess production capability to build what you're suggesting."

Battle Commander Balforr drew in a sharp breath. "If we don't, then someday we will see Human and Voltrex fleets hovering above our core worlds. They will drop nuclear weapons, annihilating our civilization. It is what I would have done to them if given the opportunity."

"What you're suggesting would require building more manufacturing facilities," replied Kaldre as he thought of where the resources would have to come from.

Everything in the Empire was aimed at handling the exploding population of the core worlds and even some of the larger colony worlds. New manufacturing facilities and even shipyards were being built but they were designed to provide ships and resources for the population.

"If we do not, the Humans and the Voltrex will eventually come for us. Already Humans ships have penetrated to our homeworld. What will the High Command say when a full sized war fleet shows up?"

Kaldre knew Balforr was correct. "I will see what I can do. As far as adding missile pods to our ships, I'll see what Commander Malborr thinks about that."

"I must have the missile pods if my ships are to defeat a Voltrex battleship," reiterated Balforr.

"While I work on that, I need you to find that last Human ship. It must not leave our space with the information it has gathered."

Balforr nodded. "I will find it and when I do I will destroy it."

"One more thing," Kaldre said, watching Battle Commander Balforr. "One of the manufacturing facilities here in the Traxis System has been building some seventy-megaton fusion missiles with a slightly longer range than our current missiles. Once we have enough I will send a cargo ship out to your fleet with a supply of the new missiles."

Balforr looked pleased at this announcement. "Those will help significantly. I will have those missiles placed aboard the new warships under my command. I will keep you informed on the search for the Human ship."

Kaldre watched as Battle Commander Balforr returned to his flagship. The Battle Commander truly hated the Humans.

Kaldre hoped that hate wasn't driving Balforr to take unnecessary risks or to make unsubstantiated statements. Standing up, Kaldre decided to go over to the main shipyard and to speak with Commander Malborr. Balforr's suggestion about the missile pods did make sense. He would see what Malborr thought of it and how difficult it would be to accomplish.

-

Battle Commander Balforr made his way back to his flagship, the *Conquest*. If High Commander Kaldre followed his recommendations about adding the missile pods to the new ships being built in the shipyards, he was confident they would be able to take on a Voltrex battleship and win, especially if they were equipped with seventy-megaton missiles. With a wicked smirk he knew his eventual revenge against the Humans for his defeat in conquering their world would someday be avenged. In time he would turn Earth into a smoking cinder and hunt down every member of that infernal species.

-

Leaning forward in his command chair, Captain Dolan watched the tactical display as the *Fury* eased out of the dust cloud it had been hiding in for over two weeks. The ship was repaired as well as the crew could. The holes in the hull had been sealed though the compartments directly beneath the damaged areas were still locked out with the emergency bulkheads and hatches shut. Some areas of the ship had cabling running along the floor to bypass damage, which wasn't practical to repair in the field.

"Report," said Mark as the tactical screen cleared showing the open space in front of the *Fury*.

"Sensors are clear of enemy contacts," reported Kia.

"All systems are powered up and working at optimum levels," added Chloe as she quickly scanned the entire ship. "All repairs are holding."

"Lieutenant Masterson?"

"Course is plotted and we're ready to enter hyperspace."

Mark looked around at his command crew. He could sense the apprehension in the air. They were deep in Trellixian space and the odds of making it back home were not good. "We'll get back," he said. "We have a good ship and a great crew. Nothing will stop us from returning to Earth. Lieutenant Masterson, activate the hyperspace drive and let's see if we can get away from these Trellixian core worlds."

Mark was convinced once they cleared the core worlds they would be much safer. He was also anxious to get to one of the hyperspace relay drones so he could send the data the *Fury* had gathered back to Earth. Once that was done the mission could be considered a success even if the ship failed to make it back.

-

Moments later the *Fury* entered hyperspace as it fled the Trellixian core worlds. All around her Trellixian warships searched for the elusive vessel with one goal in mind. Destroy the Human ship at all costs. It could not be allowed to escape.

-

Commander Balforr paced back and forth in front of the command pedestal in his Command Center as he contemplated his next move hunting down the remaining Human ship. He had gathered his fleet back into a single formation after failing to find the Human ship anywhere in the core systems. He was still convinced with the damage it had suffered the vessel was hiding somewhere close by while its crew made repairs.

"How do we find the Human vessel?" asked Second Officer Albion. "All of our searches have been negative so far and we have several thousand vessels searching. All core worlds are using their fleets to search the star systems near them."

Balforr stopped his pacing and stared at Albion. "Maybe instead of searching for these Humans we should let them come to us."

Albion had a look of confusion on his face. "What do you suggest?"

"Let's take our fleet outside the core worlds and position some task groups between our worlds and Earth. If we spread our net wide enough we should be able to detect the Human ship on its way back to their home world. We both know the ship will periodically have to drop out of hyperspace to take navigational readings. When they do, that's when we can destroy it."

Balforr strode over to the navigational console. After conferring with the helm officer he decided on a course and destination. If everything worked out he would catch the Human ship when it dropped out of hyperspace.

Several days passed as the *Fury* traveled through the Trellixian core worlds. Multiple times the ship's course had to be adjusted to avoid Trellixian warships. The ship dropped out of hyperspace near a red giant to confirm their course and to do routine maintenance on the ship's hyperspace drive.

"The Trellixians are bound to have detected us," said Lisa as she and the others took time off to eat a quick snack. "We've passed too close to so many of their warships and cargo vessels."

"It's not their cargo ships that worry me," said Brett. "However, there's a very good chance some of the warships we've passed close to could have reported our presence back to their High Command."

Kia plopped a strawberry into her mouth and then spoke. "We've passed within half a light year of over a dozen Trellixian battlecruisers. It wouldn't be too hard for them to plot our course and arrange a welcoming committee somewhere ahead of us."

"Second Officer Katana mentioned that to Captain Dolan yesterday," Brenda said. "I heard them talking about it. They're considering changing our course radically once we reach the hyperspace relay drone so the Trellixians can't predict our course."

Lisa breathed out a deep sigh. "That will delay our return home though it will be much safer."

Brett was eating a Salisbury steak with mashed potatoes. He took a bite and smiled. "At least the food on the *Fury* is pretty good. Even if all goes well we're still a good four weeks from reaching Earth. A lot can happen in that time."

"Thankfully the repairs are holding up," mentioned Derek as he cut off a generous portion of the cinnamon roll he was eating. "We still have a number of compartments sealed off for safety reasons."

"I'll be glad to get back home," said Lisa. She really missed her talks with Professor Wilkens. "When we do I have no plans on leaving Complex One for quite sometime."

Brenda nodded. "I think we all feel that way. We've had enough excitement and adventure to last a lifetime."

Brett was in agreement as well. "I'm looking forward to getting back into my research full time. I suspect we all are since that's what we were originally trained for."

Lisa took a bite of the chicken salad in front of her. "I know I'll sleep a lot better when we get back. I lay in bed at night just waiting for the Condition One alert to sound."

"I think we all do," replied Brett. "I jumped out of bed the other night and had my uniform half on before I realized it was only a dream. Then I lay there the rest of the night and couldn't fall back to sleep."

"I imagine the entire crew is feeling the same," Lisa said in between bites of her salad. "Everyone is worried and wondering if we're going to make it back home."

Lisa was just about to say something else when the alert klaxons started sounding and the red Condition One lights began flashing in the Officers' Mess. "I guess we spoke too soon," Lisa said as she stood up.

In the Officers' Mess everyone moved quickly toward the hatch. The cooks began putting the food away for later.

It didn't take Lisa and the others long to reach the Command Center and take their places.

"We're going to risk contacting the hyperspace sensor drone," Second Officer Katana informed them. "We've encountered so many Trellixian battlecruisers in the past day the captain and I both feel it's prudent to send our data while we still can."

Lisa felt her pulse begin to race. If they were doing this it seemed to indicate both Katana and Captain Dolan were beginning to have doubts the *Fury* would make it back to Earth. Lisa risked glancing over at Brett, seeing a steep frown on his face. He was obviously thinking the same thing.

-

"Stand by to transmit the data package," ordered Captain Dolan. Mark knew they were taking a risk transmitting the data to the drone. They were at the extreme range of hyperspace communication. There was also a small chance the Trellixians might detect it.

"Ready to transmit," reported Marissa. "The data is in a condensed format and will only take a few seconds to send."

Mark nodded. "Do it."

Marissa reached forward and pressed a blinking icon on her communications screen. After a moment she turned back toward the captain. "Data has been sent. It will take the drone a few seconds to receive the data and then send back a confirming response."

The seconds passed slowly by and then an icon on the communications screen began blinking.

"Data package received and forwarded," reported Marissa, sounding relieved.

Mark breathed out a long sigh of relief. If the other drones were still intact the data would soon reach Earth and General Mitchell. Their mission would be considered a success. Now all Mark had to do was concentrate on getting the *Fury* and her crew home safely and he knew that would be no easy task.

"It will be hours before the message reaches Earth," said Katana nervously. "I would recommend we change course immediately in case the message was detected."

"Do so," ordered Mark. "I want a course change of at least sixty degrees away from our present heading. We'll stay on that course for three days before we resume our heading back toward Earth."

Katana stepped over to the navigation and helm control where Brett was sitting. The two conferred for a few minutes and then Brett began making the necessary course corrections.

"We're changing our forward course by sixty-three degrees and also moving bow downward from our course by twenty-nine degrees," reported Katana. "If any Trellixian vessels detected our message that should throw them off of our course."

"Lieutenant Masterson, take us back into hyperspace," ordered Mark.

Brett touched several icons on his computer screen and moments later the Fury reentered hyperspace but on a radically different course.

"I don't believe our message was detected," reported Chloe. "The odds of a Trellixian ship being in the right spot to detect the message is less than two percent."

Mark suspected Chloe was correct. However, he still planned to take whatever precautions were necessary to keep the *Fury* and her crew safe. "Secure from Condition One and go to Condition Three," Mark ordered. At least for a few hours the crew could get some rest.

-

Battle Commander Balforr was pleased with the progress of his fleet. Since his fleet knew the safer navigation routes through the Trellixian Empire there was no doubt that his ships were moving much faster than the Human one.

"We'll be in our blockading position in two more days," Second Officer Albion reported. "Once there we'll spread our ships out in small task groups and wait for the Human vessel to trigger our sensors. Once it's done that we'll follow it and wait for it to drop out of hyperspace to take navigation readings."

"And once that happens we'll move in for the kill," replied Balforr. He could already taste the victory. It would be one more satisfying step in his revenge on the race that had sidetracked and nearly destroyed his career.

Chapter Nineteen

General Mitchell was listening as Colonel Tricia Steward reported on the recent data burst from the *Fury* in the underground Command Center.

"The ship was heavily damaged in their battle with the Trellixians in the Trellixian home system. They hid in a nebula for nearly two weeks while they worked on repairs to the ship. When they returned to the rendezvous coordinates to join back up with the rest of their fleet they found the ships destroyed. The Trellixians are currently using most of their fleet to search for the ship. Captain Dolan is taking evasive maneuvers in the hope of making it back to Earth though the odds of him doing so are not looking good."

General Mitchell looked with concern at Fleet Commander Kamuss and Admiral Edwards. "Any suggestions? Is there anything we can do to help the *Fury*?"

"The Trellixians must not be aware that the *Fury* has transmitted back her information," said Admiral Edwards with a deep frown as he considered the ramifications. "They would have to have been in the direct path of the transmission and as short as it was I doubt if they would have even noticed it. They will be using all of their resources to find and destroy the ship before it can get back here."

Fleet Commander Kamuss looked at the other two military leaders. "Those Trellixian warships in the Proxima Centauri System could become a threat to the *Fury*. At any time they could be recalled to form a barrier between Earth and the Empire. When the *Fury* passes through that barrier they will be detected and then pursued. When the ship drops out of hyperspace in the Solar System all of the pursuing enemy ships will also, probably all around the vessel in an attempt to destroy it before the vessel can reach Earth or transmit the data collected on the Trellixian core worlds."

Admiral Edwards nodded in agreement. "They won't know we already have the data." Edward's brow creased in thought. "What if we take preemptive action and destroy those Trellixian fleets in the Proxima Centauri System? That will be one less threat the *Fury* has to worry about."

"I would also recommend once that is done we send some of our heavier ships further into the Empire to meet the *Fury*," suggested Fleet Commander Kamuss. "The stealth ships we brought with us have excellent sensors. If we can locate the *Fury* we can escort her safely back to Earth."

General Mitchell looked at a tactical display showing the enemy ships in Proxima Centauri. This was from a Human battlecruiser that had scanned the system only a few hours previously. There were slightly over two hundred red threat icons. "Can we take out that fleet with few losses?" Mitchell didn't want to lose a major portion of either fleet. They were too important to Earth's safety.

"Fleet Commander Barvon will remain in the Solar System with his fleet," replied Kamuss. "In addition he will be reinforced by all of my medium and light support ships. We have the reinforcements for my fleet which arrived two days ago. I believe we can take out the Trellixian ships with few losses. There will be some but they will be acceptable."

"A portion of our battlecruisers will take part as well," Admiral Edwards said. "Our ship crews need the battle experience."

General Mitchell took a deep breath and slowly nodded. "Very well; make up a battle plan and let me know when you're ready to initiate it."

Mitchell watched as Admiral Edwards and Fleet Commander Kamuss left the Command Center to return to their respective flagships to begin planning their attack on the Trellixian fleets.

"General Briggs, have we sent a copy of the data files we received from the *Fury* to the president?" asked General Mitchell.

Briggs nodded. "Yes, shortly after we received them. We also sent a copy to Professor Wilkens. His people may be able to break the data down and give us a better idea of what we're up against."

"I had time to look over some of the data," said Colonel Henry Fields. "The population density on several of those core worlds is astonishing. We're talking about tens of billions of Trellixians on just a single planet."

"Some of those planets are covered in massive cities," added Major Jase Thomas. "From the data it appears they have built towering buildings that nearly reach into the clouds and at a guess they must go deep underground as well."

"They may have civilians living underground who have never seen the sun," said General Briggs, shaking his head. "The living space on those planets must be minimal with very limited privacy."

Colonel Steward frowned. "I don't see how anyone could live that way. It must be terrible on some of those planets."

"We'll know more when we break down the data," replied General Briggs. "There's a lot of information in what the *Fury* sent to us."

General Mitchell sat down and turned his attention to several viewscreens showing Earth. Today there were more breaks in the cloud layer than there had been in months. He could see a large part of the Pacific Ocean and most of the U.K., including the coast of France. Unfortunately even now all of those land areas were still covered in deep snow. Some forecast models were even suggesting a mini ice age might have been triggered. Mitchell hoped not; the surviving people on the planet had already dealt with enough hardships and death.

-

President Hathaway was in her office with Vice President Arnold and Professor Wilkens discussing some of the data being processed from the *Fury*.

"Sixty billion Trellixians on just one planet!" exclaimed Katelyn, shaking her head in disbelief. "How can they live like that?"

Professor Wilkens was holding a laptop on which some of the data from the *Fury* had been downloaded. "They're used to it. From birth to death they're indoctrinated into living the way they do. We have a large number of communications from the planets recorded by the *Fury*. I have a team of analysts already going over those to see what we can learn of the Trellixians' culture."

"There must be trillions of them in the Empire," said Vice President Arnold. "How can we defeat them if they possess those types of numbers? For every one we kill they can replace them with hundreds maybe thousands of others."

Professor Wilkens hesitated and then spoke in a quieter voice. "Our preliminary estimates put the Trellixian population in excess of twenty trillion."

"Twenty Trillion!" uttered Vice President Arnold turning pale. "How do we fight something like that?"

President Hathaway didn't know what to think. This news was devastating to the war effort. There were only around two hundred million people left on Earth and many of those were scattered across the globe. The Voltrex Federation had a large population on their worlds but nothing like the population the Trellixians had. In addition, the Voltrex Federation was several thousand light years distant. It made Earth seem afloat in a massive ocean filled with danger.

"Have we learned anything useful so far?" asked Katelyn, looking across her desk at Professor Wilkens.

"Not yet," admitted the professor. "We've only managed to skim through the data. We'll need several weeks at a minimum before we can give a proper report and several months before we can go through everything with enough detail to possibly recommend some type of future strategy."

"If there is one," said Vice President Arnold, leaning back and folding his arms across his chest. "Our only hope may be to place massive defenses around Earth and hope the Trellixians leave us alone."

Katelyn hoped the vice president wasn't right. The future of Earth was out in the galaxy. She realized that now. Somehow they needed to find a way to defeat the Trellixians. The solution was going to be like finding a needle in a haystack. She also wondered where the *Fury* was and if the battleship would make it back to Earth. She hoped so and she knew Professor Wilkens felt the same way. Katelyn had met Lieutenant Lisa Reynolds several times and was impressed with the young woman's intelligence. After speaking to her she quickly learned why Professor Wilkens placed such trust and confidence in the woman. It also filled her with sadness that three of the ships in the fleet had been lost. They had understood in the beginning there might be losses on this mission. Now that fear had materialized. She could only pray for those who had lost their lives.

Admiral Edwards was sitting behind his desk in his quarters speaking to Captain Nelson. "What ships should we assign to this mission?"

Captain Nelson had a small handheld computer pad in his hand. He scrolled though it and looked up at the admiral. "I would recommend we send all the ships the Voltrex have built for us: thirty battlecruisers and four battleships. That would leave us Fleet Commander Barvon's fleet as well as our Earth-built battlecruisers plus the *Annapolis*. That should be sufficient to protect Earth while they're gone. Also Proxima Centauri is only a little over four light years away. If something drastic happens here we could be back in less than a day."

Admiral Edwards took a few moments to consider Captain Nelson's recommendation. It made sense to send the larger ships as they were much more powerful than Earth's smaller battlecruisers. In case of a future attack, it was the larger ships, which would bear the brunt of defending Earth. It would be wise to get all the crews of those ships some additional battle experience.

"Make the necessary arrangements. Inform Major Brandon of our decision. We will need to deploy more of the small patrol ships to replace the battlecruisers we'll be taking off patrol duty."

"I don't believe that will be a problem," Nelson replied. "He can also increase the fighter-bomber patrols around the Earth and the Moon."

Admiral Edwards stood up and stepped over to a large colorful map of the Solar System. "We have sensor buoys spread throughout the Solar System. If any enemy ships drop out of hyperspace we will detect them instantly." The only region without sensors was the outer cometary zone.

Captain Nelson stood up as well. "We should also consider the possibility of what will happen if the *Fury* makes it safely back to Earth. There is a good possibility she will be followed by Trellixian warships. We may have another battle on our hands at that time."

"If she makes it back," said Admiral Edwards, turning around to face Captain Nelson. "You and I both know the odds of that are very low. They have a long ways to come and all of it through enemy territory."

"Maybe not all the way if we can send out a reception committee to meet them."

"But how long do we wait?" asked Edwards with his eyes narrowing. "We have no idea how long it will take them to make it back to Earth and if the *Fury* is destroyed we have no way of knowing that either."

Captain Nelson didn't reply. There was no easy or right answer.

-

Fleet Commander Kamuss had recalled all of his personnel from Earth. Lieutenant Commander LeLath was the last to arrive and he had to smile upon seeing the joyous look on her face.

"I found some new and exciting food on Earth," she said excitedly as she took her spot in the Command Center. "It has some of the most wonderful spices I've ever tasted."

"I assume you were out with Captain Dolan's sister," said Kamuss. He knew the Lieutenant Commander enjoyed trying different types of food. He didn't know if she ever ate the same thing twice.

LeLath nodded. "We're becoming very good friends. Why were we all recalled back to the ship?"

"We're going to destroy the Trellixian fleets in Proxima Centauri."

LeLath looked confused. "So soon? I thought we were going to wait until all of our ships were repaired. There are still several battlecruisers in the Human shipyard."

"The *Fury* is on her way back. General Mitchell and Admiral Edwards are concerned the enemy ships in Proxima Centauri may attempt to set a trap for the ship. We want to destroy them before that happens. Part of the Earth fleet will be accompanying us as well."

"How soon before we leave?"

Fleet Commander Kamuss looked at some data on a screen in front of him. It was a list of the Human ships that would be accompanying them. They were all Voltrex-built vessels and fully equipped with Jelnoid technology. Kamuss approved of Admiral Edward's decision to send these vessels. "Tomorrow or the day after at the latest. We don't want the Trellixian ships to leave. As soon as we're satisfied our ships and Admiral Edward's ships are ready, we'll depart."

Lieutenant Commander LeLath nodded. "I'll check with our ships. All should be finished loading missiles from the fleet replenishment vessels. Our replacement ships should be ready as well."

"We're fortunate the Federation sent extra ships to augment our fleets," Kamuss said. "We have twenty extra battlecruisers and seven more battleships. That's a considerable increase in firepower. The latest scans indicate a little over two hundred Trellixian battlecruisers in the Alpha Centauri System."

"So we just drop out of hyperspace and blow them out of space?"

"I wish it were so easy," Kamuss replied smiling. "We'll have three fleets at our disposal. I plan on dropping out of hyperspace on three sides of the Trellixian fleet formations, preventing them from maneuvering. We'll launch our missiles just outside their weapons' range. That should minimize our losses."

"I suspect they'll attempt to attack one of our fleets," warned LeLath. Some of the fighting could become ship to ship before it's over with."

"If they do the other two fleets will close the range and engage with energy weapons."

LeLath nodded. "At least we can return to Earth and repair our battle damage afterward."

Fleet Commander Kamuss looked at a star map he had up on one of the main screens. "When the battle is over I will take part of the fleet and attempt to find the *Fury*. The Trellixians will be pursuing the ship with everything they have. It may make the battle in the Proxima Centauri System look like child's play."

LeLath took on a look of seriousness. "Nothing can be allowed to happen to the *Fury*. If Captain Dolan were to be killed, it would be devastating to his sister. She has already lost so much."

"We'll try to see that doesn't happen," promised Kamuss.

It was late the next day and all three fleets were preparing to leave the Solar System. Admiral Edwards had moved his flag temporarily from the *Renown* to one of the Voltrex battleships manned by a mixture of Humans and Voltrex. Captain Nelson would remain in the system and assume command of the fleet until Edwards returned. This operation also made Edwards realize he needed to name someone a rear admiral. Once he returned from this mission, he would sit down with President Hathaway and General Mitchell and discuss that.

"All fleets are ready to enter hyperspace," reported Lieutenant Commander Lelath.

Fleet Commander Kamuss shifted his gaze to the tactical display, which was showing all three fleets. For some of the Humans this would be their first trip outside of their solar system. "Initiate hyperspace jump," ordered Kamuss. It was time to go to war once again.

-

Six hours later the four Trellixian stealth scout ships entered the Proxima Centauri System and took up positions to scan the Trellixian ships. Initial scans quickly showed two hundred and eighteen enemy battlecruisers in one large fleet formation around a small icy planet two hundred million kilometers from the star. This information was quickly transmitted back to the approaching fleets.

-

"Trellixian ship strength is as expected," reported Lieutenant Commander LeLath. "They are still at the same location."

Kamuss nodded. This would make the attack easier. "We'll drop out of hyperspace twenty-thousand kilometers from the Trellixian fleet, launch our first wave of missiles and begin to close. We will continue to launch until the Trellixians ships are all destroyed or they make a countermove to our attack." Kamuss relaxed in his command chair. It would still be a few hours before the fleets arrived at their target. That would give him time to finalize the battle plan with Admiral Edwards and Fleet Commander Masurl.

Kamuss looked around the busy Command Center. Everyone seemed calm and unafraid of what lay ahead. In this battle they would have a slight advantage in numbers and a huge advantage in weapons. His only real concern was whether the enemy fleet was equipped with fifty-megaton fusion weapons or the even deadlier one hundred-megaton antimatter ones.

Kamuss wondered what his mate was doing. They were too far away from Voltrex for easy communication. Hyperspace messages took hours to travel there and back. He missed speaking to Karina and knew that at some point in the future he needed to take some days off to spend with his family. The latest report from his son, Albor, mentioned he was stationed on a new battlecruiser and had been involved in two engagements against Trellixian fleets. Kamuss felt proud of his son as well as concerned. This war against the Trellixians could be long and extremely dangerous.

"Admiral Edwards is on the comm," reported Meela. "He has some questions about the upcoming battle."

"Transfer him to me," Kamuss ordered. "I was expecting his call."

-

Admiral Edwards finished talking to Fleet Commander Kamuss. Kamuss was in overall command of the three fleets as he had the most battle experience. He explained to Captain Anderson what Kamuss wanted to do.

"We should be dropping out of hyperspace in one hour and forty minutes," reported Captain Anderson.

"Our other ships will assume a standard offensive formation nine ships wide and four high with our battleships in the center," explained Admiral Edwards. "Upon exiting hyperspace we will target the nearest Trellixian battlecruiser with our missiles and continue to fire until we either run out of missiles or the enemy has been destroyed."

"There are no plans to close to energy weapons range unless the Trellixians force the issue. Fleet Commander Kamuss is not sure if they will withdraw when faced with a superior force or fight to the death. He believes it will depend on the Battle Commander in charge. In the past he has encountered those who will sacrifice every ship for the Empire but he has seen a few withdraw once the battle turned against them."

Captain Anderson took a long breath and then addressed the admiral. "I imagine commanding a fleet like this is a lot different than an aircraft carrier." Anderson knew Admiral Edwards was once the flag officer of the *JMS Prince of Wales*.

Edwards let out a deep sigh. "It's a lot different in some ways and in others it's the same. Back on the *Prince of Wales* everything seemed much simpler."

Anderson nodded in understanding. "I was in command of a frigate which is a lot different than this. I never imagined I would end up in space fighting an interstellar war."

"I don't think any of us imagined that," replied Edwards. "It makes one wonder what the future holds for us."

"At least we now have some powerful allies."

"Yes, we're fortunate the *Vengeance* and Captain Dolan found the Voltrex. Without them our future would have been very questionable."

Captain Anderson shifted his gaze to the tactical display showing the disposition of the fleet in hyperspace. It was comforting knowing the other ships were there. "Have we heard anything else from the *Fury* since the last data burst?"

No," replied Admiral Edwards. "There's a good chance we won't until they make it back."

The two men fell silent. They both knew the odds of the *Fury* returning to Earth were very small.

-

Battle Commander Amblinn entered the Command Center of his flagship. He stifled a yawn as this assignment was unbelievably boring. He would much rather be using his fleet out on the borders of the Empire conquering new worlds for the expansion of the Trellixian race.

"What's the latest report on Earth?" he asked as he stepped up on the command pedestal and sat down. Every few days he would send a battlecruiser to the outskirts of the system and take sensor readings. While not one hundred percent accurate at that range, they did provide sufficient information to keep track of what was occurring in the system.

The second officer turned toward Amblinn. "The Voltrex fleets are still there. We believe their ships are being repaired at the Humans' new shipyard."

Battle Commander Amblinn looked around the Command Center, noticing a number of stations were unmanned. "Where are the missing crewmembers?" Discipline was rapidly falling and he realized he needed to do something if he wanted his ships to maintain their combat readiness.

The second officer shook his head. "It's the Kriss. I suspect many of our crew are using too much of it. This assignment has been too boring and they're using the drug to pass the time."

Amblinn felt anger flow through him. He was aware of the use of Kriss in the fleet. However, it could not be allowed to effect battle readiness. "Effective immediately I want the amount of Kriss used to be limited. Any crewmember found to be under influence of the drug and not at their post will face strict and uncompromising disciplinary action."

"I will see to it," the second officer replied.

Neither officer noticed the red blinking icon on the vacant sensor console or the lights on the communications panel indicating incoming messages from the other ships of the fleet.

"Take the fleet to Battle Condition One," ordered Fleet Commander Kamuss as he watched the tactical display intently.

Instantly, alarms began sounding and red lights started flashing.

"Battle Condition one has been set across the fleets," reported Lieutenant Commander LeLath. "Forty-megaton missiles have been loaded in the missile tubes and are ready to launch."

"Ten minutes to hyperspace dropout," reported Metriic.

"Trellixian fleet is still holding position," reported Zalurr. "I don't believe they've detected us."

"Scout ships confirm the Trellixian fleet is showing no indications of higher alert status," added Meela.

Lieutenant Commander LeLath frowned. "They must be asleep at their controls. As large of a fleet as we have they should be detecting us."

"Never-the-less we'll take advantage of their failure to respond to our presence," said Kamuss as he leaned forward in his command chair. "We will initiate our battle plan and drop out of hyperspace in a three-pronged attack. If we're lucky they won't even have their shields up."

-

The three fleets continued their approach through hyperspace and then suddenly the wrenching sensation of returning to normal space was felt on all the ships.

"Report!" ordered Admiral Edwards as the viewscreens began to fill with stars.

"Enemy fleet detected! Range is twenty thousand kilometers," reported the sensor operator.

Captain Anderson turned toward the tactical officer. "Launch missiles!"

On the main viewscreen, the Trellixian fleet appeared, ship after ship lined up in formation. They were massive with each vessel 2,000 meters in length and heavily armed.

"Missiles launched," reported the tactical officer as the ship shuddered slightly from the departure of the missiles. "All ships are launching."

"Trellixian ships are beginning to respond to our presence," reported the sensor officer. "We're detecting energy shields powering up on most of their vessels."

-

In space, the missile strike slammed into the energy shields of the Trellixian vessels, lighting up space in a series of massive explosions. A number of Trellixian ships had not managed to raise their shields and these vanished in huge fireballs of released fusion energy. Across the Trellixian formation small novas appeared indicating the death of dozens of Trellixian battlecruisers.

-

The Trellixian flagship shook violently and Battle Commander Amblinn found himself flying through the air to strike the communications console. Feeling stunned, he stood back up. "What was that?" He could feel blood dripping across his forehead from a wicked cut. Alarms were sounding and red lights began appearing on the damage control console.

"We're under attack," replied the second officer as he staggered to his command console. "Three Voltrex fleets have dropped out of hyperspace around us."

Battle Commander Amblinn made his way back to his command chair and sat down. His right leg was hurting and he suspected he had fractured it in the fall he had just taken. "Return fire. Make sure all ships have their energy shields up." He noticed several Trellixian officers enter the Command Center and hurry to their stations.

"Enemy craft are still outside weapons range," reported the tactical officer.

Amblinn felt himself shaking with anger. "Advance our fleet toward the nearest enemy ships. Close the range so our missiles and beam weapons will be effective." Looking at the tactical display, he saw a number of green icons representing the ships of his fleet swell up and then vanish. He had never expected to be attacked. This was a Trellixian fleet composed of the most powerful ships in the galaxy, or at least that was what he had always believed. Watching the tactical display, he began to have doubts.

-

Missiles from several Voltrex warships struck the screen of a Trellixian battlecruiser, battering it down. Another missile slammed into the hull and exploded in a massive flash of light. Secondary explosions rattled through the ship, shaking it violently. Large pieces of glowing debris were hurled into space. Then the craft blew apart in several powerful explosions.

Another Trellixian battlecruiser broke in two from a missile strike and then both sections exploded as fusion missiles locked on and blew them apart. Across the Trellixian fleet formation wreckage was beginning to slam into shields and in some instances cause substantial damage to the vessels.

-

Fleet Commander Kamuss watched in satisfaction as the Trellixian ships died. They had been caught unprepared and were now paying the price.

"Eighty-two enemy ships have been destroyed," reported Zalurr, with satisfaction in his voice. "A number of others have been heavily damaged."

"They're moving," warned Lieutenant Commander LeLath. "They are heading toward the Human ships."

Kamuss frowned. This could be a problem. The Humans only had thirty-four ships in their fleet. The Trellixians were going to attack the smallest of the three fleets. This was something Kamuss should have seen beforehand. "Close the distance with the Trellixians. We'll take them from the rear while they engage the Human ships. With our superior weapons we should be able to destroy them before the Humans suffer much damage."

"Course set and the fleet is accelerating," reported Metriic.

Kamuss focused his attention on the tactical display. The Trellixians had left him no choice but to close the range. He would soon find out what type of missiles the enemy fleet was equipped with. "Diboll, keep up the missile fire on the Trellixian fleet. We're going to close to energy weapons range."

–

Admiral Edwards watched with a feeling of deep concern as the surviving enemy ships turned and charged toward his fleet formation.

"Admiral, what are your orders?" asked Captain Anderson.

"Keep launching missiles. Prepare to fire energy weapons as soon as they are in range. Hold our position; we can't let those ships through our lines."

"Energy weapons range will be achieved shortly," reported the sensor operator. "Their fleet is rapidly closing with ours and Fleet Commander Kamuss is coming up on their rear."

The viewscreens switched to show a magnified view of the approaching Trellixian fleet. Many of the ships were damaged with huge open rents in their hulls and on several fires could be seen burning inside.

"Enemy fleet is in extreme energy weapons range," reported the sensor officer. "Detecting missile launches."

The flagship shuddered as two fifty-megaton fusion missiles struck the energy shield, jarring the ship. The lights dimmed briefly and then returned to normal.

"Increase defensive fire!" ordered Captain Anderson. "Shoot down those missiles." On the main viewscreen, a number of enemy missiles were being destroyed by heavy defensive energy beam fire but many others were still getting through.

"The *Crayton* is reporting heavy damage," reported the communications officer.

"Have her pull back behind the fleet," ordered Admiral Edwards, clenching his fist.

On the screen, several Trellixian battlecruisers blew apart under the heavy fire of the fleet.

The flagship suddenly seemed to keel over to the side as a powerful force struck it.

"Battlecruiser *Hammond* is down," reported the tactical officer breathlessly. "She was struck by an antimatter missile."

Captain Anderson shook his head. "Those are one hundred-megaton warheads. They can pop a shield if several of their fusion warheads hit at the same time as well."

"Energy weapons range," reported the sensor officer.

"Locking on targets and firing energy weapons," reported the tactical officer.

-

In space, the region between the two fleets became filled with energy weapons fire. Fusion energy still ran rampant over the energy screens of both fleets and occasionally a more powerful antimatter weapon would detonate.

The top section of a Trellixian battlecruiser exploded and started drifting away from the ship as energy weapon fire pummeled the vessel. A few moments later a fusion missile arrived, vaporizing the center of the ship. Energy weapons fire riddled the rest of the vessel turning it into a lifeless wreck.

-

"The Humans are holding their ground," reported Lieutenant Commander LeLath breathlessly. "They've lost a couple of ships and a few others have been damaged but they're destroying numerous Trellixian vessels with their weapons fire."

"We're in energy weapons range," reported Zalurr. "Fleet Commander Masurl's fleet is approaching the remaining Trellixian vessels from our port side. They will be in range shortly. The Trellixian fleet is using fifty-megaton missiles."

Diboll touched several icons on his tactical console. "We're still launching missiles and have activated our energy weapons."

"Receiving counter fire from the Trellixians," reported Lieutenant Commander LeLath.

The *Claw of Honor* shook slightly and Kamuss looked over at Zalurr.

"We took several fusion missile hits to our energy screen. Screen is holding at 72 percent."

A sudden bright flash lit up the primary viewscreen. When it cleared the Voltrex battlecruiser *Crimson Dawn* could be seen burning. The fires quickly died as the ship's oxygen was depleted. Multiple Trellixian energy beams were spearing the vessel, tearing it apart. In a massive explosion, the ship blew up, sending debris flying across space.

Fleet Commander Kamuss' eyes narrowed sharply as he watched the viewscreens. More weapons were striking the Trellixian fleet. Massive explosions indicated dying ships. In another few minutes this would be over. The question was what would be the final cost.

"Antimatter warheads have been detected," reported Zalurr. "Not many but a few. That's what's destroyed the Human ships as well as the *Crimson Dawn*."

Kamuss could feel his heart pounding. It always did during battle. "Continue the attack. I don't want a single one of those vessels escaping."

Battle Commander Amblinn stared gloomily through the smoke-filled Command Center. His flagship was heavily damaged but still moving toward the enemy fleet in front of it. "Report!" He knew he was losing his fleet.

"We've lost one hundred and forty-two ships with most of the others damaged," reported the second officer as the flagship shook violently and several more consoles exploded in showers of sparks.

"Our own ship?"

The second officer checked the damage control console and then turned toward the Battle Commander. "We've lost 60 percent of our weapons and all but four of our missile tubes have been destroyed. We have massive ruptures in our hull and substantial crew losses. There are several out of control fires near Engineering. Fire suppression is down and we're attempting to vent those areas to space."

Before Amblinn could reply, he felt the flagship begin to shake uncontrollably, then the roof of the Command Center split open showing the stars.

-

Admiral Edwards was watching the viewscreens intently. The Trellixian fleet was lit up like furnace fire. It was burning from the front and the back and now from one side as Fleet Commander Masurl was blasting the hell out of it with his fleet.

"They won't survive much longer," commented Captain Anderson. Even as he spoke two more Trellixian battlecruisers were turned into miniature novas by the fleet's fusion missiles.

"Enemy fleet is becoming disorganized," reported the sensor officer. "I believe their flagship has been destroyed."

-

In space, the remains of the Trellixian fleet were being assailed from three sides. Ships were having a hard time maneuvering from all the wreckage and some vessels were losing power due to heavy damage. Fusion missile fire and energy beams were raking the entire fleet. The surviving ships rapidly died as the superior weapons of the Voltrex ships annihilated them.

-

"That's the last one," Lieutenant Commander LeLath reported as a Trellixian battlecruiser on the main viewscreen was riddled with energy weapons fire.

"I can confirm that," added Zalurr. "Sensors are showing all enemy ships have been destroyed."

Fleet Commander Kamuss began to relax. The battle was over and this enemy fleet would no longer be a threat to the Solar System or to the *Fury*. "What were our losses?"

"We lost three battlecruisers, Fleet Commander Zalurr lost two, and the Humans lost four," reported LeLath.

Fleet Commander Kamuss nodded. The losses were acceptable considering the number of Trellixian ships they had destroyed. "Can all ships enter hyperspace safely?"

Lieutenant Commander LeLath spent a few minutes talking to the different ships that had suffered damage in all three fleets. She finally turned back toward Fleet Commander Kamuss. "Yes, all ships are hyperspace capable though a few will need substantial repairs when we return to Earth's shipyard."

"Very well, let's get the fleet reorganized and as soon as we do we'll head back to Earth."

Lieutenant Commander LeLath stepped closer to the Fleet Commander. "What are we going to do next?"

Fleet Commander Kamuss stood up and stepped away from his command chair. "We're going to send out our scout ships and a fleet to search for the *Fury*. The Trellixians are bound to be hunting for them. If we can find them I intend to bring them safely home."

LeLath nodded. She was pleased to hear that. It would mean a lot if they could bring Jennifer's brother and his ship safely back to Earth.

-

An hour later the three fleets were in formation and made the transition back into hyperspace. Behind them they left a shattered Trellixian fleet. In the outer region of the system a lone Trellixian battlecruiser, which had been hiding behind a comet, sent a message to the High Command. Something needed to be done about Earth. The Voltrex and Human ships in the system were becoming a danger. Once the message was sent, the battlecruiser entered hyperspace and headed toward the nearest fleet base where it would download all the data it had gathered on the battle. The Humans and the Voltrex had made a major tactical mistake in not searching the system for additional Trellixian warships. The commander of the battlecruiser was certain in the future that mistake was going to cost them.

Chapter Twenty

The *Fury* dropped out of hyperspace on the outskirts of a another red giant star system. It was hoped the Trellixians would not be searching for them around such a large star, particularly this one as it was also a pulsar.

"The interference from the star should play havoc with Trellixian sensors," Lisa said. "We're having trouble with our own."

Captain Dolan looked concerned. "How far can our sensors see?" He didn't want to be completely blind in case the Trellixians were to locate them. He couldn't imagine anything worse than a Trellixian fleet dropping out of hyperspace right on top of them.

"Two million kilometers," replied Kia. "I can't pick up anything past that point. The radiation from the star is too intense."

"Can we get a stellar fix on our position?"

Brett nodded his head. "It will take awhile. We know generally where we are. We just need to sight on several familiar stars so we can plot our next hyperspace jump." This was necessary so they wouldn't pass too close to a star or other space body such as a nebula or even a black hole.

Second Officer Katana stepped over closer to Brett. She had considerable experience in these matters and usually helped him plot their course. She had been on several exploratory missions in the past where it had been necessary to take numerous readings to determine their exact location and their future course. Several exploratory missions had been lost, vanishing, never to be heard from or any traces ever being found.

"I believe the Trellixians are getting more desperate to locate us," said Chloe, turning around on her holographic pedestal to face the captain. "We are encountering more of their ships every day. It is essential we keep adjusting our course so they cannot predict it."

"That sounds good," replied Mark. "Unfortunately they know our eventual destination. I fear the closer we get to Earth, the likelihood of the Trellixians finding us is going to increase."

"There is a 72 percent chance we will be detected," confirmed Chloe.

"I'm open to suggestions." Mark looked round the command crew waiting for a response. He was open to any idea that might improve their chances of getting back to Earth.

Derek looked thoughtful and spent a few moments working at his computer and then turned toward the captain. "What if we change our electronic signature to resemble a Trellixian cargo ship? It might fool them for a while, maybe long enough to allow us to get to Earth."

Lisa nodded her head. "We changed our signature to look like a colony ship last time. They might not expect us to camouflage ourselves as a cargo ship and we've encountered numerous Trellixian cargo ships, many more than their warships or anything else. It might actually work."

"I accessed the records we have of known Trellixian colonies near Earth," said Brenda, gesturing toward her computer screen. "I would suggest we set a course toward one of them and not toward Earth. When we get close enough we can change our course and make a run for home."

Mark leaned back in his command chair. They were still quite a ways from Earth. For the last few days they had encountered growing numbers of Trellixian battlecruisers. What had saved them were the Jelnoid sensors the ship was equipped with. They managed to give them advanced warning of the presence of Trellixian warships before the *Fury* was detected so they could deviate from their course to avoid the enemy. "Go ahead and change the ship's signature. Set a course to keep us in hyperspace for as long as possible. We'll do as Brenda suggests. Find a colony world near Earth and we'll disguise ourselves as a cargo ship. With a little luck maybe the enemy will believe that's what we are and will leave us alone." It was a desperate tactic but it might just give them the edge they needed to make it back to Earth.

A little while later Lisa and the others were back in Lab Two working on the new electronic signature for the *Fury*.

"Will this work?" asked Brenda. She was helping with some of the electronics work for the electronic signature. Minor changes needed to be made to the original equipment. Two highly qualified engineers were assisting.

"Maybe," replied Brett as he stood up and stretched. "It just depends on whether the Trellixians will buy it."

Kia stopped working and looked over at Brenda. "We've encountered a lot of cargo ships recently. It will be difficult for any Trellixian warship to penetrate our disguise."

"How much longer will it take us to get home?" asked Brenda. "I'm ready to get out of this ship."

Brett laughed. "Getting space happy? I think we all would like to get off the ship to stretch our legs and breathe some fresh air. We have eight to ten days of travel yet. It depends on how often we have to deviate from our course."

Lisa breathed out a long sigh. "Once we have this new electronic signature set up maybe we won't have to change course so often. If the Trellixians believe we're one of their own cargo ships, there won't be any reason to change course."

"Lisa's right," said Brett, nodding his head. "If we can maintain our course and speed we can be back home in eight more days."

"Eight days," said Kia with a slight dreamy look on her face. "It seems like forever since we were back home. I guess eight more days won't be so bad."

"As long as the food holds out," added Derek grinning. "I think I've tried every menu item in the Officer's Mess."

Lisa checked an electronic connection and turned the power back on the electronic signature device. The two engineers who were assisting indicated everything was ready as near as they could tell.

"We may have to fine tune it a little," one of the engineers said. "But it should be working."

Derek checked his computer console and ran several quick simulations. "Everything looks fine here. Lisa, if you want to inform Captain Dolan that we're ready for a full scale test we can do so at any time."

Lisa activated her comm unit, putting her in contact with the Command Center. "This is Lieutenant Reynolds. Please inform Captain Dolan the new electronic signature for the ship is ready." Lisa listened to a reply and then turned toward the others. "We'll be staying here for a few more hours while the engineers check the hyperspace drive. It's been acting up slightly and they want to make some adjustments. They don't want it failing and dropping us out of hyperspace at an inopportune time."

Brett looked at the others. "Let's go get something to eat and take a short break. We can all meet back in the Command Center when we're ready to go back into hyperspace."

"Are we certain this signature will work in hyperspace?" asked Brenda as they started to leave Lab Two in the hands of the two engineers.

Lisa hesitated and then answered. "It should. I guess we won't know for certain until we try."

"It'll work," replied Derek confidently. "All the computer simulations indicate it will."

Kia looked over at Derek. "Let's hope so. I'm ready to get back home."

-

Captain Dolan listened as reports came in from the different department heads across the ship. This was the first time since fleeing from the Trellixian home system he actually felt safe. With all the radiation the pulsar was putting out, it would be a complete mischance if the Trellixians stumbled across them.

"How are our shields holding up to the radiation from the pulsar?" he asked looking over at Katana.

Katana checked her console and then replied. "Fine, they're holding at 92 percent. None of the radiation is getting through though our sensors are still limited."

Mark looked around the Command Center. Most of the primary crew were either eating or taking a break. He would need them all back in the Command Center when the *Fury* left the vicinity of the pulsar. "I want all the systems checked as thoroughly as possible before we leave. If this electronic signature works I intend to get us home as quickly as possible."

"The closer we get to Earth, the more Trellixian warships we're going to encounter," warned Katana, her voice sounding like a low growl. "They know where we're going and are bound to be waiting for us."

"The electronic signature might not fool them," added Chloe. "They may be expecting something like that."

"I know," Mark replied. "They may even follow us into the Solar System. That's why as soon as we get within communication range we'll contact Admiral Edwards and let him know we're coming in so they can be prepared." Mark took a deep breath. He knew they still had a long ways to go before arriving at Earth and a lot could happen between now and then. However, with a little luck they might just live to see home again.

-

Battle Commander Balforr was growing more impatient with every report that came in. There had been no confirmed sightings of the Human ship though there had been a few unconfirmed reports of an unidentified ship being spotted on the extreme range of several battlecruisers' sensors.

"It has to be them," said Second Officer Albion. "They have greatly deviated from their course to fool our search efforts."

Balforr eyes turned red as he realized he probably was not going to be able to destroy the Human ship before it reached Earth. However, this might be the time to talk the High Command into allowing him to attack the system. He could point out how dangerous it was to allow Earth to exist and to serve as a forward base for the Voltrex. With the information the Human ship had gathered on the Empire, it might be just enough to talk the High Command into sanctioning an attack in overwhelming force.

"Albion, you have the Command Center. I need to contact High Commander Kaldre with a recommendation."

Albion's eyes widened. "You want to attack Earth."

Balforr nodded. "Yes, with our new fleet and the two reserve fleets as well as whatever other ships the High Command will make available. This might be our best opportunity to finally defeat the Humans. If we can destroy Earth that will leave the Voltrex without an advanced base and greatly reduce the chance of them attacking our core worlds. I'm certain the High Command will agree to this tactic."

-

It had been six hours since Lieutenant Reynolds had informed Captain Dolan the electronic signature device had been modified to make the *Fury* look like a Trellixian cargo vessel. All of the primary command crew were now in the Command Center to see if their ruse would pay off.

"Katana, take us back into hyperspace. Lieutenant Keys, activate the electronic signature and let's see what happens. Lieutenant Masterson, do you have a course set for a Trellixian colony world close to Earth?"

"Yes, sir," Brett replied. "We can travel six days toward the colony and then adjust our course toward Earth the last two. That will be the most dangerous as there will be no reason for a Trellixian cargo ship going that near Earth."

Mark nodded. "We'll deal with that concern when we make the course change. For now, get us back into hyperspace and let's head home."

-

A few moments later the *Fury* made the transition into hyperspace and accelerated away from the pulsar at many times the speed of light.

-

For several days the *Fury* stayed in hyperspace. Seven times they encountered Trellixian battlecruisers but there was no attempt to follow them.

"Our disguise seems to be working," said Second Officer Katana, licking her face whiskers with her tongue. "There is no evidence the Trellixians have realized we're not a cargo ship."

Mark was pleased to hear this. The morale on the ship was greatly improved as it looked as if they would soon be home. "Keep us on our present course and let's hope our luck holds." Mark was already looking forward to seeing his sister. She was his only living family member. If Admiral Edwards approved, he intended to take a few weeks off. He hoped his entire crew could; they definitely deserved it.

-

High Commander Kaldre read the latest report from Battle Commander Balforr. There had been no contact with the Human ship and it looked like there was a good possibility it would reach Earth with its information. "We must take the necessary steps to neutralize Earth," he said. "We cannot allow them to become a forward base for the Voltrex, not with what they will soon know about our core worlds."

"What has the High Command said about this?" asked Second Officer Calaah. "Have they given permission for an attack?"

Kaldre nodded. "Yes, I'm sending all of the newest ships to Commander Balforr. While we haven't had the time to mount the missile pods on the inside of the ships as the Battle Commander wanted, we have managed to come up with a compromise to mount the pods permanently on the outside of the ships. Each battlecruiser will have two pods on the outer hull. Each pod will contain six missiles with seventy-megaton warheads."

Calaah looked impressed. "That will give our ships considerably more firepower until the pods have been used."

"Perhaps long enough to cause considerable damage to the enemy." Kaldre was anxious to see Earth removed as a possible staging area for the Voltrex. The High Command felt the same way after being taken by surprise at how easily the Human ship had slipped into the home system.

"Have you informed Battle Commander Balforr of the High Command's decision?"

"Yes," Kaldre replied. "The ships will be departing tomorrow. The fleets will rendezvous near Earth and after Battle Commander Balforr scouts the Humans' system he will launch his attack."

Calaah turned his attention to a viewscreen showing Battle Commander Balforr's current location as well as the location of Earth compared to the core worlds. The Empire surrounded the planet. It was also in a less populous region of the galaxy. While there were nearby Trellixian colonies, there was not the abundance of habitable worlds like there were around the core of the Empire. "It will be a great victory for the Empire."

"Yes, it will," replied High Commander Kaldre. "Though it still won't solve our problem of overpopulation."

This still greatly concerned him. He had asked several high-ranking computer scientists to run simulations of what would happen if the Trellixian population continued to grow at its current pace. None of the simulations boded well for the Empire. In every case the simulations predicted widespread civil unrest and even possible cannibalism on some of the planets. He had already implemented plans to ensure his own family had sufficient means to survive such turmoil in the Empire. He had arranged for a reserve of food to be hidden away on a small moon his family owned. It was a desperate gamble and one which could cost him his position on the High Command should it become known, but the others still refused to recognize the threat the Empire's growing population posed. Kaldre was convinced this threat was greater than that posed by Earth or the Voltrex.

Battle Commander Balforr was pleased with the response from the High Command. They had approved his attack against Earth and were providing a large number of ships for the operation. It was just as well. Balforr was certain the Human ship had already slipped past his battlecruisers and was well on its way to Earth. Heading to his quarters he was going to begin working on the plan to eliminate the planet as a threat to the Empire. He would at long last have his revenge on the Humans.

-

Captain Dolan was satisfied they could now adjust their course and head straight for Earth. They had dropped out of hyperspace and taken another navigational reading. Next time they entered hyperspace, they wouldn't drop out until they reached the Solar System.

"We're going to make it," said Katana with a relieved look on her face. She purred softly, happy they had made it through the more heavily populated part of the Empire. "The new electronic signature actually seems to be working."

"It seems so," replied Mark as he visibly relaxed in his command chair. For the first time in a number of days he felt the pressure of command lessen. In two more days they would be back in the Solar System and to Earth.

-

The next two days passed by quickly with the crew growing more apprehensive the nearer they came to the planet. When they were twenty light years from Earth Mark sent a hyperspace message to Admiral Edwards that they were coming in. Mark also informed the admiral there would be no further communications until the *Fury* dropped out of hyperspace.

"We'll drop our electronic signature just before we enter the Solar System," Mark said. "I don't want our forces to accidentally identify us as an enemy ship." It would be ironic if friendly forces destroyed the *Fury* after everything the ship and crew had been through.

-

Lisa was sitting in front of her science console. She couldn't believe that in a few more hours they would be back home. They had actually done it! Traveled to the center of the Trellixian Empire and then back to Earth. She felt great sadness at the lives that had been lost; three valuable ships destroyed by the evil Trellixians.

"We're almost home," said Kia over their private comm line. "It will be nice to finally be off this ship."

"Among other things," added Brett, smiling at Lisa.

Lisa felt her face flush. Once they were safely back on Earth and in Complex One she and Brett could continue their growing romantic relationship.

She heard Derek and Brenda both laugh. She shook her head and focused on her computer console. It would be good to be back in Complex One and at least away from the fears of war for a while. She was also looking forward to seeing Professor Wilkens.

In orbit around Earth, Admiral Edwards shook his head after he finished listening to Captain Dolan's message. Disguising themselves as a Trellixian cargo ship was brilliant. No wonder the enemy had failed to detect them.

"This new technology they've developed could be very useful," said Captain Nelson with a thoughtful look on his face. "We could disguise any ship in our fleet as a battleship. It could give us a tactical advantage in the future."

Edwards had already thought of that. "It might. We'll have to do more research on it once the *Fury* gets here and we can examine the equipment they've built."

"It seems putting those five special lieutenants on board the *Fury* paid off."

Edwards nodded. "Yes, it did. However, after this mission I doubt if we'll be able to talk Professor Wilkens into letting us have them again. He's probably correct when he says they're too valuable to risk on these types of missions in the future. They can better serve Earth doing research in Complex One. Who knows what they might come up with that would be useful to our war effort."

"We need to notify Fleet Commander Kamuss that the *Fury* is coming in."

This was true. Fleet Commander Kamuss had taken a small fleet of battleship and battlecruisers further into the Trellixian Empire in order to find the *Fury*. They were currently three hundred light years from Earth. Fortunately they had left a string of hyperspace drones between them and Earth so they should be relatively easy to contact. Admiral Edwards walked over to the communications console. "Send a message to Fleet Commander Kamuss on the *Claw of Honor* and inform him we have been contacted by the *Fury* and they should be back in the Solar System in just a few more hours. He can bring his ships back to Earth."

-

In Complex One, Professor Wilkens was ecstatic. He had just been informed the *Fury* had contacted Admiral Edwards and would be dropping out of hyperspace into the Solar System shortly. For the first time in weeks he felt the worry about Lisa and the others dissipate. They were coming home and all were safe.

"She's coming back," said Amber Stone with a pleased smile on her face. "I told you Captain Dolan would keep her and the others safe."

"I'll just be glad when they're all safely here in Complex One. I have big plans for Lisa and the others."

"I'm sure you do." Amber was glad they had received the news about the *Fury*. The professor had not been his normal jovial self for weeks. She could already see the change in the professor's attitude.

-

"Hyperspace dropout in two minutes," reported Brett as he monitored his navigation console.

"All systems are operating in acceptable ranges," added Chloe.

"Electronic signature has been turned off," confirmed Katana.

Mark leaned forward in his command chair. They were already in the outer edges of the Solar System and would be shortly dropping out of hyperspace just outside the orbit of the Moon.

The atmosphere in the Command Center had lightened just from the excitement of finally being home. Crewmembers were laughing and smiling as the long voyage of exploration was coming to an end.

"Coming up on hyperspace dropout," reported Brett. "We'll be exiting hyperspace 40,000 kilometers outward from the Moon."

"As soon as we exit hyperspace contact Admiral Edwards on the *Renown* and inform him we have arrived," ordered Mark.

"Yes, sir," replied Marissa. "Message is ready to send."

A few moments later the ship exited hyperspace as the Moon appeared on the main viewscreen. In the background the visage of the Earth could be seen.

"We're home," said Lisa with a new cheerfulness in her voice.

"Confirmed," replied Chloe. "We are 42,000 kilometers from the Moon."

"Contacts," added Kia. "I have a squadron of fighter-bombers from the Moon base coming out to inspect us as well as several patrol vessels."

"Admiral Edwards says welcome home and we're to dock with the new shipyard," said Marissa. "He will come over for your debriefing. He'll make arrangements to get the crew shuttled down to Earth for some R&R as soon as possible. He also sends congratulations to the crew for a job well done."

Mark turned on the ship's comm system from his command console. "Crew of the *Fury*. We have arrived safely back in the Solar System and will soon be docking with the new shipyard. Shuttles will be made available to transport everyone down to Earth for some well deserved time off. Admiral Edwards and I want to congratulate all of you on a job well done."

Mark leaned back in his command chair with his eyes on the tactical display. There were an unusually large number of green icons, most of them identified as Voltrex warships. Mark wondered why there were so many of them in the system and if it might signify some new aspect of the war. He would know shortly when he spoke with Admiral Edwards. Hopefully he would be able to go down to Earth shortly to see his sister. It would be nice to get away from the ship and the stress of command for a few days. Looking around the Command Center he smiled to himself. They had made it back home to Earth.

Chapter Twenty-One

Captain Dolan had been called into the president's office. He had no idea why. It had been two months since the *Fury* returned from its mission. During most of that time Mark had been staying in Complex One though he knew shortly he would be returning to his ship to resume his duties.

Reaching the president's office he was ushered in by two security guards. Going inside he was surprised to see Admiral Edwards, Fleet Commander Kamuss, General Mitchell, President Hathaway, Vice President Arnold, Secretary of State Maggie Rayne, and Professor Wilkens.

"Come in and have a seat," Katelyn said with a pleasant smile. "We have much to discuss today."

Mark sat down in the lone remaining empty chair. He felt out of place considering the others in the room. He wondered what was going on.

"I'll let Fleet Commander Kamuss begin," said Katelyn, gesturing toward the Fleet Commander.

"As you know we brought four stealth scout ships with us when my fleets arrived a number of months back. Since then an additional ten more have been sent from the Federation. I've been sending those scouts into the surrounding space out to a distance of about two hundred light years to get a good feel for the Trellixian presence around Earth. A few days ago I received some disturbing news." Kamuss hesitated and looked slowly at each person in the room.

"The scout ship *Far Strike* stumbled upon a Trellixian fleet in a white dwarf system about one hundred and twelve light years distant. There are nearly one thousand Trellixian warships in this fleet and it may still be growing larger."

Mark's eyes bulged. "That's a big part of their known fleet."

Admiral Edwards nodded his head. "We believe the Trellixians have approximately five thousand battlecruisers in their fleet. At least two thousand of them are currently involved in trying to expand their Empire."

President Hathaway took a deep breath and then asked a question. "Why do you believe that fleet is there? Do you believe it represents a threat to Earth?" She hoped not. Earth was just beginning to recover from the previous Trellixian attacks.

Fleet Commander Kamuss nodded his head. "Undoubtedly. I feel certain it's gathering for one of two purposes: to greatly reinforce their fleets in the region of space near Voltrex space to stop our advances or to attack Earth. Due to its location, I believe the attack on Earth is the most likely."

Katelyn felt as if she had been punched in the stomach. After being through so much the last few years was it about to start all over again? "What will happen if that fleet attacks us?"

"We don't know," answered Admiral Edwards, shrugging his shoulders. "Captain Dolan encountered some updated Trellixian battlecruisers in their home system. If the fleet has a large number of them we could be in trouble."

"I've ordered all Voltrex battlecruisers and battleships to remain in the system," added Kamuss. "I've also sent a request back to the Federation for a reinforcing fleet to be sent immediately."

Katelyn looked across her desk at the Fleet Commander. "How soon before it gets here?"

"Nearly four weeks," answered Kamuss, showing some concern over the time involved. "The Federation is quite some distance away."

"What do you suggest?" asked Katelyn, looking over at General Mitchell. She trusted the general's judgment. He had been a bulwark for her administration.

Mitchell hesitated and then responded. "We prepare for all out war. If the Trellixians hit us with this fleet, there is no doubt a large number of troop transports will be involved as well."

"Troop transports," said Vice President Arnold, his eyes widening. "You think they'll land troops again?"

Mitchell nodded his head. "Yes, but this time we'll be ready for them. We'll use our fighter-bombers based on the *Annapolis* and the Moon base to attack their troop shuttles in the atmosphere. We should be able to shoot most of them down. Don't forget they have to get through our planetary defense grid first and we have over eleven hundred defensive satellites in orbit."

"Plus three completed battlestations," added Admiral Edwards. Two had just been completed the previous week. "They add considerable firepower to our offensive and defensive capability."

"We have some people outside the domes," said Secretary of State Rayne. "Should we call them back in?"

President Hathaway looked at General Mitchell for his advice. The Earth's population had been drastically reduced by the Trellixian invasions. They couldn't afford to lose more.

"I would," Mitchell said. "Just to be on the safe side. Two of Fleet Commander Kamuss' scout ships are keeping an eye on the enemy fleets. If they start to move we'll know."

"Captain Dolan. You've seen these new ships of the Trellixians in action against the *Fury*. Just how dangerous are they?" Katelyn waited for an answer.

"They can't stand up to a battleship though they can cause damage," Mark replied. "As far as our battlecruisers go we still have a weapons and shield advantage though not as much as in the past. I would also expect this fleet to be heavily armed with fifty-megaton fusion missiles as well as a number of antimatter ones."

"The antimatter missiles concern me," said Fleet Commander Kamuss. "They can be a danger even to our battleships. Let's hope they don't have too many or this could be a very short battle."

"Can the shipyard and the new battlestations withstand an antimatter strike?" asked General Mitchell, looking at Admiral Edwards.

"Yes, due to their size they have sufficient power for stronger energy shields. It would take a number of antimatter strikes to knock them down and cause damage."

"How's our weapons research going?" asked General Mitchell. "Anything new?" Mitchell looked over at Professor Wilkens.

"Lieutenant Lisa Reynolds and her group have designed a new fusion reactor that is considerably more efficient than our current ones," answered Professor Wilkens. "They did much of the design work while on the *Fury*. We've run some preliminary tests and can increase the power for our warships by nearly 30 percent."

Admiral Edward's eyes widened in surprise. "That's impressive. Could our current warships handle the new reactor and extra power without problems?"

Professor Wilkens nodded his head. "Yes, the current designs for both Human and Voltrex ships takes into account an improvement in power designs though this would put us near the upper limit."

"How soon can we begin making the modifications?" asked Admiral Edwards.

"We can begin with all new construction," replied Professor Wilkens. "As a security measure we should send the specifications for the new fusion reactor back to the Voltrex Federation on a warship, preferable a battleship. We don't want these plans falling into the hands of the Trellixians."

"The new fusion reactor might help us in the future," said Katelyn. "But what about now? What do we do if the Trellixians attack?"

Admiral Edwards glanced over at Fleet Commander Kamuss and then back to the president. "We have a lot of Voltrex ships currently in the system and are holding all warships which normally serve as escorts for Voltrex cargo convoys. If we can hold out until the Federation's reinforcing fleet gets here we could defeat nearly anything the Trellixians throw at us. If they hit us now we'll just have to see. The fleets will do their best to defend Earth."

"The Voltrex fleets will do their part," promised Fleet Commander Kamuss. "We have no intention of abandoning Earth."

Katelyn turned her attention to General Mitchell. "What about our ground forces and air assets?"

"We'll have our ground forces deployed defending the pulse cannon emplacements. Our air assets will be doing the same thing. Fortunately the weather has improved markedly in the last few weeks. On most days now we're seeing some sunshine."

"How soon can we expect an attack?" Katelyn hoped the Voltrex reinforcements would arrive before the Trellixians tried to strike Earth.

General Mitchell's eyes narrowed. "To be truthful, any day. I don't think they'll wait much longer. They have too many ships in that fleet. If I had to make a guess I would say in the next week or two."

"I agree," said Fleet Commander Kamuss. "We will have some notice from our scout ships, probably about twelve to sixteen hours."

"Then I suggest we keep our people either in the domes or close by," said Katelyn, looking over at Secretary of State Raynes. "General Mitchell, I will need you to communicate the direness of this situation to our allies. This will affect all of us."

"I will do so as soon as we're out of this meeting."

-

The group spent another hour discussing contingencies and the disposition of forces. When the meeting was over everyone went back to their offices or flagships. There was no doubt the war for Earth was far from over.

-

Battle Commander Balforr felt his pulse race. On the viewscreens of his flagship he could see hundreds of Voltrex warships. This was the largest concentration of battlecruisers in the history of the Trellixian Empire.

"Quite impressive," said Second Officer Albion. "I've never seen so many of our warships in one place."

Balforr looked at the tactical display, which was covered in green icons. Each icon represented a battlecruiser under his command. There was no doubt in Balforr's mind that if he was successful in eliminating Earth as a threat his promotion to the High Command was assured. High Commander Balforr had a good sound to it. "What's the latest status on the ships we're still waiting on?"

"They'll be here early tomorrow," Albion answered. "That will give us another eighty-seven battlecruisers. There are also four cargo ships in the fleet with three of them carrying the new seventy-megaton missiles. The remaining cargo ship is full of antimatter missiles from High Commander Kaldre."

"Make sure those are spread out across the fleet with first preference given to our newer battlecruisers. How many ships have the new missile pods?"

"Only twenty-two. That's all that could be readied in time."

"Those will have to do. Their targets will be Voltrex battleships. Our other vessels can handle the battlecruisers."

"We're going to lose a lot of those ships," said Albion, pointing to the viewscreens. "The weapons on the Human and Voltrex ships are still superior to ours."

"Our numbers will carry the day. We will lose some ships but the Humans and the Voltrex will lose all of theirs. In the end we will have victory."

Battle Commander Balforr was ready for the battle to begin. As soon as the last fleet arrived with the cargo vessels, he would distribute the missiles and then be on his way to Earth. Farther out in the star system the recently arrived invasion fleet was waiting: forty more battlecruisers and seventy troop transports. After the fleet battle was over and all ground targets destroyed by orbital bombardment, the troop transports would unload their cargoes of soldiers who would sweep across the planet ensuring not a single Human survived.

-

"Do you have to leave?" asked Jennifer. Her brother had just told her he was returning to the *Fury*.

Mark let out a deep sigh. He didn't want Jennifer to worry, but there was no guarantee he would be coming back from this battle. "The *Fury* is one of our most powerful ships. I'll be back before you know it."

"You'd better," replied Jennifer, giving Mark a teary-eyed hug. "I need you, big brother."

Mark stepped away from his sister with a weak smile. It was time to return to the *Fury*.

-

Lisa was in one of the labs with Derek, Brenda, and Kia working on the new fusion reactor design. Professor Wilkens had asked them to get the plans organized so they could send a copy to the Voltrex Federation. "Are we ready?"

"Yes," Derek replied as he handed her several computer disks and a sheaf of papers. "Everything they need to duplicate our research is in there. Those disks have been formatted to work in Voltrex computers."

"How are you and Brett getting along?" asked Kia, with a sly smile. "I heard rumors the two of you are thinking about moving in together."

Lisa blushed and slowly nodded her head. "We're talking about it," she admitted. "But it's a big step for both of us."

"Do it!" suggested Brenda with an impish grin. "It will give us all more to talk about."

Lisa shook her head. The five of them were still very close and kept very few secrets. Brenda and Kia had become like sisters and Derek almost like a brother. "Some things need to be kept private." Before she could say anything more the alarms in the research lab began sounding.

A military officer opened the door to the lab looking in at the four. "A large Trellixian fleet has been detected moving toward the Solar System. The civilian concourse will be shut down in six hours for everyone's safety. Cafeterias will still be open for those who need to get a meal. You can stay here in the lab or go to your quarters but there will be no moving about the complex without permission after the concourse is closed."

Lisa felt her heart flutter. The expected attack was about to begin. While she felt safe here in Complex One she knew there were many people across the planet who weren't so fortunate. She was worried about what the next few days would bring.

-

Admiral Edwards was on board the *Renown* when he received word the Trellixian fleet was moving. It was coming at them in two sections. The first was the attack fleet consisting of battlecruisers and the second was the invasion fleet. It would be lagging several hours behind the other ships.

"Status!" He wanted the latest battle readiness reports of his fleet and orbital installations.

"We have four ships on the ground for crew rotation and maintenance," reported Captain Nelson. "All four ships will be off the ground within three hours. The battlestations are combat ready with full loads of missiles. The shipyard is buttoning up. All ships docked to it are moving away. All Voltrex cargo ships are preparing to leave. Ten Voltrex support ships and one battlecruiser will escort them. Only two are still loaded and they will return once the all clear is given."

"What about the defense satellites and the Moon base?"

Nelson checked some information on one of his computer screens before replying. "We have 1,129 defensive satellites and all are operational. The Moon base has gone to Condition Three and will be going to Condition Two in another four hours; sooner if the threat from the Trellixians increases."

Admiral Edwards thought about what to do with the twenty small patrol craft. They would only pose a minor threat to the Trellixians. "The patrol ships are to stay grounded for the time being. We may need them for later. I want the fighter-bombers armed with twenty-kiloton missiles. They're to stay out of the combat unless they see a heavily damaged Trellixian vessel. Then they are to attack in squadron strength and use their missiles to destroy it. Once any fighter-bomber has used its load of missiles it's to return to base to be rearmed."

"How will our fleets fight this battle?"

Admiral Edwards took in a deep breath. "Even though this is Earth, Fleet Commander Kamuss has far more battle experience. I am turning command over to him. It's the best way to ensure a victory."

"The latest reports from the scouts indicate we're going to be facing over twelve hundred Trellixian battlecruisers."

Admiral Edwards didn't like the odds but there was nothing he could do about it. "We have two hundred and thirty-two Voltrex battleships and battlecruisers in the system. We also have fifty-seven battleships and battlecruisers in our own fleet plus the *Annapolis*."

"Speaking of the *Annapolis*, where do we want her?"

"Put her beneath the defensive grid," ordered Admiral Edwards. "Her primary job is going to be to use her fighter-bombers and weapons to destroy any enemy missiles that penetrate the grid."

Captain Nelson gazed at one of the main viewscreens showing the Earth. A good part of the cloud layer had dissipated. Much of the ash and dust in the atmosphere had settled. Large parts of the oceans and even the landmasses were visible. "Let's hope this coming battle doesn't damage Earth again."

"That's why we're going to try to force this battle far enough away from the planet to prevent that. Fleet Commander Kamuss wants to meet the Trellixians midway between the Earth and the Moon. We'll use our long-range missiles to destroy as many as we can before we begin to fall back toward the three battlestations. We're hoping their extra firepower will be the determining factor in this battle."

"I wish the other three were finished," said Captain Nelson, looking at one of the smaller viewscreens, which showed one of the one-thousand-meter battlestations.

Admiral Edwards wished they were done as well. With six, the Earth would be much safer. As it was, they were going to have a battle on their hands trying to keep the Trellixians away from the planet.

—

Captain Dolan was back on the *Fury* along with Second Officer Katana. "Report!"

"All systems are powered up and working at optimum levels," reported Chloe.

"Trellixian fleet is expected to drop out of hyperspace in another few hours," added Katana. "Fleet Commander Kamuss has been put in charge of the fleets. We're to join Admiral Edward's fleet formation."

This didn't surprise Mark as Fleet Commander Kamuss was the more experienced flag officer. "Marissa, contact the shipyard and inform them we will be moving away." The *Fury* had been docked to the shipyard to allow the returning crew to board. "Helm, as soon as we've cleared the shipyard take the ship to Admiral Edward's fleet." Mark leaned back in his command chair. There was no doubt the coming battle could well decide the future of Earth.

—

Battle Commander Balforr felt slight apprehension as the fleet prepared to exit hyperspace in the Human star system. He had a major portion of the Empire's fleet with him. If he were to lose this fleet, it would have serious repercussions for the Empire. It would drastically reduce future expansion and Empire security until the ships could be replaced. However, he had no intention of losing the fleet. While the fleet might suffer substantial loses, removing Earth as a threat to the Empire would be worth it.

"Hyperspace dropout in twelve minutes," reported Joltan from the Helm. "We will exit hyperspace two million kilometers from Earth."

Balforr was doing this so there would be no surprises. His fleet would scan Earth and the surrounding space to ensure there were no surprises. Once he knew for certain what they were up against, the fleet would advance and engage the enemy.

"All ships are ready for combat," reported Second Officer Albion.

Balforr nodded. So far everything was going according to plan.

"We'll place Battle Commander Treela's fleet at the forefront of our formation," Balforr said. "Battle Commander Cartlen and Battle Commander Visonn will be on our flanks. Our fleet will be mixed in with the two other fleets assigned to us to make our ships more difficult for the Humans and the Voltrex to spot. The same for the twenty-two battlecruisers equipped with the new missile pods."

Second Officer Albion was silent for a moment and then spoke. "We'll be sacrificing most of Battle Commander Treela's fleet when we reach engagement range. No doubt the Humans and the Voltrex will attempt to use their extended missile range to strike our ships before we can get within combat range."

"Perhaps," replied Balforr. "However I intend to close the range as quickly as possible in order to take that advantage away. I have a plan the Humans and Voltrex will not be expecting. Our own missiles are more powerful than theirs and I've made sure all the ships in our fleets have full missile loads. Not only that, all of our updated battlecruisers are carrying a number of our antimatter missiles."

"Then it will be a battle of attrition with both sides losing ships until one is the victor," said Albion. "It will be a vicious battle."

"One we will win," replied Balforr confidently.

The Humans and the Voltrex had never fought a fleet as large as the one Balforr presently commanded. The sheer number of vessels would make the difference. Once the defending forces were defeated he would place his fleet in Earth orbit and drop nuclear weapons until the planet's ground based defenses were eliminated. Then the troop carriers would be called in and Trellixian soldiers would begin landing. Someday in the near future the planet would take its rightful place as a colony of the Trellixian Empire.

Chapter Twenty-Two

Mark was watching a timer on the main viewscreen, which was counting down to the time the Trellixian fleet was expected to exit hyperspace. The tension in the Command Center was high as everyone knew what was at stake in this coming battle. If they failed to stop the Trellixians the Earth and everyone on it would die.

"Contact!" called out the sensor officer. "Trellixian battlecruisers exiting hyperspace two million kilometers out."

"Set Condition One," ordered Mark, feeling his heart start to beat faster.

Alarms began to sound and red lights started flashing. The crew was already at Condition Two; the setting of Condition One meant combat was imminent.

"Fleet Commander Kamuss has cleared all ships for unlimited use of forty-megaton missiles," reported Marissa. "We are to launch as soon as we have a target lock on an opposing vessel. He wants to destroy as many as we can before they get within their own weapons range."

Mark was in agreement with this strategy. The Human and Voltrex missiles had nearly double the range of the ones the Trellixians possessed.

"Status of our missile tubes?" asked Mark, looking over at Lieutenant Thomas at Tactical.

"All tubes are loaded with forty-megaton warhead missiles. We can launch as soon as the enemy are within range."

On Lieutenant Thomas's tactical display, a number of red icons were blinking. Those were the missile tubes with live missiles. One touch of his finger and the missiles would start launching.

Mark looked at the primary tactical display, which was still filling with red threat icons as more Trellixian battlecruisers poured out of hyperspace. Mark began to feel deeply concerned when he realized just how many there were and how badly they were going to be outnumbered.

From beside him he heard a low growl come from Second Officer Katana. Looking at her, Mark noticed her claws were out. "Calm down, Katana. We still have a few minutes before we engage in combat."

"Sorry, sir," replied Katana, retracting her claws. "I just hate the lizard people and now we have an opportunity to kill more of them."

"Yes," Mark answered. "We're definitely going to get that opportunity." On another screen, Mark could see Earth. He was relieved his sister was safe in Complex One but just how safe would that be if the Trellixians succeeded in destroying the defending forces and began landing troops on the planet once more? Mark was determined not to allow that to happen.

Fleet Commander Kamuss gazed unflinchingly at the main tactical display as it filled with red threat icons. "Do we have a firm count on the enemy vessels?"

"One thousand two hundred and forty-three," replied Lieutenant Commander LeLath. "That's by far the largest concentration of Trellixian ships we've ever encountered."

"If our reports are correct that's nearly a fourth of their fleet." Kamuss knew if they could destroy this fleet, it would change this war dramatically.

The Voltrex themselves had nearly three thousand warships of all sizes. If this fleet could be eliminated the Voltrex Federation, using Earth as a forward base, could go on the offensive.

"Enemy ships are holding position," reported Zalurr. "Detecting numerous sensor scans."

"Scanning our defenses," said Lieutenant Commander LeLath. "They want to know what they're up against."

This didn't surprise Kamuss. "They won't like seeing three completed battlestations and the shipyard packs quite a punch as well."

"There's also the base on the Moon," added LeLath. "It's much more heavily armed than previously. It'll be a major surprise to the Trellixians."

Several minutes passed and then suddenly the Trellixian fleet began to vanish from the sensors.

Alarms began sounding and a surprised look crossed Zalurr's face. "Trellixian fleet is jumping into hyperspace!"

LeLath looked confused. "Are they leaving?"

Suddenly on the main viewscreens, Trellixian battlecruisers began appearing right in front of the fleet.

"Trellixian battlecruisers detected," reported Zalurr. "Range is five thousand kilometers."

"They're already in weapons range," groaned LeLath, realizing they had just lost their biggest tactical advantage. They've also avoided the weapons based on the Moon."

"Fire all weapons!" ordered Fleet Commander Kamuss, leaning forward in his command chair, his eyes focused intently on the viewscreens. Already the enemy ships could be seen launching missiles and firing their energy cannons.

"Targets locked and missiles away," called out Diboll. "Energy cannons firing as well. Defensive batteries are set to automatic and targeting the inbound missiles."

The *Claw of Honor* shook violently and several red lights appeared on the damage control console.

"We've been hit my multiple fusion weapons," LeLath reported. "We have minor damage to section seventeen with two compartments open to space. Compartments have been sealed off and damage control teams are en route. Those were fifty-megaton missiles."

Kamuss frowned, deeply worried. This was not how he had envisioned the battle beginning. The Trellixian hyperspace jump had been daring and unexpected.

"Fleets are fully engaged," Lieutenant Commander LeLath informed the Fleet Commander.

On the viewscreens, the front of the massive Trellixian fleet formation was lit up from the explosions of thousands of forty-megaton missiles. Occasionally a brighter flash indicated the destruction of a Trellixian battlecruiser. Kamuss had nearly three hundred Voltrex and Human ships to try to stop the Trellixian fleet from reaching Earth.

"Can we tell how many of the Trellixian ships are of the new design reported by Captain Dolan?"

"No, sir," replied Zalurr. "Not until we get closer and I can determine the difference with our sensors."

The *Claw of Honor* shook again and several more red lights appeared on the damage control console.

"We have another rupture in the hull," reported LeLath, her eyes narrowing. "Three more compartments are open to space and we have a small fire. I've sealed off the area and activated the fire suppression systems. Repair teams are en route."

"All weapons still functional," added Diboll.

A huge vibration suddenly shook the flagship. Kamuss looked questionably over at Lieutenant Commander LeLath. "The *Valiant* just blew up," she explained with a pained look on her face. "It was right next to us." The *Valiant* was a Voltrex battlecruiser.

Taking a deep breath, Fleet Commander Kamuss began issuing orders to the combined fleets. "All ships, hold your position. We must keep the enemy from reaching the shipyard or Earth. Severely damaged ships are to pull back to the rear of the formation and do whatever repairs are necessary to get back into the battle. We fight for Earth and for the future of the Federation!"

-

The battle between the opposing fleets intensified. The number of missiles striking each fleet increased even though defensive fire was destroying over half of them before they reached their targets. In the Trellixian fleet, battlecruiser after battlecruiser was being blown apart by multiple strikes of forty-megaton missiles. The entire front of the massive fleet formation looked as if it was on fire.

In the defending fleet, several battlecruisers had been lost and others damaged. Fifty-megaton missiles continued to strike the powerful Jelnoid energy screens, threatening to bring more of them down.

-

Battle Commander Treelas stared in growing dismay as his fleet was being annihilated around him. On the viewscreens of his Command Center, he watched as the *Warriors Hand* and the *Defender* were blown apart by fusion missiles. Nova-like explosions left little wreckage behind.

"Intensify our missile fire!" he ordered, hoping this would lessen the carnage being delivered to his fleet. In all of his years as a Battle Commander he had never experienced anything like this.

The *Red Sunrise* shook violently. Red lights glowed ominously on the damage control console. Alarms began sounding warnings of severe damage to the ship.

"We have heavy damage just aft of Engineering," reported the second officer. "We've venting atmosphere and several fires are burning. Fire suppression equipment in those sectors is non-functioning."

"Vent those areas to space," ordered Treelas. "We can't let those fires reach the missile storage bunkers." Treelas knew if they did they would lose the ship.

"Venting those sections," replied the second officer. A few moments later he turned toward Battle Commander Treelas. "Venting has been completed and the fires are out. There were sixty crew personnel in the sections when we vented out the atmosphere."

This didn't concern Treelas. "They died for the Empire. That is our duty as fleet officers and crew."

Treelas turned his attention back to the tactical display. He had already lost over 60 percent of his fleet with more vessels dying every minute. In the defending fleet several battlecruisers had been eliminated and others damaged.

-

In the Human and Voltrex formation, the sheer number of fifty-megaton missiles striking the shields was having an effect. Numerous fusion explosions knocked down the energy screen of the Voltrex battlecruiser *Nightwing* and then energy beam fire slammed into the armored hull, drilling deep within the vessel setting off multiple explosions. Huge pieces of hull plating were hurled away from the stricken vessel. Secondary explosions began to shake the battlecruiser as more energy beams penetrated the ship. In a fiery explosion the *Nightwing* blew apart, sending debris flying across space.

-

Battle Commander Balforr was pleased with the progress of the battle. While Battle Commander Treelas had lost most of his fleet, it had allowed Balforr's newer ships to close the range. "I want all ships to launch a continuous barrage of missiles. I also want all twenty-two of our battlecruisers equipped with the missile pods to target a Voltrex battleship. They are to empty both of their pods and time the missiles to arrive on target simultaneously. That should pop the shields, making the vessels vulnerable to our regular missile fire."

"Orders being sent," Second Officer Albion replied.

Battle Commander Balforr leaned back in his command chair with a wicked grin on his face. Now the Humans and the Voltrex would realize the real power of his fleet.

-

Battle Commander Kamuss was growing concerned as the missile barrage from the Trellixians suddenly increased to the maximum. At the same time a number of compact missile groups came through the barrage aimed at his battleships. "Target those missiles!" he ordered, realizing the Trellixian were trying to take out his battleships.

Defensive fire intensified but there were so many inbound missiles it was difficult to target the individual missile groups. With devastating effect, they slammed into the Voltrex battleships.

-

In space, massive explosions pummeled the largest ships in the defending fleet. Shields flared brightly and began to fail. As soon as they failed, additional Trellixian missiles smashed into the hulls of the now vulnerable ships. In brilliant explosions of light sixteen Voltrex battleships died and four others were heavily damaged. The Voltrex fleet recoiled at the deadliness of the attack.

"Pull us back," ordered Fleet Commander Kamuss, his face ashen with shock. "All Voltrex fleets are to pull back to the battlestations. The Human fleet is to take up defensive positions around the shipyard."

Kamuss didn't like being forced to pull back like this but he had just lost nearly half of his heaviest ships. He needed the heavier firepower from the battlestations, the shipyard, and the defensive grid to offset the loss of so many battleships.

The fleet pulled back in an orderly fashion. Missile launches and energy weapons fire continued unabated between the opposing fleets. The Trellixians tried to exploit their newly won advantage by pushing even closer to the Voltrex and Human ships.

On the ground in General Mitchell's Command Center, all the on duty personnel were watching the space battle on the huge high definition viewscreens. They could see close-ups of ships in both fleets being destroyed by relentless energy beam fire and missiles.

"This isn't going well," said General Briggs. "I don't believe Fleet Commander Kamuss thought the Trellixians could destroy his battleships."

General Mitchell looked at a viewscreen, which showed one of the smaller Human-built battlecruisers being riddled with energy beam fire. After a minute the ship simply broke in half to drift helplessly in space. "The firepower from the battlestations and the shipyard will help."

"But not enough," replied General Briggs, folding his arms across his chest. "I would suggest we make all commands ready for possible Trellixian troop insertion." Across the planet military troops were waiting for orders to move out and engage the enemy, an order all were hoping would not be given.

General Mitchell took a deep breath. He had a decision to make shortly. If the battle in space became hopeless, he was going to order Fleet Commander Kamuss and Admiral Edwards to save what remained of their fleets and withdraw. They could come back later with reinforcements to try to retake Earth if anything remained.

"Get me the president," he ordered. "I need to inform her of the progress of the battle." Mitchell wasn't looking forward to giving the president the bad news. With every passing moment it looked as if the Trellixians were once more going to be in control of the orbital space around Earth.

-

Admiral Edwards watched the tactical display and the viewscreens as his fleet took up defensive positions around the shipyard. Already the shipyard had begun to fire its weapons and launch missiles at the nearing enemy fleet. The shipyard's energy shield was raised and operating at full power. The shield around the shipyard was even stronger than the ones possessed by the battleships.

The *Renown* shook violently as its energy screen was struck by several seventy-megaton missiles.

"Shield is at 70 percent," reported Captain Nelson. "We've lost the battlecruisers *Reliant* and *London* with a number of others suffering heavy damage."

"The Voltrex fleets?" Edwards knew they had taken some heavy losses.

"They've lost seventeen battleships and twenty-three battlecruisers. Also Fleet Commander Barvon's flagship has been destroyed. Fleet Commander Masurl has taken over command of the survivors of Barvon's fleet."

Admiral Edwards let out a deep sigh. He had become friends with Fleet Commander Barvon. The large feline had a great sense of humor. The *Renown* shook again and red lights began appearing on the damage control console.

"We have several compartments open to space and a fire near Engineering," reported Captain Nelson. "I've got repair crews on the way."

The ship shook violently once more and additional alarms began sounding.

"We just lost six energy beam turrets and three missile tubes," reported the tactical officer. "Energy shield is down to 22 percent and dropping."

Captain Nelson listened intently as more details of the damage came in over his comm unit. "We have a large rupture in our hull over thirty meters long and twelve wide. There are numerous stress fractures around it."

Edwards closed his eyes briefly. If this continued the *Renown* would not last much longer. "Contact the *Fury*; I need to speak to Captain Dolan."

"I have Admiral Edwards on the comm," said Marissa, looking over at the captain.

"Put him on my comm unit," ordered Mark. He wondered why Admiral Edwards would be contacting him in the middle of the battle.

"Captain," came Admiral Edward's voice over the comm.

"Yes, sir," Mark replied.

"I am promoting you to rear admiral effective immediately. My ship has been heavily damaged and is still under attack. In case the *Renown* is destroyed you will take command of the fleet and do the best you can to defend the shipyard and the Earth."

Mark was silent for a moment, stunned by the sudden promotion and the thought that Admiral Edwards might not survive this battle. "Yes, sir," he finally said. "I will do as you have instructed."

"Good luck, Admiral," Edwards said as the comm went silent.

Mark leaned back in his Command Chair. This was completely unexpected. There were other qualified officers in the fleet. In some ways Mark wished the admiral had chosen some one else to be his successor. Looking at a viewscreen, focused on the *Renown*, he saw the flagship was under heavy attack. Several huge ruptures were visible in her hull. Even as Mark watched, several energy beams penetrated her weakening screen and striking deep inside the ship. Several explosions hurled large pieces of hull plating off into space. Mark's eyes widened as he realized the flagship was in its death throes.

-

Admiral Edwards looked around his Command Center. The crew were still at their posts doing their jobs. He felt great pride in their dedication. This was a fine crew and he wished there was some way to save them.

"Sublight drive is down," reported Captain Nelson. "Hyperdrive has been destroyed."

"This is it then," said Admiral Edwards, shifting his gaze to Nelson. The ship shook violently, throwing several crew personnel to the deck. More alarms began to sound and the damage control console was now covered in red lights. Edwards pressed the comm button, which would allow him to speak to everyone on the ship. "Crew of the *Renown*, it has been an honor to serve with you. I could not have asked for a better crew." Before he could say anything else the lights flickered and then went out.

"We've lost Engineering," reported Captain Nelson as the lights came back on dimly from the emergency batteries.

"All weapons are down," added the tactical officer.

"Life support has failed," reported the systems officer.

Admiral Edwards leaned back in his command. He knew this was it. He just wished he knew how all of this would end.

-

Rear Admiral Dolan watched with anguish as the *Renown* blew apart. One moment the flagship was there and the next it was an expanding field of glowing debris.

"*Renown* is down," reported the sensor officer in a stunned voice.

"There are no survivors," added Chloe. "You are now in command of the fleet."

Mark nodded. "All ships are to continue to fire. We will hold our position here as long as a single ship has an energy beam or a missile to fire."

-

"The *Renown* has been destroyed," reported Lieutenant Commander LeLath with great sadness in her eyes. "Admiral Edwards promoted Captain Dolan to rear admiral and put him in charge of the fleet just before the flagship was destroyed."

Kamuss nodded. He had witnessed the destruction of the *Renown* on one of the viewscreens. "Captain Dolan will make a good rear admiral. What's the current status of our fleet?"

"We've taken up positions around the three battlestations. We've suffered substantial losses and a large number of our ships have been damaged. We've managed to destroy about 30 percent of the Trellixian fleet and damaged many more of their vessels. They continue to press us."

"Have we identified their newer ships?"

"Yes, there are a little over one hundred and twenty of them. They're in the heart of the Trellixian fleet formation, making them harder to destroy. It appears the Trellixian Fleet Commander is sacrificing his other ships to destroy as many of ours as possible while limiting the danger to his newer and more powerful vessels. The newer ships are also launching seventy-megaton fusion missiles."

"More contacts," called out Zalurr. "We have more Trellixian ships dropping out of hyperspace four million kilometers from Earth."

Kamuss let out a deep sigh. "It's their invasion fleet. It will hold at its present position until it's safe for them to go into

Earth orbit." Kamuss looked at the tactical display. Even with Earth's battlestations and the shipyard he was going to have a hard time stopping the Trellixian fleet. His only real hope was that the eleven hundred defensive satellites and the hundreds of pulse cannons on the surface could stop whatever Trellixian battlecruisers his fleet failed to destroy.

On board the *Fury*, Mark grimaced as his flagships took more damage. Nearly ten percent of the compartments on the powerful battleship were now open to space. Several fires were burning out of control. So far his fleet had prevented any damage to the shipyard but he knew that would not last much longer. In the last few minutes he had lost one Voltrex-built battlecruiser and two more Earth-built battlecruisers.

"Admiral, the Moon base is launching their fighter-bombers," reported Katana.

"Major Brandon has ordered them to attack any damaged Trellixian battlecruisers they can find," added Marissa.

Mark looked at the tactical screen, which showed a host of small green icons leaving the Moon.

"Four hundred," reported the sensor officer. "That's all that are based on the Moon."

Mark knew most of those brave pilots were flying to their deaths. They would be easy targets for the defensive batteries on the damaged warships. He considered calling them off but realized that even if they could destroy a few of the damaged battlecruisers it might just be enough to give Earth a chance.

"Some of the enemy battlecruisers are launching missiles at the defense grid," warned Chloe. "Defense grid has been activated."

On the tactical screen, several hundred Trellixian missiles headed toward Earth. Energy beams from the defensive grid lanced out, destroying the majority of them. Fourteen made it to the defensive grid and detonated.

"They're trying to blow a hole through the defensive grid," said Chloe in alarm.

"Have the *Annapolis* use her fighter-bombers to cover that hole," ordered Mark, his right hand clenching in a tight fist. "We can't have any missiles getting through to Earth!"

Mark watched with anguish as the small green icons representing the fighter-bombers closed with the rear of the Trellixian fleet. Suddenly the small icons began to vanish as they came under defensive energy weapons fire from the Trellixian battlecruisers. Several large fusion explosions took out entire squadrons but the fighter-bombers continued to close with the enemy.

-

Flight Leader Captain James Rollison jinked his fighter-bomber hard to the left, dodging incoming energy beam fire. Next to him his wing mate wasn't as fortunate as his fighter-bomber was hit dead center by an energy beam. In a fiery explosion, which rapidly died away the small craft, was blown apart. All around Captain Rollison pilots were dying as the deadly defensive fire struck them.

"All Black Ravens form up on me for our attack run," he ordered over his comm unit. Three pilots answered out of the ten he had started out with. "Arm missiles and launch on my mark." Rollison had chosen a badly damaged Trellixian battlecruiser at the rear of their formation. It had several large ruptures in the hull and its energy shield was down. Reaching forward he armed the two sparrow twenty-kiloton nuclear missiles with which his fighter-bomber was equipped. On his console his targeting system showed a firm lock. "Fire missiles." From his fighter-bomber two missiles dropped away and arrowed toward the enemy battlecruiser. "All Black Ravens, head to the barn." He turned sharply heading away from the enemy battlecruiser.

Captain Rollison activated his afterburners and the small fighter-bomber rocketed forward at an increased speed. Behind him, six missiles struck the battlecruiser, destroying it. Looking at his tactical screen, he saw only two other fighter-bombers had joined back up with him. With a deep sigh, he said nothing as he headed back toward the Moon to rearm.

Rear Admiral Dolan felt his breath catch in his throat. Six Trellixian battlecruisers had been destroyed at the cost of nearly 80 percent of the attacking fighter-bombers.

"Remaining craft are returning to the Moon base to rearm," reported Marissa.

"Inform Major Brandon the surviving fighter-bombers are to remain at the Moon to help with the defense of the Moon base." There was no point in having the remaining fighter-bombers to attack again. He doubted if any of them would make it close enough to launch their missiles at the Trellixian ships.

On the main viewscreen, one of the remaining Voltrex battleships in Fleet Commander Kamuss' formation suddenly exploded.

"What happened?" demanded Mark. The ship had only been hit with a couple of missiles.

"Detecting signs of an antimatter explosion," reported Chloe. "The newer Trellixian ships have started firing antimatter missiles. Fleet Commander Kamuss has already lost a number of battlecruisers to the weapons.

Mark's shoulders slumped. If the Trellixians were using antimatter and they had a lot of the missiles then the battle was lost.

Battle Commander Balforr was jubilant. Battle Commander Treelas and his fleet were gone but he was now pushing forward, shielded by his two fleets of regular battlecruisers with Battle Commander Cartlen and Battle Commander Visonn on the flanks. Both Battle Commanders had lost a lot of ships but Balforr's ships in the center of the formation were still mostly intact. Not only that, he had just issued the order to begin using their store of antimatter weapons. Already in the Human and the Voltrex fleet formations more of their ships were dying. The computer was predicting a 92 percent chance of Trellixian victory. He would wipe out the defending fleets and leave the shipyard and the three battlestations alone. They he would stand off with his fleet and annihilate the defensive grid from long range. When the grid was gone, he would begin to bombard the planet with nuclear weapons. Victory was his and there was nothing the Humans or the Voltrex could do to stop it!

Fleet Commander Kamuss had just received word from General Mitchell to pull his fleet out and return to the Federation. Victory for the defending ships was slowly slipping away as more antimatter weapons were being used by the Trellixians.

"What do we do?" asked Lieutenant Commander LeLath. She could not imagine abandoning Earth even if it was the strategic thing to do.

"We're not leaving yet," replied Kamuss, shaking his head and trying to think of another option. "The least we can do is reduce the size of the Trellixian fleet as much as possible to give the ground defenses on Earth a chance."

Battle Commander Balforr could feel victory within his grasp. Since ordering his more modern battlecruisers to using their stores of antimatter weapons, the battle had quickly turned in the Trellixians' favor. True, many of his regular battlecruisers were still being annihilated by heavy defensive fire, but every minute more Human and Voltrex ships were being destroyed. "Fire another salvo of missiles at the Human defensive grid. Follow it up with a flight of nuclear missiles and let's see if we can hit a few targets on the surface."

"As you command," answered Second Officer Albion as he began issuing orders to the fleet's tactical officers.

Hundreds of fifty-megaton fusion missiles hurtled toward the Earth's defensive grid. Energy beam fire quickly annihilated the majority of them but thirty-eight more struck the defensive grid, creating an even larger hole above Earth. Several hundred nuclear missiles were then launched toward the opening. Even so, nearly half were shot down by energy weapons fire and the fighter-bombers from the *Annapolis*. The nimble craft were able to take out forty-seven more and defensive fire from ground-based defenses took out all the rest except three, which hit the Earth and detonated. Two were ocean strikes and one exploded above a landmass. Into the atmosphere of Earth three mushroom clouds began to rise into the air.

"It's confirmed, sir," Colonel Fields reported. "Three nuclear missiles have struck the Earth. Medium yield with two being Pacific Ocean strikes and one on the Baja Peninsula."

"So they're going to nuke us," said General Briggs grimly. "I would recommend we keep all of our troops and other military assets beneath the energy shields until the Trellixians begin landing troops."

General Mitchell nodded. "I agree. Send the orders." Mitchell then turned toward Colonel Steward at Communications. "Has Fleet Commander Kamuss responded to my recommendation that he pull the fleets out?"

"Yes, sir. He says he will once he destroys more of the Trellixian fleet."

Mitchell shook his head. "That crazy feline. I should have known he would refuse to retreat."

In space, the battle had become brutal with the two fleets now beginning to intermix. The Voltrex fleets left the vicinity of the battlestations and began to engage the Trellixian vessels in one to one combat. In this the Voltrex ships had a decisive advantage unless they were hit with several antimatter missiles. The Human fleet stayed near the shipyard as they could not afford to allow it to be destroyed. Even so, they were still under heavy fire.

Rear Admiral Dolan coughed as he tried to catch his breath. The Command Center was full of smoke as several consoles had shorted out. Several large ceiling support beams had broken free, crushing several officers and causing even more damage. Nearly half of his fleet had been destroyed and the region around the shipyard was full of drifting debris. Trellixian missiles were now impacting the powerful screen of the shipyard but so far it had remained impenetrable. The shipyard's energy cannons were firing nonstop and hundreds of missiles were being launched.

"Report!"

"Second Officer Katana shook her head. "Sublight drive has suffered damage. It's still operational but may not last much longer. Hyperdrive is out and will take twenty minutes to repair. We have numerous compartments open to space and have suffered a lot of crew casualties. We have three major fires and we're trying to bring them under control. At the moment Engineering is cut off from the rest of the ship."

"Energy screen is down to 30 percent," added Lieutenant Thomas. "We've lost half of our defensive turrets and most of our heavy energy beam projectors. All but four of our missile tubes are nonfunctional."

Mark looked around the Command Center. He knew they needed a miracle or this battle would soon be over. His stint as a rear admiral might be the shortest in history.

The *Fury* shook again and more alarms blared out; the damage control console became filled with even more red lights. His ship was dying and Mark felt great pain at the damage being done to his ship and the loss of so many crewmembers.

Alarms suddenly began sounding on the sensor console.

Mark looked instinctively toward the tactical display to see more red threat icons appearing. He felt devastated seeing them. Any hope of victory had just evaporated.

"More ships exiting hyperspace," reported the tactical officer in a subdued voice. "Exit point is just behind the current Trellixian fleet."

Mark knew this was it. Another fleet of Trellixian ships would allow the enemy to sweep right through the defenders. Even as he watched the tactical display trying to figure out what to do the red icons suddenly turned green.

"They're Voltrex!" shouted the sensor officer excitedly. "We have over two hundred and seventy Voltrex ships exiting hyperspace!"

"How?" uttered Mark in shock, looking over at Katana. "The reinforcing fleets are still nearly two weeks out."

"I have a message from Fleet Commander Lore," reported Marissa. "His fleet has been out attacking Trellixian colonies. The Voltrex Fleet Command ordered his fleet here as it was far closer than the reinforcing fleets. They did not say anything as they didn't know if he could make it here in time."

Mark felt as if the weight of the world had suddenly been lifted from his shoulders. Already the new Voltrex fleet was firing forty-megaton missiles into the rear of the Trellixian fleet. Mark knew now they had a fighting chance to win this battle.

–

Battle Commander Balforr screamed in anger as the entire rear of his fleet formation vanished in massive blasts of fusion energy. The new Voltrex fleet was undamaged and had appeared in the worst possible location. His fleets were caught between two powerful forces and he dared not split his fleets. The *Conquest* shook violently as several fusion missiles slammed into its energy shield.

"We must withdraw," said Second Officer Albion. "This new fleet is too much for our surviving battlecruisers. We have used most of our antimatter missiles and many of our ships are damaged."

"No!" replied Balforr stubbornly. "We end the Humans here and now. Fire another barrage of missiles at their defense grid. I want all ships to launch as many nuclear missiles as possible at Earth." Balforr was determined to destroy the planet at any cost.

–

Hundreds of fusion missiles in multiple waves suddenly hurtled toward the defensive grid. Defensive energy beams lashed out, shooting a large number down. The weapons began detonating high above the Earth, taking out many of the defending satellites. Then the nuclear missiles began to arrive. Energy beams shot down some of them but many made it through the now large gap in the defensive grid to be engaged by the fighter-bombers from the *Annapolis*. The Annapolis herself had moved to just beneath the massive gap in the defenses so she could use her own energy weapons to take out some of the missiles.

"Some are going to get through," reported the tactical officer as he used every defensive battery on the carrier to destroy the incoming missiles.

Captain Travis glanced at the tactical display. It was full of incoming enemy missiles. His face turned pale when he realized how many were going to get through his defenses and strike the Earth.

"Hyperspace exit vortexes are forming all around us!" shouted the sensor officer.

Travis looked at the Command Center's viewscreens and was stunned to see all twenty of the two hundred-meter patrol ships based on the Moon appear around his vessel. As soon as they were stabilized their point defense turrets began firing on the descending missiles. Travis felt massive relief. Maybe, just maybe they could get most of them.

-

Bright explosions lit up the space directly above Earth as hundreds of Trellixian nuclear missiles were destroyed. Pulse cannon fire from Earth's ground defenses managed to take out many of the descending missiles. Even so, seventeen slipped through all the defensive fire and detonated. Four exploded in Mexico, twelve in the United States and one in Southern Canada. Once more deadly and radioactive mushroom clouds rose into the atmosphere.

-

General Mitchell looked grimly at the reports. None of the protected cities with energy shields had been destroyed. Unfortunately the atmosphere was being polluted once more with dust, ash, and radiation.

"The patrol ships have formed a protective ring around the *Annapolis*," reported General Briggs. "I've ordered several squadrons of F35s into the air to help eliminate any more missiles that might get past the ships."

Mitchell did not look forward to telling the president more nuclear weapons had fallen on the United States. On the bright side at least they were all still alive and the battle in space was rapidly turning in favor of the defenders. The newly arrived Voltrex fleet had turned the tide.

Battle Commander Balforr was livid with anger. He was losing the battle. Several Voltrex battlecruisers had positioned themselves above the hole in the defensive grid and were now helping to shoot down all the missiles he aimed at Earth. On the tactical display, more Trellixian battlecruisers were dying in growing numbers with every passing minute.

"We must withdraw," said Second Officer Albion, his eyes narrowing dangerously. "If we remain, we will lose the entire fleet!"

"Then we lose the fleet!" growled Balforr. "I want the Human world destroyed. I want all ships to make a run on the planet. When we're near enough we will launch every missile we still have. We will overload their defenses and burn their world."

"That's suicide," said Albion, his hand inching toward the pistol at his waist.

"Then we die," said Balforr, his eyes focused on the tactical display. "Send the order. All ships will advance now! We will die for the Empire!"

Without hesitation Albion drew his pistol and shot Battle Commander Balforr twice in the chest. While he was willing to die for the Empire he was not willing to die in a useless suicide charge.

Balforr looked at Albion in shock before he fell off the command pedestal and to the floor to lay unmoving in a growing pool of blood

"Contact all of our ships and order them to jump back into hyperspace," Albion ordered as he stepped up on the command pedestal and sat down in the command chair. "We're leaving while we still can."

The stunned crew hesitated and then began obeying Albion's orders. Two soldiers moved over and removed Balforr's body from the Command Center.

-

Moments later the surviving Trellixian ships began to enter hyperspace. Many were too damaged to make the transition and continued to attack. The Human and Voltrex ships moved in and rapidly eliminated these in massive blasts of fusion energy. In less than ten minutes the battle came to an abrupt end as all weapons fire ceased.

-

Fleet Commander Kamuss felt his heart stop hammering in his chest. His breathing slowed back down to near normal. The adrenaline rush of battle began to subside. The battle was over and he was still alive. Even more stunning was the Voltrex fleet which had arrived and saved them from defeat. It was the fleet his son, Albor, was assigned to. Fleet Commander Lore had pushed his ships to the limit to get here in time. Many of his ships' hyperspace drives would have to be repaired or even replaced before they could leave the Solar System.

"What did we lose?" he asked, looking over at Lieutenant Commander LeLath.

"It's bad, sir," LeLath replied, her whiskers drooping as she looked at the latest reports. "Between all three Voltrex fleets we lost twenty-four battleships and one hundred and eighty battlecruisers. We've lost nearly 70 percent of our fleets. We also lost Fleet Commander Barvon and Fleet Commander Masurl. Nearly all of our remaining ships are damaged."

"What about the Humans?" Kamuss knew they had taken heavy losses as well.

"Same as us," LeLath reported. "They lost twenty of their Earth-built battlecruisers, sixteen of their Voltrex-built battlecruisers and two battleships. We have confirmed kills on seven hundred and sixty Trellixian battlecruisers. Many of the ones that escaped are damaged."

"The shipyard and the three battlestations?"

"Undamaged," reported LeLath. "The defensive grid is still 72 percent functional."

"How many nuclear missiles got through to Earth?" Kamuss knew some had. He had seen the nuclear explosions on several of the still functioning viewscreens.

"Twenty that we know of, sir," replied LeLath. "There might have been a few more. We have no reports as yet of surface casualties."

Kamuss closed his eyes and shook his head. They had come so close to losing everything, including Earth. "Begin search and rescue operations. We have a lot of damaged ships out there and some large pieces of wreckage. I want every survivor found."

LeLath nodded. The battle was over and it was time for the survivors to move on.

-

Several days later General Mitchell, Rear Admiral Dolan, Fleet Commander Kamuss, Fleet Commander Lore, and Professor Wilkens were in the president's office. Rear Admiral Dolan had asked for this meeting.

President Hathaway sat down behind her desk and looked over at recently promoted Rear Admiral Dolan. She shook her head thinking about how many good men and women had been lost in the space battle. She would miss talking to Admiral Edwards. He had always seemed so knowledgeable and charismatic. "Rear Admiral Dolan, I want to congratulate you on your promotion. There is no doubt in my mind Admiral Edwards made the right decision."

"Thank you," Dolan replied. "I'm sure I was as surprised as everyone else."

"He made the right decision," added General Mitchell with a slight nod. "Now, Admiral Dolan, why did you call this meeting?"

Mark took a deep breath and set a small disk down on the president's desk. He pressed a button and a miniature version of Chloe appeared standing on the disk.

"I asked for the meeting," Chloe said. "I have some very important tactical information to present."

"Tactical information?" said General Mitchell with a surprised look in his eyes. "What are you talking about?"

"Since our return from the Trellixian core worlds I have spent considerable time analyzing the data. Using information we gathered on incoming Trellixian vessels, particularly cargo ships, I have come up with a strategy to neutralize the Trellixian Empire."

"You know how to neutralize the Empire?" said Kamuss, his eyes widening in surprise. "We're talking about an Empire of several thousand inhabited worlds. We're looking at a war which might last for decades."

Chloe shook her head. "No, the Trellixians have a major weakness, one inherent throughout their entire Empire. One we can use to cause their entire Empire to collapse."

"What is this supposed weakness?" asked Fleet Commander Lore with doubt edging into his voice.

Chloe looked around at the group. "It's their out-of-control population. On their core worlds living space and food is at a premium. From some of the communications we intercepted we know food and even living space is being severely rationed."

"I don't see how that helps us," said President Hathaway, her brow wrinkling in a frown. "Even after this battle they still have over four thousand warships and the capability to replace those they just lost very quickly."

Chloe smiled knowingly. "Not if they have to concern themselves with a civil war."

Fleet Commander Kamuss shook his head. "I don't understand. Why would they become involved in a civil war?"

"It's actually very simple. They will be fighting over food supplies. Using the data from the courses of certain cargo ships, I was able to extrapolate the location of possibly six of the worlds they use to grow food. If we destroy those worlds, they will not have enough food to sustain their massive populations on their core worlds. Civil war will break out as they fight for the remaining food supplies. The Empire will fracture."

Fleet Commander Kamuss looked thoughtful. "Can this actually work?"

Professor Wilkens nodded. "Rear Admiral Dolan contacted me earlier and explained what Chloe had come up with. I took her data and my research group ran some simulations. She is correct. If we destroy the Trellixians' food production worlds, it will throw their Empire into chaos."

Fleet Commander Kamuss stood up. "I must contact the High Command and get approval for this. If this will work we need to strike as quickly as possible before they can recover from the losses they just suffered."

President Hathaway looked over at General Mitchell. "We might actually be able to end this war in our lifetimes."

"Sooner," said Professor Wilkens with an all-knowing smile. "The Trellixian civil war will develop quickly and be quite brutal. We will want sufficient fleet units standing by to help add to the chaos."

"We need to sneak in and take out their shipyards while they're fighting each other over food," said Admiral Dolan, nodding his head. "We can position fleets in key areas of the core worlds and destroy targets of opportunity when they present themselves. If the civil war over food is as severe as Chloe and Professor Wilkens believes it will be, the Trellixian Empire will basically destroy itself. We just need to demolish their ability to wage war in the future."

"Yes," said Chloe. "Much of their manufacturing infrastructure is in orbit around their worlds and from our scans only the shipyards are armed and possess energy shields. If we use the confusion caused by their civil conflict we can move in and destroy that infrastructure."

"You have found the path to possible victory," said Fleet Commander Lore. "I'm certain the High Command will agree to this."

President Hathaway leaned back in her chair. Just maybe she was going to see actual peace return to Earth. After all of this time there was now a growing light at the end of a long and dark tunnel. The future had suddenly become much brighter for the Human race.

Epilogue

Four months later deep in the Trellixian Empire.

Rear Admiral Dolan gazed at the world his fleet was orbiting; one of the food worlds of the Trellixian Empire. It was a world with cultivated land and several large oceans. White clouds drifted lazily in the atmosphere.

In orbit drifted the remains of twenty large stations Mark's fleet had just finished blowing apart. He had two hundred and ten Voltrex battlecruisers and forty battleships under his command. There had been very little resistance to their unexpected attack. The fourteen defending enemy battlecruisers had been quickly eliminated and then the hundreds of cargo ships and the orbital stations had been destroyed with fusion missiles. A few cargo ships had escaped but not many. Mark knew five other Voltrex fleets were at this very moment attacking five more of the Trellixians' food worlds.

"There are four major cities on the planet," Chloe reported. "All are involved in food production in some manner. I estimate there are only about twenty million Trellixians on the entire planet."

Second Officer Katana stood gazing at the ship's main viewscreens. "It's a beautiful world. It's a shame we have to destroy it."

Mark nodded in agreement. The world was very similar to Earth as it once had been. Looking around the Command Center of the *Fury*, Mark prepared to give the order which would destroy a planet. The *Fury* had only recently gotten out of the repair dock. The ship was fully repaired and there were no signs of the severe damage she had suffered in the battle.

"Stand by to launch fusion missiles," he ordered. Fusion missiles were going to be used since they wanted to deprive the Trellixians of this food source permanently.

"We'll target the four cities first and then commence a systematic bombardment of the entire planet," replied Katana.

Mark drew in a deep breath and then gave the order. "Launch missiles."

The *Fury* vibrated slightly as the first missiles were launched. Around the *Fury*, the other ships in the fleet began to launch missiles as well. A few moments later the first explosions began to shake the planet. Massive mushroom clouds began to rise up into the atmosphere. Powerful blast waves spread across the surface, leveling everything. Forests and farms burst into flame from the intolerable heat of fusion explosions. In less than twenty minutes the damage was done. What was once a vibrant and living planet was now a scorched and dead world.

"Mission accomplished," reported Katana. "Sensors indicate there is nothing surviving intact below. All plant life will be dead within a week and animal life within ten days."

Mark nodded. He didn't feel proud at what he had just ordered. However, it had been necessary if they wanted to end this war. "Take us to our standby location. We will wait now and see what happens in the Empire."

The plan was very simple. He would take his fleet to a nearby white dwarf system and wait. Voltrex stealth scout ships would monitor the Trellixian core worlds to see what the results of destroying six of their food production worlds were. Once civil war broke out Mark would use his fleet to take out as much of the Trellixian orbital infrastructure as possible. While he was doing that the other five Voltrex fleets would be doing the same. If all went as planned in six months or less the war with the Trellixian Empire would be over.

-

Two months later.

High Commander Kaldre was in the primary shipyard above Traxis Three. He was standing in the observation room, which gave him a clear and unrestricted view of the planet below. The atmosphere was turning gray from all the fires raging on the surface. With the Human and Voltrex destruction of some of the food worlds the Empire depended upon chaos had erupted on nearly every core world. Massive civil unrest had broken out as food rations were cut even more. Starving Trellixians had formed into huge mobs and stormed the food warehouses. In days all the food was gone and then the mobs turned on one another. Anyone hoarding food was sought out and killed and their supplies taken. Reports of widespread cannibalism had been confirmed. Attempts to send the military in to quell the riots had failed. Already the casualty count was in the tens of billions and rising rapidly. Fires were burning everywhere and growing worse with every passing day.

"The ships are loaded, High Commander," reported Commander Malborr. "We can depart whenever you're ready."

Kaldre turned away from the large observation window. He was taking all the updated ships in the system and going to the small moon where he had a habitation dome capable of growing food. Some of the shipyard personnel would be going along as well as they would be useful in maintaining the technical systems for the dome. He had already sent word to his family to join him there. Kaldre knew several other High Commanders were doing the same while still others were fighting one anther over the remaining resources. There were daily reports of battles between opposing Trellixian fleets.

"Let's go then," he ordered. High Commander Kaldre knew this was the end of the Empire. The Humans and Voltrex had struck where no one expected. The Empire would collapse and even many of the outer colony worlds with large populations would fall as well. Kaldre suspected the Humans and the Voltrex would take advantage of the chaotic situation to eliminate most if not all of the outer colonies. Whether anything of the Empire would manage to survive was doubtful. For the time being Kaldre would withdraw to his secret moon retreat and stay there. Once everything calmed down he would send out ships to see if anything remained. If it did, he would try to recreate the Empire but it would be a much different one. Population growth would be controlled and the worlds would have to learn to survive on what they could produce themselves. The conquest of other worlds and the destruction of sentient races would become a thing of the past. They would defend themselves but they would not attack others.

An hour later High Commander Kaldre left the Traxis Three System for the last time. Behind him, he left a world on fire as hungry mobs swept across the planet. After he left he did not see the Voltrex fleet which dropped out of hyperspace and methodically destroyed all the shipyards and orbital stations around Traxis Three and the other planets. Once its work was done, the Voltrex fleet jumped back into hyperspace to go on to its next target.

Six months later.

President Katelyn Hathaway was down in the valley near the large mountain that protected Complex One. The sun was out and most of the snow had melted. It was quiet and peaceful. All across the planet things were beginning to return to normal. The city domes were down and people were beginning to move back out into the countryside. Crops had been planted and animals were grazing on some of the lush pastures which had returned.

"It's hard to believe the war is over," said Maggie Rayne, who was walking next to Katelyn. "I never thought I would live to see this day."

"None of us did," replied Katelyn as she bent over to pick a wildflower blooming on the valley floor. In the distance, she could hear the twitter of birds and the dim drone of insects. "I spoke to General Mitchell earlier. The Trellixian Empire is pretty much a thing of the past. Most of their fleet was destroyed in the civil war and Rear Admiral Dolan and the Voltrex fleets with him have obliterated nearly all of the Trellixian shipyards and orbital infrastructure. The Voltrex Fleet Command is going to keep several large fleets patrolling Trellixian space to ensure the Empire does not resurrect itself."

Maggie stopped and stared at a hawk circling in the air. "So, what do we do next?"

Katelyn grinned. "We build a new capitol. Soon we'll have elections again and just maybe I can retire. I may even build a cabin here in the mountains somewhere." Looking up, Katelyn could feel the warm sun shining down on her face. It was good to be alive.

-

Lisa Reynolds was having lunch with Professor Wilkens.

"I understand you're getting married."

Lisa nodded. "Yes, Brett and I have set a wedding date. With the war coming to an end we didn't see any reason not to."

"I'm happy for you," the Professor said with a pleased smile on his face.

"We'll still be doing our research," Lisa promised as she took a bite of her salad. "Nothing there will change."

Professor Wilkens cut off a small piece of steak and chewed it, looking thoughtful. "I think I can arrange some time off for you and Brett to have a proper honeymoon."

Lisa nodded happily. Her life had finally turned around. "There is one more thing I need to ask you."

The professor looked at Lisa expectantly. He had no idea what she could want.

"I want you to give me away at my wedding." Lisa waited breathlessly for the professor's response. "I want you to walk me down the aisle."

Professor Wilkens' face broke out in a big grin. "I would be delighted to."

Lisa felt excited at the prospect of her wedding. Her dreams were coming true and she was now looking forward to a long and happy life.

-

Deep in the Trellixian Empire on a cold and desolate moon, High Commander Kaldre was making plans. In orbit, there were eighty-seven battlecruisers of the most recent design. Already he had sent ships to several nearby worlds to check on their status. Most of the rioting had come to an end with the populations drastically reduced. A quick survey had indicated all the orbiting infrastructure had also been destroyed. The Humans and the Voltrex had been very thorough with that.

In another year or two he would move out and take over those nearby Trellixian worlds. He would use them as his center of power and then gradually expand from there. He would become the leader of a new and more realistic Trellixian Empire. At some point in time, he would have to contact the Humans and the Voltrex and sign some type of peace agreement. At least this way his people would survive though in a much different Empire.

-

Rear Admiral Mark Dolan watched the viewscreens as Earth appeared. His fleet was back from Trellixian space after accomplishing its mission. Now he just wanted to go down to Earth and see his sister. The last time he had been down to Earth Jennifer had introduced him to one of her friends he had found intriguing. He just might give her a call and see if she would be interested in going out to dinner.

"What are your plans now?" asked Mark, looking over at Katana.

Katana grinned her large feline smile. "Finding a mate and raising lots of cubs," she replied. "For me the war is over and I'm going to retire. My family has big plans for me and I intend to return to them as soon as I can."

Mark nodded. "I'll miss you. You have been an outstanding officer."

Mark turned his attention back to the viewscreen. While there was still a lot to do the war was pretty much over. There might be a few small actions in the future but nothing like what they had just went through. On the screen, the blue and white globe of Earth beckoned. It was time to go home.

The End

If you enjoyed Earth Fall: Empires at War please post a review with some stars. Good reviews encourage an author to write and also help sell books. Reviews can be just a few short sentences, describing what you liked about the book. If you have suggestions, please contact me at my website, link below. Thank you for reading Earth Fall: Empires at War and being so supportive.

Note from the Author: This book came out late due to the fact I suffered from severe Kidney failure in June. I was hospitalized for over three weeks and unable to write for nearly two months. I am now on home dialysis and have begun writing again. Once more I'm sorry for the delay.

Special Announcement # 1!!

Due to numerous requests The Originator Wars will continue in a new series. (The Originator Wars: Explorations) If you want to continue to follow the exploits and adventures of the Special Five, Ariel, Clarissa, and the others in the Slaver Wars, Lost Fleet, and Originator Wars series the first book should be out sometime in February of 2019. Once again I want to thank everyone for your support in my writing and all the wonderful emails I've received.

Thank You

Raymond L. Weil

For updates on current writing projects and future publications, go to my author website. Sign up for future notifications when my new books come out on Amazon.

Website: http://raymondlweil.com/

Follow on Facebook at Raymond L. Weil

Special Announcement # 2!!

Galactic Empire Wars: Final Conflict (January 2019)
This will be a short novel to wrap up some unfinished story lines in the series.

Other Books by Raymond L. Weil
Available on Amazon

Moon Wreck (The Slaver Wars Book 1)
The Slaver Wars: Alien Contact (The Slaver Wars Book 2)
Moon Wreck: Fleet Academy (The Slaver Wars Book 3)
The Slaver Wars: First Strike (The Slaver Wars Book 4)
The Slaver Wars: Retaliation (The Slaver Wars Book 5)
The Slaver Wars: Galactic Conflict (The Slaver Wars Book 6)
The Slaver Wars: Endgame (The Slaver Wars Book 7)
The Slaver Wars: Books 1-3

-

Dragon Dreams
Dragon Dreams: Dragon Wars
Dragon Dreams: Gilmreth the Awakening
Dragon Dreams: Snowden the White Dragon

-

Star One: Tycho City: Survival
Star One: Neutron Star
Star One: Dark Star
Star One

-

Galactic Empire Wars: Destruction (Book 1)
Galactic Empire Wars: Emergence (Book 2)
Galactic Empire Wars: Rebellion (Book 3)
Galactic Empire Wars: The Alliance (Book 4)
Galactic Empire Wars: Insurrection (Book 5)
Galactic Empire Wars: The Beginning (Books 1-3)

-

The Lost Fleet: Galactic Search (Book 1)
The Lost Fleet: Into the Darkness (Book 2)
The Lost Fleet: Oblivion's Light (Book 3)
The Lost Fleet: Genesis (Book 4)

The Lost Fleet: Search for the Originators (Book 5)

-

The Star Cross (Book 1)
The Star Cross: The Dark Invaders (Book 2)
The Star Cross: Galaxy in Peril (Book 3)
The Star Cross: The Forever War (Book 4)
The Star Cross: The Vorn! (Book 5)

-

The Originator Wars: Universe in Danger (Book 1)
The Originator Wars: Search for the Lost (Book 2)
The Originator Wars: Conflict Unending (Book 3)

-

Earth Fall: Invasion (Book 1)
Earth Fall: To the Stars (Book 2)
Earth Fall: Empires at War (Book 3)

(All dates are tentative)

Galactic Empire Wars: Final Conflict (January 2019)
This will be a short novel to wrap up some unfinished story lines in the series.
The Originator Wars: Explorations (Book 1) February 2019

ABOUT THE AUTHOR

I live in Clinton Oklahoma with my wife of 44 years and our cats. I attended college at SWOSU in Weatherford Oklahoma, majoring in Math with minors in Creative Writing and History.

My hobbies include watching soccer, reading, camping, and of course writing. I also enjoy playing with my five grandchildren. (Soon to be six!!) I have a very vivid imagination, which sometimes worries my friends. They never know what I'm going to say or what I'm going to do.

I am an avid reader and have a science fiction / fantasy collection of over two thousand paperbacks. I have always enjoyed reading science fiction and fantasy because of the awesome worlds authors create. I can hardly believe I'm now creating those worlds as well.

Made in the USA
Lexington, KY
28 January 2019